Praise for
STARFIST I: FIRST TO FIGHT

"CAUTION! Any book written by Dan Cragg and David Sherman is bound to be addictive, and this is the first in what promises to be a great adventure series. *First to Fight* is rousing, rugged, and just plain fun. The authors have a deep firsthand knowledge of warfare, an enthralling vision of the future, and the skill of veteran writers. Fans of military fiction, science fiction, and suspense will all get their money's worth, and the novel is so well done it will appeal to general readers as well. It's fast, realistic, moral, and a general hoot. *First to Fight* is also vivid, convincing—and hard to put down. Sherman and Cragg are a great team! I can't wait for the next one!"

—RALPH PETERS
New York Times bestselling
author of *Red Army*

By David Sherman and Dan Cragg

Starfist
FIRST TO FIGHT
SCHOOL OF FIRE

By David Sherman

Fiction

The Night Fighters
KNIVES IN THE NIGHT
MAIN FORCE ASSAULT
OUT OF THE FIRE
A ROCK AND A HARD PLACE
A NGHU NIGHT FALLS
CHARLIE DON'T LIVE HERE ANYMORE

THERE I WAS: THE WAR OF CORPORAL HENRY J.
    MORRIS, USMC
THE SQUAD

By Dan Cragg

Fiction

THE SOLDIER'S PRIZE

Nonfiction

A DICTIONARY OF SOLDIER TALK
GENERALS IN MUDDY BOOTS
INSIDE THE VC AND THE NVA (with Michael Lee
    Lanning)
TOP SERGEANT (with William G. Bainbridge)

Books published by The Ballantine Publishing Group
are available at quantity discounts on bulk purchases
for premium, educational, fund-raising, and special
sales use. For details, please call 1-800-733-3000.

SCHOOL OF FIRE

Starfist
Book Two

David Sherman
and
Dan Cragg

A Del Rey® Book
THE BALLANTINE PUBLISHING GROUP • NEW YORK

A Del Rey® Book
Published by The Ballantine Publishing Group
Copyright © 1998 by David Sherman and Dan Cragg

http://www.randomhouse.com

Library of Congress Catalog Card Number: 97-95003

ISBN 0-345-40623-0

Manufactured in the United States of America

First Edition: August 1998

OPM 15 14 13 12 11 10 9 8 7 6

For

Our Mutual Friend,
J. B. Post

If it wasn't for him,
these books would
never have been written

SCHOOL
OF FIRE

PROLOGUE

The approaching sounds of snapping twigs and wet fronds squelching under rushing feet came to Commander Hing's ears. He didn't turn to look toward their source. If it was some fool of a Feldpolizei trooper coming through the forest, the man wouldn't live long enough to reach his position, except as a prisoner—his fighters would see to that. Most likely, Hing thought, it was one of his guerrilla band's scouts returning with the hoped-for report of a small Feldpolizei patrol approaching the ambush site.

Hing kept his eyes idly roaming the road that cut between the shallow-sided hill his position was on and the equally low hill that rose from the road's other side, while his mind ran through all the possibilities. A commander who considered all the things that might go wrong could devise plans to turn each possible wrongness to his advantage.

The sounds came closer and closer and finally stopped, punctuated by the thump of a knee hitting the ground a meter from where Hing lay concealed in a clump of grospalms.

"Commander, it must be true what we have heard, the Feldpolizei has a new commissioner," a gasping voice said.

At last Hing turned his attention from the road and looked at the speaker, Fighter Quetlal, the scout whose hasty approach had snapped so many twigs, squelched so many fronds. The commander raised an eyebrow questioningly.

Quetlal was grinning broadly. The heaving of his chest quickly subsided; the members of the guerrilla band were well-accustomed to physical exertion in this heat and humidity. He made his report.

"They are not wearing camouflage, Commander. They are not even wearing plain green or tan to help them hide among the trees." His grin broadened and his eyes glittered. "There are a hundred of them. And they are all wearing orange tunics and sky-blue pantaloons. You can tell the officers by the plumes on their helmets!"

A hundred, normally too many for his company—but in that formation they might be easy to defeat. Commander Hing instantly thought of something that might be wrong, even with a new Feldpolizei commissioner as foolish as this one was said to be. "How do you know the ones you saw are not a diversion?"

Fighter Quetlal grinned more widely than seemed possible and bobbed his head in a quick nod. "I thought of that myself, Commander. As soon as I saw them I thought they must be a diversion. But search as I might, I could find no one. Nor could the other scouts with me."

Hing slowly shook his head one time. The oligarchs were getting more and more foolish in their conduct of this war. Where had they gotten the idea that sharp-looking parade ground troops made the best fighters? Did they really think fancy uniforms would frighten fighting men?

"How long?"

"They are marching briskly in a column, Commander. Much faster than we would move through the forest. If I had seen us where I saw them, I would say at least a half an hour. As they are marching down the middle of the road, I must say bare minutes."

"How watchful are they?"

"Their eyes are straight ahead, as though they are passing in review. They are even carrying their blasters at right shoulder arms."

"Scouts? Flankers?"

Fighter Quetlal shook his head. "They have two point men twenty meters ahead of the column; that is all of their security." He barked a short laugh. "The point men must think they are ready, though they march straight ahead—they carry their blasters at port arms."

"Have you passed an alert?"

"As I came along our line, Commander. I told everybody."

"Then continue along our line and tell the rest of the company." Hing turned back to the road; Quetlal was dismissed. The scout hastened to do his commander's bidding.

Commander Hing's fingers absently caressed the stock of his blaster, fondled its firing lever. His was one of the few modern weapons possessed by the grandiosely named Che Loi Brigade of the Peoples Liberation Army, and the only one in this ambush. The rest of the sixty brigade members with him were armed with obsolete projectile rifles, which was a major reason for this ambush—to take modern weapons from the corpses of the oligarchy's Feldpolizei. Normally, with only sixty men he would let a hundred Feldpolizei pass unmolested. But with them marching in formation as they were, they were far too tempting a target to let go. Soon, in bare minutes, Hing's fighters would strike a mighty blow, and strike further fear into the hearts of the oligarchy—and become better armed.

"That imbecile sends us to our death," Patrolman Perez muttered to the man at his side.

"Only if they lie in ambush," Patrolman Troung replied equally quietly, "and are not frightened off by our blasters." He wanted to spit, but Captain Rickdorf's discipline was too severe for him to take the chance. He rolled his shoulders slightly to ease the way his burden weighed on them. "I'm more concerned with how my armor makes me sweat."

"Quiet in the ranks," Shift Sergeant Ruiz called out softly from his position marching alongside the column of twos. Instead of a blaster on his shoulder, he carried a sergeant's saber at trail in his hand. "We don't want any bandits in the area to hear us and run away before we can catch them."

Captain Rickdorf, marching erect at the head of the column, gave no sign that he'd heard the patrolmen talking. But he had heard, and he would remember. He promised himself that Perez and Troung—he knew their voices—would be disciplined for talking out of turn, as an example to the others, when they returned to the headquarters of the 407th GSB—Grafshaftsbezirk—precinct. Then he put aside thoughts of troopers so undisciplined that they talked in the ranks, and thought of the absolute surprise that would overcome the bandits when they finally saw his magnificent company, and the panic that would grip them when his men's blasters rained fire and destruction on them. He knew in his heart that Commissioner Schickeldorf was absolutely right: a well-drilled, well-armed, splendidly uniformed force will always strike fear into the hearts of an undisciplined bandit rabble—the very sight of such a force could spur the bandit rabble into flight. Even if the bandits attempted to fight, their projectile weapons would be useless against the body armor his men wore under their tunics. He nodded inwardly, confident that this brief expedition would rid the Bavaran Hills Province of its bandit problem forever.

Captain Rickdorf saw that the road ahead cut between two steep-sided, thickly wooded hills. Just the kind of place where he knew the bandits liked to set their ambushes. He smiled inwardly as he thought of the shock the sight of his troops would induce in the bandits if they were indeed in ambush there. He hoped they were. This expedition could well earn him a decoration directly from the hand of Commissioner Schickeldorf—and a much-desired promotion and transfer out of this forsaken hills province.

Fighter Quetlal had barely left Commander Hing's position when the brigade leader heard the slightly ragged *tramp-tramp-tramp* of marching feet coming along the road below. He listened for a voice, but heard no one counting cadence. So they know how to march, he thought. We shall see soon how well they know how to die. His men knew how to lie in ambush, invisible from the road—none would fire his weapon until Hing blew his whistle.

Two troopers, as splendidly popinjayed as Fighter Quetlal had promised, strutted into sight. Sunlight filtering through the tops of the towering hochbaum trees that grew between the clumps of grospalms dappled their tunics to the flowing color of old gold. Their marching legs *swish-swish*ing along made their sky-blue trousers ripple like fast-flowing water in a clear, shallow stream. Hing shook his head; they were indeed marching erect, eyes straight ahead, blasters at right-shoulder. "Fools," he muttered, dismissing them, but his eyes lingered hungrily on their weapons. Soon the fighters of his brigade would put those modern weapons to far better use than these comic-opera Feldpolizei ever could.

Twenty meters behind the point men, the rest of the column snaked along the road, marching two men abreast. This was so foolish; Hing suspected their commander would have had them marching three or four abreast had the road been wide enough.

Their commander, oh yes. He was the most glorious popinjay of them all. His tunic was piped with gold cord, gold epaulettes jounced on his shoulders, and a fourragère—a braided gold cord—swirled around and dangled from his shoulder. A veritable kaleidoscope of medals adorned his left breast. Broad bands of silver ran down his trouser legs. It hardly seemed possible, but the saber scabbard that hung from his tasseled belt looked to be of precious metal as well. The saber he carried point up against his shoulder looked like a purely ceremonial blade, not a fighting blade at all—as though a sword was a weapon to use against blasters or even projectile weapons.

As the officer passed below Hing's position, the guerrilla commander turned his attention to the column proper. Had he known that Captain Rickdorf thought his guerrillas would be surprised, he would have agreed with him. He was very surprised by the sight of this marching column of the Wanderjahrian Feldpolizei. They marched as if on a parade ground, their blasters for the moment uselessly propped on their right shoulders. When he blew his whistle, Hing thought, half would be dead before any of them could move their weapons into firing position.

Hing counted the ranks of Feldpolizei as they marched past him. When his count reached twenty-two, he put his whistle to his lips. At twenty-three he sucked his chest full of air. At twenty-four, near the center of the double line of

Feldpolizei, when all were well within the killing zone of the ambush, he blew.

Thunder rippled all along the hillside as the fighters of the Che Loi Brigade opened fire at the marching column. Here an orange-tunicked man thudded screaming to the ground, clutching his thigh where arterial blood pulsed brightly from a bullet hole. There another spun about, his shattered arm spraying red. A brilliant rosette of bone and brain and blood blossomed on the forehead of a third man before he collapsed. Others staggered from the bullets that thudded into their bodies, but kept their feet as their body armor spread and absorbed the kinetic energy of the blows.

"Troop! Face to the right!" Captain Rickdorf and his platoon officers shouted above the din of gunfire.

"Front rank, kneel!" Rickdorf calmly snapped his order.

The lieutenants echoed the command as they briskly assumed their positions at one end of their platoons. The shift sergeants stood their places with their men, ready to relay commands and keep the men in good order.

"Lay your fire in a swath!" Rickdorf commanded, and the junior officers echoed him.

"By ranks. Front rank, fire! Rear rank, fire!"

Crackling plasma flashed from the nozzles of the front ranks' blasters and struck the hillside in a random pattern, followed quickly by an equally random pattern from the blasters of the rear rank. There were one or two screams from guerrillas charred by bolts, but the screams were quickly cut off by death or shock. A thin mist instantly spread raggedly on the hillside as the fire of the plasma bolts vaporized the moisture in the wet leaves and damp earth. Flames briefly shot up here and there, but quickly went out, as the recent rains had made the forest too wet to burn.

"Line your fire," Rickdorf commanded. Neither he nor his men could see their attackers; they had to fire together to make sure they covered the hillside. "Front rank, ten meters up the hillside, fire!" The front rank fired again. This time its bolts struck in an irregular line along the hillside, some in the clumps of grospalms where the guerrillas hid, others uselessly in the lightly carpeted ground between them.

"Rear rank, leapfrog five meters, fire!" The rear rank fired its volley, and its bolts spattered in a lightning-bolt jagged line along the hillside five meters above the first line.

Here and there along the two lines of Feldpolizei, men staggered or bent as bullets spent their energy against their armor, a few screamed in agony from the pain of bullets that tore into arms or legs. Their screams were not matched from the hillside. Only a few troopers fell from chance hits in their heads.

"Front rank, leapfrog, fire!"

"Steady, lads," Ruiz said, loud but calm, as he marched casually behind the rear rank. "They are only an ill-armed rabble. We will easily beat them. Steady. Keep up your disciplined fire." Other shift sergeants said much the same to their men.

Commander Hing saw how the troopers reacted to the body blows of his men's bullets, and understood almost immediately why they remained standing and continued to fire. Maybe he should have let them pass. But maybe he and his guerrillas could still win the fight. "They're wearing body armor," he shouted. "Aim for heads, arms, legs."

Elsewhere along the ambush line he heard others cry out the same order, some so quickly he knew he wasn't the only one to see and know. The guerrillas shifted their aim from the center of their targets to the extremities, and troopers started falling.

The Feldpolizei stood or knelt in patient ranks for the space of one more volley before individuals among them began to notice above the crackles of blasters and bangs of rifles screaming from within their own ranks and a lessening of their plasma cracks.

"I told you!" Perez shrilled at Troung.

"Keep firing," Troung shouted back.

Terror rapidly mounted in his heart, and Perez glanced to the side—if anyone broke ranks, he would run with them. He looked just in time to see Shift Sergeant Ruiz's face erupt and splatter blood and brain from two bullet hits. Perez shrieked in horror and panic at the sight. He dropped his blaster and ran. By some miracle, he reached the shelter of the trees alive.

Captain Rickdorf, head held high, swept his gaze across the hillside. The bandits must be higher on the hillside than he guessed; their fire wasn't slackening. "Rear rank, leapfrog ten—" He never finished the command. Simultaneously, one bullet tore through his throat, a second shattered his right temple, and a third shot between his open lips and ripped out the joint that held his skull to his neck bones.

The bullet that hit Rickdorf in the throat continued its deadly flight unimpeded and spent itself in the shoulder of the trooper standing next to him. That man staggered and fell to his knees. The force of the blow knocked his blaster out of his hands and turned him half about, where he saw the captain's lifeless body bounce as it hit the road's surface. He screamed, more in shock at seeing his commander down than because of pain. Struggling to his feet, he tried to run away, but felt the mounting pain of his wound and was too unsteady for flight. He blundered into the men next to him.

From the hillside, the guerrillas saw the troopers falling now and cheered. On the road, more and more of the troopers heard and saw the men to their sides no longer firing, either down or breaking ranks.

Abruptly, with their captain dead, the surviving Feldpolizei who were able, ran.

"Get them!" Commander Hing screamed. "Kill them before they get away."

The guerrillas rained fire at the fleeing Feldpolizei, most of whom had thrown away their weapons to speed their flight. Many of them fell, dead from head shots or crippled with shattered legs. Some dropped to their knees and faced the hillside with their arms upraised in surrender.

"Cease fire, cease fire!" Hing shouted as the few who managed to dodge his fighters' bullets disappeared into the trees on the opposite hillside or around a bend in the road. He stood and bounded down the hill. On all sides his fighters came with him.

Commander Hing looked up and down along the road, between the clumps of grospalms and the scattering of spikers on the opposite hill. There were more than seventy, maybe more than eighty, troopers down—dead, wounded, or surrendered. And there were more than ninety blasters scattered about. It was a most gratifying sight.

"Lieutenant Pincote," he said as his second in command approached. "How many casualties?"

Lieutenant Sokum Pincote showed teeth filed to points when she smiled at him. "Only six, Commander."

"Six fighters dead is nothing to smile about, Lieutenant," he snapped at her. "I don't care how many Feldpolizei we kill, the life of one fighter is of greater value."

Pincote's lips snapped shut. "Yes, Commander. I know that. I was merely expressing pleasure at our victory. We can now properly arm nearly half of the brigade."

Hing looked back at the corpses and casualties littering the road and nodded.

"What will we do with the wounded?" Pincote asked. "Shall I kill them?"

Hing didn't bother to even shake his head. "We are not murderers. Leave them. We don't dare stay here long enough to tend them. The unwounded survivors can bandage them."

Ten minutes later the fifty-four members of the Che Loi Brigade who survived the fight were carrying their burden of ninety-three blasters and the charred corpses of their six dead comrades under the trees, heading for a narrow, steep-sided valley that was hidden from the current orbits of the planetary government's surveillance satellites. Soon they would join the other 240 members of the Che Loi Brigade back at their base camp, where the satellites could never see them, no matter what their orbits.

CHAPTER
ONE

Thorsfinni's World is a water world studded with islands small and large. High in its northern hemisphere floats Niflheim, an island approximately the size and shape of the Scandinavian peninsula on Old Earth. Niflheim is the center of Thorsfinni's World's Viking-based civilization and home to better than three-quarters of its population. In northern Niflheim the summer temperature rarely broaches 25 degrees on the Celsius scale, its winter temperatures often reaching that degree on the minus side of the scale. Niflheim is a wet place, rainy when the temperature is warm enough for liquid precipitation, snowy the rest of the year. And all of Thorsfinni's World smells of fish.

Niflheim. Outpost of Human Space. Home of the 34th Fleet Initial Strike Team, Confederation Marine Corps. When the Marines of 34th FIST weren't off on a campaign on some other world, they spent most of their time in the field, either on Niflheim or one of the other islands, training for operations they might not ever be called upon to execute. Even if they trained for something they would never have to do, their commanders felt the most important thing was that they trained.

"So that's what we're going to be doing for the next two or three days," Ensign vanden Hoyt said at the conclusion of his briefing to the men of the third platoon, Company L, 34th FIST. A wry smile crossed his lips and he added, "Or what *you'll* be doing, I should say. Any questions? Problems?" He peered carefully through the steady rain in the direction of the men—his men, his first command. All he could make out were their indistinct faces through what looked like undulating sheets of water. Their heads seemed to hover in the air. Ten years in the Corps and he was still sometimes startled by the illusions created by chameleon field uniforms.

There were no questions and only one problem, but it wasn't voiced. Lance Corporal "Hammer" Schultz caught the eye of the platoon sergeant, Charlie Bass, and shook his head slightly. Bass replied with an almost imperceptible head bob. The problem was dealt with.

"All right, then," vanden Hoyt said when nobody spoke up, "Staff Sergeant Bass will make the assignments. Then you can get back under shelter until it's time for you to go back into the rain." He stepped aside to let Bass take front and center.

"First squad," Bass said without preamble, wanting to get out of the rain as badly as anyone else in the platoon, maybe more so. Twenty-odd years as a Marine had taught him when being uncomfortable was good, and when it wasn't. "Chan, I'm sticking you with MacIlargie and Godenov, so you also get Schultz. Go someplace and dry off," he said, glancing at the low, dark sky, which showed no sign of breaking, and shook his head. "Or at least get out from underwater until you get your assignment. Van Impe, you have Lonsdorf. You also get Neru and Clarke from guns . . ."

Chan and his three men didn't hear the rest of the assignments. As soon as their names were called, Chan gathered his men and they slogged through churning mud for shelter.

"You should be in charge here," Chan said to Lance Corporal Schultz. "You're senior to me, and you've got a lot more experience."

Schultz grunted. He didn't want to be in charge. He was exactly what he wanted to be, a lance corporal, a man not in command in any way. His function in life, as he saw it, was to be a fighter, not a leader. The Confederation Marine Corps was filled with men well-qualified to be officers and noncommissioned officers, more than there were slots to fill. Schultz was an excellent fighter; so far as the Corps was concerned, he could remain a lance corporal until he retired, if that's what he wanted.

Shelter was a low tent made from three polymer sheets stretched over a framework of strong synthetic rods. The four Marines had to crouch to get inside, and almost had to huddle together for all of them to fit. Chan turned on the radiant heating unit that sat in the center of the tent while Schultz secured the entrance. Wind buffeted the tent and the rain drummed on it, making conversation difficult—but at least they had a chance to dry out. The four sat cross-legged around the heater and in minutes their fronts were dried. Then they turned around. Their backs weren't quite dry when the flap opened and Charlie Bass crowded in, extending his open arms toward the heater as he moaned with pleasure.

"There used to be a disease called rheumatoid arthritis," he said. "Cold and wet made your joints swell up and hurt. If bio-engineering hadn't eradicated it, I'd probably have it and be aching in every joint in my body," he twisted his back to ease rain- and wind-stiffened muscles, "instead of just feeling like I've been turned into a piece of soggy wood." The others chuckled at his joke.

"All right," Bass said, abruptly all business. "Mike Company's making a sweep. Third platoon's going to stop them. Here's your part of it . . ."

This phase of the two-week exercise was a three-way force-on-force for the three companies of the FIST's infantry battalion, with the other units of the FIST in support of all three companies. Kilo and Mike Companies were acting as complete units in opposition to each other. Company L was playing an irregular force, broken down into four-man teams that would act in opposition to Kilo and Mike. Commander Van Winkle, the battalion's commanding officer, wanted to test the junior men, so the officers and NCOs of Company L were acting as umpires, and each four-man team was headed by a lance corporal.

A Dragon, the Marines' ubiquitous amphibious armored vehicle, dropped off Chan and his team twenty-five kilometers northeast of the company's bivouac area. In addition to their weapons and simulators, they carried light packs with little more than two days of rations. Due to vagaries of local weather conditions, the sun was shining brightly where the Dragon dropped them off and the rocky ground underfoot was dry; it hadn't even rained overnight there. The team was in a clearing in the midst of sparse vegetation that grew to twice the height of a man. The main plants in the area resembled Earth scrub-pine trees.

Chan checked the time. "We don't know how long it'll be before somebody gets here," he said, "or if it's going to be a platoon or a whole company or anything else. We need to find a position where we can watch all approaches from under cover." He scanned the area as he spoke, orienting himself, looking for recognizable landmarks, building a mental map of the unfamiliar scene.

Nothing that resembled grass grew on the rocks under the pine tree look-alikes, just a spotty coating of pale green, lichen-like stuff. Spindly plants whose stems didn't look strong enough to hold themselves upright grew from cracks in the forest floor. Flitterers that could have been butterflylike birds, or birdlike butterflies, flew from tree to tree. Smaller buzzers that could easily have been mistaken for Earth insects by anyone but an entomologist zigged and zagged their way among the lower flora of the forest, stopping here and there to absorb whatever passed for nectar on Thorsfinni's World.

Chan looked to Schultz for help.

Schultz merely shrugged and said, "You're in charge," which was no help at all.

This wasn't realistic, Chan thought. Irregulars should know the area they were in, and he'd never been there before. Maps didn't tell you what was really there. After a moment, he said, "That tor over there," pointing toward a low hill barely visible through the trees to the northwest. "That seems to be the highest ground around. That's probably our best starting place. If nothing else, we can take a look around from there." He looked at his men as he talked. Schultz was walking slowly—almost invisibly—about, examining the terrain with the eye of an experienced infantryman. Godenov was listening intently. MacIlargie had a quizzical expression on his face and didn't seem to be paying any attention. He had the kind of face that should have been framed by long, tangled hair, and a mustache with ends that drooped to below his chin wouldn't have seemed out of place—but Marine regulations required short hair and forbade mustaches that long.

"Are you listening to me, MacIlargie?" Chan snapped.

"What's that smell?" MacIlargie asked.

Taken aback by the unexpected question, Chan sniffed. He hadn't noticed any aroma that might indicate danger. "What smell?" he asked. "I don't smell anything."

Godenov, a big young man, deceptively soft-looking, took a deep breath. He didn't smell anything either.

Schultz seemed to pay no attention to the exchange—he knew what MacIlargie noticed and that it was irrelevant.

"That's what I mean," MacIlargie said. "Something's missing." His face lit up with a broad smile as he realized what it was. "Okay, now we see how sharp you are. What's missing? If you can't tell that, you're not going to be very good on patrols when we go on operations for real." He grinned at the others.

Godenov got it first. "The air doesn't smell like fish!"

"Izzy, if I was in charge, I'd make you my second in command," MacIlargie exclaimed. "You get out here in the toolies, you gotta be sharp, and you're the only one who figured that out."

Chan simply looked at MacIlargie's grinning face, hovering in the middle of the clearing like the last glimpse of a Cheshire cat. MacIlargie, like Godenov, was on his first assignment after Boot Camp. Both had recently joined the platoon as replacements for men lost on the FIST's last operation, peacekeeping on Elneal. Chan himself had been on four combat operations, including one with the 34th FIST. Schultz was more experienced than he was.

MacIlargie staggered, then almost fell, and yelped. Schultz, in his deceptively casual, almost invisible way, had come near and hit him with an elbow—hard. Schultz's disembodied voice mumbled something that might have been an apology but probably wasn't.

MacIlargie recovered his balance and spun toward where he thought Schultz was. For a second it seemed he'd attack Schultz if he could find him. But only for a second. He remembered what Schultz looked like when he was visible—Schultz moved languidly and seldom had much to say, but he exuded a dangerous self-confidence that gave strong men pause.

Chan spoke up: "We're going to that hill. MacIlargie, take point. Godenov, bring up the rear. Now. Move it out."

Schultz gave Chan a look that said, I should have the point. Chan said again, "MacIlargie, move out." Then he added to Schultz, "This is training. He needs the experience."

Schultz nodded, satisfied that Chan understood that if it had been a real operation, he was the one who would take the most dangerous and important spot in the patrol column.

The tor was closer than it had looked. It was a broad, low platform of limestone, forced upward in terraces by an upwelling of magma deep below the surface. Scree dotted the ground at the foot of the tor's steep side.

MacIlargie stopped at the foot of the hill and looked back at Chan, uncertain what to do next.

Schultz brushed past both of them and started climbing the eight-meter cliff to the first terrace.

Chan looked back and saw Godenov's face hovering as he stood watching.

"Watch our rear, Godenov," Chan said. "That's the rear point's job: watch the rear."

Godenov started. "Oh." He turned around and dropped to one knee to peer into the thin trees behind them.

Even though he could barely make out where Godenov was, Chan saw that he wasn't in position to effectively watch the rear. He shook his head and wondered what they were teaching recruits in Boot Camp these days. Surely he'd been better than that at field craft when he went on his first assignment. He briefly considered taking the time to show the young man how to pick a better position, but instead said to MacIlargie, "Follow the man."

Schultz's climbing noises indicated he was already over the

top of the first terrace. Chan flipped down his infras so he could watch his men. When MacIlargie was halfway up the first terrace, Chan sent Godenov after him. He then gave the trees near the base of the hill a quick once-over. When his infras didn't show anything man-size in them, he followed.

The higher terraces and slopes were older than those below. As the Marines climbed, it became easier because the increased erosion made the slopes gentler. Here and there crevasses and cave mouths dimpled the tor.

Once, when they were close to each other, Schultz said to Chan, "I know this place. If we have to, we can hide."

It didn't take long to approach the top. "Off the horizon, people," Chan said when he saw two man-size pillars of rock above. He was crouched below the top, as he knew Schultz was.

One of the rock pillars rippled, and MacIlargie's face appeared above it. "What do you mean?" he asked. "We're wearing chameleons, nobody can see us."

"Chameleons pick up the nearest colors," Chan said, "not what's behind you. You look like a man-made pile of stone up there."

Rocks seemed to shift as MacIlargie shrugged. "A man-size pile of rock doesn't have to be a man, it's just a pile of rocks."

Chan flipped down his infras. "These tell me you're a man, not a pile of rock," he said. "Off the top of the hill."

MacIlargie snorted. "You've got to be less than a kilometer away for infras to show enough detail."

"Hoppers have infras that can pick out a man as far as the horizon. Get down." Godenov had already dropped down to the military crest of the hill.

MacIlargie's face disappeared and his rock pile rippled as he turned in a circle. "I don't see any hoppers out there," he said as his face reappeared.

"You don't know anything about evasive flying, do you?"

MacIlargie yelped and his face dropped through the space that no longer looked like a man-size pile of rocks. Then his shocked, frightened face skittered down from the top of the hill and came to rest next to Chan.

Schultz's voice came from MacIlargie's other side. "That's how you get someone too dumb to live to do what you tell him to. Either that or blast him." He had slithered unseen to the top and knocked MacIlargie's feet from underneath him, then dragged him down.

"Hey, don't do that!" MacIlargie shouted, and swung a fist at Schultz, but the other man had already moved away.

"Calm down, MacIlargie," Chan said, putting a restraining hand on the new man. "When Marines don't follow orders, somebody can get hurt. On a real operation, not following orders can get Marines killed."

"No need to knock me down like that," MacIlargie muttered. "You want me to do something, all you got to do is say so."

"What do you think I was doing?" he snapped. Chan shook his head, then switched his attention back to the mission. "Everybody, four corners. Use your infras, use your magnifiers, use your bare eyes. And listen. Mike Company, or part of Mike Company, is out there somewhere. We damn well better spot them before they spot us. Schultz, far side. MacIlargie, right, Godenov, left side. Do it now." Through his infras he watched his men moving away. He'd give them a minute or two to get into position, then go around and check them. Especially the new men, to make sure they were behind rocks that would reduce their heat signatures.

Everyone was well-positioned when Chan made his rounds—even MacIlargie, who didn't seem to understand how vulnerable even a man in chameleons and a blaster shield could be. On his way back to his own position, Chan scouted routes between positions to see how they could move about while exposing themselves as little as possible. Then he settled down to watch, listen, and wait.

Once the Marines settled down, tiny things, gnatlike flitterers, gathered around their still bodies. Landed on them, got inside their clothing, crawled about, itched and annoyed them, made them focus inward, close at hand. As the waiting, watching, and listening time lengthened, the Marines found their attention diverted from the horizon and surrounding landscape to their very near airspace and skin. The new men were the first to begin waving their hands to dispel the flitterers, to pluck them off their skin, pull them out of their clothing, to crush them between fingernails when all else failed. After more than an hour of watching nothing happen out there, even Chan began paying attention to the bugs. Eventually, Schultz too was delousing himself. It took a lot to get Schultz to shift his attention from the mission to tiny bloodsuckers; to him they were simply part of being in the field. And a lot less dangerous than people.

After half a day of boredom and delousing, Chan noticed aircraft humming somewhere in the distance. The humming quickly grew louder. He looked around but didn't see anything from his position.

"Heads up," he murmured into his helmet comm unit, "aircraft coming. Who sees them?"

A couple of seconds passed before someone whistled over the team's comm net, then MacIlargie's voice said, "I see ten hoppers. They're coming straight at us."

"Nobody move," Chan ordered. Keeping under cover as much as possible, he rushed to MacIlargie's position. As the new man had said, ten hoppers were coming at them. They were flying just over treetop level, less than two kilometers away and closing fast. He shivered.

"Hold your positions," Chan said into his comm unit. "Maybe they'll pass over us and keep going." If that happened, he knew he and his men would have a long walk trying to follow them. But if that many hoppers landed anywhere nearby, the reinforced company they must be carrying would be far too many for his four men to deal with.

The formation began orbiting a small clearing two hundred meters away, and the hoppers touched down two at a time to disgorge passengers.

MacIlargie said, "We need to even the odds a bit." He checked the simulator on his blaster, raised it to his shoulder, took aim at the nearest hopper, and fired at it before Chan could stop him.

"Oh, no," Chan groaned. "You just got us killed."

The laser beam the simulator transmitted hit the hopper, and sensors on the aircraft signaled the crew that their bird was hit, where, and how badly. The pilot radioed his squadron commander that he'd been hit and the direction the fire had come from, then made a quick landing to off-load the squad and half of the infantrymen his hopper carried. He immediately lifted off again to treetop level and headed back toward base at half speed, which was as fast as the simulated damage the hopper sustained allowed it to go.

Another hopper, carrying extra weaponry instead of passengers, broke from the formation and spun toward the tor. It opened fire with its simulators, peppering the side of the tor with random fire until its infras could pick out and zero in on the "enemy."

MacIlargie gulped and his eyes bulged at the sight of the oncoming hopper and the fire it was spraying in their direction.

"I could have told you that was going to happen," Chan said dryly. "Dumb guy." Then he thought frantically about what to do next while MacIlargie fired a shot at the hopper as it swooped past them. MacIlargie missed.

"You just gave them our position," Chan told him. "They'll fry us on their next pass."

"No they won't," Schultz's voice said. "Maneuver toward me. I know a way out of here." MacIlargie ran upright, fast enough that Chan's reaching hand couldn't grab him and pull him into cover.

Chan made his way using as much cover as he could. The escort hopper came back around the side of the tor and swept the area he and MacIlargie had just vacated. Continuing the circuit, its fire reached the narrow opening in the hillside the four Marines ducked into just as Chan, again bringing up the rear, was diving through it. A couple of hundred meters away the last of the hoppers was off-loading its passengers, and the reinforced company was deploying for an assault on the tor to mop up any of the "enemy" who weren't killed by the escort hopper.

MacIlargie and Godenov huddled near the entrance, exclaiming to each other about their narrow escape from the hopper.

"Now you know why nobody makes the mistake of firing at Marine hoppers more than once," Chan snarled.

MacIlargie looked at him innocently and shrugged. "It seemed like a good idea at the time."

Chan shook his head patiently. "Now what do we do? Hope they give us a chance to surrender, or do we go out in a blaze of glory?" he asked sarcastically. He quickly looked around. The cave appeared to extend only three or four meters into the side of the tor.

"Neither," Schultz said. "Follow me." He scuttled to the back of the cave, past MacIlargie and Godenov, and seemed to melt into the rock wall on the left.

"Where'd he go?" Godenov exclaimed.

"You coming with me or not?" Schultz's muffled voice echoed from the wall.

Chan brushed past the two men to examine the wall where Schultz had disappeared. "Well, I'll be. Come on, you two."

Situated where it couldn't be seen until you were right on top of it, a crack just wide enough for a man to squeeze through opened into the side of the cave. Chan pulled and pushed his way through, and for a brief moment thought he was going to get stuck. MacIlargie, smaller, got through more easily. Godenov, like Chan, almost got stuck.

"Hey," MacIlargie exclaimed when he was in the crack, "it's dark in here. How are we going to see where we're going?"

After a couple of meters the narrow slit opened into a room larger than the cave mouth. Schultz was patiently waiting for them. They could see his face easily in the greenish illumination from a sphere in his hand the size of a tennis ball, a non-issue, civilian glowball. It wasn't a bright light, but in the darkness of the cave it was enough to see by.

"Never go into the field without your own personal glow-ball," he said to the new men. "If you live long enough, you might learn these things."

"Why wouldn't we live long enough?" MacIlargie asked.

"Because you're stupid. If you don't make a mistake in training and get yourself killed, someone else might kill you to keep you from getting him killed." He turned to a tunnel leading away from the entrance to the room. "I hope none of you are claustrophobic," he said over his shoulder. "It gets tight in a few places back here."

"Wait a minute," Chan said sharply. "Where are we going?"

"This way." Schultz pointed at the tunnel.

"Where does 'this way' go?" Chan asked. He didn't want to admit it, but in fact he was claustrophobic.

"To the other side of the tor. This place is honeycombed. We can come out anywhere we want."

"Yeah, and if it's honeycombed, we can get lost anywhere too. And how do you know it's honeycombed?" Schultz was a hard, cold man. The fact that Chan wanted to argue with him was a measure of how afraid he was of being in a cave.

"I've been here before. There are markers we can follow." He walked toward a shadow on the other side of the room and toed a small cairn. "Like this." He ducked and disappeared into the shadow—the mouth of a passageway.

"You better be right," Chan muttered, "because if I get lost or stuck in here and die, I'm coming back to haunt you." Then, louder, he said to MacIlargie and Godenov, "Follow him."

The tunnel was low enough that they had to crouch to get through, but they didn't have to crawl—the crawling and slithering came later. This first tunnel curved gently to the left, then took a sharp right and emptied into another cavern, which had two exits.

Schultz didn't hesitate before picking one and heading for it.

Nervous sweat was beginning to bead on Chan's forehead. "Are you sure you know where you're going?"

"I'm sure."

"I don't see any of those markers you said were there."

"You're not looking," Schultz said as he slid into the exit he'd chosen.

"I see it," MacIlargie said as he hurried after Schultz. His boot tapped the cairn as he passed it and knocked it over.

Godenov gave Chan a glance that was half excited and half scared, then followed.

"Muhammad's beard," Chan muttered. He shrugged out of his pack, dug in it for his glowball, then paused momentarily to repile the cairn. He hoped it didn't matter what order the rocks went in, because he couldn't remember how they'd been piled before MacIlargie knocked them over. "Wait for me," he said as he sidestepped into the crack in the wall. It was another tight squeeze, and he resolved that he wasn't bringing up the rear again—if he got stuck, he wanted someone behind him as well as in front so he could be pushed or pulled in either direction to get free.

Time seemed to suspend its normal movement, and it felt like they were spending the beginning of an eternity making their way through the rock passages. But it took less than one hour standard to make their way to the other side of the tor. They squeezed sideways through vertical and near-vertical cracks, slithered on their bellies through horizontal ones. Here they had to clamber up, there they gingerly climbed down. Most of the time, though, they duckwalked or crawled on all fours; few of the passages were high and wide enough for them to walk erect. Now and then they passed through chambers so small only three of them could squeeze in, but one of them was big enough to hold a platoon. Chan never got permanently stuck, but there was one briefly harrowing spot where he couldn't move forward or aft until he let all the air out of his lungs and was push-pulled through with his sweat serving as lubricant. Schultz noticed how wet he was and how he stank of fear, but only grunted.

When they reached yet another small room, Schultz took off his helmet, then turned off the glowball and returned it to his pack. "Wait a few minutes," he whispered to the others. "The exit's right on the other side. We'll let our eyes adjust until we can see some light, then follow it."

"We're not out yet," Chan said. "And there's still a whole company out there looking for us."

Schultz's helmetless head was now visible as a shadow on a shadow, and Chan saw him shake it. "They're not still looking for us here. Only a couple other people know about these caves. Either they're searching every opening on the other side of the tor or they think we managed to evade all their sensors and get away."

"Uh-huh."

At last, diffused light was visible on the far side of the room.

"Let's go," Schultz said. They followed him through the crack. The crack turned, dropped, and became a narrow tunnel that emptied directly onto the hillside next to a mid-size boulder. Schultz dragged himself out, then helped the others gain the open air.

"We made it," Chan said, immensely relieved. He shook himself, enjoying the feeling of nothing pressing in on him. "Now we need to find out where Mike Company went to so we can do a number on them."

"We're right here," came a voice from above and behind them. "Drop your weapons or you're dead."

They looked back and up into the faces and blasters of a Marine squad.

"You didn't really think you were the only ones who knew about the caves in there, did you?" the Mike Company squad leader asked.

Suddenly, the air smelled of fish again.

CHAPTER TWO

The communications console bleeped insistently beside Kurt Arschmann's elbow. He frowned, his train of thought interrupted. Damn. These production accounts for his plantations were complicated. How could he get through them with these interruptions? He could have given the accounts to his staff to review, especially now that he was burdened with the duties of Chairman of the Ruling Council, but for seventy years he'd personally reviewed the accounts every quarter, and he wasn't about to stop now.

"Yes?" he demanded impatiently. The dark complexion and jet-black hair and mustache of Kalat Uxmal appeared instantly on the console screen. People of Arschmann's social stratum still noticed such things, although, after two hundred years of intermarriages on Wanderjahr, mixed lineage—in Uxmal's case Pakistani and Mayan—had become accepted, even among the elite. Kalat's narrow features always reminded Arschmann of a rat, but he kept the unkind thought to himself. Kalat was too valuable to Arschmann as his private secretary to hold his mixed heritage against him or to mock his unfortunate physical endowments.

"Excellency, a matter of the utmost urgency—"

"What is it, Kalat? Spit it out!" Arschmann fumed.

"Excellency, I should really tell you about this in person," Kalat answered. Arschmann looked at the image of his secretary on the screen, glanced again at the overseer's report, and drummed his fingers on his desktop. "Very well. Come up at once."

As the door to Arschmann's private sanctum hissed shut

behind him, Kalat seemed to glide across the richly carpeted floor. That was another thing about Kalat that Arschmann had observed with annoyance over the years: he seemed always to creep about, so deferential and obsequious, but popping up at your elbow when you least expected it. Real men walked with purpose, unafraid, confident, spoke their piece clearly and moved on. But like many powerful men who prized efficiency and loyalty, Arschmann could not do without Kalat. The man was always there when needed, and nothing seemed too complicated for him to handle. He was really more a chief of staff than a secretary. Arschmann ran a big hand through his thick blond hair.

"Excellency, I have the most terrible news to impart." Kalat bowed slightly but remained silent. Arschmann sat behind his desk, waiting for Kalat to continue.

When he did not, Arschmann sighed. "*What* is the news, Kalat?" Arschmann asked in a tired voice.

"Excellency, in brief, your nephew is dead."

Arschmann just stared at Kalat for a long moment. "Which nephew, precisely?" he asked in a small voice.

"Excuse me, Excellency. Captain Rickdorf."

The color drained immediately from Arschmann's face. He had trouble speaking. Then, in a voice so quiet Kalat had to lean forward to hear it: "How?"

Briskly, Kalat outlined the details of the ambush conducted by the Che Loi Brigade of the Peoples Liberation Army in the Bavaran Hills Province. As his secretary concluded, one part of Arschmann's whirling mind realized Uxmal was enjoying his role as the bearer of sad tidings.

Both men sat, silent, for a long time. Rickdorf had been a favorite nephew. The boy had always been a pompous fool and a very poor choice as an officer of the Feldpolizei, but his love of the active life and his open admiration for the "Germanic" virtues of his forebears had endeared the young man to his uncle. Not smart enough to attend a first-class university off-world, as was the practice among the landowning class on Wanderjahr, young Rickdorf had attended a military school in the capital, where he excelled at riding, shooting, and fencing, but not at tactics or history. No one had ever thought his appointment as an officer of Feldpolizei, the paramilitary force created to deal with the guerrillas, would have ended so tragically. In fact, the young man's father considered the Feldpolizei an ideal place to keep his son out of trouble.

And now he and nearly a hundred of his men were dead!

Arschmann rested his head in his hands. "Do we know who conducted the ambush?"

"Excellency, our intelligence sources believe the bandits were under the command of Fernando Hing."

Arschmann's hands flew away from his face and he sat straight up.

"Goddamnit, the son of my cousin has murdered my nephew. And I put that son of a bitch through school!" Secretly, though, he was glad it hadn't been the other way around. Although Hing was an obstacle to Kurt Arschmann's ambitions, he admired Hing for his efficiency and dedication—primary virtues for a man, in Arschmann's opinion.

Then Arschmann took a deep breath and gathered himself. There was work to do. This incident would give him the leverage he needed. "Kalat, I want you to assemble the Council immediately," he said. His resonant baritone carried to the far corners of the spacious room.

"Excellency, on such short notice . . . I could easily arrange a satellite conference in just a few minutes . . ."

"Goddamnit, Kalat, I want them *here*, in person, and I said immediately! I don't need to spread the news; if we know, the whole world knows what happened out there. We need to discuss what to do about it, and I won't do that over a satellite hookup where someone might be listening in. I want them all here by tomorrow morning. Make that very clear. Those who are visiting their plantations on other continents can fly back this evening. See that it is done."

Back in his own office, Kalat Uxmal smiled. He would make the calls necessary to convene the Council tomorrow. My God, he thought, that a poor boy like himself, from the barrios of Brosigville, could have risen to such a position of power and influence! But first he had to get a message to a person right there in the capital. Kalat chuckled.

"Thank you, sweet Karl," Arschmann whispered when he was alone again, as if addressing the man in the portrait on the wall of his office. Briefly, he considered smoking a pipe of thule, but he had no business celebrating in view of the news that had just been delivered. In fact, he had already forgotten about the late Captain Rickdorf.

This thing with the Peoples Liberation Army, or whatever fancy name they were going under, had taken a very bad turn. They should have taken immediate and decisive action against the guerrillas years ago, as he had advised at the time—imprisoned them, shot them, exiled them, whatever it took. But no one believed a handful of overeducated college radicals could ever pose a serious threat to the government of Wanderjahr, especially not when the Confederation had just granted them an unrestricted license to export thule to every world in Human Space. Not when unparalleled prosperity was about to catapult Wanderjahr from a third-class developing world into an economic competitor with the oldest and most advanced members of the Confederation of Worlds.

What do these fools want? Arschmann mused silently. Democracy? That was a system where fools were allowed to elect other fools and cowards to ruin their lives for them. Sharing of wealth? That only guaranteed everyone would be poor. Land ownership? Pigshit! What would the peasants of Wanderjahr know about managing their own property? Independence? What was that but pure economic survival of the fittest? Unionizing of the plantation workers? Good God, didn't they realize that a union would only create power and prosperity for its bosses and nothing for the peasants? No, what the bandits wanted was power all to themselves, Arschmann concluded, and if they got it, they would ruin the economy and social order painstakingly established on Wanderjahr by his forebears over two and a half centuries. And, more important, their seeking power put the bandits in direct competition with him.

Kurt Arschmann glanced at the hologram portrait of Karl Eschmann Wanderjahrer that occupied an honored place on one wall. Dressed in the antique formal garb of the late twenty-second century, the old explorer seemed to stare through him. Arschmann was descended from Wanderjahrer through a female line of his family. His own fierce blue eyes matched those of the revered patriarch. Otherwise there was no physical resemblance. There was even less between them philosophically. Where Karl Wanderjahrer had been a philanthropist and a visionary, Kurt Arschmann was a businessman.

Karl Wanderjahrer was the descendant of a long line of German Christian evangelicals belonging to a sect calling itself the United Brotherhood. They believed in hard work, the glory of God, and the dignity of man. Viciously persecuted in ancient times, the church found spiritual renewal in America, where it flourished long before the Second American Civil War. It had reestablished itself in its native Germany long before Karl Wanderjahrer was born in Neu Kaiserslautern in 2101.

The Brotherhood did not eschew the fruits of its labor. Quite the contrary. Over the years many of its families became very wealthy, including the Wanderjahrers. By the time Karl came into his inheritance at the age of forty, he had already developed plans to fulfill one of the Brotherhood's most cherished dreams: the creation of a world where their descendants could live in peace with one another, free from the persecutions that had plagued the sect since its founding in the fifteenth century.

With the purchase of the starship *Dr. Elly Brosig*, Karl's and the Brotherhood's dream became a reality. Chartered by the Confederation of Worlds as an exploration and survey vessel, the *Brosig* actually accomplished much good work extending the outer envelope of Human Space during the fifty-year period it took Wanderjahrer and his companions to find the right world for their settlement. When the world later to be known as Wanderjahr was discovered, it fit all the criteria the Brotherhood's vestrymen had established as necessary for settlement: far from the space lanes of the day, habitable by humans without the necessity of terraforming, and an environment capable of supporting an agricultural economy. Initial surveys reported a fauna possibly inimical to humans, reptiloid creatures vaguely reminiscent of the Cretaceous period of Earth's geological past, but the vestrymen decided the beasts of Wanderjahr could be controlled, so an immigration company was established.

Karl compromised on a name for the new world. Arguing that it was too egotistical to name the place obviously after himself, no matter how much he deserved the honor, he suggested Wanderjahr, a play on his own name and on the German word "Wanderjahre," a journeyman's years of travel. Unlike so many staid and serious members of the Brotherhood, Karl Wanderjahrer did have a sense of humor.

But the Brotherhood, never a very numerous sect even after the persecutions had ended, soon realized that it could never recruit enough colonists from among its own members to make the venture work. Besides, even among the most faithful communicants, there were many who just would not leave Earth for life on a remote and possibly dangerous new world.

So Karl suggested, and the vestrymen accepted the suggestion readily, that they recruit from among Earth's underprivileged. They settled on peoples of Latin America and Asia known to be hardworking, energetic, and hardy people who would not find the intensive labor required to establish a self-sustaining agrarian economy on a virgin planet too unfamiliar a way of life. Young families were preferred, but single men and women with valuable skills such as doctors, engineers, technicians, and mechanics were also accepted. The prospective colonists were screened carefully by a Board of Colonization, and every individual accepted had to agree to undergo conversion and faithfully apply the religious doctrines and beliefs of the Brotherhood. Happily, most of the immigrants found the Brotherhood's doctrines far less onerous than those of the faiths in which they had been raised.

Return transport was not part of the agreement. Still, people came in the thousands.

Life on Wanderjahr was not easy at first, and tragedy struck

within only a few years of the first settlement when the wise
and charismatic Karl Wanderjahrer was carried off in the jaws
of a ravening beast. Then, less than fifty years later, the enormous cost of supporting the colony bankrupted the Board of
Colonization, and the immigrants suddenly found themselves
on their own in a remote quadrant of Human Space. Through
determination and necessity the colonists held on, year after
year pushing settlements farther from Brosigville, their first
town. Crops imported from Earth flourished in Wanderjahr's
lush climate, and the local fauna and flora, when it wasn't
eating the colonists, proved edible itself, so starvation was
never a likelihood. Of necessity in those early years, the many
cultural groups settled on Wanderjahr—the descendants of the
Incas and Aztecs from the mountains of South America and
Mexico, Indians and Pakistanis from that huge subcontinent,
Vietnamese and Cambodians from the Mekong Delta region—
intermingled.

The original German families kept mostly to themselves,
although there was some intermarriage with the other immi-
grant communities. Race was not the barrier that separated
them. The barrier most Wanderjahrians found impossible to
cross was that the Germans were the bosses and everyone else
their employees.

Government on Wanderjahr was decentralized. The ruling
families ran their properties as individual fiefdoms called
Staats, administering justice and local government from their
home cities with total autonomy. A Ruling Council was established to deal with interplanetary trade, political relations, and
common interests such as tariffs for offworld imports, common security, and intra-Staat affairs. The Ruling Council consisted of nine representatives, the heads of the nine families
that owned all the arable land on Wanderjahr. Chairmanship of
the Council rotated among its nine members. The Council
members selected an ambassador to the Confederation of
Worlds, and all his activities were subject to their supervision
and approval. Four years earlier, the Confederation had delegated as its ambassador to Wanderjahr an aging diplomat
ready for retirement. The man was a joke among the oligarchs,

but the Confederation's ambassador nonetheless, and living proof that Wanderjahr had at last been accepted into the community of worlds.

English was the lingua franca on Wanderjahr, as it was throughout the Confederation of Worlds. The Brotherhood never thought to impose German on its colonists, since it believed a man should talk to God in whatever language he was most comfortable with. Along with the languages the original colonists brought with them to Wanderjahr, they also perpetuated the cultures of their native lands on Earth. English was taught in all the schools on the planet, and government business was conducted in English, but so long as the oligarchs could communicate somehow with their employees, they didn't care what languages they spoke at home.

The lower echelons of local government often resembled those of the places on Earth from which the majority of the local inhabitants' ancestors had come. So the mayor of a town where Hispanic people had established themselves might be referred to as its alcalde, while the chief official of a town where Germanic descendants prevailed might be called its Burgermeister. These arrangements existed, of course, only at the pleasure of the local oligarch, who ultimately held the real power within his Staat.

Nothing changed when thule was discovered and other Confederation worlds began to trade with Wanderjahr for the valuable commodity. At first the oligarchs' chief worry was suppressing the illegal production of the drug for home consumption and export. Local police forces, known as Stadtpolizei or metropolitan police, were used to deal with the illicit trade, turning a blind eye to those smugglers who could buy them off, while rigorously suppressing the ones who could not. Until the outbreak of the rebellion, an army and navy had been considered unnecessary.

The Christian evangelical spirit that drove early settlers like Karl Wanderjahrer soon dissipated, to be replaced eventually by a watered-down state-sanctioned "ministry" preaching that what one gave to Caesar was as important as what one owed God; homegrown religious cults sprang up among the people.

The portrait of old Karl Wanderjahrer seemed to glare balefully down upon him, Kurt Arschmann reflected as he brooded in his office.

And now, some 250 years after the old man first set foot on this world, now, as the oligarchs had virtually within their grasp the most profitable trading franchise in all of Human Space, those goddamned radicals had to go and kill Captain Rickdorf and nearly a hundred of his men!

"All right, Kurt, we all know what happened, just what the hell can we do about it?" Klaus von Hauptmann barked once the Council members had seated themselves. Klaus affected the mannerisms of a nineteenth-century Prussian Junker, even to the extent of carrying a riding crop everywhere he went, although the few horses there once were on Wanderjahr had long since become tasty snacks for the larger reptiloids. He was known to be quick to apply the crop to the backs of subordinates. He also considered the Wanderjahrian Feldpolizei nothing more than a convenient hiding place for the leading families' idiot sons, and shared not a bit of sympathy with Arschmann over the loss of his worthless nephew. The Peoples Liberation Army had found Hauptmann's plantations a fruitful source for recruits despite the private army he maintained to keep his workers in line. And the "von" in Hauptmann's name had been added by his grandfather, to bolster his own image, not as a legitimate connection to the ancient German royal line.

"I assume we'll ask for outside assistance." Lorelei Keutgens smiled. Kurt acknowledged the old matriarch with a nod, thinking, The goddamned bitch is right on cue! "Lori" Keutgens, in contrast with Hauptmann and some of the other members, took care of her people and donated generously to the appropriate charities. The guerrillas had had the least success proselytizing among her workers.

"Humph," Max Ficker snorted. "That damned Feldpolizei is less than worthless, always has been. Damned waste of money. Damned comic-opera buffoons." He turned quickly to Arschmann, remembering that Captain Rickdorf had been the Chairman's nephew. "Sorry, Kurt, I meant no insult to your family." Within the Council, Ficker was tolerated because he had inherited his lands. But as a manager he was worthless, giving control of his holdings to factors and spending most of his time gambling and scandalizing the countryside with his endless amours.

Arschmann merely nodded, then waited for the others to voice their opinions.

"Jesus our Savior protect us," Gretel Siebensberg sighed. "Why now, of all times, just as the Confederation has granted us the franchise to export thule without restrictions?" Gretel was a throwback to Karl Wanderjahrer's ancient faith. Extremely otherworldly, she had restored the faith of her fathers throughout Freidland, her Staat, spending large sums on churches and charities for the benefit of her workers. But she was also a sharp businesswoman.

"Money," Turbat Nguyen-Multan interjected. "The bandits smell money, and with money comes power." Multan was an anomaly among the ruling families, the descendant of entrepreneurial Pakistani-Vietnamese ancestors. He ruled his Staat, Porcina, with the iron fist of a warlord. "These people claim ideology is their religion, but it isn't. Power is." The Feldpolizei, which was controlled by the Ruling Council and could be deployed anywhere it was needed on Wanderjahr, was never invited onto Turbat's lands. Like Hauptmann, he believed in settling scores by himself. He had turned his own Stadtpolizei into a private mercenary force. But unlike Hauptmann, who was not so draconian in his methods, Turbat protected his interests simply by killing anyone who even seemed to be out of line.

"Speaking on behalf of Herr Mannlicher, the bandits have legitimate grievances," Carmago Kampot Khong, Helmut Mannlicher's factor, said. Hauptmann and Multan snorted derisively. The others just stared at the Mexican-Cambodian half-breed. He was Mannlicher's trusted subordinate and had served Mannlicher faithfully his entire life, as other members of his family had served the Mannlichers from the time of the original settlement. The old man was not able to attend the meeting himself because he was only days, perhaps hours, from death. At the age of 140, Helmut Mannlicher was only one generation removed from people who had actually known Karl Wanderjahrer. When Mannlicher died, it was generally expected that Khong would share the vast holdings with the old man's own children, and then he would be a power to reckon with on his own. While not at all religious, Mannlicher had believed all his life in the value of labor and the dignity of the laborer, and Carmago Kampot Khong too was devoted to that philosophy. The bandits had found no foothold in their territory either, but Mannlicher believed the oligarchy could survive the crisis only by sharing its power with the people, and he had long advocated a dialogue with the guerrillas.

"Well, they are a problem," Hans Rauscher ventured timidly. He glanced apprehensively at Hauptmann and Multan as he spoke. The guerrillas were causing him great problems by destroying his crops and suborning his laborers. They were successful among his people not because Rauscher's workers were oppressed, but because they were neglected, and Rauscher, a weak and indecisive man who could not fight his own battles, depended entirely upon the Feldpolizei for security.

"Yes, and I go along with Lori. We should ask for outside help," Manfred Kaiserstuhl said. Kaiserstuhl was a compromising old charlatan who could always be counted on to take the easiest solution to any problem, preferring to buy his way out when that was possible. This approach had worked well with the guerrillas, who took the money he gave them to leave his properties alone and used it to finance their operations in other Staats while recruiting actively among his workers.

"Brothers and Sisters," Arschmann said, using a linguistic formality that had originated with the United Brotherhood almost a thousand years before, "I propose this: we dispatch an urgent message to Ambassador Misthaufen directing him to approach the Confederation of Worlds requesting military assistance—"

"But their Constitution forbids direct military intervention in member worlds' internal affairs," Lori Keutgens exclaimed.

"Except in the most extreme cases, and we are not yet that bad off," Rauscher interjected.

"Yes," Arschmann agreed. "But we will not ask for 'intervention,' only 'assistance' in the form of equipment and training for the Feldpolizei. It would be a short-term mission at most, and if the bandits mount any assaults while our men are being trained, the offworlders will have to act to protect themselves, thereby eliminating our problem for us. In any event, once they leave, the Feldpolizei can carry on the process of rooting out the bandits. Let the bandits suffer some casualties, and their zeal for living in the hinterlands will dissipate quickly enough."

"We do not need the Confederation Army here," Multan snorted.

"Send in the Marines?" Hauptmann laughed.

"Precisely," Arschmann responded. "I suggest we recommend asking for a small contingent of Confederation Marines, what they call a FIST, or something like that, to help train our men. They've done that before on other worlds and are famous for it. The Marines will obey their orders, and if they have to fight, they will make the bandits sorry they were ever born. Are we agreed on this course?"

"No foreign troops shall ever set foot in Porcina," Multan said.

"But do you agree, my dear Turbat, that those who wish for such help have the right to ask for it?"

Multan thought for a moment. "Yes. But none will ever come into Porcina," he repeated.

"All right, then, we are agreed. Nevertheless, there are some details we need to work out," he said.

"Rules of engagement and command authority?" Multan laughed, shaking his head. He had been wondering how long it would take Arschmann to get around to these all-important details.

"Yes," Arschmann said.

"The Confederation will impose strict conditions if they agree to deploy Marines here," Lori Keutgens said.

"Yes," Arschmann replied. "I suggest we instruct our

ambassador to agree to the following: the Marines will take over complete command of the Feldpolizei, lead it, and train it. They will have the power to demote and promote."

"Who cares, so long as they do not set foot in my domains," Multan said. Hauptmann nodded his agreement vigorously.

"Then we are agreed on this?" Arschmann polled the other members, who each nodded approval.

"Finally, the local police forces," Arschmann began. "You all have them and control them as you see fit. I want mine completely retrained, as we are doing for the Feldpolizei. I will ask the Confederation for a team of professional police officers to be assigned here, same ground rules as for the Marines. Since Brosigville is within Arschland, they will start here. Any objections? Anyone else wish to participate?"

"Never! Never, never, never! Not in Porcina!" Multan raged, banging his fist on the table.

"Very well," Arschmann replied softly. "Anyone else wish to comment?"

"I am with Multan." Hauptmann glowered.

"Well, Turbat," Lori smiled sweetly, "some of us don't have quite the stomach for police work that you and Klaus do."

"None of you have 'stomach'!" Multan growled. Then he glared at Arschmann, who'd expected his reaction; a real police force in the capital would put the screws to Multan's clandestine business interests there, and Turbat Nguyen-Multan was not one to take that interference lightly, even though the operations were a personal insult to Arschmann since policing the capital city was his responsibility.

"Very well, then, to summarize," Arschmann sighed. "The Marines will operate under no restrictions. They will command and train the Feldpolizei, but no Feldpolizei or Marines will be allowed into Porcina. Those of you who wish may join me in asking the Confederation to provide professional police training for our Stadtpolizei, under the same rules as apply to the Marines." He looked in turn at each of the Council members and no one demurred. "Then it is agreed. I will draft a communiqué today and submit it to each of you for final

review. A courtesy copy will be furnished to Ambassador
Jayben Spears, of course."

Several of the Council members laughed outright when
Arschmann mentioned the Confederation's ambassador by
name. A stooped, gangly, slightly bowlegged man, Ambassador Spears was famous on Wanderjahr for eating his way
through official receptions without apparently gaining much
weight, and delivering advice in terse and very undiplomatic
language. He could consume prodigious quantities of wine
without showing any ill effects except that his language then
became even more undiplomatic. Twice, to the great amusement of Lori Keutgens, he had brazenly asked her to marry
him, once at a formal dinner party and another time at a
funeral. Lori liked Spears, not because he flattered her with his
attention, but because he always spoke the truth and never
minced his words. And diplomatic protocol required the
Ruling Council to inform him of any instructions passed to its
ambassador for presentation to the Confederation Council.

"Kurt," Lori Keutgens ventured, "I agree to all your pro-
posals, but before all these others here assembled, I want to say
that inviting these Marines to come here will change everything. I don't know if that will be good or bad."

Nobody said anything in response to her statement, but all
knew that when Lori Keutgens spoke, she usually knew what
she was talking about. A bachelor, Arschmann had often considered proposing to Lori after her husband had been killed.
But years passed and he had never made the proposal because
he knew the strong-willed woman would be difficult to
manage. He would deal with her eventually, though. Things
were about to change, all right. He smiled at Lori. She smiled
back. Arschmann had the uncomfortable feeling she knew
what he was thinking.

"We must do something," Rauscher said lamely. He was
delighted with Arschmann's suggestions; if the Marines
were successful, he could have the protection of a revamped
planetary Feldpolizei at little cost to himself. He turned to
Arschmann: "Draft the communiqué."

"Very well. Friends, I need only remind you that these

deliberations must be kept entirely secret until the Marines deploy and start their work. Please, no incautious remarks?"

Arschmann then summoned Kalat. Two minutes after a smiling Kalat left the Council room, word of the deliberations was on its way to his contacts in the city. Just as Kurt Arschmann expected it would be.

CHAPTER
THREE

Two days after Chan and his patrol were captured, the exercise ended. And Ensign vanden Hoyt had his first chance to talk to Chan and the men he'd led into the cave. The platoon commander shook his head sadly. Staff Sergeant Bass stood a pace to his left, arms akimbo, glowering at them.

"Whose bright idea was it to shoot at a hopper formation?" vanden Hoyt asked.

Schultz turned his head and glared at MacIlargie. Godenov edged away from MacIlargie.

Chan swallowed nervously. He didn't think it mattered whose idea it had been; as the man in charge the mistake was his responsibility. He opened his mouth to say so, but MacIlargie spoke first.

"It seemed like a good idea, sir. Look, sir, there were ten hoppers. I figured if we each took out one it would cut the odds against us almost in half." A wild grin split his face. "If it worked, it sure would have shaken up the rest of 'em. That had to be all of Mike Company, and the four of us might have been able to stop the whole company by ourselves."

"Haven't you ever heard about escort hoppers?" vanden Hoyt asked with exaggerated patience.

MacIlargie shrugged uncomfortably. "They all looked the same. I didn't think they had a gunship with them."

Bass couldn't take it anymore. In two strides he was nose-to-nose with MacIlargie. "If one of them looked like a gunship, everybody would know which one to shoot at. Or were your D.I.s deficient in their training and nobody told you that?"

MacIlargie flinched. "I forgot," he said in a small voice.

"YOU WHAT?" Bass bellowed.

"I forgot."

"Louder, I can't hear you," Bass roared.

"I FORGOT!" MacIlargie shouted.

Bass shook his head and took a step away, muttering, "He forgot. That young man's going to get people killed." Then he spun back to Chan. "You were in charge," he shouted, "why'd you let him do something so stupid?"

"Because I didn't think he was that stupid," Chan snapped back defensively.

Bass blinked. That was a good answer, but he still got in the last word. "Never underestimate anybody's capacity for stupidity." With a quick glance at vanden Hoyt, he returned to his previous position and resumed his glower.

Vanden Hoyt silently studied the four of them for a long moment, then calmly said, "You had a frightening experience when MacIlargie fired at that hopper. Now you know why almost nobody ever fires on a hopper formation—and nobody is ever stupid enough to do it a second time."

He gave them time to dwell on that before continuing. "Third platoon failed to achieve its mission—to stop Mike Company. In part because the first of our teams to come into contact with them, the team that could have done the most to tie them up while the rest of the teams maneuvered to hurt them, got itself caught immediately and put Mike Company on full alert." He looked directly at MacIlargie and added, "I hope at least some of us learned something."

The full company stood at ease in morning formation behind its barracks. Everyone wore the dull-green garrison utilities that hadn't changed much in appearance from the field uniforms of the twentieth century. Captain Conorado, the company commander, stood front and center, the company's other officers arrayed behind him. Gunnery Sergeant Thatcher was at his post to the left of the officers. Even Top Myer, the company first sergeant who was rarely seen at morning formation, was present.

"We have a deployment," Captain Conorado announced.

There were few murmurs and fewer visible reactions in the ranks. Most of the men had been on enough previous deployments for the announcement to be almost routine. The only thing out of the ordinary was that a new mission had come so soon after the last one. "In three days, 34th FIST will board ship for transit to Confederation member world—" He looked at the paper in his hand to make sure of the name. "—Wanderjahr." That did cause murmurs—if the skipper had to double-check the name of the place they were going to, it must really be out of the way. "All I can tell you about the mission at this time is Wanderjahr has an insurgency problem and has requested Confederation assistance."

Conorado looked sharply to his left. "Company Gunnery Sergeant," he barked, "front and center!"

Gunny Thatcher snapped to attention, took three brisk steps to his front, pivoted, and marched to the company commander.

"Company Gunnery Sergeant, the company is yours," Conorado said sharply.

"Sir, the company is mine," Thatcher acknowledged. "Aye aye, sir." He brought his hand up in a sharp salute.

Conorado returned the salute equally sharply, executed a training manual about-face, and marched toward the entrance to the barracks. The other officers and the first sergeant fell in behind him.

Thatcher about-faced and barked out, "Comp'ny, a-ten-TION!" He quickly scanned the company. There were a few new men who had never deployed before, but most of them had already been in combat. His chest swelled; he knew they'd acquit themselves well once more, whatever this mission entailed. "Platoon sergeants, you have your orders. Comp-NEE, dis-MISSED!"

First and second platoons broke ranks and headed for the barracks to begin preparations for the deployment.

Before third platoon got away, Bass snapped out, "As you were, third platoon." The men, who had already broken formation, shuffled back into position. None of them stood quite at attention, though they were all attentive. Bass waited until the rest of the company was far enough away that he could speak without shouting. "Claypoole, Dean, on me." The two men stepped out of ranks and ran to stand at attention in front of him. Bass looked to his left, to the first squad leader. "Sergeant Hyakowa, the platoon is yours. Get them ready."

"Aye aye," Hyakowa said. He stepped to the front of the platoon and dismissed the men from formation. As they left they all looked at Bass and the two men standing in front of him, wondering what was up.

"The skipper wants to see you," Bass said when the others were gone. "So let's go and see the skipper."

Claypoole and Dean looked at each other. Dean wondered if Claypoole had screwed up in some way and gotten them both in trouble. He wished they were in their dress scarlets with their medals shiny on their chests, not that they had many, only two apiece. But one of those two was a Bronze Star, won for bravery in the face of the enemy. Still, he thought an officer wouldn't be as hard on a man whose chest showed he was a hero.

Claypoole had no idea why the company commander wanted to see them. But he knew neither of them had done anything wrong.

"What's he want us for?" Dean asked as the three of them headed for the barracks.

"He didn't say" was all Bass replied.

Claypoole and Dean stood at attention in front of Captain Conorado's desk, staring at a spot on the wall above and behind the seated company commander. Bass stood casually behind them. Ensign vanden Hoyt stood at one side of the desk, Top Myer at the other side with his arms sternly folded across his burly chest.

Conorado looked at the two PFCs expressionlessly and thumped the end of a stylus on his desktop a few times. He didn't look happy. "At ease," he said after a moment. He smiled slightly at the two young Marines who now looked at him nervously. "Relax, you're not in trouble."

Dean was visibly relieved. Claypoole perked up.

"I've got a special job for the two of you. You know that FIST HQ got hit hard by raiders on Elneal, don't you?"

"Yessir," they said together.

"I heard they got chopped up pretty bad," Claypoole said.

Dean grimaced at Claypoole's forwardness. Top Myer glowered at Claypoole; Bass nudged him in the kidney.

"You heard right," Conorado confirmed. "They lost so many men who haven't been replaced yet that Brigadier Sturgeon has ordered each company-size unit in the FIST to detach two men to FIST HQ for our upcoming operation. After all due consideration, and full consultation with the company's officers and senior NCOs, I've picked you two."

Dean blanched at being told he was going to leave the company.

"What?" Claypoole exclaimed. "We didn't do anything wrong, we're good Marines. How come you want to get rid of us?"

Conorado held up a hand to forestall reaction from the others in his office. "As you were, PFC," he said in a commanding voice.

"Aye aye, sir." Claypoole snapped to attention, followed half a beat later by Dean.

"I said 'at ease,' so relax. That's right, Claypoole, you didn't do anything wrong." He leaned back in his chair. "The brigadier was very specific about the kind of men he wants. Sharp, intelligent, quick learners who have been on at least one operation and know how to fight. You two fit that description. You probably know that headquarters types think that infantrymen are pretty dumb. Well, they think that because we routinely do things they're afraid to do. The fact that each of you has a Bronze Star should impress them enough for them to show you some respect." He sat straight again and said briskly, "I'm giving you this assignment because I know you'll do a good job and will reflect well on this company. Then, when you rejoin us, you'll be able to do that much better a job because you'll have a deeper understanding of what goes on at higher levels. Do you have any questions?"

"Nossir," Dean said. Claypoole shook his head.

"Good. Then you're dismissed. Get all your gear ready and report back to the office at fourteen hours. Top Myer will arrange for your transportation to FIST."

When they were out of the captain's office, Dean pulled Corporal Doyle, the chief clerk, from where he was supervising PFC Palmer in getting the company office ready to mount out. "Did you hear that?" he asked.

Doyle pulled a face. "Yeah, I heard."

"You should be the one going to FIST," Claypoole said, disgruntled. "You know all that office stuff."

"You're a quick learner too," Dean said. "You proved that when you were humping across the Martac Waste with us." Corporal Doyle, the company's senior clerk, had been with the two of them, Staff Sergeant Bass, and four other Marines on a patrol on Elneal that was involved in some of the fiercest fighting in that campaign. Like the others, he had earned a Bronze Star for heroism.

"Right," PFC Palmer broke in. "I think he should have picked you too." Before Corporal Doyle joined the company, Palmer had been the chief clerk—the only clerk. He wanted to be top dog again. They ignored him—Palmer was only a clerk, not a fighting Marine. Doyle was "only" a clerk too, but he had fought alongside the blastermen, and they had a respect for him they had for no other clerks.

"Well," Doyle said, "they didn't pick me. But listen, if they need someone else, put in a good word for me, will you?"

"You know we will."

Claypoole clapped Doyle on the shoulder and the two left the office to pack their gear, grumbling about being picked for office duty.

On the appointed day, the 34th Fleet Initial Strike Team boarded Essays, the navy's surface-to-orbit shuttles, and lifted off to mate with and board the medium cruiser CNSS *Denver*.

"A cruiser?" MacIlargie asked. "What are we doing on a cruiser? Do they expect us to man the crow's nest and repel boarders?"

"Shut up, MacIlargie," said Corporal Dornhofer, his fire

team leader. "You wouldn't understand even if somebody told you." To himself, Dornhofer was wondering the same thing. Why were they going on a medium cruiser instead of a troop transport?

But they had neither time nor energy to worry about the reason. They had to get to their quarters, stow their gear, and prepare for the first jump. All of which was more difficult than it should have been since they weren't familiar with a cruiser's layout and the ship was in null-g orbit.

The *Denver* was a confusion of sounds: metallic pings rang throughout the ship from crews working on its hull to repair the ravages of interstellar flight; gears clanged as great chain drives mysteriously moved strange objects to unknown destinations; sweaty chief petty officers bellowed orders at greasy sailors to urge them on in their portside preparations; motors whirred and squealed as bulk movers shifted loads from hither to yon.

Not a man among the thousand Marines of 34th FIST had a good idea of what the bustle around them was all about. All they could do was allow the navy ratings to snap them into draglines, then float along behind them through endless passageways to wherever they were bound. Some of the passageways went this way, others that, still more in a third dimension. Under powered flight within a planetary system, some passageways would go fore and aft or side to side while others went up and down. During time in warp-space some horizontals would become verticals, and vice versa. The Marines had no way of knowing which was which at this time, and few of them cared; they knew they wouldn't spend much time wandering the ship.

Eventually they reached the holds where they were to be berthed. Holds, not troop compartments. The *Denver* was a combat ship and had compartments for its crew, not for passengers. At least the holds had berthing, row upon row of narrow cots stacked five high. Lockers were just small-item containers stacked between the cots. The Marines didn't voice much in way of complaint, most of them having suffered worse accommodations at the hands of the navy. Even the officers and senior NCOs didn't feel badly used at finding that their quarters were sections of the holds incompletely walled off by stacks of small-item containers.

"Secure your gear," the platoon sergeants bellowed as they propelled themselves through the air in their platoon areas.

"If it can fit in your lockers, fit it in your lockers," the squad leaders shouted as they flitted from man to man, slowing only to show the newest men how to do it. Blasters, truly safetied because their batteries wouldn't be issued until the end of the journey, were locked into place at the heads of the cot stacks. Crew-served weapons were secured in the senior NCO quarters.

The Marines were given less than a half hour to settle in before Klaxons blared and a well-modulated female voice announced, "The ship is about to leave port. For safety's sake, everyone secure yourselves into your launch couches. I say again, the ship is about to leave port, secure yourselves in your launch couches."

"Launch couches?" someone shouted. "What launch couches?"

"Belay the mickeymouse, people," the platoon sergeants and squad leaders ordered. "Everybody, in your cots." The platoon sergeants added, "These aren't automatics, strap yourselves in," and the squad leaders took up the cry. Fire team leaders hustled their men into their cots, made sure they were all strapped in, then took care of themselves. The squad leaders checked the fire team leaders' work, then secured themselves. The last Marines to strap in were the platoon sergeants. In Kilo Company, one platoon sergeant wasn't fast enough and the abrupt acceleration of the *Denver* slammed him to the deck, breaking his arm.

It took two days for the *Denver* to reach its first jump point, where its crew and passengers were subjected to the trials of transition into warpspace. A day after that, each company was assembled separately in whatever area its commander could locate for a briefing on the upcoming mission. Company L was lucky enough to get the ship's gym.

* * *

The ship's gym wasn't the largest space on the *Denver*, and the exercise apparatus and fitness-testing equipment that filled it made it seem smaller. But it was big enough. Squad leaders picked spots and had their men make themselves comfortable on the machines or the surrounding floor space. They were packed tightly, but didn't have to sit on each other. Unobtrusively, the platoon sergeants stood at the main hatch, blocking egress to anyone who might have ideas about skipping the briefing. Gunny Thatcher blocked entry to the shower room by himself. A small platform was set up at the secondary entrance, which led to officer country, and Top Myer stood on it, burly arms folded across his beefy chest, looking over the men of Company L. Everyone quickly quieted under the first sergeant's scrutiny and looked attentively toward him.

Noises came through the hatch at Myer's back. He looked toward it, then faced the company again and bellowed, "COMP-ny, A-ten-TION!" just as Captain Conorado, followed by the other officers, burst through the hatch. Myer stepped off the platform to give the captain space. All present scrambled to their feet and snapped to as close an approximation of attention as they could manage in the cramped space.

"As you were," Conorado shouted as he bounded onto the platform. He stood feet spread and arms akimbo, bent forward slightly at the waist, looking every bit the Marine combat commander as his men settled themselves back down. Then he took a long moment to look around the compartment, giving the impression that he looked each man directly in the eye. The other five officers, who stood against the bulkhead behind him, looked at their own men.

"We are on a nominal training mission to the world of Wanderjahr," Conorado finally said when everyone was back in place. He didn't shout, but his voice carried loud and clear to every man in the compartment, undampened by the 120 bodies that filled it. "There is an internal conflict under way on that planet. Officially, the Confederation classifies it as a rebellion, not a civil war. Wanderjahr's ruling oligarchy calls it banditry. Wanderjahr doesn't have an army, it has a heavily armed paramilitary police force called the Feldpolizei, which is German for 'field police.' The Feldpolizei are getting their tails whipped by the opposition forces, whether they are bandits or rebels. The oligarchs have requested that the Confederation send in Marines to train the Feldpolizei in combat tactics so they can fight more effectively." He shook his head. "From what I've read in the reports, it sounds like the Feldpolizei go into the hills and try to use urban riot control measures to fight guerrilla bands. As you can imagine, that doesn't work very well. We are going to teach them how to fight like soldiers." He had to pause as his Marines nudged each other and whispered what an easy job they had coming up if all they had to do was teach cops how to fight like soldiers; that they'd probably wrap it up in a week or so and then pull some liberty.

"All right, belay the mickeymouse," Conorado ordered after a few seconds. "We're going to teach them how to be good soldiers, the kind who can do serious fighting. One thing that means is, when the Feldpolizei sends out patrols against the guerrillas, we will go with them to make sure they do it right." He held up a hand to forestall any questions. "You will not be going along as noncombatant advisers. I won't subject any of my people to that kind of danger—and neither will the brigadier. Any Marine who goes into the hills goes as a fighter.

"Now, we estimate that this operation will last three months. I know, I know, three months isn't anywhere near as long as the training you had to become Marines. But the Feldpolizei is already organized along paramilitary lines, and they have probably mastered the basics of garrison soldiery and know how to use weapons, so those are things you won't have to train them in. This will be more on the lines of an advanced infantry course. And the newest one of you knows a lot more about being an infantryman than almost any of them. When we reach Wanderjahr there will be a short period of orientation and organization. Then you will be assigned to the Feldpolizei units you'll be training.

"I saw questions on some of your faces when I mentioned the ruling oligarchy. It's an unusual form of government that few, if any, of you, have ever seen before. I'm going to let the first sergeant cover that when he gives you his orientation. First Sergeant, the company is yours."

Myer leaped onto the platform as Conorado stepped down from it and bellowed, "COMP-ny, A-ten-TION!" The officers were gone before the Marines could get to their feet. Myer let them stand at attention for a moment while he glared at them. He glared not because he was angry, but to sharpen their attention on him and what he had to say.

"At ease." He clumped his feet on the platform—it wasn't big enough for him to pace on—as though collecting his thoughts. Then he glowered out at the company. "I was watching you while the skipper was talking, and I got the distinct impression that most of you think this is some kind of candy-ass operation we're going on, that it'll be the easiest thing anyone ever did to earn a campaign star on his Marine Expeditionary Medal. Well, if that's what you're thinking, jettison it right now. We could be walking into a meat grinder. The rebels win every time the Feldpolizei fights them. And the Feldpolizei is armed with blasters and other modern weapons, and the rebels are mostly armed with projectile weapons. That's right, men armed with antiques are routinely whipping men with modern arms. Think about it, and think about why it's possible. Now, most of what I'm going to tell you to help you think about what we might be up against isn't stuff you'll find in any diplomatic area study or official intelligence report. It's what I've learned or figured out from my unofficial sources. Unfortunately I haven't been there myself to know absolutely what I'm going to tell you, but my sources are generally pretty reliable.

"One reason the rebels keep beating the Feldpolizei is many of the oligarchs and their families see commissions in the Feldpolizei as a convenient job for male offspring who aren't smart enough for anything else." He paused and raised his eyebrows at the sounds of surprise from the men. "That's right. The Wanderjahr Feldpolizei commissions its officers directly from civilian life; they don't have to prove themselves by being enlisted men first like our officers do. The troopers, that's the junior enlisted men, all come from the middle and lower ranks of Wanderjahrian society. They've got a morale problem because of this sharp class distinction.

"The guerrillas, on the other hand, have intelligent, highly educated leaders, most of whom studied offworld, several of whom studied military history, and a few have served in the Confederation forces.

"Now, most of you have probably never heard of an oligarchy, so I'll take a moment or two to describe it for you. It's an odd form of government, one that's cropped up very few times in human history.

"Most of you are from democracies or republics, places where the citizens have a voice in how their government functions and what it does; places where any citizen can enter government and rise to the highest ranks. Some of you are from monarchies, where you have a hereditary ruler and aristocrats—and the rulers have a sense of noblesse oblige, an obligation to take care of their people.

"Well, an oligarchy isn't like either of them. I won't bother describing the classical oligarchy, just this one. On Wanderjahr a few people, the heads of just nine families, own the whole world and share power with no one. Each is a totally autonomous dictator in his or her own geographic area, and they only get together for matters that concern all of them. There is very little vertical social movement. There is no independent judicial system to which a citizen can apply for relief from an unjust oligarch. The citizens have no voice. Before you start thinking I'm contradicting what I said earlier about the guerrilla leaders being educated offworld, the oligarchs send the brightest of their subjects to school so they'll be better servants. This brought about some unanticipated consequences, and they don't know how to deal with them. They're calling us in to save them from the error of some of their ways. This is in some ways a very political operation. If they don't like what we're doing, they can send us away—not that we won't be doing a good job, mind you, but they might see some things we'll be doing as threatening." He shook his head. "Given the organization of the Feldpolizei, I don't see how we can do the job without relieving a good many of the officers of their commands, and you can be sure that will upset more than a few of the oligarchs.

"I should say a few words about who these oligarchs are, from whom they're descended. First off, they're German. Those of you from Earth are probably aware that Prussia, Bavaria, and Hanover are collectively referred to as 'Germany,' even though they're separate geopolitical entities. For those of you who slept through your history classes, that's because until the middle of the twenty-first century they *were* one country.

"The Germans have always been a tough bunch. Way back in the time of the Caesars, when they were just a few barbarian tribes, the Teutons and Alemanni stopped the Roman advance into northern Europe, stopped them dead in their tracks.

"Once the Germans became more or less civilized, they were a bunch of independent little kingdoms, principalities, and dukedoms. They entertained themselves by doing a lot of warring against each other and their non-German neighbors. But none of them were powerful enough to be truly dangerous on a wide scale. It wasn't until they got unified as one nation in the second half of the nineteenth century that they made the rest of the world sit up and take notice. That's because they started trying to take over. At some point in their history—it probably began back when they stopped the Romans—they started convincing themselves that they were better than anybody else, some kind of 'Master Race.' They were certainly highly advanced technologically, they had some of the best scientists throughout history, and they knew warfare and were highly innovative at it.

"Well, their first successes as a unified nation emboldened the Germans, and in the early twentieth century they tried to take over all of Europe and started what came to be called World War One. That was the most widespread, most devasting war the world had ever seen. They invented and used the most horrific weapons mankind had conceived to that time. Millions upon millions of men were killed throughout Europe. Fortunately for the rest of the world, the Germans were over-confident and ended up losing because they took on too many enemies. World War One was so terrible that the rest of the advanced nations swore off war. But not the Germans. They rebuilt, reconstructed, invented newer and deadlier weapons and tactics, and twenty years after losing World War One started another world war, one far vaster than the first one.

"This time, Germany was partitioned after it was finally beaten. That stopped them. For a while. Forty-five years after the end of World War Two, Germany was reunited. They bided their time and it was a half century before they started another world war, even bigger than the first two combined." Top Myer shook his head. "They just didn't learn that they weren't big enough or tough enough to take on the whole world. Anyway, after that war, Germany was permanently partitioned.

"The way this looks to me is, historically, every time a large enough portion of the world's Germanic population has been united under one government, they've tried to take over the world. Well, on Wanderjahr, the Germans own the damn whole thing. You can work out the implications for yourselves.

"I've got to add something here so I'm not misunderstood. When I talk about the Germanic peoples, I don't mean any individuals. Individually, Germans are like any other people: there are saints and sinners, decent people and scoundrels. It's only when you get enough of them together that the Germans become dangerous to everybody else. Lance Corporal Schultz, for example, is of German descent. I like Hammer Schultz. He's one of the finest, most decent human beings it has ever been my privilege to meet. He's a good man, he's a good Marine. I've enjoyed drinking with him a few times. I wouldn't object to him marrying my daughter—don't you get any ideas there, Hammer! But make an army of him, and he'll make me fear for all of Human Space.

"On Wanderjahr, we have a world the Germans own. They think they know it all, they think they're always right, they believe anyone who doesn't agree with them is necessarily wrong. So bear that in mind while we're trying to turn their Feldpolizei into a proper fighting force.

"There's one other thing you have to be aware of on

Wanderjahr. The planet's home to many very big animals. Some of them have very large teeth and eat meat. Fortunately, there's not many of those. Most of these beasts are plant eaters, and some of them look pretty docile. Don't be fooled. If a docile, twenty-ton plant eater accidentally steps on you, it'll kill you just as quickly as a five-ton meat eater that thinks you're just the right size for an after-dinner mint.

"That is all. COMP-ny, A-ten-TION!" Top Myer glared out at the company for a moment, wondering how much of what he said got through to them. Enough, he hoped, to prevent some needless deaths. "Dis-MISSED!"

Company L's officers listened to Top Myer's briefing over the intercom in Captain Conorado's quarters. Ensign vanden Hoyt looked at his company commander wide-eyed at what the first sergeant had to say.

Conorado saw his newest officer's expression and chuckled. "You think that was something?" he said. "You should have heard the briefing he gave before our last operation. He began that one with, 'We're going up against a bunch of bloodthirsty savages.' The Top isn't interested in giving accurate historic lectures, and he might not always have everything right—and he certainly has a unique point of view at times. But that doesn't matter.

"You see, the first sergeant hates having Marines wounded or killed. He feels every injury or death deeply, personally. What he does in his briefings is try to get the attention of the men, to focus them on the upcoming operation so they'll be as alert as possible. I don't care what he tells them, as long as it makes them sharp and keeps them alive."

CHAPTER
FOUR

The force of the explosion hurled Dean from his console onto the floor, where he lay stunned for several seconds, his ears ringing while debris, dust, and papers swirled all around him. Realizing he was not seriously injured, he jumped to his feet, looking for Claypoole.

"They missed!" Claypoole grinned lopsidedly from where he sat slumped against the communications equipment. Blood trickled from a small cut just above his right eyebrow, caused by flying glass. Claypoole scrambled to his feet and began brushing dust and plaster flakes from his utilities.

"Stay away from those windows!" Commander Peters shouted. Fortunately, like the other two in the small office, he'd been facing away from the windows when the bomb went off, and so sustained only some minor cuts from the flying glass. "Come on, let's check to see if there are any other casualties!"

Before he could exit the small cubicle that had been designated as FIST F-2 section, Brigadier Ted Sturgeon stuck his head in the door. "Okay in here?" the FIST commander asked. His thin red hair was white with plaster dust. "Don't anybody go outside the building until I give the all clear," he added, and then pounded off down the corridor to check on the other elements of his headquarters staff.

Dean felt an overwhelming urge to stick his head outside the blasted window, to see what was going on in the street three stories below, where the bomb had just gone off. Shouts, screams, and the roar of burning fires filtered up to him through the smoke and dust. Commander Peters laid his hand on

Dean's shoulder. "If these guys know what they're doing, Dean, there'll be another bomb out there somewhere, set to go off when the rescue squads arrive and survivors start to pour out of the buildings onto the street. There's nothing we can do about it now but lie low. Later Brigadier Sturgeon'll work with the alcalde and the police, work out the emergency procedures. But we're too new here to do anything."

"Hell of a welcome," Claypoole said, grinning as he brushed debris off his workstation.

Commander Peters couldn't help smiling. At first, when the two grunts had been assigned to him as replacement "intelligence analysts," he'd been dubious. But the FIST commander had given him no choice. Left to him, Peters would have taken men from the Psychological Operations section to replace the hospitalized analysts. But the brigadier, who emphasized that all Marines were qualified infantrymen before they were anything else, had put the psyops men, along with the men from the gun and transportation companies and the composite squadron, into the field as part of the mobile training teams supporting the line companies training and leading the Wanderjahrian Feldpolizei units. In fact, for this mission, to get as many men in the field as he could, the brigadier had ordered Commander Van Winkle, of the infantry, to assign as much of his battalion staff as possible to duty with the various Feldpolizei garrisons as commanders and shift leaders. He told his now drastically reduced staff, "It'll be good for you to be overworked here in Brosigville. Make the time go quicker. Keep you out of trouble."

Reluctantly, Commander Peters had been forced to admit that with lots of hard work and constant supervision, he could probably get by with only two gifted amateurs to help him with his duties. Yet during the trip from Thorsfinni's World, he'd come to appreciate the pair's quick intelligence and their willingness to learn. He liked Dean's serious attitude toward the unfamiliar work and his curiosity about intelligence operations in general. Claypoole, who was also a fast learner, complemented Dean's seriousness with a bubbling sense of humor and an optimistic outlook.

And Dean and Claypoole had been with Charlie Bass on Elneal. The story of how the platoon sergeant had led his men across the desert and fought it out hand to hand with the Siad chieftain was already a Marine legend, and Commander Peters was fascinated by the story as the two PFCs told it.

For their part, Dean and Claypoole had come to respect the narrow-shouldered, hawk-nosed intelligence officer and to appreciate what he did for their commander and his staff. He was an easy man to work for, thorough in all he did, had infinite patience, and was always ready to explain. He was a highly educated, contemplative man who often failed to pay close attention to his uniform, leaving flaps unfastened and once coming to work without any insignia of rank on his collars. When Claypoole diplomatically pointed this out, the commander blushed and smiled with embarrassment but thanked Claypoole for noting the discrepancy. In time they came to think they were "taking care" of their new boss, a widely traveled officer who could expound learnedly about the political and military situation on any of a dozen worlds.

Their bitter disappointment at being detailed to the staff and separated from their buddies in Company L's third platoon had faded somewhat by the time the contingent reached Wanderjahr. The two were soon caught up in the hectic life of the staff officers, where everything was done at the double quick. Brigadier Sturgeon, normally seen in the line companies only during inspections or on other formal occasions, was a familiar figure and a dominating presence on the staff. Often during the flight to Wanderjahr he would come into the F-2 section and lean casually against a bulkhead, chatting easily with the commander. At briefings, Dean and Claypoole sat proudly in the rear of the room, staring at the backs of the battalion and company commanders' heads. Once, on his way out, Captain Conorado nodded at the pair and flashed them a conspiratorial wink. For the two enlisted men, that acknowledgment was more satisfying than a medal. It meant he was satisfied they were proving an asset to the staff since their conduct there reflected well upon his company.

"Well, I'm getting a little tired of people blowing up my office," Commander Peters said with a grin, referring to the mortar attack that had wiped out his staff when the FIST was fighting the tribesmen on Elneal. "How's that cut on your head, Claypoole?"

"No worse than yours, Commander," Claypoole replied. For the first time, Peters noticed dried blood on his collar and put his hand to the side of his neck. It came away bloody from a gash just below his left ear. "How're you, Dean?" he asked.

"Sir, if I were any better, they'd investigate—"

The second bomb detonated. Since all the loose material inside the building had been blown away by the first explosion, the men were only stunned by the shock wave of the second one. Now all three rushed to the window and looked down into the chaos in the street below. Dean clearly saw an armless man stumbling and screaming in the street, the severed brachial arteries pumping his blood away in bright spurts. As Dean watched, the man collapsed amid the rubble and lay still.

"Holy God," Claypoole muttered. Commander Peters's face was ashen.

Dozens of people had been killed and mutilated in the blast. Just as Peters predicted, they had emerged from the buildings after the first bomb, only to be caught by the full force of the second device. The first rescue units on the scene had also been caught in the blast, and their burning vehicles added fuel to the inferno raging in the street. The commander felt no satisfaction over his prescience, unless it was that they were not among the casualties; he felt only a sickening sense of failure that he hadn't been able to warn those people down below. Suddenly Dean lurched back from the window with an involuntary shout. He'd just noticed a man's severed hand, badly burned, resting on the ledge inches from his nose.

"We can't stay here anymore," Peters said as he headed for the doorway. Dean and Claypoole followed him out.

Brigadier Sturgeon was assembling the staff by the stairs. "We've offered help from our own medical people, they're experienced in handling trauma injuries like these," he said, "and all the fire and rescue units in the city are on their way here. The hospitals are also standing by. We'll give what help we can to the civilian authorities. You all know combat first aid. First goddamned thing tomorrow, I'm moving our headquarters to the port, where we can establish our own security. I should have known better than to have moved us in here." He led his staff down the stairs and out into the street.

Horror greeted the Marines when they stepped out of the building. Bodies and body parts lay everywhere. Many wounded were in agony. For a moment Dean just stood, gaping stupidly at the carnage all about him, and quickly lost sight of Claypoole and the others as they fanned out to assist the victims nearest them. He stumbled forward into the carnage until he spotted a policeman trying with badly shaking hands to apply his belt as a tourniquet to a woman's severed leg. Shaking off his stupor, he rushed forward to help. When they'd stanched the flow of blood there, they tried to assist a badly burned man nearby, but he was already in shock, and when they tried to move him to a more comfortable position, Dean could clearly see the man's spine and his lungs through a jagged gash in his back, just below his left shoulder. Despite his injuries, the man kept insisting he could get up and walk, and Dean had to help the policeman restrain him while the man fought them weakly and muttered in a language Dean couldn't understand.

"I—I think I know this man," the police officer mumbled almost inaudibly as they tried to make the victim's last minutes as comfortable as they could.

During the next hour they assisted numerous other victims. Later, Dean couldn't recall clearly the exact sequence of events during that time, only disjointed individual scenes of horror that coalesced into a continuous montage of blood and mangled bodies. One memory that made him wince long afterward was the sight of a man's body blown completely in half, the jagged bones of his shattered pelvis a brilliant white against the burned flesh of his legs. Tendrils of intestines, the remains of his colon, looking like strings of overcooked pasta, stuck up through the pelvic bones, while his genitals hung down between his legs, burned black by the heat of the blast.

As the medical rescue units began arriving in force, somebody established a triage and Dean helped the policeman, whose name was Gonzales, carry the wounded to the first-aid station established on the bombed-out ground floor of a nearby department store. Gradually order began to appear. Dean and Gonzales paused for a few moments to rest. Dean stared down at his hands, which were caked with dried blood. The policeman lit a cigarette and inhaled deeply. He offered Dean a drag.

"What is it?" Dean asked, suspicious at the way the cigarette seemed instantly to calm the policeman.

"Thule," he answered, offering him the cigarette again.

"Sorry," Dean replied. "We're not allowed to take that stuff on duty."

The policeman shrugged. "Me neither, but fuck the regulations," he said in thickly accented English. He took another deep drag. He waved an arm at the destruction around them, and Dean suddenly wished that he could take a drag.

He noticed, then, a figure walking slowly, apparently aimlessly, amid the debris. Occasionally the man would reach down, pick up a bit of twisted metal, study it for a few moments, then toss it away. Gradually he neared where the two were standing, and Dean recognized him then as Chief Long, the burly, disheveled civilian policeman who'd been sent along with the 34th FIST to command and train the Stadtpolizei, the metropolitan—as distinct from the field—police force in Arschland, Chairman Arschmann's Staat. The chief looked up at them and nodded in a friendly manner, as if their meeting were nothing more than a chance encounter on a quiet street.

Long held up a piece of blackened and twisted metal in one hand. "We can find out what kind of bomb this was by analyzing this fragment," he announced. He slipped it into an evidence envelope. "But the question I must ask, gentlemen, is,

'Who did this?' We haven't been here two days. Oh, make no mistake about it, this bomb was meant for us. But this mission was top secret from the start, so whoever planned this had to know about our coming for a long time, and also had to know we were going to be headquartered over there." He nodded toward the ruined facade of the government building. "Well," he sighed, and the right side of his face twitched in the rictus that for him passed as a smile, "you boys get any ideas, give me a call, eh?" He waved casually at the two men and shambled off. His rotund figure was soon obscured by clouds of smoke still drifting away from burning vehicles.

Dean watched the policeman disappear down the street. It must have been the guerrillas who set off the bombs, he thought. It made sense. After all, the Marines were here to deal with them, and the guerrillas just struck first. He'd ask Commander Peters about it. But Long had made a good point. How did they know where the headquarters would be when not even Brigadier Sturgeon knew that until two days ago? Were they that well organized?

Joe Dean continued to stare after Chief Long. For the first time since the bombs went off he felt a clutch of fear in his gut.

Several days after the bombing, when the FIST headquarters had just relocated to its new facility at the port, Brigadier Sturgeon stuck his head into the F-2 office and said, "Rafe, get your gear and come along with me. I've been summoned to the palace of the great nabob."

"I take it you mean Chairman Arschmann has asked for a visit?" Commander Peters asked.

"Yep. Bring these two with you." He winked at Dean and Claypoole. "Claypoole, you drive, and Dean can ride shotgun."

"Aye aye, sir!" the pair shouted and jumped to their feet, grabbing equipment harnesses and weapons. Since the bombing, every Marine on Wanderjahr, even the headquarters staff, went everywhere armed and ready to deliver immediate fire.

"Shake a leg, Marines," the brigadier added. "Ambassador Spears will meet us at Arschmann's villa, and nobody wants to keep him waiting." The joke was lost on the two enlisted men, but Commander Peters grinned. The brigadier had come to like Jayben Spears, the Confederation's ambassador to Wanderjahr. The ambassador had some very strange personal mannerisms, but once the FIST commander got to know him, he discovered Spears to be meticulously honest, straightforward in his speech, and objective to a fault, unlike any other member of the Confederation diplomatic corps Sturgeon had ever met. And of all people, Ambassador Spears was the last who'd ever complain about being kept waiting, especially if there were free food and drink to keep him occupied.

Claypoole threw himself behind the driver's console and punched in his PIN. The onboard computer immediately flashed that it was ready. For security, he told the computer the names and ranks of his passengers and their destination. This information was instantly acknowledged by the headquarters communications section, which would be monitoring their progress and recording their conversations, as would the watch onboard the *Denver*, in orbit.

A heads-up display appeared on the windshield. Claypoole pressed a button on the steering yoke and vehicle status data were replaced by a map of Brosigville. "Best route, Chairman Arschmann's home," he said. A bright yellow route line appeared on the map. A pulsing green dot showed their location. The display was constantly updated by the string-of-pearls, the geosynchronous satellites placed into orbit by the navy upon their arrival.

They covered the eight kilometers from the port to downtown Brosigville in only a few minutes. A city of about 250,000, and the oldest settlement on the planet, Brosigville was a beautiful place. Settled originally by several waves of Hispanic immigrants, the general appearance of the city's buildings reflected the architecture of Latin America. The suburbs consisted of high-grade roads dotted with spacious residential lots on which sat modest but comfortable villas inhabited by the city's large middle class. The less affluent citizens lived in apartment dwellings on the outskirts of the city. The city center was devoted exclusively to shops, cafés, business establishments, and government facilities. With a mean annual temperature of 55 degrees Fahrenheit, the weather was seldom unpleasant at that latitude. As it was local summer, most people were dressed casually.

The Marines had found the people easygoing, friendly, and openhanded. The locals seemed intensely but politely curious about the Marines, their families, the worlds they'd come from, their experiences in the Corps. To Dean and Claypoole, the young women they saw in the streets and at work in the port area were exotically beautiful, always showing white teeth through friendly smiles, black eyes glittering like diamonds as they tossed long black hair sassily about their shoulders.

Kurt Arschmann's palace, where he lived and from where he ruled Arschland and exercised his authority as Chairman of the Ruling Council, sprawled along a high ridge six kilometers on the far side of Brosigville from the port. They were waved through the main gates by the security guards. Noting the light weapons the men carried and the unimpressive defensive positions they manned, the Marines concluded the guards' function was to alert the main house to the presence of intruders, not to stop them.

As the brigadier's landcar came to a halt at the top of a long, tree-lined circular driveway in front of the main entrance, the mansion's white stucco walls and carefully landscaped verdant lawns were impressive in the bright sunshine. Three other vehicles were parked to one side of the driveway, their operators lounging about beside them, smoking and talking in low voices. The cars were painted bright colors, and some sported brilliant pennants and flags from their bumpers. "Some spread," Claypoole muttered as Brigadier Sturgeon hopped out and started up the long staircase to the main door.

"You stay here," Commander Peters told the enlisted men. "Go over there, mingle with the drivers, find out what you can about who's here and what's going on. Do some real intelligence gathering for a change."

A wiry, thin-faced little man opened the main doors as the two officers approached the top of the stairs. "Kalat Uxmal, at your service, gentlemen," he said, bowing deeply in greeting.

"Please follow me. His Excellency is waiting for you in the Gold Room."

Gold Room? Sturgeon mouthed silently to Peters and shook his head. Four people, three men and a woman, waited for them. Uxmal bowed the Marines through the doors into a sumptuously appointed study decorated in shades of gold and yellow. The sunlight streamed in through windows over-looking an intricately landscaped garden that seemed to extend for a hectare or more behind the house. The windows were open and a sweetly scented breeze flowed in steadily from the sun-warmed flower beds outside.

"Brigadier Sturgeon!" A muscular blond man stood up and moved from behind the desk where he'd been sitting. The woman, a very handsome athletic lady of about seventy-five, with long blond hair, rose from her chair and smiled at the two Marines. The third occupant, a heavyset, dark-skinned man whose black hair was cropped close to his skull, kept his seat and observed the Marines through half-closed eyes. Finally, there was Ambassador Jayben Spears, who jumped to his feet as the Marines entered the room, a warm smile on his bearded face and a large glass of wine in one hand. The ambassador was a vigorous one hundred years old, with a slight paunch; his closely cut hair and beard were gray interspersed with strands of dark brown. All his life he had refused the simple procedure that would have cured his farsightedness, and insisted on wearing spectacles that gave him a permanently owlish look, when they weren't sliding down his nose and making him look like an absentminded professor.

Brigadier Sturgeon had met with Kurt Arschmann several times already. "Sir, I think you met Commander Peters, my intelligence officer, at the welcoming ceremony several days ago," Sturgeon said. Arschmann shook hands warmly with Peters.

"Gentlemen, this lovely lady is Lorelei Keutgens," Arsch-mann said. "As head of Morgenluft Staat, she is a member of the Ruling Council, and, I am happy to say, my very good friend." Arschmann bowed toward the stately woman. Lorelei extended her hand to Brigadier Sturgeon, who took it gently in his own. Her skin was smooth and warm and her grip firm.

"Let me say, gentlemen, how very happy I am to have you here. Brigadier, your men have already landed in Morgenluft and begun their work with the Feldpolizei garrisons there. I am deeply impressed." To Brigadier Sturgeon's surprise, she continued to hold his hand, squeezing it firmly at each word. He wondered if that was a greeting peculiar to the people of Wanderjahr, but saw that when she took Peters's hand, she gave it a warm businesslike shake and let it go. Brigadier Sturgeon, who was not married, could not help feeling a bit flattered at the attention. Then he smiled to himself: This woman knew whom and how to flatter.

"And this other gentleman," Arschmann said, turning to the man lounging in his chair, "is Turbat Nguyen-Multan, also a member of the Ruling Council and one of our most important landowners and producers of thule." Multan made no move to shake hands with the Marines, just nodded casually at them. "Multan is here on other business today," Arschmann went on, "but I asked him to stay for this meeting. You may have noticed that he was unable to attend the welcoming ceremony I arranged for your arrival.

"Ambassador Spears you already know," Arschmann continued.

Spears nodded pleasantly and waved a free hand at the Marines. With the other hand he popped a piece of kiwi into his mouth. "I never pass up free eats," Spears commented to no one in particular.

Brigadier Sturgeon was beginning to understand why Spears had been shunted off to a backwater post. At formal diplomatic functions his conduct must have been scandalous. Another reason the brigadier liked the man.

"Please be seated." Arschmann motioned the two officers to chairs drawn up close to his desk. A servant came in with another tray of refreshments. Sturgeon indicated he did not want any, and Peters, who could have used a cool beverage himself, followed his commander's lead, shaking his head no. The servant padded silently out of the room.

"Brigadier Sturgeon," Arschmann began, "we here on Wanderjahr are direct in our business and official relations, so forgive me if what I am to say seems abrupt. In a word, I wish you to move your headquarters back into the city."

Sturgeon nodded affably. "I understand, Excellency, but the answer is no."

"He is as direct as you are, Kurt!" Lorelei Keutgens laughed. The brigadier noted that she had a delightful laugh. He smiled back at her. Multan only snorted. For him that was as close as he ever came to laughing.

"But, Brigadier, our agreement with the Confederation specified that you would make your headquarters in the capital city, so we could better communicate and plan your activities," Arschmann said. He glanced at Spears, attempting to solicit the diplomat's agreement. Spears merely shrugged, then sipped at his wine.

"Yes, Excellency, but my orders are discretionary," Sturgeon replied. "It is my opinion as commander of this force that the safety of my Marines comes first. Dead Marines are of no value to you or to the Corps. I can better protect my headquarters against terrorist attacks like the one a few days ago, and so we'll have to remain at the port until we have eliminated the people who are responsible."

"That's right," Spears confirmed around a mouthful of fruit.

Arschmann was flustered. "But, sir, surely you understand the, ah, incident of the other day, ah, requires your stabilizing presence in the city, until the, ah, metro and field police forces achieve the state of competency for which—"

"That'll take a while," Lorelei said dryly. Arschmann affected a brief smile, but the look he gave her would have killed a subordinate.

"Yes, yes, of course, but until then, well, it would make our citizens feel more secure, Brigadier, if your men were living among them instead of sequestered at the port."

"Sir, I am deeply saddened that any of your people were hurt in that bombing. Sincerely. But the bombs were meant for us, not them. Your people are actually safer with us outside town.

Besides, my headquarters staff, even with its small security force, could provide no safety for your townfolk."

"Exactly!" Ambassador Spears said.

"Well . . ." Arschmann could see that the brigadier would not budge, especially since the Confederation stooge, Ambassador Spears, seemed to be firmly behind everything he was saying. "Well, very well, Brigadier. Now, I wish to discuss with you the measures you'll take to retrain our security forces. I have some ideas that—"

Sturgeon held up a hand, silencing Arschmann in midsentence. "Excellency, excuse me, but that is not your area of expertise. Certainly I would welcome any advice you might have as time goes on and we get a feel for just what needs to be done. But until then, I am taking over these forces. My officers and noncommissioned officers will assess what is needed to transform your men into a first-class fighting force—and then they will do just that. Chief Long, who is occupied in the city and couldn't come with us today, will do the same for your metropolitan police force. We will brief you on a regular basis. Those are the terms of our agreement, and I will stick to them."

"Quite so, quite so," Ambassador Spears said, nodding his head sagely from where he sat, working on his second glass of wine.

Arschmann pursed his lips and then nodded briefly. "Are you sure you won't have some refreshment?" he asked. He had concluded that the only way to deal with this Marine brigadier was to treat him as an equal.

"A cool drink, sir? If that would be convenient?" Sturgeon asked. Instantly, the servant was back with his tray of refreshments.

Multan cleared his throat and leaned forward. "Brigadier, your men are very tough fighters, are they not?" Sturgeon looked at Multan silently for several seconds, but before he could reply, the oligarch continued, "You have, how many, one thousand men under your command? Will that be enough? These bandits are more numerous, I think."

Commander Peters thought: This guy knows a lot about us.

Sturgeon took a long sip of his cold drink, a delicious combination of the juices of several fruits native to Wanderjahr. "Sir, my men know their jobs." He looked directly into Multan's eyes. "We don't look for fights, but when one comes our way, we fight to win. Now, madame, gentlemen, I must be leaving. There is much to be done." He rose, bowed slightly to Arschmann, and walked out of the room. Peters hurried to keep up with him.

Behind them in the Gold Room, Kurt Arschmann smiled. Things were proceeding perfectly.

Before they reached the main hallway, Lorelei Keutgens caught up with them and laid a restraining hand on Brigadier Sturgeon's arm. "Brigadier," she said softly but urgently, "will you come to visit me soon? I will send my own suborbital. It is very important."

"Why, yes, madame, if you wish. We have our own air transportation. We'll arrange a visit with my operations officer."

"Thank you. But make it soon. And, Brigadier, watch out for Multan."

"We aren't even going into his Staat," Peters volunteered.

"Watch out for Multan," she repeated, then turned and walked down the corridor.

Sitting in a nearby alcove just off the main corridor, obscured by some large potted flowers, Kalat Uxmal sipped his own cool drink and smiled.

Ambassador Spears caught up to the Marines in the parking lot outside. "I think you can trust the Keutgens woman, Brigadier," he began without preamble, "but don't trust Multan—and for the life of the sainted martyrs of N'ra, don't trust Arschmann."

Sturgeon looked hard at the ambassador, wondering if he'd drunk too much wine.

"I've been here four years, Brigadier," Spears said, "and I know you can't trust these oligarchs . . ." He ticked the names off his fingers. "And as far as Kurt Arschmann is concerned, well, as your Marines might say, he's dirtier than the south end of a northbound kwangduk."

With a wave, Spears jumped into his own car and left the two officers staring after him. It was not the obscenity of the metaphor that astonished the Brigadier as much as the fact that a senior member of the Confederation diplomatic corps could talk like a Marine.

"Whatcha smokin'?" Claypoole asked as he sauntered up to the drivers lounging around their vehicles. They looked uncomprehending at first and then one smiled and said, "English!" Claypoole nodded. "Thule!" one man answered, and offered the Marines a drag on the cigarette. The smoke from their cigarettes was pleasantly aromatic, tinged with a very faint sharpness that reminded Dean vaguely of burning grass.

"No thanks, fellas, on duty we aren't allowed," Dean said. The man looked bewildered and then smiled and put the butt back into his lips.

"You. Marine. You smoke?" a short, burly man with closely cropped black hair and several nasty scars on his head barked. He stuck his jaw out aggressively at the pair, as if challenging them. One hand rested lightly on the butt of an old-fashioned handheld blaster, an ugly, inefficient weapon compared to the ones the Marines carried, but still deadly. Between his shoulder blades hung a machete, its rugged handle sticking up above his left shoulder. To the Marines it seemed an awkward, uncomfortable thing to be carrying around, but evidently the man took much pride in it.

"Yeah," Claypoole answered, producing a fresh cigar from a cargo pocket. "Best 'bacca they grow on 'Finni's. Smoke?" The rough-looking man turned his lips down and waved the cigar away. Claypoole generously offered it to the other two, who politely declined. He shrugged and lit up, sucking the smoke deep into his lungs. The three Wanderjahrians watched him curiously. "Tobacco kill you," the ugly one muttered darkly. "Thule no hurt."

"You drivers?" Dean asked, pointedly ignoring the unwanted medical advice.

"No, we whores!" one of the men answered, and began to

laugh loudly. The other two laughed along with him and slapped him on the back.

Dean grunted and made a wry face. "Guess that's one for him," he said to Claypoole out of the side of his mouth. He tried again: "Whom do you drive for?"

"Mistress Keutgens," one of the men answered. Dean had compiled a dossier on her for Commander Peters. Seventy-five, five grandchildren; two girls, three boys, eldest a grand-daughter, nineteen. Husband and only child killed five years ago in an aircraft accident. Reportedly the richest woman on Wanderjahr. Her holdings were in the southern hemisphere of the planet, about an eight-hour flight by suborbital from Brosigville. Good-looking woman for her age. Solid reputation all the way around.

"Me Multan," the ugly one said proudly, thrusting his chin forward again.

Claypoole suppressed an urge to land a fist on that arrogant chin. "Nice name," he said.

"No!" the man barked. "Multan my master!" He said it as if Claypoole were a complete idiot. "I am Garth. I drive much and well for him."

"Nice haircut you got there, Garth. Ever been in the Marines?" Dean said, trying to lighten the tension. Garth just stared at him in stony silence. "Well," Dean went on, "what brings you guys up here?"

"Meeting. Much talking," the Keutgens driver replied. He shrugged as if what was being discussed by his mistress was too far beyond his comprehension to be of interest.

"You. Marine. You work for redhead guy?" Garth asked, obviously meaning Brigadier Sturgeon. The guy was observant.

"Yes, our brigadier. Tough man," Claypoole answered.

"You, Marine, you tough too?" Garth asked. He grinned broadly. The two Marines were startled to see that his teeth had all been ground to sharp points.

"Ummm, well, fellas," Claypoole began, staring at Garth's teeth, "we don't go around lookin' for fights, but one comes our way, yeah, we kick ass."

The look on Garth's face indicated he did not quite understand the meaning of the expression. He motioned at Claypoole's holstered blaster. "You show me, Marine."

Claypoole rested his hand on the holster flap and leaned close to Garth's face. "Sorry, shitbird, but regulations say if I draw this weapon, well, I'd just have to kill you with it." He pronounced each word very carefully. Startled, Garth stepped backward and bumped his rear hard against the side of his vehicle. Claypoole smiled fiercely.

"Well, fellas," Dean said with feigned heartiness, "been good talking to you. We gotta go now!" He grabbed Claypoole's elbow and pulled him in the direction of their own car.

"Jesus X. Muhammad," Claypoole hissed, "Elneal all over again!"

"Well, at least we're not back in the desert."

"Yeah, but that ugly bastard back there belongs in the desert, and I bet if there's one anywhere on this planet, that's where you'll find him hiding out."

Behind them the man named Garth straightened up slowly and glared after the Marines. Then he smiled with real amusement and spit on the ground.

Back at the brigadier's vehicle, Claypoole slid in behind the driver's console. "Let's go to Juanita's tonight," he said to Dean.

"Rachman, we've only been here about a week and you already found a place?" Dean asked. He'd been too tired the few nights they'd been off duty to do anything but sleep.

"Yep. They have beer there, and the girls . . ." He rolled his eyes and laughed.

"Lemme drive," Dean said. "Come on, Rock, don't hog all the fun."

"Nope. Brigadier designated me as the driver and—"

"Move over, Marine!" Brigadier Sturgeon shouted, startling Claypoole. "I'm driving this thing. You can't hog all the fun for yourself. You men climb in back," he said as he punched his PIN number into the computer. "And keep a sharp lookout. I think some people real close by don't like us very much."

"You got that right, sir," Claypoole muttered as he climbed into the back, undoing the flap to his blaster. He turned and grinned fiercely at Dean, who stuck his middle finger out at him.

CHAPTER
FIVE

"Aren't they pretty," MacIlargie said under his breath from the end of first squad's rank.

Dornhofer and Van Impe, next in line, ignored him, but from where he stood in formation on the other side of Dornhofer, Godenov whispered back with awe, "I never thought I'd see uniforms brighter than our officers'."

"Quiet in the ranks," Chan stage-whispered. If he'd been standing closer to Godenov, he'd have given him an elbow in the ribs.

Ratliff flicked his eyes left toward Chan and thought the lance corporal was going to be a good influence on his new man. Now if only Van Impe would help Dornhofer the same way.

"Gorgeous," MacIlargie said softly. "And they stand at attention so nicely too."

"Knock it off!" Van Impe said.

Sergeant Hyakowa didn't seem to move a muscle, but his soft voice came clear to first squad from where he, as senior squad leader, stood at ease in the platoon sergeant's position to the front of the platoon. "Don't make me turn around, people." Second and third squads, in their ranks behind first, knew Hyakowa wasn't speaking to them.

MacIlargie thought a few moments of silent admiration of the Feldpolizei might be advisable.

Three companies of Wanderjahrian Feldpolizei faced third platoon from the other side of the parade ground of the 257th Feldpolizei Grafshaftsbezirk—police precinct. The "pretty" that made MacIlargie speak up was the combination of orange

72

tunics over sky-blue pantaloons of their uniforms. The leaders of the two units met midway between the field police formation and the Marines. The uniforms of the Feldpolizei battalion commander and his staff, with their flouncing plumes, glittering fourragères, sparkling silver pantaloon stripes, and gleaming saber scabbards, contrasted sharply with the dull-green garrison utility uniforms of Ensign vanden Hoyt and Staff Sergeant Bass.

"Your men make a magnificent spectacle on the parade ground, Commander," vanden Hoyt said, with no trace of irony in his voice.

"The 257th Battalion is the best in the Feldpolizei," Commander Vankler replied haughtily. He was shorter than the Marine officer, yet managed to look down his nose at him. He was deeply insulted that the Ruling Council had saddled his battalion with this platoon of offworld mercenaries—he knew no better word to describe soldiers who meddled in the military matters of an independent world—who had no idea of whom his men were fighting, or why. And it galled him to the core that a mere ensign, the lowest possible rank for an officer, even less than a lieutenant, should be placed in training command of his battalion—and that he and his ragamuffin platoon would pass judgment on their fighting ability! This Confederation Marine probably knew nothing of the tactics developed by Commissioner Schickeldorf, to say nothing of the military philosophy behind it. The training of his battalion was properly the responsibility of his operations officer, Inspector von Holfmann, who was doing a splendid job.

"Permission to speak, sir," Bass said in his best diplomatic voice. He didn't bother to wait for permission, but continued, "As excellent as your men obviously are on the parade ground, we came to see how they perform in the field. We were told we would be given a demonstration of their fighting prowess."

Vankler glared at the impertinent enlisted man. If this, this . . . *sergeant* were in his command, he'd have his stripes—all of them—and the man would spend the next ten years cleaning the stockade latrines with a toothbrush. Preferably the very toothbrush he used to clean his teeth! But Commander

Vankler was absolutely forbidden to take any disciplinary action against the Marines, no matter how insubordinate they might prove—some moron had placed the mercenaries completely outside his chain of command even though they were to be given command authority over his men! With effort, he got his anger under control and gave his reply to vanden Hoyt—the man might only be an ensign, but at least he was an officer.

"We have a demonstration prepared for you. If you will accompany me." Vankler turned abruptly and marched briskly toward one end of the parade ground, his staff rushing after him.

Bass and vanden Hoyt exchanged glances, then followed, not quite as rapidly.

"Move your men," Vankler snapped back at them. "They're in the way."

Bass looked back toward the platoon and waved an arm at Hyakowa in the hand signal that told him to move the formation to the end of the parade ground near the reviewing stand. The Marines picked up their light packs, helmets, and blasters and followed to the side of the reviewing stand.

The Feldpolizei battalion's parade ground was the size of four soccer fields. For this occasion the reviewing stand, which was normally placed in the center of the barracks side of the long axis, was at the far end, near the entrance to the battalion's camp. A small airfield with pads for four hoppers was at the remaining side.

The long side of the parade ground, where third platoon had stood watching, was fronted by a forest such as few men of third platoon had ever seen. Thick-trunked trees towered one or two hundred meters into the sky. Branches radiated out of the massive trunks in tiers, the lowest beginning more than twenty meters above the ground, the highest spread wide and thick enough to blot out sections of the sky. The smallest saplings of the giant trees seemed to be no shorter than ten meters. Wherever these giants stood far enough apart for sunlight to penetrate to ground level, clumps of smaller trees grew, but the tops of the tallest of those didn't reach the lowest branches of the giants. The trees resembled nothing so much as palm trees from old Earth, palms that had grown fat and lazy from easy living. A fringe of downward-slanting frondlike leaves some two-thirds of the way up their trunks made them look like they were wearing grass skirts. The trees were what the Wanderjahrians called hochbaums and grospalms. What little underbrush grew on the mostly bare forest floor was fuzzy and indistinct in form, vaguely resembled ferns, and varied in height from shoe top to taller than a man.

Before they reached the reviewing stand, Vankler crisply turned to his operations officer and said, "Prepare the demonstration, Inspector von Holfmann."

"Yessir!" Von Holfmann saluted his commander's back, then turned and marched to the front of the battalion formation and began barking commands at the company officers.

From somewhere in the distance beyond the woods came the honking cry of something very large. The Marines on the ground at the side of the reviewing stand cast curious looks in its direction. Vanden Hoyt and Bass tried to classify the sound like old infantrymen: how far away is it, who is it, will it have any immediate effect on us?

The Wanderjahrians ignored it, so the Marines returned their attention to the parade ground in time to see the Feld-polizei formation begin its maneuvers.

The 257th's company commanders spun about to face their companies and barked crisp orders. "Form combat ranks!" the commanders of companies A and C shouted.

"Prepare for reserve!" cried the commander of Company B.

Instantly, the front rank of Company A, on the left side of the battalion formation, pivoted to its right and marched until its last man was just beyond the other two ranks. The rear half of that rank faced front, while the front half executed a round-about to re-form behind it. As soon as the first rank was out of the way, the company's second and third ranks stepped briskly forward so the company was re-formed into two ranks. On the right side of the formation, Company C mirrored Company A's maneuver. When both companies were re-formed into two lines, they faced each other and marched forward until they met, then pivoted back toward the front. At the same time,

Company B re-formed into one line ten meters behind the first two companies.

"A complicated maneuver," vanden Hoyt whispered to Bass.

Bass thought drums should be beating a tattoo in the background. "Too complicated to do under fire," he agreed.

While the companies were changing their formation, von Holfmann marched to his position, which was centered behind the two forward companies. The entire maneuver was completed in less than thirty seconds. Von Holfmann sharply looked to his left and to his right, then straight to the front.

"Firing positions!" he barked. The Company A and B commanders echoed his command. The front rank of Feldpolizei troopers dropped to one knee and the men raised blasters to their shoulders. The second rank took offhand shooting positions. The rear company remained standing at port arms.

"Prepare for advancing volley fire!" von Holfmann shouted. He looked along the lines of the battalion, then shouted, "Fire by ranks. ADVANCE!"

The front rank fired a volley from its blasters. The second rank immediately stepped forward so its members were between the kneeling men and fired another volley. Von Holfmann commanded again and the kneeling men stood and stepped forward two paces, dropped to one knee, and fired. The second rank repeated its earlier maneuver. Then both ranks repeated. The reserve company followed in trace.

The first volley of plasma bolts struck a ragged line a hundred meters wide on the parade ground surface halfway to the trees. The second volley hit ten meters beyond the first. Each successive volley scorched the parade ground ten meters beyond the previous one.

When the first volley fired, Vankler said condescendingly to the Marines, "Don't worry, they're firing at low power. I have no need to melt the surface of my parade ground."

Bass and vanden Hoyt nodded noncommittally; they'd already noted the low power of the shots.

Advancing and firing by alternate ranks, the battalion reached and was firing deep into the forest in less than a minute. Several small fires started in the undergrowth and a clump of the fat palms had its skirts singed off, but Vankler seemed totally unconcerned about the damage to the ecosystem.

"Imagine yourself a bandit," Vankler said. "Imagine you see a battalion of such splendidly uniformed men snap into assault formation so briskly and advance toward you firing in disciplined volleys. How do you think you would react?" He cast a scornful look at vanden Hoyt.

"Well, sir, if I was a simple bandit, poorly trained and ill-equipped, and badly outnumbered, I'd likely panic and run."

Vankler snorted and looked proudly at his battalion. "That is exactly how the bandits have been responding when they have met my men in the field."

Vanden Hoyt nodded. "But recently a Feldpolizei company from the adjoining GSB met a large group of guerrillas and was nearly wiped out."

Vankler jerked as though slapped. He glared at vanden Hoyt. "That was not my battalion. That was the 407th. The company involved was led by an incompetent. It was an isolated incident."

Bass said nothing, but found it interesting that Vankler felt the need to justify himself. Instead, Bass pretended to be interested in the way von Holfmann was reassembling the battalion into its parade formation.

Vanden Hoyt calmly looked at the Wanderjahrian officer and said, "Commander, the guerrillas are growing in strength. They are becoming better equipped—with weapons taken from the Feldpolizei. They do not use tactics that lend themselves to defeat by serried ranks firing in volleys."

"We have defeated them in every instance we have encountered them!"

"You have faced small, isolated groups that couldn't stand and fight. Still, according to the reports I've seen, in each instance they have caused casualties in your ranks. And it appears they have caused more casualties to you than you have to them. When they mass in any strength, which they will, if you try to fight them this way they *will* defeat you."

Vankler sputtered and his face turned deep red. This was

exactly the reaction vanden Hoyt counted on. "With your permission, sir, we have prepared a demonstration of our own. We have brought enough fire- and hit-simulators to equip your entire battalion. My platoon," he waved an arm at his Marines, "under the command of the platoon sergeant—that's a total of twenty-six Confederation Marines—will take on your battalion. We may not decisively score a victory, but I believe we will severely injure your battalion while taking few casualties of our own. Simulated casualties, of course."

Vankler looked as if he were about to have a stroke.

The Wanderjahrian commander was right where vanden Hoyt wanted him to be, and he made his ultimate appeal to Vankler's pride and vanity. "Sir, if we do not, I will report to my superiors that this battalion doesn't need our training."

Some of the red drained from Vankler's face. He glared down his nose at the taller Marine officer and snarled through gritted teeth, "Your platoon will be slaughtered. You will see that we have no need of your training."

Still calm, vanden Hoyt replied, "Yessir, we shall see." He looked toward the forest fronting the parade ground. The small ground fires he'd seen earlier seemed to have gone out. He turned to Bass. "Platoon Sergeant, if you will prepare the platoon."

Bass came to attention. "Aye aye, sir." He saluted, executed an about-face as sharp as the best of the Feldpolizei, and marched off the reviewing platform to the men of third platoon.

"Let's do this thing," Bass said softly as he reached them. The Marines grinned at him, and many of them made remarks about the gaudy Feldpolizei, remarks he ignored. He led them into the woods, to where a clump of palmlike trees was dense enough to conceal them from the parade ground. A few of the Marines, remembering the honking of something very large, eyed the woods cautiously.

The simulators third platoon brought with it were in one of the ground-effect vehicles that had carried them to the 257th base. Vanden Hoyt oversaw their distribution to the 257th's company officers, made sure the shift sergeants understood that the simulators made a crack like the discharge of a blaster when fired, and a humanlike scream when they registered a hit on the wearer. He brought a few simulators back to the reviewing stand to show to Commander Vankler and his staff, to explain their workings to them. Lastly, he wandered through the ranks of the battalion to make sure everyone was wearing the detectors right and had the shot simulators properly fixed into the battery wells, from which the firing batteries had been removed, and onto the muzzles of their weapons. It took half a standard hour to outfit everyone with the unfamiliar training equipment. Finally they were ready.

By then Vankler had regained his composure and again looked every bit the Prussian officer he imagined himself to be. "Line your men up," he snapped at vanden Hoyt. "This should only take a few seconds."

"Sir, my men are ready, but Marines don't line up and fight in the open any more than the guerrillas do. They're over there, in the trees."

"It doesn't matter. We'll make short work of them." Vankler turned to an aide and murmured something to him. The aide raced to von Holfmann to relay the commander's instructions. Vankler wanted to lead this demonstration himself, but couldn't if the Marine officer was leaving his command to his number two—and an *enlisted* number two at that! Almost, he thought, it was a waste to have this demonstration under an inspector; he should give it to his most junior lieutenant. But it was too late: von Holfmann was already barking the orders that put the battalion into its assault formation.

As before, two companies lined themselves into two ranks and the front rank dropped to one knee. Von Holfmann barked a command and the front rank's blasters crackled with simulated fire. Just as the second rank stepped between the kneeling men of the front rank, the sound of crackles came from the forest, followed instantly by a dozen very loud and piercing screams from the Wanderjahrian ranks. Troopers throughout the battalion formation jumped in surprise and looked about— mostly those near the men whose simulators screamed.

Von Holfmann and the company commanders had to bellow their commands several times before the battalion was again facing front and moving forward in their disciplined manner. But it took time, time the Marines in the forest used to shoot more of them. When the second rank stepped between the kneeling men of the front rank a second time, an entire platoon from the reserve company had to move forward to fill gaps in the ranks caused by the simulated casualties. The Feldpolizei fire had yet to reach the nearest trees.

Vankler was infuriated. He screamed at von Holfmann and waved an arm, trying to instruct him to forgo the advancing fire, to raise it so the shots would go into the trees where the Marines were. Von Holfmann looked at his commander and gave his head a bewildered shake before he understood. Several more simulators screamed by the time von Holfmann adjusted his men's fire. More than half of the reserve company was now in the firing ranks. Yet more simulators screamed as the battalion continued its methodical advance across the open field.

Vanden Hoyt listened carefully; it sounded as if only a squad was firing at the formation. He wondered if Bass had split the platoon. He wondered what Charlie Bass had up his sleeve and restrained a smile.

As their simulated casualties mounted, the Feldpolizei moved less sharply and their fire became less coordinated. From the angles the Wanderjahrians were holding their blasters, the Marine officer saw that most of their increasingly ragged fire was either too high or too low to reach anyone in the trees. He still didn't smile, but he couldn't hold back a quick shake of his head.

Most of the reserve company was filling gaps in the front ranks by the time the battalion had crossed two-thirds of the distance to the trees. That was when all hell broke loose. Crackles so close together they blended into a screech came from two points somewhere in the vicinity of the small airfield opposite the reviewing stand, and were answered by a cacophony of screaming simulators in the battalion's rapidly thinning ranks.

Vanden Hoyt didn't restrain his smile this time—he might have known that Bass would have the men change into their chameleon uniforms as soon as they were out of sight—the Feldpolizei were being fired on by men they couldn't see to shoot back at.

"WHAT!" Vankler shrieked. "Where is that coming from?" He craned his neck and leaned from side to side, trying to spot the guns that were raking his battalion with enfilade fire. He saw nothing but the hopper landing pads. More and more of his men dropped as their simulators shrilled that they were hit. The troopers, rattled by the sound of fire from two directions, and dazed and confused by the piercing screams of the simulators, shouted screams of their own and looked about madly, unable to see who was shooting at them. After a few seconds one man, totally unnerved by the shrilling of so many simulators, threw down his blaster and ran, screaming. A few others, equally confused and unnerved, broke and ran with him. Soon the entire battalion was fleeing in rout.

The fire from the airfield stopped for a few seconds when the formation finally broke, then there was a short burst and all the simulators vanden Hoyt had brought to show to Vankler and his staff screamed.

Apoplectic, Vankler spun on vanden Hoyt. He thrust an arm out, finger pointed between the Marine's eyes. "You, sir," he sputtered, "are under arrest. I will have your hide at a court-martial!"

"With all due respect," vanden Hoyt said, "you can't do that, sir."

"I am the battalion commander here. This is my Grafshafts-bezirk. I can do anything I want!" He twisted around and screamed at a junior officer, "Tell Inspector von Holfmann to issue power packs and have the troopers load their weapons. All of these offworlders are under arrest!"

In response to a string-of-pearls radio call from Staff Sergeant Bass, Commander Van Winkle, 34th FIST's infantry battalion commander, commandeered the nearest hopper and flew directly to the 257th Feldpolizei Grafshaftsbezirk. He left in such a hurry that only his sergeant major and three junior enlisted men as guards were able to accompany him. Van Winkle made three radio calls while in transit, one to Charlie Bass for an update on what was happening. When he arrived, some twenty minutes after Commander Vankler placed Ensign vanden Hoyt under arrest, he found a stalemate that had to be defused before it broke.

Commander Vankler and his staff, along with the "arrested" Marine officer, still stood on the reviewing stand. One company of Feldpolizei was nervously arrayed in front of it. The other two companies were in assault formation along the barracks side of the parade ground. Sensors in the hopper showed Van Winkle that chameleoned Marines were spread out inside the trees and behind cover in the airfield. He knew from Bass's call that the Marines had also stripped off their simulators and were fully armed. If a skittery trooper accidentally pressed the firing lever on his blaster, a bloodbath would destroy any chance of the Marines gaining the confidence of the Feldpolizei. He ordered the pilot away from the airfield and had him land the hopper in the middle of the parade ground, which was almost a mistake; only a sharply shouted command from Commander Vankler kept his men from opening fire on the descending hopper.

Van Winkle jumped out of the bird while it was still several feet above the ground. Sergeant Major Parant was on his heels. As he marched toward the reviewing stand and looked at the men on it, he was glad he and the sergeant major had just returned from a reception. Their dress reds, bloodred tunics with gold trousers for the commander and navy blue with a broad red stripe down the seam for the sergeant major, would make a more positive impression on the gaudily dressed Feldpolizei commander and his staff than would Marine field—or even class A—uniforms. Nervous troopers shifted to make a path for the senior Marines.

Van Winkle bounded up the stairs to the reviewing stand. Barely glancing in his direction, he said to vanden Hoyt, "I'll speak with you later, Ensign." He stopped at attention directly in front of Vankler.

"Sir, I am Commander Van Winkle, battalion commander of these Marines. What happened?"

Gratified to have an officer of proper rank on whom to vent his spleen, Vankler roared in a voice that carried to fully half of his men, despite the fact that the man he was addressing stood less than arm's length in front of him.

"These insubordinate underlings of yours have made a mockery of a combat tactics demonstration by my battalion. First they mocked my battalion as being parade ground troops rather than fighters, then they denigrated their parade ground sharpness. Then these—these offworlders had the effrontery to tell me, in the presence and full hearing of my staff, that our tactics, which were developed by the commissioner of the Feldpolizei himself, are ineffective against bandits!" He had to pause briefly because the roar of an approaching V/STOL aircraft drowned out his words. "The very bandits against whom my men have won the field repeatedly!" Vankler's face was rigid when he began, but grew florid and animated as he spoke; his voice rose in pitch as his animation increased.

"Then as a final insult, this ensign of yours had his men dress in chameleon uniforms and arm themselves with guns, neither of which the bandits have, and assault my battalion from unexpected directions!" Vankler was nearly screaming when he finished, which seemed a fitting accompaniment to the roar of the V/STOL aircraft that was settling on one of the landing pads in the airfield.

Van Winkle ignored the spittle that sprayed his face and retained his composure during the eruption. When the other concluded his tirade, Van Winkle said in a steady voice at normal speaking volume, "This is a very serious matter indeed, Commander. Might we retire to your office to discuss the situation and what to do about it?"

"I will see him court-martialed." Vankler stuck his arm out at vanden Hoyt.

"You and I, we will determine exactly what steps we must take to reach a satisfactory resolution to the humiliation your battalion suffered today."

"We will indeed." Vankler pivoted and marched off the

reviewing stand, toward the administration building, which was between the main gate and the barracks. He ignored the ground vehicle that was racing toward the reviewing stand from the airfield.

Van Winkle gave vanden Hoyt a hard look, but said nothing to him. Instead he turned his attention to the man who got out of the car and climbed onto the reviewing stand. The Feldpolizei officers snapped to attention and saluted the newcomer.

This officer, even more splendidly decked out than the 257th's officers, swept his gaze over the Wanderjahrians and demanded in a crisp voice, "Who's senior man here?"

"I am, sir," one said, and swallowed. "Inspector Bladhortz. I'm the executive officer."

"Well, Inspector, it appears we have a situation on our hands."

Bladhortz swallowed again. "Yes sir, it does."

"And you must be Commander Van Winkle," he said to the Marine.

"I am, sir. And whom do I have the honor of addressing?"

"Chief Inspector Kleinst. We spoke on the radio."

"Yessir. Thank you for getting here so quickly." Chief Inspector Kleinst was the commander of all Feldpolizei forces in Arschland.

"We have a matter and a man which must be dealt with. I am the man to do it." Kleinst looked toward the administration building in time to see Vankler disappear into it. "Let us first defuse matters here." He included Bladhortz in what he said next: "Shall we have our men stand down?"

"I think that would be the best, sir," Van Winkle said.

"Yessir," Bladhortz said. "A splendid idea, sir."

While Bladhortz left the reviewing stand to see to the unloading of the weapons of the Feldpolizei, Van Winkle turned to Parant. "Sergeant Major, will you see to our men, please?"

"Aye aye, sir." Parant leaped off the reviewing stand and strode toward the airfield, which was where he thought Bass was most likely to be.

"You stay here," Van Winkle said to vanden Hoyt. "You

don't move." He said it loudly enough for all of the Feldpolizei officers to hear.

"Aye aye, sir," vanden Hoyt replied.

Van Winkle and Kleinst marched to the administration building.

Sometime later a runner came with a summons for Ensign vanden Hoyt.

Commander Van Winkle leaned back in Commander Vankler's chair, behind the Feldpolizei commander's desk, fixed vanden Hoyt with a steely gaze, and let the junior officer stand sweating at attention for a long moment. The chair swiveled and tilted, had a high back and armrests, and—most amazing—was upholstered in some sort of splotchy green leather. He had been surprised when he first entered the battalion commander's office. All the furniture was upholstered in leather in colors he'd never seen on a live animal. One visitor chair was an iridescent blue, another was yellow with mauve stripes, a settee was speckled orange. Even the desktop was covered with a red and beige skin. An impossibly large lizardlike head hung high on one wall.

Van Winkle drummed his fingers on the desktop; the skin that covered it was amazingly hard. Abruptly, he leaned forward. "Whose bright idea was it to turn invisible and then hit those amateurs from the flank with guns?"

"Sir," vanden Hoyt barked stiffly, "it's my responsibility."

"Yes," Van Winkle said slowly, "you were the officer in charge, it was your responsibility. But that's not what I asked. Whose idea was it?"

Vanden Hoyt said nothing.

"Ensign, did you issue the order to change into chameleons? Did you issue the order to make that flanking maneuver?"

"No, sir. But I'm responsible, sir."

Van Winkle shook his head. "We've already settled that. Whose idea was it?"

"Sir, I wasn't privy to that decision."

Van Winkle looked at him expectantly.

"Sir," vanden Hoyt said when the silence stretched long

enough to make him uncomfortable, "I can only assume it was Staff Sergeant Bass's idea. I haven't had communications with him since I sent him to put the men in the trees for our demonstration."

Van Winkle nodded. "Thought so. It has all the markings of a Charlie Bass operation." He added softly, as though speaking to himself, "If it wasn't for stunts like that, he'd probably be a colonel today." Then briskly he said, "Sit down, Ensign. You're not being court-martialed. Vankler doesn't have the authority to arrest you, and you know it."

Vanden Hoyt sat gingerly on the edge of a chair upholstered in pebbly-surfaced gray leather with ochre markings.

"Relax, Ensign. We lucked out." Van Winkle stood. "No, no, sit." He waved vanden Hoyt back down when the junior officer jumped to his feet. "You're off the hook. Drink? You probably need one." He went to a cabinet and examined its contents. "Hmmm. No, we're going to stay away from thule. Surely he's got something alcoholic in here." He pulled out two glasses and rooted about among the bottles and cans of various grades, brands, and flavorings of thule and its attendant paraphernalia. Then, with an exclamation of victory, he pulled out a nearly full bottle of an amber liquid. He read the lable, then turned with a smile. "Scotch. Real Earth scotch. Single malt! Is that all right?" He poured.

Vanden Hoyt nodded in confusion. What was going on? Vankler wanted to court-martial him. Where was the Feldpolizei commander? For that matter, where was Chief Inspector Kleinst?

Van Winkle served a glass to vanden Hoyt, then pulled a visitor chair close to him and sat. "Well now. Without talking to any of the Feldpolizei other than Vankler, I'd say your platoon made a very dramatic impression on the 257th. Would you agree?"

Vanden Hoyt sipped at his scotch and nodded. "Yessir."

"As the situation turned out, you made a strong impression on Chief Inspector Kleinst, as well."

"Ah, sir, where is he? For that matter, where is Commander Vankler?"

Van Winkle grinned. "That's where we lucked out. The chief inspector is in another room, reaming Vankler a new one. You see, Vankler is a close adherent of Commissioner Schickledorf's theories of warfare. Chief Inspector Kleinst thinks Schickledorf's tactics are more dangerous to their practitioners than to whoever they're being used against. The way your platoon devastated the 257th today is all the proof Kleinst needed to scrap Schickledorf's doctrine in Arschland. And Vankler's outburst is exactly the excuse Kleinst needed to fire him. Which is what he's going to do when he finishes reaming him out. This means Company L will have a free hand in its training of the Feldpolizei in Arschland. I hope I have similar luck in the other Staats I'm responsible for." He knocked back the rest of his drink, stood, and held his hand out.

Vanden Hoyt hesitantly stood and shook it.

"Give Charlie my best. And get on with your training program." With that, he left.

CHAPTER
SIX

Brigadier Sturgeon, true to his word, moved his headquarters into an old warehouse complex at the Brosigville port the morning after the bombing. By nightfall his drastically reduced staff had been completely ensconced in its new quarters. Of the 150-odd men usually assigned to a FIST command staff, Brigadier Sturgeon had less than eighty in the new facility, and of them, Dean and Claypoole, as privates first class, were the lowest ranking.

The building was in a cul-de-sac at the end of a long, narrow roadway that was under surveillance around the clock. Everyone entering the complex passed through surveillance devices that detected explosives and weapons; nothing was permitted in the main building unless it had been screened and carried in by the Marines themselves. All other vehicular traffic was diverted to a parking lot more than a hundred meters from the main entrance, and passengers had to walk from there. Not even a knife could be taken into the headquarters undetected. Surveillance radars mounted on the roof and tied in to the string-of-pearls satellites in orbit around Wanderjahr would give adequate warning if the complex were to come under fire by projectile weapons, which could then be quickly neutralized.

Between working for Commander Peters by day and mandatory security duty at night, the team of Dean and Claypoole had hardly any free time to themselves. All the Marines, officers, NCOs, and junior enlisted men lived inside the headquarters; some, such as the communications and aviation personnel, set up their sleeping units at their workstations so they could be available around the clock. Dean and Claypoole were allowed to pick an empty storage room for their quarters, an unaccustomed luxury for Marine infantrymen, who in garrison lived in barrack complexes, each fire team in its own room but each complex containing hundreds of other men. There was always somebody popping into the fire team rooms, and the common areas were constantly astir with men playing cards, talking, horsing around. And back in garrison, everyone's life was strictly regulated by the training and deployment missions of their units. Here, when off duty, they were all by themselves. Compared to the hubbub of barracks life, the silence in the building was disturbing at first. The big recreational event of the day for all the Marines on the staff was mealtimes. The mess section had been left fully staffed because the brigadier believed Marines worked best on a full stomach.

"Gentlemen," Commander Peters announced early one morning about a week after the move to Brosigville, "the brigadier and I are flying into the hills today. You deserve a break. Be back in the building in time for guard mount tonight." The two looked at their new boss for about five seconds before grabbing their covers and side arms and bolting out the door.

Outside, Claypoole skidded to a stop near the entrance to the motor pool and stood looking into it with a bemused expression.

"Hey, get a move on," Dean shouted when he noticed Claypoole wasn't still with him. "The town's this way."

Without looking at him, Claypoole waved at Dean to come back.

"What?" Dean demanded as he closed the gap.

"We're going in style." Claypoole turned his head and grinned at Dean.

"What do you mean?"

"The section landcar."

"We can't use that. It's for Commander Peters's official use."

"Sure we can. We work for him, he sent us on liberty, we're on official business for him."

"But—"

Claypoole didn't wait to hear Dean's objection. He darted to the F-2's landcar, which was only a few meters inside the motor pool, got in, and drove it out. "Get in," he said as he stopped next to Dean and opened the passenger-side door.

Dean protested, but climbed in anyway. Once they were on their way he said, "The commander didn't say we could take his car off the port!"

"He didn't say we couldn't," Claypoole responded. "Don't worry, the communications center knows where we'll be every second, and if they need us or want to call us back, they can do that. So far as I know, nothing around here's off-limits to us—yet."

Dean considered that for a moment and shrugged.

The Brosigville spaceport occupied thousands of hectares and was a small city unto itself. Just outside its main gate was the village of Rosario, a suburb of Brosigville. "We're going to Juanita's," Claypoole announced as they were perfunctorily waved through the gate.

Claypoole guided the landcar down a tree-lined boulevard and turned up a side street. It ended abruptly in a cul-de-sac. "Damn!" Claypoole muttered, turning the vehicle around. "Turned too soon. I've only been out here once before," he added, smiling awkwardly. Dean just made a face and kept his silence.

Juanita's was nestled among a row of shops and cafés about a kilometer from the gate. Behind it the neighboring low hills, heavily wooded with grospalms and spikers, rolled away toward the city. The setting was more rural than urban, and the small businesses served mostly local residents, nearly all of them employees at the port. Juanita's was a haven for the men and women from the shuttle craft that were constantly coming and going at the port. Just then, in the middle of the morning, the place was nearly deserted.

"Place jumps after dark, or at least it did the one time I was in here," Claypoole said as he pushed aside the beaded curtains that hung over the doorway. "We'll have a few beers and some breakfast, okay?"

"I don't have much money," Dean said.

"Don't need much." Claypoole pulled out a wad of Wander-jahr marks. Each mark was worth about one-third of a Confederation credit, the currency in which the Marines were paid. "A mark will get you a whole breakfast," Claypoole said. "Twenty-five fennies for a beer." There were a hundred fennies to a mark. The Wanderjahrian currency system was based on the German mark of Old Earth, but over the generations since the original settlement, the German word pfennig had become "fenny." Upon their arrival, the Marines had been permitted to convert fifty credits to marks, not that any of them ever expected to get much chance to spend the money in Brosigville or anywhere else on the planet.

Inside Juanita's it was cool and quiet. The air was circulated by large ceiling fans that rotated lazily.

"Welcome, Marines!" a large brown woman sitting at a cashier's station shouted warmly.

"Juanita!" Claypoole exclaimed. "You remembered me!"

"Yes, Mr. Kaypole. You bring friend?" Claypoole introduced Dean, who shook hands modestly with the big woman. Hearing the greetings, several young women came in from the sunlit patio at the rear of the café and gathered around the Marines.

"Employees!" Claypoole winked at Dean. "Breakfast, please, Juanita." As soon as the Wanderjahrian breakfast—boiled and baked meats from animals native to the planet, fresh bread, and a variety of luscious fruits—was served, the young women, idle and bored during the daytime, crowded around the Marines' table, chattering excitedly among themselves and eagerly urging various dishes upon the two men. One of the fruits, a long skinny white melon they referred to as a "Canfil watermelon," was especially delicious. Filled with a thick, creamy white juice, extremely sweet, and rich and seedless, they scooped it out eagerly with large silver spoons.

"Buddha's brown balls," Dean whispered, "this is embarrassing!" A very beautiful girl, who said her name was Magdalena, sat next to Claypoole and laughed merrily as she tried to feed him pieces of fruit. Claypoole immediately dubbed her

"Maggie," and before she could react, planted a wet kiss full on her lips. The other women shrieked with laughter and the brown-skinned Maggie blushed so hard her face turned almost black. She slapped Claypoole on the cheek, hard. The blow echoed throughout the dining room and brought tears to his eyes. Then she kissed him back very long and very hard and laughed.

Rising suddenly, Maggie took a musical instrument, something like a banjo, off the wall and began to sing a lively ballad in three-four time. Her voice was a surprisingly good soprano and she plucked the instrument's strings expertly. The other girls laughed and began to keep time by clapping their hands.

"What language is she singing?" Dean asked.

"It is the old language our ancestors brought here," a girl who called herself Jallalla said. "The song is about a man who comes home and finds that his wife has run away with his best friend."

"Oh, how sad!" Dean replied.

"He is singing about how much he misses his friend." Jallalla laughed.

"Oh," Dean said.

Jallalla leaned close to Dean and said, "No, that is not what she is singing at all. She sings about your friend and the song is very dirty."

"Oh," Dean replied. "Why doesn't anybody ever sing a song like that about me?"

Jallalla leaned even closer and whispered into his ear, "Come back tonight and I will sing a song like that about you too, and nobody else will hear me but you."

Done with breakfast, the Marines ordered beer. It proved to be weak and lukewarm. Brewing was an art the original settlers had not brought with them from Germany. "Reindeer piss!" Dean exclaimed. He was used to the full-bodied brews of Thorsfinni's World. Claypoole made a face and pushed his glass away. "Guess we'll order water," he said.

"No, no," Maggie, who had finished singing and returned her banjo to its peg, protested. "Smoke thule with us!"

Claypoole made another face and shook his head. The

Marines were forbidden to use thule on duty and discouraged from using the drug off duty. Maggie lighted up a cigarillo and sucked the smoke deep into her lungs. Exhaling, she offered it to Claypoole. He looked at the beer and he looked at Maggie, and took the cigarillo. "Mmm. 'Finni tobacco is better," he said, exhaling a thin blue cloud of smoke, "and this doesn't do any . . . Hey! Dean-o, try this shit!"

Dean took the cigarillo and drew on it. The smoke tasted sweet and caused a pleasant tingling sensation as it passed into his lungs. He blew it out through his nose. The smell and taste reminded him of flower blossoms but not so cloying. He remembered the faintly acrid aroma from the day he'd talked to the drivers who'd been smoking it at Arschmann's mansion and noted it seemed to be missing now. "Do you have different, uh, grades of thule, I mean very good, not so good?" he asked one of the girls.

She smiled and nodded. "But this thule is very good quality," she said.

A feeling of great peace and satisfaction settled over Dean. But at the same time his senses remained alert, keen. He took another drag and then another. The intensity of the feeling did not increase. Jallalla said, "You smoke thule long time, feel very good while you smoke, but go back to normal when done." She smiled at Dean and draped a brown arm about his neck. He could clearly see the fine black hairs on the back of her arm. He took her hand in his and thought he could feel the blood pulsing through her fingers. "Thule a little different for each person," Jallalla told him.

"You bet!" Claypoole answered, feeling an erection beginning.

"But nobody ever fight when using thule," the third girl, Auca, told them.

"It sure doesn't cut down on hormones!" Claypoole laughed as his hand caressed Maggie's considerable frontage. She squeezed his earlobe—hard—in return.

Dean felt himself slipping into a state of euphoria. While he remained acutely conscious of everything about him, even the mundane objects in the room took on the appearance of brilliant works of art. He regarded the still-full beer glass before him on the table and marveled at how wonderfully the bubbles proceeded from the bottom to join the thin head of foam just under the rim. How could he have been so insensitive as to think this was an inferior brew? He sipped some of the beer. It still tasted like reindeer piss. But good, very good.

Dean smiled up at Jallalla, who was now sitting very close to him at the table. She leaned closer and nibbled on his earlobe. "Come back tonight?" she whispered, and then slowly kissed him. Dean closed his eyes and tasted the girl's lips. Her teeth brushed lightly against his and he felt a pleasant electric shock at the contact.

"Hey," Claypoole shouted, "everybody out back! C'mon, we're gonna spend the day on the patio!"

The next hour was the most pleasant Joe Dean could ever remember. Juanita's patio extended for fifty meters behind the dining room and was surrounded by a lush garden. Chairs and tables were spaced at wide intervals. Half a kilometer beyond the garden the verdant hills began. At that time of day the sun was pleasantly warm, so the five of them sat at one table in the shade of a vine-covered trellis, drank cool fruit punch, smoked thule, laughed, bantered, and spoke of home and family and friends. Claypoole recited the events of their recent adventures on Elneal as the girls listened with wide-eyed attention. He promised to introduce them to the magnificent Charlie Bass, and he really meant it.

Dean was lolling with one arm about Jallalla and the other around Auca, puffing on his second cigarillo, totally at peace with himself and the entire universe, regarding with a deep sense of well-being the stunning natural beauty of the green hills beyond the patio. The girls, puffing on their own cigarillos, sighed contentedly.

Dean remembered his friend, Fred McNeal, who'd been killed on Elneal. He thought how much Freddie would've enjoyed Wanderjahr and Juanita's. But this time, for a change, remembering his dead friend did not fill him with sadness. He tried to conjure a mental image of McNeal, but it kept going out of focus, and Dean realized Fred's features were already beginning to fade in his memory. No matter, Freddie had died bravely, and when it was his own time to go, Dean knew, he wouldn't be afraid.

Maggie, meanwhile, had put her mouth close to Claypoole's ear, to tell the lance corporal the only news short of promotion he ever wanted to hear. She whispered, "Come with me to my room. Now."

Then Dean saw a bright flash on the distant hillside, and he lurched forward, pulling the two women with him to the ground. Three more flashes winked from the hillside in quick succession. The first bullet smacked into the table where Dean had been sitting, plowing a furrow through the wood, then ricocheting off the paving stones in a bright flash of sparks and fragments. The second went through the hole punched in the wood by the first one and spanged harmlessly off the paving stones. But the third round hit Maggie just behind her right ear and exited the other side of her head in a spray of blood mixed with bone fragments and chunks of brain. The fourth round whizzed harmlessly past Claypoole's right ear.

In the next second the distant *pop-pop-pop-pop* of the discharges reached their ears. And then Claypoole was on his feet, holding Maggie in his arms, her red wet blood smeared all over his face, uttering a scream of rage and despair so terrible it made Dean's blood run cold.

Quickly, Dean got the others inside the café, and after a few moments Claypoole came to his senses and they drew their weapons, prepared for an assault, but none came and no more shots were fired at them. They comforted the two hysterical girls as best they could while waiting for the police and emergency units. The thule did not help at all in these circumstances. Juanita fluttered about, muttering to herself, "Bad things happen now you Marines come here, bad, bad things!" Dean wanted to shut her up, a rising sense of anger and frustration mounting inside him, but he could think of nothing to say that would silence the woman who only a little while earlier had welcomed them so warmly.

They had dragged Maggie's body inside with them. Now

she lay in a corner, draped with a cloth hastily snatched from a nearby table, dark blood slowly pooling beneath her head. Her feet stuck out from the sheet. One still wore a sandal; the other was bare. Dean looked steadily at the one bare foot for a long time. She had manicured her toenails, he noticed. She would never do that again, or sing a song either, or laugh, or . . . He thought again of McNeal and shook his head sharply. He was losing it. He focused his mind on the royal ass-chewing they'd get when Brigadier Sturgeon found out about the day's events.

Claypoole kept his mind as nearly blank as he could. He lay prone just inside the door to the patio, his weapon leveled at the rear of the patio, watching for movement from the direction of the nearby hills.

Dean went over to Juanita. "Did you call the police?" he asked.

"I call them! I call them!" she exclaimed, then broke into sobs. Dean put his arm awkwardly around her and she rested her head on his shoulder.

That's how they were standing when the first police vehicle roared up outside and uniformed officers, weapons drawn, burst in through the door. Dean wondered just what they'd been told had happened when two officers rushed up and grabbed him by the arms. A third removed his blaster from its holster. Instantly, the place was full of police officers. Three more pulled Claypoole up from the floor. Claypoole snatched his right arm free and delivered a roundhouse blow to the side of the second officer's head, but his legs were kicked out from under him and he crashed to the floor with two policemen on top. The man he'd hit took an electric prod from his equipment belt, set it on stun, and was about to deliver a knockout shock when a powerful voice sounded from the doorway.

"Halt!" Everyone froze. Two men entered, one short and trim and wearing a uniform, the other much larger and dressed in loose civilian clothes. The big man walked to the center of the room and ordered the officers to release the two Marines. Dean was pleasantly surprised to see it was Chief Long.

"Lads, I want you to meet Commissioner Alois Landser, chief of the Brosigville Stadtpolizei and the man responsible for law enforcement through all of Arschland," Chief Hugyens Long said. Landser, a spare, gray little man with a black goatee, clicked his heels loudly and bowed slightly as he was introduced. He wore an immaculate uniform, a sky-blue tunic with black trousers sporting a bloodred stripe down the outside seam of each leg. His black leather Sam Browne belt shone with polish, and a silver badge of office glittered brightly above his left breast pocket. A smart visored cap, bill polished to mirrorlike perfection, was held tightly under one arm. The other policemen who swarmed through the café and out the back toward the hills were dressed similarly, except that lieutenants and below wore white tunics.

"I beg you to return with me to headquarters for the making of personal statements, gentlemen," Landser announced. Long laid his hand gently on the commissioner's shoulder. "That won't be necessary right now, Alois," he said. "We'll just sit here and talk to the lads a bit."

"But, my dear chief—"

"Sit down, Alois. Relax." Long smiled and pulled up a chair. He turned it around and draped his arms over the back. Compared to Landser, Long looked disheveled, wrinkled clothes hanging loosely about his large frame. He sported no visible gear, just a capacious jacket over civilian trousers, but when he sat down, Dean clearly saw the large handheld blaster slung under his left armpit.

Landser also took a chair, but he sat in it stiffly, primly, as if afraid to wrinkle his trousers. Long's informal way of conducting serious police business frustrated the little man. He was a capable officer, but subjected himself to very restrictive rules of conduct that never permitted him to relax while on duty—and seldom when off. But he could obey orders. And he was obeying them now, because Long was chief of police at Chairman Arschmann's express instructions.

"Remember, Alois," the chairman had told him the day Hugyens Long had arrived and presented his credentials, "this man is now in charge. You will be his understudy. You will learn to do things his way, Alois, or you are out. Out at *his* discretion. I have given him total independence and the authority to act as he sees fit to completely reorganize your force. I want my police to be the best on the planet, and if you do not go along with Chief Long, you are finished. I don't care that your family has served mine faithfully for generations, Alois. This is a totally pragmatic matter. It is business. You will not mess it up."

At first Landser had been so insulted at his master's command that he'd considered quitting on the spot. Only strong self-discipline and the fact that his family *had* served the Arschmanns for generations had enabled him to keep his silence—and his job. Landser's family was not a prominent one, but it was respected, and his blood was completely German. Landser felt he was being treated like one of the common mixed-bloods. Most galling was the fact that his fate had been put into the hands of an offworlder. It had taken him a full day to get control of himself. He sensed that things on Wanderjahr would change somehow, with the Marines there, and he intended to be around to take advantage of whatever altered circumstances presented themselves in the future.

So now Alois Landser sat dutifully at a small table in Juanita's café. He would learn something from this offworlder. Meanwhile, his resentment against Arschmann smoldered.

"Tell me what happened," Long asked the two Marines.

Dean looked at Claypoole, his face white but his eyes burning with suppressed rage, and decided to do the talking for both of them. In a few words he told the policemen the story. During the telling, various police officers approached the chief and whispered information into his ear. Long simply nodded and the officers disappeared.

"How did you know to duck at the flash of the first shot?" Commissioner Landser asked.

Dean shrugged. "I've been shot at before by those kinds of weapons, on Elneal. I guess when I saw that first flash, my instincts took over."

"Claypoole," the chief said, "do you have anything to add?"

"I will kill whoever did this," Claypoole muttered, his voice tense with anger.

Chief Long nodded. "Let us do a little more work on this before you start shooting up Brosigville, Marine."

"Fuck," Claypoole muttered.

"Look, lads," Chief Long began, "I'm here to teach these people how to conduct police operations. That's something I know how to do real good. You Marines are here to teach the Feldpolizei how to fight, which you do real good. But either of you guys get in my way and you're history. Okay?"

"Sorry. Okay," Claypoole answered.

"These officers who've been whispering in my ear as you were talking located the sniper's position, about eight hundred meters straight out the back door. He was shooting from the limbs of a spiker tree out there. No shell casings, few footprints, that's it. Evidently he had plenty of time to get into position. He probably used a semiautomatic projectile rifle firing caseless ammo. The guerrillas have them. Who knew you were coming here today?"

Claypoole shrugged. "Nobody." Dean nodded.

"Then they were being watched," Long said to Commissioner Landser, who nodded. "They were watching your compound, and when they saw you leave, they followed you. Did you see anybody suspicious along the way here?"

"No, sir," both Marines answered.

"Put some agents in the vicinity of the Marine headquarters, Alois. Perhaps we can watch the watchers."

"We have our informant network too, sir," Landser said. "I will put out the word."

Chief Long smiled and thought to himself, Yes, Alois, you do have your "network," and if it's the last thing I do, I'm going to find out what's in it. He returned his attention to the Marines. "Your Commander Peters and I are spending a lot of the Confederation's credit here to establish an intelligence network. Once it's up and going, we'll share information, but for now, Commissioner Landser's agents are all we have. It's not a bad network either."

Beside him Landser nodded and thought, Good enough to stick a certain prominent old bastard where it'll hurt.

"Okay, been a long day for both of you. I am really sorry it had to end this way. Whoever did this meant to hit both you and the girls. The first two rounds seem to have been meant for Dean, but the shooter fired the third one at Miss Magdalena. The fourth was meant for you, Claypoole, but he missed. Sometime in the next few days, you lads come by headquarters and see me. We have some details to wrap up. Now you better get back to your own HQ and leave this mess to us."

The pair rose. "One thing, Chief . . ." Claypoole said. Long nodded. "When you find out who did this and you go to get him, I want to be there. Will you let me? I promise, no trouble. But I want to be in on it."

A long moment of silence passed before Long replied. He looked steadily at the two Marines. Claypoole's utilities were stained dark with Maggie's blood. Chief Long could read the character of any man. These were good lads. "All right," he said.

After the two Marines left, Landser turned to Chief Long. "The shooter did want to hit the girls, didn't he? He wasn't shooting just at the Marines. That impresses me as a very important fact."

Chief Long nodded slowly. "I think he missed Dean because light travels faster than a bullet and Dean reacted quickly when he saw the first muzzle flash. Christ, what reflexes! That second shot was insurance, but yes, the third one was right on target. He wanted to kill the girl, maybe even more than either of the Marines."

"Bandits? Cause terror and resentment here in the Brosigville suburbs?" Landser asked.

Long grunted. "Have the guerrillas been doing much of that?"

Landser thought for a moment. "No. Propaganda, yes. Sabotage, some. But outright murder to intimidate? No. It might be a new tactic, a desperate move now that the Marines are here to help the government."

Chief Long rose from the table and clapped Landser on the shoulder. "Alois, let's go back and think this whole thing over."

Landser sat at the table a moment before following Chief Long outside. Who could it have been but the bandits? he wondered. He did not know Chief Hugyens Long very well yet, but he sensed the chief's instincts were very good.

With the resiliency of youth reinforced by very hard combat experience that had taught them people close to you get killed, the two young Marines were able to put the bombing and Maggie's shooting in the background and go on with their duties. Still, Claypoole knew he wouldn't rest easy until her death was avenged. It wasn't that he'd gotten to know Maggie at all well, or that their budding relationship, as superficial as it was, had been cut short. What made him angry was the fact that an innocent life had been destroyed by some dumb shit with a rifle who couldn't even hit two man-size targets at eight hundred meters. He'd never had a projectile weapon in his hands in his life, although he'd seen the Siad warriors on Elneal use them to good effect. But he knew if he did ever use one, he'd be sure he could hit something with it.

After a long and very one-sided talk with FIST Sergeant Major Shiro about unauthorized trips in official vehicles, the two returned to duty very subdued. All Commander Peters said to them was, "You did well under the circumstances."

Two days later, Commander Peters allowed them to visit police headquarters. After they went over the events for the investigative team Chief Long had assigned to the case, the big policeman escorted them to his newly established forensics lab.

"How much do you know about the police organization on Wanderjahr?" Long asked as they walked from his office to the lab.

Claypoole shrugged. "There are field police and city police."

"We advise the field police and you advise the city police," Dean added.

"Close enough," Long said. "Originally there were no 'field' police. They only came into being when the insurgency started.

With no army to speak of, the oligarchs had to create some kind of armed body that could cope with it. The metropolitan police forces were neither equipped nor trained to do that. All the cops on this planet go to the same police academy. Each Staat has its own force and runs its own training program, but essentially the curriculums are about the same. That's something I'm working on. But basically the metropolitan police forces here are pretty good. They know the basic patrol and investigative techniques about as well as any police force anywhere else in the Confederation."

"I hear the field police are a bunch of comedians," Claypoole said.

"They're being led by fools," Long replied. "After basic police training, the men selected for assignment to field battalions go to an infantry-type school that's run by the Ruling Council. The field police are commanded by an officer appointed by the Council, and it operates independently of the oligarchs' Staat governments. That's a good concept. Where it's screwed up is, the field police are commanded by idiots. I think your Brigadier Sturgeon will look into that," he added dryly.

They were at the lab. Chief Long paused just outside the door. "This is the Brosigville Stadtpolizei forensics lab. Do you know anything about police forensics?"

"That's how you figure out who committed the crime?" Claypoole ventured.

Chief Long nodded. "That's about it. But it's a science unto itself that includes a lot of things besides taking fingerprints and looking at footprints. A forensics expert can look at the details of a crime scene and tell you volumes about what happened there. For instance, the pattern of blood spots at the murder scene can tell him how the crime was committed, even how tall the murderer was."

He led them over to a workbench and picked up a twisted metal fragment. "My forensics people did a chemical analysis on this fragment," he told them, holding up the piece of metal. "I brought a good team along with me to teach the Wanderjahrians how to set up their own lab—and imagine my surprise when I discovered they already had some very well-qualified people here." The portly policeman chuckled as he sat down at the workbench. "At least one of Arschmann's nephews has brains. He got the old man to fund a pretty sophisticated forensics program for this police department. Technologically, these guys are way behind most other Confederation worlds' police force forensics teams, but they've got the basic techniques down pat."

"Lean closer." The two Marines peered over the chief's shoulders. "There was enough chemical residue on this fragment that we were able to figure out what kind of bomb it was," Long said proudly, turning the fragment slowly in his gloved fingers.

"Why the gloves?" Claypoole asked.

"The stuff stinks, and when you get it on you, it's hard to get off. Smell it. Besides, it's been a rule for hundreds of years that you don't handle any kind of evidence with your bare paws."

Claypoole sniffed gingerly and drew back quickly. Chief Long laughed and held the fragment out to Dean. "Won't hurt you, lads!" The odor coming off the scorched bit of metal was tantalizingly familiar to Dean. He knew he'd smelled it before, but couldn't remember where.

"Constantine!" Long shouted. A short, gray-haired man in a smock turned from where he was explaining to a group of police recruits the mysteries of latent fingerprints. "Yes, Chief?" He excused himself from his students and limped over.

"This is Lieutenant Pete Constantine, gentlemen. Lost his right leg in a shoot-out with terrorists on Chilban last year. He's my explosives expert, best damn man in that field you'll find anywhere in the Confederation."

"What happened to the terrorists?" Claypoole asked.

"Killed 'em all," Constantine answered. "Got 'em with a grenade of my own invention," he said proudly. " 'Course, I was a bit too close when it went off." He shrugged, patting his right leg. "But I got the job done. Nerve grafts haven't quite healed up yet, but I'll be back on full duty anytime now. Look at this arm." He tapped his right forearm. "Lost that in a lab accident about ten years ago. Good as the real one now. And this eye," he tapped his left eye, "took a fragment when a device I was defusing went off prematurely. Can see with it better than I could with the old one. How can I help, Chief?"

"Give our Marine friends here a rundown on the bomb that was used against their headquarters, will you?"

"PETN w/M," Constantine answered. "Pentaerythritol tetranitrate with Monroite mixed to military specifications. Until about a hundred and fifty years ago PETN was a standard explosive compound used in military munitions. Then they developed Monroite, and that gave the PETN more stability while increasing its power. Don't see it much anymore in modern military munitions, not since plasma weapons came into use, but it's still plenty available.

"I estimate these bombs generated a shock wave traveling at about eight thousand meters a second at a temperature of somewhere around five thousand degrees Centigrade. It was that blast wave that got everyone. Pretty respectable, but you'll notice the explosions did little structural damage to the buildings. Not intended to. They were set off to get people in the open. The blast waves dissipated rather quickly. Oh, they destroyed things in the street and blew in the frontage on the lower floors of the buildings, but you don't bring buildings down by setting off bombs in the streets outside. The first one we think was in some kind of handcart, one of those fruit-vending carts you see in the streets around here all the time. The second, larger bomb was in a landcar about a hundred meters up the street from the first, where it was protected from the first blast. Both were detonated remotely; we found enough of the detonator components to establish that fact."

"How will you catch the guy who did it?" Dean asked.

Chief Long sighed. "That, my lad, is the question. They use PETN w/M explosives. The whole thing has the earmarks of a rebel terrorist attack. But I don't know . . . Whoever did this knew precisely where you'd be moving, and had plenty of time to set things up. Same with whoever shot at you guys the other day. I've discussed this with Commander Peters. We know the guerrillas have cells in the city here, but I'm not sure they have the logistics to pull off a thing like this even with advance notice. You lads figure that out for me and I'll buy you both as much cold beer as you can drink."

Claypoole picked up the bomb fragment again and sniffed at it. "Smells like burning rags," he said. "Um, no, not rags, more like burning grass. Yes. Funny."

"That's the Monroite residue. Leaves a strong, almost indelible odor. Get it on you, you just wear it for weeks afterward. You spend even a little time handling that stuff and it gets all over you."

"I've smelled it before!" Dean exclaimed. The three men stared at him. "Yes! Here, since we've been on Wanderjahr. Damn. Where?" He turned to Claypoole, who just shrugged.

"Take your time, Mr. Dean," Chief Long said. "Make sure. You remember where you smelled this odor, and we might have our bomber."

And then it came to him: Chairman Arschmann's parking lot, the three drivers standing there smoking thule. "Garth!" he blurted out.

CHAPTER
SEVEN

Staff Sergeant Charlie Bass didn't have any problems with the orders that came down from FIST headquarters; he thought they were exactly the orders that would allow the Marines to accomplish their mission. But others had problems with the orders, and that created problems for him. As soon as the platoon was dismissed after Ensign vanden Hoyt read the orders, Sergeant Hyakowa, the senior squad leader, and all three of his fire team leaders approached Bass. A very angry Lance Corporal Dave Schultz reached him first.

"No! I won't do it!" Schultz shouted. "I'm not an NCO! I don't want to be an NCO. I'm exactly what I want to be, and that's a lance corporal. I won't do it. You can court-martial me if you want to, but I won't do it!"

"Now, now, Schultz, calm down." Bass patted his hands on the air in a placating gesture. "Nobody's asking you to fill the role of a noncommissioned officer." He didn't bother looking to first squad's NCOs for help; he knew they wouldn't give him any. Why should they? He knew *he* wouldn't offer any help if he'd been in their position.

Schultz glared. "That's sure what it sounds like to me."

"Hammer, you are the kind of lance corporal every junior Marine strives to become. Before you were a lance corporal, you were one of the best PFCs who ever served in the Corps. When you were a private, you were so good your superiors couldn't wait to promote you to PFC. You are the best at what you are, at what you do. That's what you want to be, what you want to do. Nobody has any argument with that, nobody wants to try to make you be something you don't want to be."

"Well, what do you think making me a squad leader is?"

Bass shook his head. "Not a squad leader, the Feldpolizei doesn't have squad leaders. You're going to be an acting shift chief."

"That sounds like a squad leader to me."

"It's not a squad leader. Nobody's making you a squad leader."

"That's right, and nobody's going to either. I'm a lance corporal, not a sergeant."

"Listen to me, Schultz," Bass said more calmly than he felt. "I said you're the best. And I meant it. Do you agree with me that these Feldpolizei aren't very good as fighters?"

Schultz snorted. *Not very good* wasn't the way *he'*d put it.

"Do you agree they need to be trained?"

Schultz looked toward the empty parade ground where the 257th Feldpolizei Battalion had made its abortive assault on one platoon of Marines. "Wrong question. *Can* they be trained, that's the question."

"They can be trained. They may never be as good as Marines, but they can be trained."

Schultz grunted; he'd believe it when he saw it.

"Think back. Who were your drill instructors in Boot Camp? They were some of the best Marines you've ever served under or with, right?"

Schultz nodded grudgingly.

"It's the same here, maybe even more so. We need the best people to train them. And you're the best."

Schultz challengingly looked Bass in the eye. "So put me in a classroom."

Bass shook his head. "A classroom won't do it. The FPs are involved in a counterinsurgency war." Bass had tired of constantly using the cumbersome German name for the Wanderjahrian field police and gave it an English abbreviation. Thus, in time-honored military tradition, was born a shorter name for the local paramilitary force. "They can't be taken out of the field for classroom work. Besides, what you know can't be taught in school. What you know has to, can only, be taught in the field. On patrols. I am going to give you a shift of FPs to teach."

"As squad leader."

"Not as squad leader." Bass silently thanked the stars for the subtle semantic difference between *squad* and *shift*. "They don't have squads, they have shifts. And you'll be a teacher."

"If all I'm doing is teaching them, how come I'm getting an FP sergeant's warrant?"

That was really what Lance Corporal Dave Schultz was unhappy about. He was a career lance corporal; he didn't want to be a corporal, much less a sergeant. But in order for the relatively few Marines of 34th FIST to do a proper job of training the many thousands of men in the Feldpolizei, they had to be integrated into the FP units. One platoon of Marines was assigned to each battalion, and at that, there weren't enough Marine platoons to go around. The Marine platoon commander and sergeant worked with the FP battalion commander and his staff. One squad was assigned to each company in the battalion, one three-man fire team to each platoon. The Marine-sergeant squad leader had to teach the FP captain company commander, and the corporal fire team leaders the lieutenant platoon leaders. That left the lance corporals, PFCs, and privates the responsibility of training the shifts and their leaders. But it wouldn't do to have an ensign teaching a commander, a sergeant teaching a captain, a corporal a lieutenant, or a private a sergeant. So Brigadier Sturgeon, with the agreement and assistance of the Confederation ambassador to Wanderjahr, Jayben Spears, secured the appropriate commissions and warrants in the Feldpolizei for all of his Marines. And that made Lance Corporal Schultz extremely unhappy. The way Ensign vanden Hoyt had worded it when he told his men about the arrangement, Schultz interpreted it to mean he was being promoted to sergeant. It wasn't vanden Hoyt's word choice that made Schultz think that, though. Schultz would have reached that conclusion no matter how the order was worded.

"That's right, *FP sergeant's* stripes. You're not going to be a sergeant in the Marines," Bass reiterated. "You'll still be a Marine lance corporal. But you need the FP stripes to make sure the men you're teaching obey . . . ah, make sure they listen when you tell them something."

"The Eagle, Globe, and Starstream on my collar brass should be enough to tell them to listen up when I speak," Schultz said.

Bass nodded. "Right, you know that and I know that," he said with the arrogance common to those who served in elite forces. "But not everybody knows it. Some people need to see the rank insignia to be impressed. So you're going to be wearing sergeant's stripes." He held up a hand to stop whatever objection Schultz was about to make. "They're not real sergeant's stripes, not *Marine* sergeant. They're FP sergeant's stripes. Look at it this way. An FP sergeant knows about half as much about fighting as a Marine recruit who's made it halfway through Boot Camp. Don't think of it as an unwanted promotion, think of it as a bust."

Schultz knew that wasn't true, but having just said in effect that any Marine outranked an FP sergeant, he couldn't very well argue the point. He gave in—but not graciously.

Schultz wasn't the only problem Bass had to deal with regarding the Feldpolizei promotions. As soon as Schultz stomped away, Corporals Ratliff and Dornhofer jumped in.

"No!" Startled at simultaneously speaking so vehemently, they looked at each other. Dornhofer dipped his head, deferring to Ratliff as the senior of them.

"Godenov isn't good enough to lead a *one*-man kitchen police detail, much less run a fifteen-man police shift," Ratliff declared. "The man's a natural-born follower." He looked at Dornhofer as though to say "your turn."

"Make MacIlargie a shift sergeant, and you'll have the most screwed up, most troublemaking shift in the entire FP," Dornhofer stated.

In a less heated, less demanding, more conciliatory tone, Ratliff continued, "Besides, it's really not fair to our men to expect an inexperienced junior man to train and lead a fifteen-man shift." He wasn't for an instant fooled by Bass's claim to Schultz that the Marines weren't acting in leadership positions.

"Right." Dornhofer saw what Ratliff was thinking. "Make us a headquarters group and we'll supervise the FP shift sergeants along with teaching the lieutenant."

Bass shook his head. "We need to have Marines actually be in the leadership positions, otherwise we'll just be advisers, and history shows us that doesn't always work very well. Besides, Brigadier Sturgeon wants it that way, and when a man with a nova on his collar says he wants something done a certain way, I don't argue the point."

All four junior NCOs stared at him dumbfounded. They knew very well that Charlie Bass did things the way he thought they should be done, no matter who wanted them done a different way.

Ratliff was the first to recover. "Right," he said. "You don't argue the point, you just go ahead and do it your own way."

Hyakowa, silent to that point, gaped at Ratliff. He'd been thinking the same thing, but hadn't thought it was a good idea to voice.

"You just be glad I didn't hear that," Bass snarled. He felt a blush spreading on his face.

Leach, who'd been quiet to this point, said, "Staff Sergeant Bass, they're right. This isn't going to work. You and Ensign vanden Hoyt are going to be too busy teaching the new battalion commander and his staff how to run combat operations to supervise the platoon. Sergeant Hyakowa is going to have his hands full running the company headquarters. The three of us will be so busy with the lieutenants," a smile flickered across his face as he thought of himself supervising an officer, "we aren't going to have much time to help our men."

Hyakowa jumped in for the first time. "As much as I hate to say it, they're right. This arrangement puts too much of a burden on the junior men. There's simply not enough of us to go around."

"But there are," Bass said. "We're getting reinforced."

The junior NCOs glanced at each other. What reinforcements was he talking about?

"Doyle and Stevenson are being assigned to us . . ."

"The company clerk and the driver?" Leach and Ratliff squawked.

Dornhofer nudged Ratliff.

"Oh, right," Ratliff mumbled. "Doyle, he's okay." Ratliff ruefully remembered that Doyle had a Bronze Star and he didn't.

"I'm giving Stevenson to second squad to replace Claypoole. You get Doyle to fill in for Dean because you've got two men who've seen him in action and trust him." The two he was talking about were Dornhofer and Chan, each of whom had also won a Bronze Star in the action where Doyle had gotten his. "DuPont," Bass said, naming the platoon communications man, "will help Wang with the lieutenant, which will free him to help you so you can properly supervise your men. So, you see, there's no problem. You've got enough men." Bass turned to leave, but didn't complete his turn before Ratliff and Dornhofer were objecting again.

"Doyle's okay, DuPont's okay," Ratliff wasn't so sure about Stevenson, "but Godenov's still not good enough."

"That goes triple for MacIlargie," Dornhofer said.

Bass turned back, planted his fists firmly on his hips, and leaned forward aggressively. His eyes stopped briefly on Hyakowa and each of his fire team leaders to make sure they knew he was addressing all of them. "We are Marines. From the beginning, way back when Marines carried muzzle-loading projectile weapons and sailed oceans on wooden ships, Marines have always done more with less than anyone else. Marines have always faced problems others said were insolvable. *Schultz* has a problem with our assignment. That means," he looked Leach in the eye, "that *you* have a problem. Godenov is a problem," staring at Ratliff, "*your* problem. MacIlargie is a problem," to Dornhofer, "*you* have a problem." Then to Hyakowa: "Your fire team leaders have problems, that means *you* have problems." Back to all of them: "You are Marine noncommissioned officers. You have centuries of history behind you, centuries of Marine NCOs solving the unsolvable. So solve your damn problems!"

Bass spun about and marched toward the administration

building, where he and vanden Hoyt had set up their headquarters.

He knew that sometimes the best way to deal with problems was to kick them back to the subordinates who brought them to you.

Not everybody in first squad had a problem with the orders. Chan—not only a lance corporal, but a junior lance corporal—was startled by the orders that incorporated the Marines into the Feldpolizei as its officers and NCOs. Then he started thinking about it. He quickly got beyond the elite arrogance of "We're Marines, of course we should be in charge" and got to the implications. This was going to be a difficult job, he knew that almost instinctively. It was going to put to the test everything he knew about being a fighter, everything he thought he knew about leadership, and it was going to force him to learn a lot in a very short time. It didn't take long for him to stop thinking and start smiling. He hadn't realized it before, but it was exactly the kind of challenge he had joined the Marines for. He was going to enjoy his assignment. And somehow, some way, he was going to succeed at being a squad leader tasked with turning a bunch of glittery amateurs into professional soldiers.

The real problems began as soon as the Marines started trying to train the Feldpolizei.

"But if we dress in green, like you do, how will the bandits see us coming?" Acting Assistant Shift Sergeant Alauren asked Acting Shift Sergeant Chan, the Marine who'd supplanted him.

"That's the idea," Chan said patiently. "If they don't see you coming, you'll be able to catch them."

"But how will we find them if we don't march in formation?"

"When you march in formation like you've been doing, that means they get to pick the times and places to fight. When they do that, they hurt you."

"But they always run away when we fight them."

"Not until after they cause casualties," Chan said, still with patience.

"But we win, even when we have men wounded or killed. If that wasn't the case, why would they run away?"

"Because they aren't trying to beat you, they're trying to hurt you and wear you down."

"But we are winning. If we weren't winning, the bandits would fight to beat us."

"They will beat you if you keep using the same tactics you've been using," Chan said. His patience was wearing thin.

Alauren blinked and looked at Chan blandly. It was obvious he didn't believe the Marine.

"A couple of days ago, your entire battalion faced one platoon of Marines," Chan said coldly. "We let you have the first shot. If we'd been using live ammunition instead of simulators, most of you would be dead now. And you didn't manage to hit *any* of us."

The muscles at Alauren's jaws bunched and his eyes turned hard. He hadn't yet forgiven the Marines for that embarrassment. He might never forgive them.

Chan realized he was off to a bad start.

"You," Schultz snarled, glaring at a randomly selected trooper. "Hit that target." He pointed at a man-size ferrocrete block standing in front of a ten-meter-high berm a hundred meters away on the firing range.

The chosen trooper paled. He swallowed and his knees shook as he stared at the ferocious Marine, hoping that he wasn't really the one picked. But he was. He fumbled a battery into the well of his blaster and raised it to his shoulder.

"NO, you idiot!" Schultz roared. He took the few steps between him and the trooper and ripped the weapon from his hands. "Don't you know anything about range safety?" he growled in a hardly milder voice. "Never load your weapon until you're in position on the firing line. Keep your muzzle pointed downrange at all times." He grabbed the trooper by the front of his tunic and dragged him to the firing position, where he slammed the blaster back into his hands. The blaster bounced off the man's chest and would have clattered to the ground if Schultz hadn't caught it.

Schultz closed his eyes and breathed slowly while he counted to ten. When he opened his eyes, he held the blaster out for the quaking Wanderjahrian to take. "Now, mister," he said, the strain of not yelling evident in his voice, "load your weapon, aim at your target, and kill it." He stepped back and watched as the trooper fumbled a battery into the well, put his weapon to his shoulder, pointed it downrange, and pressed the firing lever. He then looked to see where the plasma bolt hit. Steam rising a good four meters from the target showed where it hit.

"You missed," Schultz began softly. "You weren't even close enough to make him keep his head down." As he spoke his voice rose. "If that was a man and he knew how to shoot, you'd be dead now!" His voice was at full scream before he reached the last word.

He jerked the blaster from the unfortunate trainee's hands, popped the battery out of the well, and thrust the weapon back at him with a snarled "Don't you dare drop it." He shoved him back toward his position in the shift formation and pointed wildly at another. "You! On the firing line!"

The second shooter missed by nearly six meters. Schultz howled. The third victim called to the firing line was shaking so badly his shot went completely over the backdrop berm.

Schultz's complexion was normally a dull copper. It was becoming maroon.

"Sir," Acting Assistant Shift Sergeant Kharim said, his voice cracking because it took every bit of courage he could muster to address Acting Shift Sergeant Schultz, "that is not the way we have been trained to shoot."

Schultz spun on the man whose place in the organization he'd taken. In two long strides his nose was mere inches away from the Wanderjahrian's. "You've been trained?" Schultz shouted, spraying the Feldpolizei sergeant's face with spittle. "Not that I can see."

Kharim swallowed. "Sir, if I might demonstrate."

Schultz's eyes bored into the man's. Emotions, mostly

anger, fury, and frustration, roiled his face. Abruptly he took a step back and swung an arm at the firing line. "Show me," he snapped.

Kharim swallowed again, then stepped to the front of the shift. "Shift, attention!" The members of the shift snapped to. "Advance on the firing line!" They briskly stepped forward. Kharim was now standing a pace behind the center of the line of his shift. "Load!" Fourteen pairs of hands sharply loaded fourteen blasters. "Shoulder arms!" They brought their weapons sharply to their shoulders, muzzles pointed down-range. "Ready!" Kharim looked to his left and to his right. "FIRE!" Fourteen blasters crackled as one.

Schultz watched their scattered hits, groaned, and closed his eyes. "Two hits," he mumbled. "The whole damn shift fired at one target and only two of them hit it." He opened his eyes and saw Kharim standing at attention in front of him.

"Did you see, sir? We hit the target."

"I want to see it again."

This time Schultz stood off to one side, where he could watch down the line of shooters. Kharim went through the routine of volley firing again. Again the hits spattered on a ragged line across the target. Again two of the fourteen bolts hit the target.

Acting Assistant Shift Sergeant Kharim turned and faced Schultz, head held high in triumph. "Sir, that is how we have been trained to shoot."

Without a word, Schultz stepped toward the line of FPs and snatched the blaster from the nearest man. He waved an arm to move the men back from the firing line, then twisted to point his left side downrange, threw the blaster into his shoulder, aimed, and pressed the firing lever. *CRACK!* He hit the target square. He dropped onto one knee without moving the blaster from his shoulder, fired again, scored a second hit. He fell back into a sitting position, took quick aim, and blasted the target a third time. He threw himself forward onto his belly and hit it again. He popped the battery from the well, hopped back to his feet, and tossed the blaster in the direction of the man from whom he'd taken it.

"That is how I have been trained to shoot," he snarled. "That is what you will learn to do." He paced the shift line, glaring at each man in turn. "I watched you," he said as he paced. "I saw what you did. Every one of you had both eyes open! You can't aim with both eyes open!" He grabbed a blaster and stepped back where everyone could see him. "Do you see this?" He jabbed a finger at the blaster's front sight. "To aim, you look at this through this." He poked a finger at the optics tube that was the rear sight. "When you are looking at the front sight through the rear sight, and your target is lined up with them, you will hit the target every time. You're lucky any of you hit it at all, the way you were shooting.

"You fired two volleys. Fourteen shots each time. Each time you got two hits. Do you know what that means? That means you *missed* six times out of seven! You missed," he shrieked, "a man-size target, standing in the open, at one hundred meters! I'd expect a bunch of civilians who'd never handled a blaster before to do that well!

"Give me a half-hidden man at one thousand meters and I won't take seven shots at him. Do you know why?" he screamed. "Because before I get to my seventh shot there won't be enough of him left to shoot at!"

He stomped along the line again, this time checking to make sure all weapons were unloaded. Satisfied there wouldn't be any accidental shootings, he began the training again.

"Put your weapons on your shoulders. Close your off eye. Look at the front sight through the rear sight."

Acting Shift Sergeant MacIlargie tried to keep his face blank as he scanned the shift he was assigned to, but he couldn't keep the tip of his tongue from poking out of the corner of his mouth when he looked at the former shift sergeant, Acting Assistant Shift Sergeant Nafciel. Ordering around a bunch of FPs, telling them to do things their regular shift sergeant would never tell them to do, was going to be more fun than he ever thought he'd have as a Marine. And giving the former shift sergeant the same orders, and making him do the same things, was going to be even better. Him, ordering a sergeant around! Oh yes. MacIlargie could hardly keep from bouncing with glee.

"All right," MacIlargie began. He had to clear his throat to keep the laughter out of his voice. "The first thing we're going to work on is movement through wooded terrain." He looked at their uniforms and shook his head. "Of course, it doesn't matter how *you* move; dressed like that, a blind man could see you in the middle of the night. One good thing, it'll make it easier for me to see what you're doing so I can correct your mistakes. Not that I need your bright uniforms to be able to see you, you understand."

This time he couldn't help himself; he laughed and shook his head at how much fun this was going to be.

"Okay, listen up. Imagine there's a squad of guerrillas moving through the woods there." He pointed to the nearby trees. "They don't know you're here. You need to sneak up on them and catch them and set an ambush for them to walk into. Understand?" He nodded yes for them. "Okay, let me see you do it." He stepped off to the side to watch the shift snoop and poop through the woods.

The FPs looked at each other, then aligned themselves and started into the woods. MacIlargie's jaw dropped. They were marching erect, their blasters held at port arms.

They can't keep this up, he thought. Just give them until they reach the trees, then they'll break formation and start sneaking.

The FPs ran into trouble as soon as they reached the trees. The woods weren't thick enough to keep them from carrying their weapons at port arms, but there was enough undergrowth that they couldn't maintain their straight-line dress. They spent more time looking to their sides, trying to maintain their positions on line, than they did watching where they were going. Their feet kept getting caught by vines and low-lying branches. After the third one fell, MacIlargie called them back.

The troopers couldn't help but look embarrassed when they reassembled in front of the Marine. None of them met his eyes, which was just as well, because this time he didn't even try to keep amusement off his face.

"Okay, that's the way you used to do it," MacIlargie finally said. "But there's other things you know how to do that will be useful in this training. It just depends on why you're doing something. Look at it this way: you're not in formation, going against the enemy. It's Seventh Day night and you want to go into town, but your shift sergeant is pissed off at you and said you have to stay in the barracks and clean your bright-work. Go back into the woods and show me how you'd keep from being spotted by your shift sergeant."

The FPs looked at each other, shocked by MacIlargie's instructions. The former shift sergeant stared at him with mixed hatred and horror.

Then one of the troopers said, "This is the way we'd do that."

MacIlargie grinned.

"Adel yer lep, yer ri', yer lep!" Godenov's voice rang across the parade ground. "Lep, ri', lep! Column left, HARCH!" The Marine marched in place while the double column of the second platoon's second shift smartly executed his command and turned in front of him. As the last two men began their pivots to march in the new direction, Godenov pivoted himself and stepped out to maintain his position to the left of the marching FPs. "Adel yer lep, yer ri', yer lep!" They made an incongruous sight, the Marine in his dull-green garrison utilities putting the orange-and-blue-clad Feldpolizei shift through parade ground close order drill. "Right flank, HARCH!" The FPs pivoted as a unit and marched on-line rather than in-line.

Godenov marveled. He'd never seen a unit that size march so sharply. And more marvelously, they were doing it to his command! His eyes shined and his face glowed with joy and pride.

Fifty meters away, Sergeant Wang Hyakowa's eyes didn't shine, neither did his face glow. Hyakowa's eyes were slitted and his face hard-set. Rather than showing joy and pride at how one of his most junior men was so sharply putting the Wanderjahrians through their paces, his face projected anger and danger. He waited until Godenov's maneuvers had the

PFC facing him, then made a hand signal that said, "Come here."

"Acting Assistant Shift Sergeant Lahrmann," Godenov commanded, "break rank and take command."

The temporarily displaced shift sergeant stepped sharply out of his position at the head of the column and marched at its side. "Loup, rahp, loup," he picked up, calling the cadence.

Spine erect, shoulders back, head high, Godenov marched to Hyakowa. The joy and pride in his eyes blocked the image of his squad leader's anger and dangerousness from his vision.

"What are you doing?" Hyakowa asked in an ominously soft voice when Godenov reached him.

"Drilling my shift, Sergeant Hyakowa." Godenov positively beamed.

Hyakowa closed his eyes for a second. When he reopened them, he tried again. "Specifically, in *what* are you drilling them?"

"Close order drill." Hyakowa's expression still didn't register on Godenov, who wondered what the point of the question was.

"Parade ground close order drill."

"That's right."

"Something they already know how to do."

Godenov nodded eagerly.

"Why are you teaching them something they already know how to do?"

Godenov blinked rapidly several times. The question was unexpected, and for the first time he realized that his squad leader might not exactly be happy with what he was doing. He thought quickly. "I'm having them do something they already know how to do," he explained, "in order to teach them something they don't know."

It was Hyakowa's turn to be surprised. "And what is that?"

"I'm training them to take orders from me."

Hyakowa blinked. His expression eased as he thought about Godenov's explanation for drilling the shift in something they were already expert at. It made sense of a sort. Certainly it was a better explanation than what *he'd* thought—he'd thought that

Godenov was putting the shift through close order drill because he had no idea how to teach them fieldcraft or marksmanship. He nodded once, briskly. "Carry on, Godenov," he said. "Just make sure they learn that lesson fast. We'll be taking them on patrols in a few days, and then they'll have to know a lot more than how to march in formation."

"Aye aye, Sergeant." Godenov about-faced, located his shift, and began marching in its direction to resume the close order drill. When he got a few paces away he breathed a sigh of relief. For a moment there, he'd been afraid that Hyakowa was going to guess the truth—he was marching his shift because he had no idea how to teach them anything they didn't already know.

CHAPTER
EIGHT

The suborbital flight to Oligarch Keutgens's Morgenluft took about an hour. Brigadier Sturgeon announced without warning that Commander Peters would accompany him on the trip. "And bring your two assistants," he said, nodding at Dean and Claypoole, who were busy creating a database on a computer terminal.

"But, sir, they're working up a very important informant database Chief Long's sharing with us. The sooner we get that information—"

Brigadier Sturgeon shook his head and held up a hand. Although he had the highest respect for Commander Peters as an officer on his staff, he had the infantryman's profound disdain for military intelligence types. Over the years, military intelligence had never given him much help in tactical matters, and he hadn't forgotten that in the recent scrape on Elneal, the entire fleet intelligence apparatus failed to discover that the Siad war chief, Mas Shabeli, had gotten his hands on Raptor attack aircraft.

"The database'll keep," Brigadier Sturgeon said. "I ain't going anywhere on this planet without some fire support, and right now your two are the only men I can spare from headquarters duty to go along with me. This'll be an overnighter, so bring some personal gear and your dress uniforms, we'll be expected to look pretty at dinner down there. And extra energy packs for your weapons. Saddle up, Marines, we leave in twenty minutes."

Dean grinned at Claypoole and they both jumped eagerly to their feet.

" 'It'll keep,' " Commander Peters mimicked Brigadier Sturgeon after he had departed. "Nobody appreciates the work I do around here," he muttered.

"Cheer up, sir," Claypoole said from the doorway. "Maybe you'll find true love on this trip, Commander." He darted into the hallway before the officer could respond.

Morgenluft lay in the tropical zone, but Schmahldorf, Keutgens's capital city, was situated in the higher elevations of her northernmost lands in the foothills of the Gaiser Mountains, so it did not suffer from the high humidity that plagued the lowlands.

Schmahldorf, named after Karl Schmahl, a missionary martyred in the witchcraft hysteria that swept the region two centuries before—the one episode of civil unrest to mar the planet's history before the rebel movement took root—was a beautiful city of about 100,000 inhabitants. Since Keutgens's people made their living mainly from agriculture—thule was their major cash crop—Schmahldorf's only industries were small and light, the kind that support an agricultural economy. The pace of life in Schmahldorf was very slow compared to that of Wanderjahr's other Staats. While the city had long since outgrown the physical and social dimensions of the farming village it had once been, Lorelei and her forebears had insisted on calling the place Schmahl's Village, *dorf* in German. This not only kept alive the memory of the courageous missionary, but helped preserve the bucolic outlook of the capital's residents.

The people's appreciation of the arts and their love of education reflected Lorelei Keutgens's own interests, and the intellectual life of the citizens of Schmahldorf was the most vigorous on the planet. So was their interest in politics. Morgenluft was the only Staat on Wanderjahr where the citizens freely elected the local governments. The guerrillas had the least influence in Morgenluft, and the prosperous and independent lifestyle of Lorelei's people was a source of annoyance to some of the other oligarchs, who feared what would happen in their own Staats if her ideas on political and economic democracy ever took root there.

Lorelei and her family were present to meet the Marine commander as he and his small party emerged from the landing port.

"Brigadier Sturgeon!" she exclaimed warmly. "How very pleasant to see you again!" She extended her hand, which the brigadier took and lifted briefly to his lips.

"You know Commander Peters, madame," the brigadier said, "and these two stalwart Marines are Privates First Class Dean and Claypoole." Dean and Claypoole came to attention.

"My, Brigadier, they are heavily armed! Do you expect trouble during your visit?" Her eyes flashed laughingly.

"No, ma'am, of course not. But if there is trouble, they can handle it. You're fighting a war on this planet, and if I'm to be a target, I plan to shoot back."

Lorelei Keutgens nodded briefly. "Well, we've had no trouble from the bandits here, Brigadier, and I don't expect any—from them, anyway. May I introduce my family? Here is my oldest granddaughter, Hway." She gestured toward a very pretty, dark-haired woman of about twenty, who smiled and curtsied at the Marines. The remaining three children, two boys, one nine and the other twelve, and a girl of fifteen, smiled self-consciously at their grandmother's guests. All seemed to have inherited Lorelei's finely chiseled facial features, but not her light complexion or blond hair.

"My villa is about twenty kilometers outside the city," Lorelei said after the introductions were made. "I have arranged transportation for us—you didn't bring one of your Dragons with you too, did you, Brigadier?" She laughed. All the Marines laughed too. "How long can you stay?"

"We've got to be back in Brosigville tomorrow, I'm afraid," Brigadier Sturgeon replied.

"What a shame! And by the way, gentlemen," she announced, shaking a forefinger at all four of the Marines, "the next man to call me 'ma'am' or 'madame' goes to bed without any supper tonight! From now on I am 'Lori.' "

Brigadier Sturgeon was not a man who put much store in rank and titles. While he would never tolerate a subordinate's calling him by his first name, he judged everyone, especially his men, by what they could do, not by the devices and badges of their rank. Lorelei Keutgens was the equivalent of a head of state, and as a matter of diplomatic protocol, far outranked even the commandant of the Confederation Marine Corps, much less a brigadier of Marines, even one with the special powers Brigadier Sturgeon had been given for this mission. Besides, Lorelei Keutgens was probably the most intelligent and capable leader on the planet, at least in the brigadier's estimation.

"Well, Lori," Brigadier Sturgeon bowed politely, "my first name is Theodosius and you may call me Ted." With that, she wrapped her arm around Brigadier Sturgeon's and led the party to meet her cabinet ministers and the waiting transportation.

A rotund, red-faced man with longish red hair, a functionary for one of Keutgens's ministers, stood in the rear of the small party of dignitaries she had summoned to greet Brigadier Sturgeon. "Zitze's guests have arrived," the fat man said into a handheld communicator.

"Are they who we were told they would be?" the disembodied voice on the other end of the transmission asked.

"Herr Ludendorf," the caller responded. "Herr Ludendorf" was a code name for Brigadier Sturgeon. "Zitze" was a code name for Lorelei Keutgens.

"Damn!" the man on the other end exclaimed. There was a slight pause. "Hmm. A slight complication. Very well. Proceed with your welcoming party. The more the merrier." The instrument went dead.

Far above Wanderjahr on board the *Denver*, every electronic transmission from anywhere on the planet was being monitored by an intercept officer. Her computer was programmed to identify key words, phrases, and names, and alert her to them. If the name of any Marine appeared in a transmission, for instance, a warning would flash on her screens and that message would be read and analyzed. Any transmission mentioning weapons, explosives, even military tactics, was instantly flagged for analysis, and all suspicious circumstances were quickly reported to the Feldpolizei or the Stadtpolizei for investigation. Programs were available to translate messages in any human language, and the computer constantly searched for words and strings of text in all of them, in case someone was using a little-known dialect to pass coded instructions to recipients; there was no cryptographic system known to the Confederation that the *Denver*'s computers couldn't break.

The intercept officer and her assistants normally reviewed hundreds of messages every day. The names Ludendorf and Zitze meant nothing to the analyst's computer, and no one on board the *Denver* was at all interested in parties on Wanderjahr.

Unlike Chairman Arschmann's estate outside Brosigville, Lori's home was modest. Nevertheless, it was still a palace compared to anything Dean had ever seen on Earth. After the men were shown their rooms, everyone gathered on a spacious patio behind the main building for refreshments.

"Hway, would you take the children and show our guests," she gestured at Dean and Claypoole, "about the house and gardens, while the Brigadier and I get better acquainted? Dinner," she included everyone, "is at sundown."

"Take your weapons with you," Brigadier Sturgeon said, "and check with me every ten minutes when you're outside the house." Lori made as if to protest, but Brigadier Sturgeon held up a hand. "We're Marines, Lori, and as long as we are on this planet we're all under arms."

After Lorelei's grandchildren had escorted Dean and Claypoole back into the house, the oligarch turned to Commander Peters. "Your brigadier is just as stubborn as my late husband." She smiled. Peters, who could neither agree nor disagree, cleared his throat nervously and sipped his wine.

"How long has he been gone?" Commander Peters asked, realizing too late that he'd brought up what could be an unpleasant topic.

"Oh, five years. My dear Tran died in an aircraft crash that also killed my son, who was my only child, and his wife.

Thank God the grandchildren were with me that day or I'd have lost everyone in this world who is dear to me."

"Tran? Your husband was . . ."

"Vietnamese, Ralph."

"Yes, hmmm." Peters rubbed his chin. That was unusual on Wanderjahr, a woman of one of the ruling German clans marrying outside her own ethnic group.

"Yes, Tran's father was one of my father's most trusted overseers. The Trans virtually grew up in my house. Young Tran and I spent a lot of time together when we were children. That was permitted. When we married, I kept my maiden name, of course. To have taken my husband's name would've been taboo in Wanderjahrian society, me being from a German family, and he—was not. I was an only child. My mother died when I was eight. My father would've opposed our marriage had he lived, but he died—of cancer, something unknown in your world anymore, gentlemen—when I was nineteen, and left me his estates. Tran and I managed them as we managed our marriage, with love and attention and infinite patience." She laughed. "But what of you, gentlemen? Tell me about yourselves."

Sturgeon shrugged. "We are what you see. Two broken-down old Marines. We go where our orders send us and we carry them out when we get there."

Lori regarded the Marines frankly for a long moment. She was wearing a silken one-piece dress that hung in folds from her neck to her feet. Its sleeves fell back from her elbows, revealing strong tanned forearms slightly dappled with tiny golden hairs. "Have you never wanted to marry, raise a family, Ted? A man is not complete until he has a family."

"I always thought a man wasn't complete until he got a battalion command," Sturgeon answered facetiously. When Lori failed to pick up on the joke, he continued quickly, "Well, maybe someday. I just haven't had time to cultivate relationships. And in many ways, Lori, my command is my family."

Lori smiled. "I know," she said, "that is the kind of man I see you as, Ted. Your Marines are lucky." She sipped her wine and winked at Commander Peters. "Well, maybe now you will have an opportunity to 'cultivate relationships,' as you put it?"

Before Sturgeon could formulate a reply both witty and polite, Peters cleared his throat. "Lori, something's been bothering me lately. When we met at Chairman Arschmann's villa, you warned us not to trust Multan. But recently Ambassador Spears warned us not to trust Arschmann. Just whom can we trust?"

"Ah! Business!" Lori exclaimed, amused at the expression of relief that came over Sturgeon's face. "Trust no one," she said. "Well, you can trust me, of course. And the bandits."

At this, both Marines shot their eyebrows up. "Excuse me?" Peters's surprise was evident.

"Yes, the bandits. Oh, I don't mean trust them not to shoot you down if they can, but when it comes time to talk, they'll talk. But with Multan and Hauptmann, and even Kurt Arschmann, the time to be wary of them is when they talk."

"I haven't had a chance to follow up on what Ambassador Spears said, but why should we be wary of Kurt Arschmann? It was he who convinced your Council to ask for our help."

Lori was silent for a moment, slowly turning her wineglass in one hand. "I have known Kurt Arschmann all my life," she said at last. She spoke slowly, pronouncing each word carefully. "I admire Kurt very much. But he is the most dangerous man on this world. Your Ambassador Spears is a very perceptive man." She smiled briefly, remembering how he had boldly asked her to marry him. "He is dangerous because he is intelligent and very ambitious and he will let nothing stand in his way to get what he wants."

"And what is that?" Commander Peters asked.

Lori was about to answer when Dean's voice crackled excitedly over the brigadier's communicator.

Once inside the house, the boys took charge of Claypoole, in whom they sensed a playmate, and left Dean alone with Hway. Hway's sister, Gudla, remained disconsolately stuck with the boys. A smaller but even prettier version of her older sister, Gudla felt cheated when Hway appropriated Dean. Reluctantly, she followed Claypoole and her brothers, leaving Dean and Hway alone in the living room.

The pair stood for a moment in the high-ceilinged living room, and then Hway suggested they tour the formal gardens. "Grandmother is famous on Wanderjahr for her interest in horticulture," Hway said.

As they turned to go outside she asked, "What is your given name?"

"Private First Class," Dean answered without thinking. "Uh, just a joke, miss," he mumbled when he saw the bewilderment on Hway's face. "That's an old Marine Corps joke. My name is Joe and I'd appreciate it if you'd call me that."

"Joe," she said reflectively, and nodded. "Please call me Hway. 'Miss' sounds dreadfully formal."

"Joseph Finucane Dean," Dean said, "that's Finucane with a terminal e."

"With a terminal e." Hway nodded. "Well, Joe with the 'terminal e,' let's go see my grandmother's gardens."

The gardens stretched for several hectares around Lori's home and displayed both native and Terran species. The Terran trees and shrubs were all carefully labeled with their Latin names, and the Wanderjahrian species were tagged with the names the early colonists had given them. Groves of trees and larger shrubs had been artfully placed between luxuriant flower beds. Teams of gardeners labored at intervals among the flowers, waving cheerfully as the pair passed on the flagstone walkways.

In a beautiful grove of Wanderjahrian flora stood the life-size statue of a man. They paused before it. On the pedestal was a name. "Tran Van Hue," Dean read.

"My grandfather," Hway announced.

"Oh." Dean had wondered where Hway had gotten her high cheekbones and slightly olive complexion. He looked at the features on the statue, then back at the girl.

"I remember my grandfather. I was fifteen when he died. My grandmother misses him very much."

"I don't know much at all about my grandparents. My father's been dead a long time too," Dean volunteered. "My mother died recently, when I was on a mission on a planet called Elneal."

"I'm so sorry, Joe. Do you have any siblings?"

"Naw. Just me. I'm the last of the Deans."

"You have no family, Joe," Hway said sadly.

"I guess not, unless you figure the guys in my squad and my platoon. There's old Claypoole, we're pretty tight. And there's Staff Sergeant Bass. Best platoon sergeant in the Corps. Top Myer, he's our first sergeant, he's tough, but fair. And our Old Man, Captain Conorado. Boy, Hway, they don't come better than those Marines! And since we've been with the headquarters, I've developed a lot of respect for Commander Peters and Brigadier Sturgeon too. Why, you couldn't ask to serve under a better officer and . . ."

Dean's face had begun to glow with pride as he talked about his Marines. Hway regarded him with a quizzical smile as he rattled on. Suddenly aware that he'd started babbling, or that Hway would think he had, Dean stopped in midsentence and blushed. She probably thinks I'm a damned schoolboy on his first date, Dean thought, embarrassed.

"Well, I miss my mom and my dad too, Hway," he said, "but life has to go on, you know. And right now the Corps manages to take up most of my time, so I seldom think about my family anymore."

Hway took Dean's hand in hers. "I am named after my grandfather's ancestral home, the city of Hway in what used to be Vietnam back on Old Earth. Many centuries ago American Marines fought a big battle there to free my father's ancestors. Perhaps you know about that war? It ended badly for my father's people, but things have a way of working out through time."

Dean was stunned. He certainly had heard of the Battle of Hue, fought in 1968, nearly five hundred years ago. He wondered if somehow he and this beautiful young woman standing in this grove on a world infinitely remote in time and space from her father's ancestral home might represent a confluence of human history, the closing of some kind of vast, cosmic cycle. He shivered with the thought, which was both delicious and a bit scary.

"Let's go watch the sun set!" Hway abruptly said. "About a kilometer on the other side of the woods that border this garden, cliffs overlook the Fotzi River! We'll have a beautiful view of the Gaiser peaks and the setting sun. We'll be back at the house in plenty of time for supper!" With that, dragging Dean by the hand, Hway started off for the woods.

The rays of the setting sun cast brilliant fingers of light between the trunks of the ancient hardwood forest as the pair emerged on the cliffs above the river. The view from there was absolutely breathtaking. The snowcapped peaks of the Gaisers, their tops a fiery orange in the dying sunlight, jutted skyward thirty kilometers to the north.

"Oh, this is beautiful," Dean whispered. He thought, Man, if any of the guys ever heard me talking like that, they'd think me a limpdick for sure! But the truth was, Joe Dean would've said anything to please the young lady beside him. He wondered how impressed Hway would've been had he said something like a "real" Marine, the way they talked back in the barracks: "Yeah, hot shit, honey. Now let's swap some spit!" Instantly he was reminded of Juanita's, back in Brosigville, and Maggie, lying on the stones, blood and brains oozing out of the bullet hole in her head. He forced the horrible image out of his mind. To give himself time to calm his nerves, he got a cigar out of a pocket and went to light it.

"No, Joe," Hway said, putting a hand on his arm. "Don't make fire here. We haven't had rain in months, everything's dry, you could start a forest fire."

He put the cigar away unlighted, sighed, and tried simply to enjoy the view. Yes, the scene really was beautiful. Its wild beauty reminded him of the northern regions on Arsenault, the Confederation training world where he'd gone through Boot Camp. A cold wind blew up from the river valley below, and without thinking, Dean held Hway close to his weak side, his blaster gripped firmly at sling arms over his right shoulder.

They stood like that for ten minutes. Meanwhile Dean

became very conscious of the slim figure by his side, her arm now firmly around his waist.

"Don't you think we should be going home now?" he asked at last. "I'm getting a bit hungry. How about you?"

Hway sighed. "A few minutes more, Joe. I've always loved this place, and I'm leaving Wanderjahr soon for school. I don't know how long before I can come home again."

Their reverie was broken by a metallic clatter from somewhere to the rear of where they were standing. Dean remembered a long sloping meadow off that way, sweeping down to the river several hundred meters below. He stiffened as he heard a man's voice carried to them on the wind.

"What is it?" Hway asked, startled. Dean unslung his blaster and automatically set the charging level at full power. "Get behind me," he ordered the girl. He released the weapon's safety. "Stay close," he said as he walked carefully back into the woods. Fortunately, the light was fading quickly, and it was almost dark under the towering trees. The large meadow, however, was aglow with the final rays of the setting sun. Up from the river marched a steady column of black figures carrying weapons.

Dean fell to one knee and spoke into the communicator strapped to his wrist. "FIST Six Actual, this is . . . this is . . ." Dean did not know what call sign to use. "PFC Dean. Sir. Over."

"FIST Six Actual. Go, Dean," Brigadier Sturgeon responded.

"Six Actual, be advised, sir, approximately forty armed men approaching your position from about one klick to your northeast. Are they supposed to be there? Over."

Sturgeon looked at Lori for an answer. She gave him a confused look and shook her head. "I don't have any armed people on my grounds."

"That's a negative," Sturgeon said into his comm unit. "Give me details. Over."

"Six Actual, they're in some kind of uniform I don't recognize. They're armed with projectile weapons. I have good cover. Will take them under fire. This is, uh, Dean, out. Sir."

Dean did not wait for the Brigadier's reply. "Run for the house, Hway, run as fast as you've ever run in your life!"

Dean crawled to the edge of the trees, where he could get a clear view of the approaching column from cover. He angled his body behind a massive trunk, took aim at the man leading the column, and fired. The bolt slammed into the man's chest and left a gaping hole all the way through. The remaining men instantly returned a surprisingly heavy volume of very accurate fire at him. Dean had to drop behind cover so fast he barely noticed the smoke that began to rise from a tree as the plasma bolt that cut through the man he'd killed smoldered in its drought-dried side. Bits and pieces of tree trunks showered down upon him as bullets exploded close above where he lay.

Dean scuttled backward, turned, and low-crawled to the trail he and Hway had walked up. The trees between him and the approaching men were absorbing most of the bullets. Then the nearly missed memory of the tree that began to burn from his first shot clicked on him—Hway had told him the forest was dry and could burn easily. He fired a rapid series of bolts at a tree with upturned, spiky leaves. The tree began to smolder and broke into flame. He then shot more bolts into clumps of undergrowth and set them afire. He smiled. That'll keep the bastards awhile! he thought. Doubled over to present as small a target as possible, he ran back toward the house.

Brigadier Sturgeon leaped to his feet. "Dean! Dean!" he said into his comm unit. "Get out of there! Do you hear me? Come back here! Dean?" The brigadier cursed and switched his comm unit to the frequency he was assigned to communicate with the *Denver*. "Bridge! This is FIST Six Actual. What do you see?"

"Bridge," a laconic voice answered from the orbiting *Denver*. "FIST Six Actual, we see several dozen men one point five kilometers to your northeast. Appear to be a work party but have dispatched a drone to confirm. Wait . . . Seems you have the beginnings of a forest fire between your position and theirs. Do you need assistance, FIST Six Actual?"

Lori was on her feet now too. Her face had gone white at the sound of the shooting, but she could also see flames and smoke from the burning forest. "They've set my forest on fire!" she screamed. "God's goddamned balls, those trees are hundreds of years old! Brigadier—"

"Lori," he said quietly, "that fire's going to save our lives." He changed the channel on his comm unit. "Claypoole!" he shouted into it.

"This is Claypoole, sir!"

"Where the hell are you?"

"Downstairs with the kids . . ." Claypoole had been watching an ancient flatvid starring John Wayne, *The Horse Soldiers*.

"Get out here. Now. How many kids with you?"

"Three, sir. Dean and Hway are outside somewhere."

"Out here. Now, Marine! Bridge!" he snapped. He switched back to the command circuit. "Do you see any other activity?" he asked the *Denver*. "How about along the road to Schmahldorf?"

"Negative, FIST Six Actual. Drone confirms forty-three men armed with projectile weapons. Shall we take them out for you?"

"Negative, negative, negative!" the brigadier shouted into his communicator. He made a mental note to ask the *Denver*'s captain why the watch had not acted sooner to confirm the nature of the approaching "work" party. "I have people out there. Stand by." He turned to Lori. "Do you have guns here, and do you have any servants who know how to use them?"

"No, Ted, I don't."

"Where's the nearest Stadtpolizei station?"

"Schmahldorf," she answered. "But the Stadtpolizei in my jurisdiction have only side arms."

"Great. Well, we'll change that as soon as I get us out of this mess. Bridge, can you contact the Stadtpolizei in Schmahldorf and alert them to our situation here?"

"Negative, FIST Six Actual. We have no channel to them. We can ask Chief Long to relay a message through Stadtpolizei channels. Over." Brigadier Sturgeon bit his tongue. Somebody should have anticipated this problem.

"I can call them from here," Lori offered.

"No. They'd be cut to pieces. Bridge, alert them but have Chief Long emphasize, I say again, emphasize they are not to come down the road to Keutgens's estate. Is that clear?"

"Roger, FIST Six Actual. They are not to proceed down the road to Keutgens's estate. Further orders?"

"Yes. I want a landing party to block the road fifteen kilometers outside Schmahldorf and to wait there for further orders." If he did have to call in a laser strike on the area, the extra five kilometers would give the landing party a good margin of safety.

"Roger, FIST Six Actual. Landing party on the way to block your road fifteen kilometers outside the capital."

"What's your plan, sir?" Commander Peters asked.

"I don't have one, Commander. We'll plan as we go. But it'll be nice to have that landing party nearby." They would be down in under a half hour.

Claypoole came running up, followed by Gudla and the boys. Faces white and eyes staring, the children ran to their grandmother and looked up anxiously at the three Marines. A group of about a dozen servants and workers had gathered nervously in one corner of the patio, and now an elderly, dignified man approached the trio.

"Mistress," he addressed Lori. "What is happening? How may we help?"

Lori looked to Sturgeon. "This is Hector, my major-domo," she said.

"Hector, can you find transportation for all these people?" Sturgeon asked.

"Yes, sir. We have a lorry that we often use to transport—"

"Get them in it and drive to the city. We'll meet you there. Go. Now." Hector hesitated, looking to Lorelei Keutgens.

Lori nodded. "Go, Hector, now. Don't take anything with you. Just get out of here."

"Claypoole, take Mrs. Keutgens and her grandchildren, load them into our landcar, and drive like hell until you get to Schmahldorf. Here, I'll trade you my side arm for your blaster."

"Sir! Dean's out there somewhere." Claypoole gestured

toward the rising glow to the northeast, more prominent now that the sun was almost completely down. "Can't I go after him?"

"No. Our responsibility now is to these civilians." The brigadier paused as he began to unstrap his equipment belt. The frustration in Claypoole's eyes was evident. "Marine, your friend has bought us time, we won't waste his sacrifice by wasting that time. You take the civilians back to Schmahldorf. Commander Peters and I will find Dean."

It had been a long time since the brigadier had used a shoulder weapon in combat, but already he was thinking like a squad leader: he was interested neither in who the men were nor their objective, only in stopping them. His instincts told him they were after Lori and her family, and it was only bad luck—for the attackers—that he and his three Marines just happened to be there. The fact that he was the FIST commander and should protect himself from harm never occurred to him. His executive officer could take over the mission if he was killed. His only thought now was to join up with Dean and conduct a fighting withdrawal until reinforced by the landing party.

"Ted," Lori said in a very small voice, "is my granddaughter with your young Dean?"

"Yes, Lori, I'm afraid—"

"Grandmother!" Hway shouted as she jumped the hedges bordering the patio and stumbled up to the adults. "Joe is back there. Forty men with guns. He's fighting with them now! You have to help!" Her words came in great sobs as she tried to catch her breath.

Joe? Claypoole silently mouthed Dean's first name. That sly bastard, he thought, and smiled despite himself. "Sir? Let me go after Dean. Please?"

"Ted, I'm not leaving this place until you get that boy out of there," Lori said, her tone of voice clearly implying she meant it. "Besides, you can't go running around out there like a private! Hway can lead Clayton back to where Dean is."

"Claypoole, ma'am," Claypoole interjected respectfully.

Brigadier Sturgeon hesitated. Plan as you go? "Hway, can

you—would you be willing—to take Claypoole back to Dean?" Hway was insulted that Brigadier Sturgeon would even doubt her willingness to go, but then, he didn't know her. She nodded yes. The brigadier turned to Claypoole and exchanged weapons with him again. "Go." He nodded toward the fire. Claypoole and Hway ran off the patio into the garden.

Sturgeon turned to Commander Peters. "Ralph, take Mrs. Keutgens and the children, get in that landcar, and take them to safety."

"But, sir—"

"Godfuckingdamnit, Commander!" Brigadier Sturgeon shouted. "Get your asses into that car and get the fuck out of here and do it right the fuck now!" Shocked by his commander's language, but energized by it, Commander Peters scooped up Lorelei Keutgens and the remaining children and without another word ushered them into the house.

"FIST Six Actual," the bridge watch officer drawled, "do you need fire support? Over."

"No, goddamnit, Bridge! Shut up until I ask you!" Those goddamned space squids are enjoying the hell out of all this, I bet, Sturgeon thought. He laughed abruptly and ran to the hedges, where he crouched and drew his side arm.

In the light of the forest fire behind him, Dean recognized Hway and Claypoole coming up the trail. "Rachman!" he shouted, his joy evident. He grabbed Hway and kissed her full on the mouth before he realized what he was doing. She did not protest.

"My, you work fast." Claypoole grinned.

"Joe!" Hway whispered. "Brigadier Sturgeon is waiting for us back at the house. Hurry! We don't have any time to waste!"

Dean looked at Claypoole, who grinned and patted his blaster. "How come you get all the fun, boot?" he asked. The forest fire was growing behind them now as flames leaped from tree to tree and shrubs ignited from the heat. The wind had picked up too and was fanning the flames straight toward them.

"They'll have to get around that," Dean said, meaning the

fire, "and right now we're in more danger from the fire than from those men. I got one of 'em, though."

They ran down the trail as the fire roared and howled behind them. The flames had now turned the darkness into the light of day, and they could feel the heat on their backs as they ran. Hway tripped and fell and Dean swooped her up with one hand and propelled her onward before him.

Brigadier Sturgeon saw the trio outlined against the flames as they ran through the gardens. "Come on, come on!" he shouted as they jumped the hedge. They ran through the house and out into the driveway. Sturgeon took the driver's seat in a landcar parked there. A civilian vehicle, it didn't need a code to be started. "Claypoole," the brigadier shouted, "ride shotgun! Dean, cover us through the back window!" Then he turned to Dean and said: "Marine, you do good work." He put the vehicle into forward, and they roared off down the road to Schmahldorf, headlights cutting through the blackness.

Smoke from the forest fire rolled overhead, obscuring them from the sensors on board the *Denver*.

"Stop!" Hway shouted before they'd gone more than three kilometers. Sturgeon mashed the braking lever and the car slewed to a halt. "My grandmother's car! Back there, off the road!"

Sturgeon shifted into reverse and backed slowly down the road.

"There it is!" Claypoole shouted, coughing from the smoke.

Several dark objects lay beside the road. Sturgeon's heart skipped a beat. "Cover me," he told Claypoole, and grabbing a glowball from a cargo pocket, he approached the car. It was empty. Four bodies lay crumpled on the shoulder. Three of them were burned beyond recognition. The fourth belonged to Commander Peters. Sturgeon kneeled beside his intelligence officer. The commander's right arm and leg were missing. "Ralph," he whispered, reaching for the commander's throat to feel for a pulse.

"I fucked up," Commander Peters whispered. "They got the woman and the kids." He spoke with difficulty. "I tried to . . . to . . ." His voice trailed off.

"Ralph, did you see which way they went? Ralph?" Sturgeon felt for the commander's pulse again. It was there, throbbing weakly, but he'd passed out.

Dean and Claypoole crouched on opposite sides of the road, weapons facing outward, searching the darkness for movement. The brigadier motioned them to him. "Search along the sides of the road. They've got Mrs. Keutgens and the children. We'll have to go after them."

"What about Commander Peters?" Dean asked.

The brigadier motioned toward the body behind him. "He got three of them. He's hurt bad, but there's nothing we can do about that now. Our first priority is Mrs. Keutgens and the children."

Hway came up. "Do they have my grandmother and my brothers and sister too?" she asked.

"We're going after them," Brigadier Sturgeon said. "Bridge," he spoke into his communicator.

"Bridge aye, FIST Six Actual."

"Take out the villa. Alert the landing party. Tell them to get up here quick once the fireworks are over. I have a badly wounded officer who needs immediate medical attention."

"Roger that, FIST Six Actual." Dean and Claypoole threw themselves flat and Sturgeon pulled Hway down into the roadbed and covered her body with his own.

A brilliant, incandescent swath of light arced down from the heavens as everything behind them disintegrated in a flash— Dean counted "one thousand one, one thousand two, one thousand three"—and a roar. The ground shook so violently the four were bounced into the air. An extremely hot shock wave howled over them and then it was dark again, except for the fires that burned at intervals throughout the rubble of what had once been Lorelei Keutgens's estate. Even the raging forest fire had been consumed in the blast.

"FIST Six Actual, this is Bridge. Ready for next fire mission."

"Stand by," Brigadier Sturgeon said. Hway got shakily to her feet.

"Our home . . ." She gasped as she saw what had happened.

"Everything . . . gone!" She looked up at Brigadier Sturgeon with tearstained eyes.

"I'm sorry, Hway. I had to even the odds," the brigadier said.

"But my grandmother . . . ?"

"I had to take a chance, Hway. I'm betting the kidnappers didn't have time to get them back to the house. I'm pretty sure that's where they were going to meet up with the main body."

"Brigadier!" Claypoole shouted. "Sir, a trail. Bush all trampled down. It heads back toward the villa."

"Dean, stay with the girl. Give what aid you can to Commander Peters. Don't get shot by the landing party."

"I know what to do, sir."

Five bodies lay sprawled grotesquely in the bushes about half a kilometer off the road. Lying nearby, trussed and gagged, were Lori Keutgens and her grandchildren.

"Thank God!" Lori choked when Brigadier Sturgeon had cut her bonds and pulled the gag out of her mouth.

"What happened here?" he asked, but he already knew. He also knew he'd taken an awful gamble and won.

"I couldn't see what happened, but when that great light flashed, they dropped us. Then this roar and a terrible heat wave, like an oven, passed over us and the men just fell down dead. There was this awful smell afterward." Lori spoke between coughs, wiping tears out of her eyes.

Brigadier Sturgeon smiled, confident she couldn't see it in the dark. "You were close enough to the ground that it missed you and fried their brains. That smell is burnt human flesh and hair."

"Wh-What was that explosion, Ted?" Lori asked.

"I had to prevent those ambushers from joining the main body, Lori. I called in a laser strike on your villa."

Lori gasped.

"I had to, Lori," Sturgeon said quietly. Gently, he laid a hand on her shoulder. When she began to cry, he held her close to his chest. Claypoole diplomatically gathered up the children and led them back toward the road, where the landing party had already arrived. What the brigadier did not mention was that he had taken a big gamble that the ambushers who captured the Keutgenses had not already joined the main body when the plasma strike came down. Otherwise, Lorelei Keutgens and her grandchildren would now be drifting in the wind along with the molecules of the attackers.

"Oh, *liebchen* ... I—I mean Ted," Lori sobbed. "That was our home ... everything ..." She shrugged helplessly, "gone ..." She was crying so hard he could hardly understand her. "All my family's history since it came here was in that house! Goddamn those men, Goddamn them, Goddamn them!" She pounded her fists against the brigadier's chest. Then an expression of intense hatred contorted her face. "Goddamn him, I'll fry his ..." Just as suddenly, she laid her head against the brigadier's chest.

"Lori, my men, the *Denver*, did what they had to do. Don't blame them for this. Blame me, if you must." Lori clenched her fists and bit her tongue. It wasn't the Marines she meant. "Lori, you can rebuild, but most important, you and your grandchildren are safe."

"Goddamned right we are!" She stiffened in his arms. "And we're going to stay that way!" She relaxed against the brigadier's chest. "Yes, we can rebuild." She sighed. "I guess this changes the rules of war here on Wanderjahr, doesn't it, Ted?"

"It sure does," Sturgeon responded, "now they've pissed me off!"

Brigadier Sturgeon summoned Dean to where he'd set up a temporary command post beside one of the landing party's Dragons. "Son, what you did out there was really stupid, do you know what I mean?" he said without preamble. Dean stood dumbfounded.

"Sir, I—I—"

"You should have kept the ambushers under surveillance and withdrawn to the house, where we could've organized a defensive position or an ambush of our own and maybe held them off until reinforcements arrived."

A long silence ensued. "Yessir," Dean answered after he'd had a chance to think the brigadier's words over. "But, sir, I just did what first came into my head. I was there and they were coming on. And I did delay them, sir."

The brigadier smiled. "You sure did, Marine. What you did required a lot of guts, I give you that. You deserve a medal, but I can't submit a citation to Fleet based on what was really an incredibly brave but very dumb act, can I?" He pretended to think for a moment. "Go get Claypoole."

When the pair returned, he said, "PFC Claypoole, since when do you give orders to a brigadier of Marines?"

"Sir, I—I—"

"And since when does a Marine who has a perfectly good head on his shoulders throw it all away to compound a stupid mistake made by one of his buddies? I mean talking me into letting you go charging off after Dean here."

"But sir, I—I—"

Brigadier Sturgeon waved Claypoole into silence. "Very well. I can't decorate you two, because it'd make me look stupid. So I'm promoting both of you to lance corporal." The two gaped at the brigadier in astonishment. "I know, you're both thinking, 'How can he promote two stupid Marines like us?' How indeed." The brigadier feigned a sigh of exasperation. "I have faith in you. I think you both have potential. You may even make good corporals someday. Now go and clean yourselves up."

The next two days were a flurry of activity as Brigadier Sturgeon, Chief Long, Lorelei Keutgens, and Chairman Arschmann conferred by video hookup about strengthening security. Within minutes of the landing party's arrival at the ambush scene, Brigadier Sturgeon had the Bridge patch him through to his executive officer in Brosigville, to whom he fired off a string of orders to be passed on to every Feldpolizei training team. He asked for and immediately received permission from the *Denver*'s captain to keep the landing party, about a hundred sailors and Marines, indefinitely. They would beef up physical security at key installations where his force would be too busy training the Feldpolizei to worry about it.

The attack had outraged everyone. Since none of the perpetrators had survived, it was generally assumed the bandits were responsible. The citizens of Morgenluft loudly demanded retribution. Chairman Arschmann was calling for Brigadier Sturgeon to organize a flying column to attack immediately.

The morning after the attack, Brigadier Sturgeon sat in a suite in one of Schmahldorf's best hotels with Ambassador Spears and Chief Long, discussing the options.

"Hold off," the ambassador urged. "This is too pat. We don't know it was the guerrillas. Arschmann protests too much, I think."

"He's right, Ted," the big policeman said.

"I never intended to do anything else," Sturgeon said. "My orders are to train the Feldpolizei, and that's what I'm going to do. We'll deal with the guerrillas when the time comes, but through the Feldpolizei, not on our own.

"Another topic: Hugh, I don't have an intelligence officer anymore. Peters was a fine officer, but he's out of the picture for the duration of this operation, and I won't get a replacement for him from HQMC until probably long after this mission is over. Will you handle that for me from now on? I'll give you his files, his office, and his two helpers."

"Dean and Claypoole? Sure, I'll take them." Chief Long laughed, a big rumbling noise deep within his chest. "I'll make detectives out of those lads yet!"

"Joe?" Hway sat opposite Dean at a table in a modest restaurant in downtown Schmahldorf. Dean was leaving in the morning and he was depressed because it seemed he wouldn't see Hway again for quite a while, if ever. For the first time in his life the thought of military duty annoyed him.

A very solicitous maître d' hovered over their table, anxious to please. Everyone in Schmahldorf had been trying to make the Keutgens family feel at ease among them. But the maître d's attentions were beginning to annoy the young couple. Hway waved him away, and reluctantly he retreated to his kiosk.

"Joe," she began again, leaning across the table and whispering loudly, "I'm going with you to Brosigville tomorrow."

Dean shot straight up in his chair.

"Yes!" Hway laughed, seeing how the news had so quickly brought Dean out of his funk. "My grandmother is sending me to live with my granduncle there. He operates a huge truck farm just outside the city, very near the port . . . uh, very near where your headquarters is located, I think."

Dean grinned foolishly, entirely consumed by this delightful news. "What's a truck farm?" he asked, because he didn't know what else to say.

"Vegetables," Hway answered impatiently.

Dean's grin increased. "Wonderful," he almost shouted. "What kind of vegetables?"

"Tomatoes and things! Joe! Don't you realize what this means?"

"Yeah," Dean said, and reached for Hway's hand across the table. "What are tomatoes?"

Lieutenant Constantine sat next to Commander Peters's bed in the *Denver*'s sick bay.

"I'd shake hands with you, Lieutenant, except I am—was right-handed," Commander Peters joked.

"I know the feeling. Chief Long asked me to pay you this visit, Commander. Dean and Claypoole say hello."

"I think I know why," Peters said. "You're gonna tell me to hang in there and one day I'll be as 'good as new.' "

"Yep. Well, since you know what I was going to tell you, might as well leave." They both laughed.

Then Peters became serious. "What's it going to be like, Pete?"

The anguish on Peters's face brought back painful memories to the policeman. "The worst part is the psychological readjustment. The medics'll give you wonderful biotech prostheses to replace your lost limbs, but it's going to take some effort on your part to accept them because they won't be *you*. But believe me, Commander, you can be restored to full duty, if that's what you want."

"Who's taking over my duties as F-2?" Peters asked abruptly.

"Chief Long, with Dean and Claypoole to help him. And me."

"Good. Lieutenant? You tell those two grunts if they fuck up, when I get back I'll kick their asses good!" Commander Peters pretended to think about that for a moment and then added, "Belay that, Lieutenant. I guess I wouldn't have a leg to stand on after all." They laughed.

Constantine knew that Peters would be just fine.

CHAPTER
NINE

Acting Shift Sergeant Schultz felt naked. He wasn't naked, of course, not festooned the way he was with extra battery packs for the blaster hanging on his pack straps. The pack itself was filled with two days' rations and a change of socks, along with odds and ends of equipment, official and unofficial. A bayonet and a knife—and another hidden inside a boot—an emergency medical kit and two quarts of potable water were suspended from his belt. A hundred feet of tightly coiled rope hung off one shoulder, and a map kit filled with a GPS locator, an old-fashioned lensatic compass, a civilian-manufacture sat-comm radio—not to mention actual maps—were clamped under the opposite arm. His accoutrements were topped off with a squad leader's helmet that contained not only the infrared, magnifying, and light-collecting face shields and squad-level communications that he was used to, but also company-level communications and heads-up displays that allowed platoon and company command elements to transmit situation visuals to him.

No, he wasn't naked. Schultz just felt that way because he was going into the hills after guerrillas wearing his dull-green garrison utilities instead of the field chameleons that would have made him effectively invisible.

The Marines of first squad were on the military crest of a hill, the highest place they could stand without being silhouetted against the sky, half a kilometer southeast of the 257th Feldpolizei's base. They were gathered around Sergeant Hyakowa for their final briefing before taking Company A of the 257th Feldpolizei on a two-day training and combat

145

patrol. None of the Marines was looking at Hyakowa; they were all looking at the FPs, who waited uncomfortably at the foot of the hill.

"They're looking better than they did a week ago," Acting Company Captain Hyakowa said of the green-clad FPs. He swallowed nervously; he wasn't as confident as he sounded.

"Anything would be an improvement over how they were a week ago," Acting First Platoon Leader Leach said.

"They still can't shoot," Schultz grumbled, and spat off to the side.

"Let's hope they've learned something more than just how to wear new uniforms," Acting Second Platoon Leader Ratliff said.

"They have," Acting Third Platoon Leader Dornhofer said.

Corporal Doyle, who found himself in the very odd and even more uncomfortable position of acting shift sergeant, declined to say anything.

"They'll know a lot more at the end of these two days," Chan said.

"If any of them live through it," Schultz grumbled.

MacIlargie was quiet—at least he didn't say anything. But his eyes glowed, the tip of his tongue stuck out of the corner of his mouth, and he jittered in anticipation of the patrol.

Godenov shivered. He was going to be leading fifteen men in a potential combat situation and didn't look forward to it. Damn, even if they weren't very good at it, every one of these troopers had seen more action than he had—which wasn't hard, because he'd never been in a real firefight.

None of the other men in the squad had any comment to make.

"All right," Hyakowa said. "You all know what we're going to be doing. If there are no other questions, join your units. We'll run a comm check as soon as you're in place." He looked at each of his men. Only one or two looked back at him. Mostly, they looked at the Wanderjahrians they were about to take into the hills. Each of the six shifts would be taking a different route, but they'd be close enough to support each other if any of them ran into a situation they couldn't handle alone. If they could keep up with each other, that was. If the Marines could handle them properly and keep the FPs from getting hopelessly lost. Hyakowa shuddered at the thought of the many things that could go wrong. He knew the Wander-jahrians were also unhappy with what they were doing. Most of them found the very idea of patrolling the woods without being in their normal formation frightening almost to the point of terror.

Dornhofer was the first to move. "Let's do this thing," he said, and stepped off toward the first platoon's command element.

Almost as though that were a parade ground command, everyone began descending the hill toward their platoons and shifts. Hyakowa stood calmly watching them. Doyle was the last to leave the hill, so he was there when Hyakowa got a transmission.

"Random One-six, this is Random Six-five. Over."

"One-six. Go, Six-five," Hyakowa said, using field-expedient communications rather than textbook procedure. He was clearly excited as he listened to Acting Battalion Executive Officer Charlie Bass, call sign Random Six-five. He whistled softly at the end of Bass's message, then said, "Roger, Six-five, I'll pass it. Over." He nibbled on his lower lip and looked pensively out into nowhere as Bass signed off.

Doyle had no idea what the message was, but if the normally impassive Hyakowa reacted to it that way, it had to be bad news for the men of third platoon. Bad news? It had to be *terrible* news. Hey, he, Corporal Doyle, was the company's senior clerk. He had no business going into a situation where he'd be facing a large force of guerrillas—especially not with a company of partly trained rural policemen who barely knew which end of their blasters was the hot one. So it had to be bad. The string-of-pearls had detected an overwhelming force of guerrillas closing on them while they stood here waiting. No, that couldn't be it. If guerrillas were approaching, Hyakowa would be giving orders, getting everybody ready to fight right now. So what was it? He quaked as he imagined what could be worse yet: The guerrillas had attacked the spaceport outside Brosigville and wiped out the FIST headquarters! They were left with no way off-planet! They were stuck here, a few Marines on some backwater world that even Captain Conorado hadn't ever heard of! How long would it be before anybody noticed that the FIST wasn't making its reports? It was how far, three weeks, to the nearest civilized planet? That was the fastest a message could travel from here to there. Then it would be more weeks or months until Fleet headquarters was informed that 34th FIST missed a report. And Fleet wouldn't do anything over one missed message, they'd wait for two or three reports to go missing. How often were messages sent to Fleet headquarters, once a week? Less often? Then weeks, maybe months—probably months—after Fleet realized something must be wrong, a rescue mission would finally be mounted. Jesus Muhammad, it would be a year—longer than that, more than a year, a year and a half—before anybody got to Wanderjahr to pull the survivors out! If there were any survivors! Doyle's knees shook so badly he felt like he was about to collapse.

"You know where Morgenluft is?" Hyakowa asked into the absolute silence that had descended around Doyle.

Morgenluft? What did that have to do with the spaceport getting taken out and them being stranded here? Doyle's throat was too constricted for him to speak. He simply nodded.

"Brigadier Sturgeon was visiting Oligarch Keutgens's home earlier today," Hyakowa said slowly.

Doyle looked at him oddly. This didn't seem to have anything to do with the predicament he imagined they were in.

"Guerrillas pulled a raid on it." He looked at Doyle. "Dean and Claypoole were with the brigadier." He shook his head slowly. "Somehow, they managed to beat off the guerrillas."

All the tension flowed out of Doyle. Well, that wasn't so bad. A raid on a whole different continent. Hey, that didn't affect him, it didn't put him into any danger at all! Everything was all right here. The sun was shining, there was a nice breeze wafting by, and third platoon was about to go for a walk in the woods with a few hundred local guys. God was in his heaven,

Muhammad in Paradise, and Odin was probably getting drunk again in Valhalla. No problem.

Doyle was so euphoric at his unexpected reprieve from catastrophe that he didn't think of any of the implications of a guerrilla raid on a continent that didn't have a guerrilla problem. Nor was he at all concerned that the raid just happened to take place at the very time the FIST commander was on the scene. It didn't even register on him that Dean and Claypoole were in the fight.

"Oh, yeah, well . . ." Doyle couldn't think of a thing to say.

"The brigadier got out, all right," Hyakowa continued, looking back down the hill toward the Marines and FPs who were waiting for him to tell them to do something. "No word on Dean and Claypoole, but there were casualties."

That got through. "Dean, Claypoole? Casualties?" he squeaked. He knew those guys. Dean and Claypoole were good Marines—no, great Marines. They were almost friends of his. He'd been to hell and back with them! And they were casualties? *No!* They couldn't be!

Hyakowa almost decided this was a bad time to pass the word to the rest of his men. Then he glanced at Doyle and realized they'd find out from him anyway, and most likely get a garbled version of the story. He flicked on the all-hands channel on his radio and used Bass's message for his comm check. Everybody got the straight scoop. Except Doyle, who convinced himself that Dean and Claypoole were dead.

Hyakowa gave the order and Company A, 257th Feldpolizei, headed into the hills for its combat/training patrol.

"Commander," the scout, Fighter Quetlal, gasped as soon as he was admitted to the half-finished chamber that served as Commander Hing's office. Quetlal was out of breath from running the last fifteen-kilometer leg of the communications route between the 257th precinct headquarters and the headquarters of the Che Loi Brigade.

Hing waved a hand to tell the scout to sit on one of the stools that squatted on the duckboard flooring of his office. "Relax, Fighter Quetlal, catch your breath," he said more calmly than he felt. It was frustrating to have to rely on runners for most of his information, but the Confederation's string-of-pearls surveillance satellites prevented using radios for communication with the scouts. "You have run far, refresh yourself." He gestured at his clerk to give Quetlal a bottle of beer. "When you can speak without wheezing, give me the message."

"Yes, Commander," Quetlal gasped. Gratefully, he accepted the bottle of cold brew and gulped half of it down immediately. That was one of the benefits of delivering a message to the commander from a great distance—Hing always gave the messenger a bottle of beer. If the message was long enough, or could be made long enough, he often got a second bottle.

Hing waited with patience he didn't feel. Quetlal brought news of what was happening with the 257th Feldpolizei, information that he badly wanted. But he knew that the 257th GSB was far enough away that the information could wait a moment or two while his messenger composed himself. Besides, the kind treatment only served to enhance his reputation among the men.

Hing was seated at a small field desk, though the chamber was large enough for a full-size desk. He thought it was better for a guerrilla commander to present an image of austerity. A counter and shelves along one wall of the chamber contained banks of communications equipment, mostly unmanned now that the guerrillas had to restrict their radio use. A small, low bed lay on the opposite side of the chamber; Hing slept where he worked, to be available at all times. Mounting both 3-D and flatvid viewers, a low table stood out from the wall behind and to the side of Hing's desk. The largest piece of furniture in the chamber was a conference table that took up most of its middle. Several officers were seated around it. The chamber was illuminated by rows of glowballs anchored to the unfinished rock ceiling.

Lieutenant Sokum Pincote had sprung to her feet the instant Quetlal was admitted to the chamber, and now stood tensely, almost vibrating like a bowed violin string. Her lips were drawn sharply back, exposing her pointed teeth. Hing knew she wouldn't have given Quetlal time to catch his breath, she would already have his message and be pressing him for additional details. And, Hing knew, that was why she would never be the commander of any unit larger than a sixty-man company; she didn't know how to treat the fighters so they respected her and willingly obeyed her orders. The fighters under her command obeyed out of fear, and soldiers frightened of their own commanders weren't always the best fighters.

Confederation Marines had arrived a week earlier at the 257th GSB to train the Feldpolizei, that much Hing already knew. That, and that the Marines had assumed command positions within the battalion. What kind of success they were having, what the Marines were training the Feldpolizei to do, and what their training schedule was, those things he did not know. He hoped that Quetlal's message would tell him some of those things.

Quetlal took another gulp of beer, wiped a dirty arm across his mouth, and began.

"Commander, the Marines at the 257th are teaching the Feldpolizei real tactics. I have a vid of their training." He reached into a pouch on his belt and handed over a capsule.

Hing kept his face expressionless; the man should have given this to him to look at while he caught his breath. There would be no second bottle of beer for Quetlal, no matter how long this debriefing took. Hing tossed the capsule to his clerk, who immediately put it in the viewer. An image formed almost instantly. Despite its three dimensions, the image was fuzzy and slightly blurred; its colors were off, and there were areas of glare in which the eye could make out no detail. Obviously, the recording had been done into bright light from deep shadow, and a telescopic lens had been used because of the distance.

The few Marines in the vid were difficult to see because of their dull-green uniforms, but the Feldpolizei stood out clearly in their orange and blue. There were two training sessions on the vid. Hing chuckled as he watched the Marines attempting to teach the lackeys of the Feldpolizei how to use aimed fire with their blasters. He laughed aloud at how confused the troopers were on the parade ground when they were being instructed on how to move without being in straight lines, and then stumbled in the forest when they tried to move through it in other than a column on a road. If this, which was nothing, was all the Marines had managed to accomplish in a week, perhaps the Liberation could be won before the Feldpolizei became a force that had to be reckoned with.

Then he noticed the date stamped into a corner of the vid—it had been made six days earlier. He grimaced. It was almost worthless, it gave him no information on what they could do today. Well, he thought, one week isn't long enough to uproot bad habits formed over many years. And it did give him one piece of usable information—the Marines would be as hard to see in the forest as his own fighters.

"Do you have any newer information?" Hing asked when the vid had run its course.

"Yes, Commander. The Marines and two companies of the 257th have gone out on patrols in the vicinity of the GSB headquarters."

"Two companies? How many Marines are with them?"

"It looked to be two squads."

"Two squads," Hing repeated pensively. The Marines used ten-man squads. That meant twenty Confederation Marines were in the field with the Feldpolizei. The Marines had a reputation as ferocious fighters, but could twenty of them stand up to his entire brigade? No matter. Even if they could, they would be too busy trying to lead the incompetents of the Feldpolizei to do any fighting of their own.

Quetlal bobbed his head. "It was difficult to tell for certain how many were Marines, Commander. The Feldpolizei were wearing the same green uniforms as they. Even their own officers were dressed in green."

Hing stared at Quetlal for a long moment. This could cause a serious problem, if his fighters couldn't distinguish between the Marines and the Feldpolizei. "How were they moving? Were they in columns like usual?"

"No, Commander. They were in route march formation." Route march formation. Spread out and staggered, rather than in a neatly aligned, tight column. Weapons ready rather than right-shouldered. Eyes watching their surroundings rather than straight ahead. The Marines had taught the Feld-polizei a great deal in only one week.

"How far are the patrols going?"

"I was told they are on two-day patrols."

Hing glanced around the room. His entire staff was present. "Fighter, you brought important information. You may rest now."

Fighter Quetlal understood that he was being dismissed, and he scampered from the chamber.

"Two days," Hing mused as soon as the scout had left. "We can do nothing to them this time, it would take too long for our fighters to get into position. But now that we know what the Marines are teaching the Feldpolizei, we can prepare for the next time they go out. Here is what I want you to start planning . . ."

Route march, that's how the scouts told Commander Hing the Feldpolizei were moving. Well, there was route march, and then there was route march.

As practiced by good soldiers, such as the fighters of the Che Loi Brigade, it was a spread-out formation in which one burst from a gun could not hit more than a few men, one small chemical-reaction explosive couldn't take down more than one or two. More than that, it meant to be alert and perhaps to move stealthily or silently, ready to shift at an instant's notice into a fighting formation, whether offensive or defensive.

As done by true professionals, such as the Confederation Marines, route march was spread out, but it accomplished more. When the Marines were on route march, they were almost completely silent and nearly invisible—even when wearing garrison utilities rather than chameleons. For the Marines, route march was a fighting formation from which they could attack or defend in any direction with virtually no notice.

When attempted by amateurs, which the 257th Battalion of the Wanderjahrian Feldpolizei certainly qualified as, well . . . Did "gaggle of geese" mean anything?

* * *

The tip of MacIlargie's tongue peeked out from between his lips. He could hardly believe what his widened eyes were showing him. Quickly, he shifted his focus from near to far and turned in a circle to see if anyone was watching—or close enough to see if he looked. The area he and his shift were moving through was barely thick enough to be called forest. It was studded with the giants the Wanderjahrians called hoch-baums, bunched with the fat, skirted palms known as gros-palms, and had randomly placed spikers, trees a little taller than the grospalms, which had spiky leaves that stuck straight up out of their horizontal branches. On the ground in between were scattered bushes that vaguely resembled ferns. But the forest was thick enough that MacIlargie couldn't see more than a hundred meters in any direction. Even using his infras, he couldn't spot anyone other than the men of his own shift. But there were others nearby; he could hear them. Somewhere to the north he heard Schultz bellow his displeasure at some hapless trooper who wasn't moving to his satisfaction. Nearer, but still out of sight to the south, he heard bodies crashing through underbrush, and a muffled thud and yelp as someone tripped and fell.

MacIlargie returned his attention to his own shift. His fifteen men were slowly, inexorably, scattering. Every one of them was watching where he was stepping—none kept an eye on anyone else in the formation, so they were drifting slowly apart from each other. Not a one ever seemed to spare a glance at the surrounding flora or terrain to look for any enemy who might be approaching—or lying in ambush.

"I've seen little children move better than this on a picnic outing," he told himself.

Silently, feeling his way with feet accustomed to seeking for trips and traps and finding their own way, he moved away from his shift. At thirty meters he turned and walked parallel to them—as parallel as he could to men who were drifting away from each other in all directions. He wondered how long it would take for any of them to notice that he wasn't in the formation anymore. He wondered how long it would take before any of them could spot him once they realized he wasn't there anymore. He wondered what kind of joke he would pull on them when they couldn't find him.

Godenov was dismayed. Not to mention scared. His shift was on one flank of the spread-out company formation, one of the positions most likely to first encounter guerrillas. Unlike MacIlargie's shift, the members of Godenov's shift were looking outward. They were also bunched up so tightly they were constantly blocking each other's view and bumping into each other. If they walked into an ambush, one burst from a gun would kill most of them. And then where would he be? Godenov wondered. Dead, that's where. He had to get them to spread out, had to get them to be aware of where they were relative to each other. And still keep close watch on their surroundings. Was that possible? Godenov shivered.

Chan helped another trooper who had tripped over some unseen obstacle back to his feet. While Chan's expression was placid to a casual glance, worry was there to see for anyone who knew what to look for. The men of his shift were properly spaced and staggered; he'd managed to teach them that much in the few days he'd had to train them. And each divided his attention between the man he was behind, to maintain contact and distance, and the flanks—he hoped when they looked off to the sides, they were actually looking for people who shouldn't be there, and not just seeing trees and bushes. The problem they were having was, they didn't seem to be able to look around without ignoring where their feet went. So far only two had fallen, but whether he looked ahead from his position near the middle of the ragged line or to the rear, he always saw at least one trooper tripping or stumbling over some obstruction he hadn't noticed.

He had to do something about the situation before something seriously bad happened. While he was alert for any sign of an enemy, and ready to take instant action if they came across any, he didn't expect this patrol to encounter any of the guerrillas. His main concern was that one of his men might break an arm or leg in a fall—or worse, impale himself on a branch upthrust from one of the fallen trees that lay about. He was concerned not only because he'd have trouble forgiving himself if one of his charges was injured, but also because he knew if one of them suffered a serious injury, that would make the FPs even more reluctant to learn what he was trying to teach them.

He whistled softly, just loudly enough for everyone to hear. When his men looked at him, he gave the assemble-here hand signal. In a moment the whole shift was standing at attention in two ranks in front of him.

Chan shook his head sadly. These men had had entirely too much bad training.

"Never stand at attention in a parade ground formation in the field," he said quietly. "That makes you entirely too easy a target. I don't want to have to explain to Ser—ah, Acting Company Captain Hyakowa—how I got some of my people killed."

Some of the troopers glanced uneasily at each other. A few shuffled their feet nervously. None broke formation.

"Spread out, get low," Chan instructed. He demonstrated getting low by kneeling on one knee. "Some of you watch the rear, some watch the flanks, some watch behind me. Don't look at me, just listen. I'll tell you what we're going to do. Then I'll show you."

"Acting Shift Sergeant," one of the troopers asked, "are we allowed to look at you when you show us what it is you will show us?"

Chan briefly closed his eyes and counseled himself in patience. "When I show you, you'll have to look," he said when he reopened his eyes.

Lance Corporal Schultz was in as vile a mood as he'd ever been in. These numskull Wanderjahrian FPs couldn't do a damn thing right, not unless it was looking parade ground sharp and marching in straight lines. He'd spent almost a whole week trying to teach them how to shoot and how to move, and it looked like they hadn't learned a damn thing.

They couldn't maintain proper distance from each other, they kept wandering off, every other step they tripped over things a blind man could see in the middle of the night. And they made so much noise the guerrillas could hear them two hard days' march off! He couldn't understand why this war hadn't already been lost. By God, Schultz thought, if the 257th is an example of the Feldpolizei, give me a FIST and I'll take the whole damn planet in a week. Week and a half, tops!

As distracted as he was by his vile mood, Schultz still had the discipline to watch and listen for danger—he had better; he suspected he was the only one in the shift who was!

All morning long, and now well into the afternoon, he'd been hearing the sounds of things, big things, blundering through the woods. At first he wanted to take the shift on a flanking maneuver to deal with whatever this potential danger was, or at least send scouts out to determine exactly what it was. But Acting Assistant Shift Sergeant Kharim assured him, insisted actually, that there was no danger, that what he heard was merely grazing cows. Kharim showed none of the fear Schultz had seen in the local forces he'd worked with on other operations when they tried to convince him that the bad guys who were out there weren't there, because the local forces were afraid to face them. Maybe Kharim was right about the cows.

That didn't mollify Schultz very much. He didn't trust cattle. Cattle were things you ate, and then you used their hides to make boots. No matter how placid something was, if it was facing the prospect of being eaten, it could get brave in a hurry and attack. Besides, he remembered entirely too well the time three years earlier when a regular army unit on Eritreafra had used Earth-evolved humpbacked cattle as cover for an approach to the Marine position, and then as a shield when they attacked the 28th FIST. That was an operation Schultz had been on. No, he didn't trust cattle at all. But he saw that Acting Assistant Shift Sergeant Kharim was almost laughing at him for his concern about the cattle—"cows" was the word Kharim used—and if he laughed, that would have created a discipline problem Schultz didn't want to have to deal with on a patrol.

So he dropped the matter, and kept an ear cocked to the blundering sounds.

A mild breeze was wafting through the woods, ruffling the leaves and swaying the fronds of the grospalms. So what with the constant small movement wherever he looked, the distraction about the "cows," and his near constant grumbling to himself about the inadequacy of the Wanderjahrian FPs, Schultz didn't notice that a patch of foliage some fifty or sixty meters to the flank was much denser than anything else he'd seen this day until it ambled about ten meters to one side.

"Alert right!" Schultz screamed as he spun toward the moving foliage and dove to the ground into a firing position. What he saw through his blaster's sights made his eyes bug and his mouth gape.

He lowered his blaster and lay there looking at the moving wall of foliage for a long moment. It wasn't really foliage, it was fauna. No, make that faunum, *one* fauna. It stood on four legs the same thickness and tan color as the grospalm trunks, and as tall as the middle-sized spikers. Where the legs met the massive body, the coloring changed to mottled green with flecks of red and blue. The massive, tapering tail that stuck straight out from one end was buff on the bottom, mottled green on the top. At the other end, a sinuous neck snaked its way to a smallish head that seemed to be mostly mouth. The mouth was placidly chomping on the succulent leaves of hochbaums.

Schultz had been to Old Earth and seen an African elephant in a zoo. He'd thought it was huge, with its four-meter height. He went on an operation to Xanadu and saw the roc, a six-meter-tall biped that vaguely resembled the flightless birds of Earth. On Hell, he'd seen the beelzebub, a five-meter monstrosity that looked like it was designed by the makers of an ancient Japanese flatvid he once saw.

This creature made them look puny. It was at least eight meters high at the top of its arched back, and twice that from the tip of its tail to its chest. He tried to tell himself it wasn't that big, it couldn't be that big, it had to be closer than it looked, that a trick of the light made it seem farther away. But he knew that wasn't true, this thing really was that big.

A tittering behind him finally broke through, and Schultz twisted around. The entire shift stood there. Most of the men were calmly looking at the huge animal. A couple of them were looking at him. Three or four were watching their surroundings—a small part of Schultz's mind registered that those three or four were doing something he'd been trying to teach them. All of them had straight faces; he couldn't tell who had laughed.

"It's only a cow, Acting Shift Sergeant," Kharim said calmly. "Nothing for us to be concerned about."

Schultz looked at Kharim for several long seconds before saying, "All right, that's a cow. Let's get moving again, we still have a patrol to run."

Kharim nodded and began giving the orders that got the troopers back into formation and moving.

Schultz got to his feet. Before moving out with his shift, he gave the "cow" a long look. He remembered Top Myer's briefing aboard the *Denver*, when the first sergeant mentioned the large animals that lived on Wanderjahr. He'd thought he was ready, but seeing something that huge for the first time was far different than hearing about them. Then he looked at his blaster and thought about firing it at the behemoth. He concluded that all the puny weapon would do was piss it off—if it even noticed it was being shot.

A few minutes later it occurred to him that on every world he'd ever been on or heard of, the grazing animals that were the equivalent of cattle were food animals. Food animals were preyed on by carnivores. He wondered what kind of animal preyed on something like the cow he'd just seen. For the first time, Schultz was frightened.

CHAPTER
TEN

Dean's mind was not on his work.

Claypoole didn't notice his friend's lack of attention until several days after their return from Morgenluft. When the FIST sergeant major announced they were going to work for Chief Long henceforth, Claypoole at least had been thrown into a tailspin.

"Sergeant Major," Claypoole protested, "we're Marines, not policemen!"

Sergeant Major Shiro, a man with huge shoulders and a prominent stomach, shifted his tobacco wad to the opposite side of his mouth and glared at him. "I know what and who you are, Claypoole." He expectorated into a container he kept handy at his desk. All Marines loved tobacco products. "The brigadier says yer goin', 'n' yer goin', it's that plain god-damned simple, Marine. Lookit it this way, you get your own vehicle and ye'll be workin' fer a civilian.

"Okay. Clean out Commander Peters's—may God help that poor man's recovery—office. Yer gonna have to do all this 'cause he's in no condition to give you and Dean advice from the *Denver*. Download all his computer files and gather up any paperwork he had in there 'n' take everything up to police headquarters in town. You need any of the hardware, take it with you on hand receipts. You'll work outta police headquarters until further orders. Ye'll be billeted here and I'll expect you to take yer turn on all the duty rosters. You may be spending yer days in town, but you'll be responsible for knowing what's in the Plan of the Day, just like any other Marine. Ya need to be excused from any duty"—*spoot-tang!* a brown glob of spittle arced neatly into the sergeant major's tiny spittoon—"have Chief Long or Lieutenant Constantine call me and I'll square it away. Now move out."

After the pair had departed, FIST Sergeant Major Frederico Shiro wiped a droplet of tobacco-stained saliva from one end of his mustache. His mustache pushed the limit of what Marine Corps regulations would allow, but nobody, not even Brigadier Sturgeon, would ever point that out to him. He shook his head. Charlie Bass had called him three times already, Captain Conorado twice, asking if they could have the pair back. After that fracas at the lady oligarch's place, he understood why the brigadier had said no. Privately he'd have recommended against the brigadier waiving time in grade requirements and battalion quotas to promote the two privates, but he admired their spunk. The idea of one Marine taking on forty men appealed to his sense of pride in the Corps. He had done something just like that when he was a young PFC.

"Fred," Brigadier Sturgeon had told him when he'd asked him to handle the temporary reassignment of Dean and Claypoole, "officers are the brains of the Corps, but you give me a junior enlisted man who can think for himself and I'll trade him for any three ensigns, and that includes me when I was one!" After that the sergeant major knew the pair weren't going back to their company anytime soon.

Claypoole had thought it strange Dean didn't jump into it with him in the sergeant major's office, but he forgot about it as they launched into the details of shifting their workstations to police headquarters. Just as the sergeant major had said, though, they were assigned Commander Peters's landcar as their own transportation, and as they drove it uptown that first day, Claypoole rattled on and on that it was a great break for them since he fully expected, working for civilians, they'd get what no other Marine on the deployment would see until they got back to Thorsfinni's World—time off.

"Man, we'll see the sights!" Claypoole nudged Dean beside him as he guided the car through the late-morning traffic. Dean grunted noncommittally. "Hey, are you sure you ain't picked up a fever or something?" Claypoole asked. He turned to look at Dean, who just sat there staring ahead. "Nope. No," Dean answered. "I'm okay."

"Well, we'll see the sights," Claypoole continued. "You know, Dean-o, these little brown girls here are, well, I don't know, more friendly than those big-breasted blondes back on Thorsfinni's World. We are gonna get laid, partner!"

"Wouldn't you rather be back with the platoon?" Dean asked listlessly.

"Yeah!" Claypoole answered quickly. "Sure. But hell, Dean-o, we're here, my man, and we ain't going anywhere but here, so we may as well settle down and make the most of it. Besides, so far on this deployment, we've seen more action, you and me, than any other Marine. We don't have to back up to the pay table!"

Matters came to a head the next day. Dean had taken the landcar to fetch more computer equipment from the office at the port while Claypoole worked in their new office, setting things up. A trip that should have taken him forty-five minutes took him three hours. When he finally returned, Claypoole accosted him.

"Where the hell you been?" he shouted.

"Huh? Rachman, I just stopped off for a little while. Calm down, will you?"

Claypoole looked closely at his friend. His uniform was rumpled and dirty, and he had an expression about his face, an air about him as of a man who had just done something—secretive.

"You been seein' that girl," Claypoole shouted, slapping his forehead. "I shoulda known. She's the reason you've been wool-gathering since we came back from Morgenluft."

"Her name is Hway, Rachman," Dean said, his face coloring.

Claypoole began to feel his temper slipping too. "Dean-o, snap out of it. I'm depending on you. We not only work together, we gotta cover each other's asses too. I don't want to depend on some gigolo with his mind on pussy when he should be thinking about watching my back. What would've happened to us at Juanita's if your mind had been on pussy when the sniper fired at you? What would've happened to the brigadier and the rest of us if you'd been swapping spit out there on that ridge the other night? Jesu, Dean, and you ain't even fucked that girl yet!"

Dean's face went white. "Goddamn you, Claypoole!" he shouted. "You ever, ever say anything about my girl like that again, and I'll ... I'll ..." He turned away quickly and smacked a fist into his palm.

Claypoole stepped over to where Dean was standing, grabbed him by the shoulder, and spun him around. "Now, you listen to me, you goddamned boot. No, shut the fuck up and listen! You're a Marine, you're on a combat deployment, and you got your duty to do, and you will do it, Dean. Besides, what are you going to do?" Claypoole's voice dripped with sarcasm. "Marry the bitch? You can't! It's against regulations. Quit the Corps? Fine. You just gotta get her to wait seven more fucking years and she'll be all yours."

Dean stood rigidly, staring at Claypoole, his own eyes bulging.

"You snap out of this, Dean, or I ain't workin' with you no more. I mean it!" He paused to catch his breath. "You poor, dumb shit," he continued, calmer now. "All you can do is just fuck that cunt and forget it."

Dean's fist landed squarely in the middle of Claypoole's mouth and the two went down in a thrashing tangle of arms and legs and rolled on the floor. Lieutenant Constantine, who'd been sitting in his cubicle nearby and had heard everything, stepped through the door, a bored expression on his face. When he separated them, he needed to use a stun stick to get their attention.

Claypoole had been wrong about the intimacy between Dean and Hway.

Dean followed Hway's directions to her granduncle's farm carefully. That the place was almost on the way to the port facility made it easier for him to justify the digression to himself. The side trip would only take a few minutes, it wasn't like going AWOL, and nobody would know because he'd programmed the detour as "official police business." Chief Long had told him and Claypoole that they'd be doing a lot of traveling around the city and its environs as his intelligence aides, and Dean thought of this little visit as a "test run." That he'd filed a false report, a court-martial offense, bothered him, but in his own mind the prize was worth the risk. He comforted himself with the thought that since Brigadier Sturgeon liked him, if he was found out, the punishment wouldn't be that severe.

Hway's granduncle's farm proved in fact to be fifteen kilometers beyond the port, and the road was tricky to drive. And Dean got lost twice. He did not dare call for help using the onboard communications system since he knew the transmission would be monitored. When he finally saw the long, tree-lined, winding drive leading up to the cluster of one-story stucco buildings on the crest of a ridge that Hway had described, he knew he'd found the place at last. His pulse beat quicker at the thought of seeing her again.

Hway's granduncle was a sturdy man of about seventy, with a firm handshake and a friendly smile. "Welcome to my home, Mr. Dean," he said. "After what you have done for Hway, consider this place your home too for as long as you are on Wanderjahr."

Emil Keutgens, Hway's grandmother's younger brother, wanted to hear all the details of Dean's recent adventure, so the young Marine was forced to sit with him, his wife Helga, and Hway as he tried to retell the story as quickly as possible in order to get some time alone with Hway. Emil's wife, a pudgy blonde with a perpetual smile, who kept nodding while Dean talked, occasionally interrupted the narrative by asking if he would like something to eat. Each time, Dean politely refused, until he realized he was hurting the woman's feelings, after which he relented and a huge snack was immediately produced. Not at all hungry, Dean forced himself to eat a sampling of cakes and sandwiches which under any other circumstances he'd have found delicious. But now they filled his mouth like old newspapers.

"Uncle," Hway said at last, "maybe I could show Joe your tomato crop?"

"Ah," the old man responded with a deprecating wave of his hand, "what warrior would be interested in tomatoes, eh, Lance Corporal Dean?"

"Oh, no, sir," Dean replied at once, swallowing a half-chewed mouthful of cake, "I've never seen tomatoes before, sir. Sure, I'd be interested." Dean smiled so widely the old farmer thought at first his young guest might not be completely right in the head. But his wife had seen the furtive glances between the Marine and her niece, and she knew the young couple wanted to be alone.

"Emil," she said, "let them walk a bit." It was an order. Emil shrugged, as if to say, In the house you are the boss.

"I don't have much time, Hway," Dean said once they were outside. "I've got to go to the port and pick up some office equipment and then take it downtown, but I just couldn't come this close without dropping by to see you."

Hway frowned. "Joe, is it all right for you to be here?"

"Sure," Dean answered quickly, and Hway knew it was not all right.

"Joe," she took his hand in hers, "I don't want you to get into trouble over me."

"I won't, I won't," he assured her quickly. "Let's see those tomatoes."

The tomato fields, which were near ripening, stretched for nearly a kilometer in all directions around the farmhouse. Supported on frames, the plants stood more than a meter high, and the red fruits hung down from the stems like balls bigger than a man's fist. Each plant seemed to support a dozen or more of them. After walking a few meters down one of the rows, they lost sight of the farmhouse completely.

Dean pulled Hway close to him and they embraced; they kissed; they melted into each other. The next thing Dean knew, they were kneeling between the rows of plants, his equipment belt hanging from a nearby tomato frame. Dean had not had sex with a woman since before the deployment to Elneal, and that was with one of Big Barb's girls back in Bronnys, on Thorsfinni's World, nothing like the passion that gripped him now. When Hway reached out to guide him in, he lost it instantly. "Sorry, sorry!" he gasped. He sat down, his legs entwined with Hway's, and tried to catch his breath. Hway's chest heaved too and her face was flushed. "My great big Joe," she whispered. After a while they did it the right way.

They lay in the dust between the rows of tomatoes, chests heaving.

"First time?" Dean asked. He'd never had a virgin before, so he had no idea what sex would be like with one.

"No," Hway answered nonchalantly, brushing a strand of hair away from her face. Joe was instantly disappointed to know he was not the first man in her life. He almost wanted to demand to know who the man was, but as quickly realized he couldn't ask a question like that. "How about you?" she asked.

"Uh, no, no." Dean realized then how foolish he was to be disappointed that Hway had been with someone before him.

As if she sensed what was going through his mind, Hway laughed. "Who was it?" she asked bluntly.

Astonished that she would ask, Dean faltered. "Um, a couple of girls I knew back home. Nothing serious." He was not about to tell her of the whore back on Thorsfinni's World. "And you?"

"Oh, just a local boy. A very pleasant boy, Joe, but nothing like you." She patted Joe's extended leg. "He's dead now," she added matter-of-factly, and Dean felt relief, then was ashamed of himself for it. After a few moments she said, "Joe, we'd better be getting back. Won't they miss you at your office?"

Dean was putting his equipment back on. "Huh? Oh, yeah, let me help you up." Awkwardly, they got to their feet and rearranged their clothes. They stood facing each other, she with a wayward strand of black hair hanging down in front of her face, a small rivulet of perspiration working its way slowly down one side of her jaw. Impulsively, Dean grabbed her again and pressed his body hard against hers. He could feel his pulse beating rapidly again. He covered her mouth with his own. She moaned and returned the kiss but then pushed him away.

"Joe, I don't want you getting into trouble over me."

"Don't worry about it," he told her, brushing dust off his

utilities and straightening his belt. He glanced at his watch. He should have been back at the Stadtpolizei headquarters an hour ago.

"Joe, before you leave, have one of these." Hway offered him a medium-size tomato she'd plucked from a plant. "Maybe it'll cool you down." She laughed. It was warm from the sun and felt heavy in Joe's hand.

"How do you eat these things?" Dean asked, turning the tomato curiously in his hands.

"Bite into it through the skin. Be careful! They're juicy!"

Dean bit into the red orb. Instantly, his mouth was filled with the rich pulp and its tangy juice. He took another bite and then another. It was the most wonderful natural vegetable he'd ever eaten. Hway laughed as she watched him consume the whole tomato in only four bites. He leaned awkwardly forward, so the juice wouldn't get on his uniform.

"They're grown using a method developed by the famous agronomist Dawid Canfil. He could take ordinary fruits and vegetables, Joe, and turn them into miracles. Take some back for your friend, Clayton," Hway said, and she picked three more. "One thing, Joe, they're very rich and they can go right through you until you get used to them." Dean had no idea what she meant but didn't want to show his ignorance by asking. They walked back to the farmhouse, Hway carrying the tomatoes in her dress and Dean trying to look unruffled, as if they'd just spent the last few minutes talking casually about the crops. Self-consciously he worked at brushing the dust off his uniform.

Uncle Emil did not seem to notice the smudges and dust spots on his niece's clothing. Helga noted the signs but said nothing, only nodded at her niece. Dean took his leave of the old people politely, promising to return soon. Carrying the freshly picked tomatoes in a sack, he climbed reluctantly into his landcar and, waving to Hway, who stood demurely between her grandaunt and -uncle, he drove back down to the main highway.

All the way back to Stadtpolizei headquarters Dean whistled and sang. He couldn't wait to tell Claypoole about his afternoon and share the tomatoes with him. But Claypoole threw cold water over everything.

After he'd determined that it was Dean who'd started the fight, Chief Long dismissed Claypoole and told Dean to sit down. He asked for an explanation, and Dean told him everything.

Chief Long scratched behind his ear and let out his breath. "You screw up like this one more time, laddie, and I'm sending you back to Brigadier Sturgeon. You know what that would mean? It would mean you'd spend the rest of your enlistment at the depot on Thorsfinni's World, kicking boxes and counting energy packs."

Dean squirmed in his seat. He knew what the chief was telling him was true. Oh, Brigadier Sturgeon liked him, had even promoted him, but AWOL was a court-martial offense, and so was misuse of Confederation property, which he'd also done when he used the landcar for personal business without permission. What he'd done that afternoon was a lot more serious than the joyride he and Claypoole had taken the time they went to Juanita's, and Dean knew it.

"I know, sir," Dean answered.

Chief Long regarded the young Marine for a moment. "Maybe you think working for me is a snap, lad? Maybe you think because I'm a policeman I'm a lot easier to tolerate than your FIST sergeant major?"

"No, sir!" Dean answered quickly. "It's just that I had the chance to go see her and . . ." He paused and thought for a moment. "Yes, I thought I could get away with it, sir. I didn't think you'd find out, and you wouldn't have if Claypoole and I hadn't gotten into it out there. But, sir, I never thought working for you would be any kind of picnic."

"I knew where you were all the time, lad." Chief Long sighed. "All our police vehicles are tracked whenever they're on the road. Commissioner Landser knows Emil Keutgens well. He practically lives at the tomato farm."

Dean's mouth fell open at the news. "Sir, then why didn't you—"

"I was going to talk to you about it at some point, but then you and Claypoole started flinging snot at each other out there. I was going to wait and see if you'd make the same mistake twice. Will you?"

"No, sir! But, sir, I don't know what to do! I love Hway! I know I do! I've never felt like this about any girl before. What do you—"

Chief Long held up his hand. "Stop. I will not give you any advice, lad. You've got to work this out for yourself. I'm sorry. That's another part of growing up. You've proved you're a brave young man. Now prove you can control yourself, or you'll never make a good cop or a good Marine. What did Hway tell you to do, by the way?"

"She said she didn't want me to get into trouble over her."

"Then she's a lot smarter than you are, laddie. All right, Dean, I'm going to tell you two things, and you listen very carefully. One: we have a lot of work to do and little time to do it in. I need your promise you'll give all your waking hours and some of your sleeping ones to Lieutenant Constantine and me. You don't, you're out. What do you say?"

"I give you my promise."

Chief Long nodded. "Two: we may have a lull from time to time. When we do, I'll let you take a police car and you can visit your girl. Now go, and sin no more. And make up with Claypoole."

Dean stood up and gave Chief Long a smart hand salute.

But making up with Claypoole was not that easy.

By the time Dean returned to their work space, the swelling above his right eye was both very noticeable and painful, and Claypoole's lip was swollen. Several times Dean was about to strike up a conversation with Claypoole but hesitated. Problem was, Dean realized Claypoole had been right, and he felt stupid about starting the fight, but it was hard for him to admit it. So they spent the rest of the day working at their stations, communicating only in monosyllables and avoiding each other's eyes.

Since neither was scheduled for duty at FIST HQ that

night, they went straight to their quarters before curious Marines could ask them where they'd collected their recent wounds. They were still not speaking when it came time for lights out. Dean lay in his rack for a long time, staring up at the darkness. He tossed first to one side, then the other.

"Rachman," he said at last. "Are you asleep?"

"Not now," Claypoole replied sarcastically.

"Well, youuumwere um, rightumboutallthat."

"What?"

"I'm sorry! You were right to chew my ass out! I was wrong to swing at you. I'm a fucking idiot. Jeez, Rachman, I am sorry, I really am."

"Light!" Claypoole said. His reading light came on. He swung his feet over the side of his rack. "Well, I shouldn't have talked about your girl that way. I'm sorry too." He got up, opened the cooler, and took out two one-liter bottles of Reindeer beer, passing one to Dean. He then retrieved two of his precious cigars and gave one to Dean. They sucked on the beers and lit up.

"What am I going to do, Rachman?" Dean asked. Anguish was clear in his voice and on his face.

"You've got to do your duty, Dean-o. As long as you wear that uniform, you're a Marine, and that's it. Listen, I've seen plenty of other guys take the big fall because of a girl." Actually, he hadn't, but he'd heard about such things from older Marines. "And I don't want to see that happen to you."

"I wish we'd never been sent up here by the Old Man."

"Yeah. But we're here just the same. Besides, Commander Peters was one hell of an officer, and this old cop ain't half bad, is he? And on top of all that, you got us promoted." He gestured at the new lance corporal's chevrons on the utilities hanging on the wall. "It was you got us promoted, Dean-o, all I did was follow along to cover your ass."

Dean laughed. He was already feeling better. It wasn't all due to the beer and the tobacco either. "Ah! I got something here for you!" he said, remembering the tomatoes he'd brought back from the farm. He handed one to Claypoole.

"I heard of these," Claypoole said, examining the fruit. "They're supposed to be good. Never ate one."

"Careful, they're full of juice," Dean warned.

"Gawdamn!" Claypoole exclaimed as he bit into the tomato. The juice ran down his chin and dripped onto the floor. He ate the entire tomato, including the stem, in several huge bites. Finished, he wiped his mouth with his undershirt. Dean ate one, then Claypoole finished off the third and belched contentedly.

Dean stepped across the narrow space that separated their bunks and stuck his hand out. "We watch each other's back from now on, Rachman."

Claypoole stood up. "Right! Like we've always done. Like Marines do it!" They shook.

Later, just before drifting off to sleep, Dean was snapped back into full consciousness by a roar from Claypoole's bunk.

"Ah, ah! Damn! Damn!" Claypoole shouted. "That fuckin' tomato!" he screamed.

"Whaa ... ? Omigod, what's that smell!" Dean sat bolt upright in his rack.

"I went to fart and, and—lookit my rack! Oh, gawdamn sumbitch!" Cursing and dragging his bedsheets along behind him, Claypoole stumbled into the head.

Dean laughed so hard the tears streamed down his face. It wasn't so much that what had happened to Claypoole was so funny—it was—as that everything was now back to normal between them, and the relief Dean felt was enormous. He would work their situation out with Hway somehow. "Omigod!" Dean gasped after a moment, then rushed after Claypoole into the head. Alas, he was too late.

CHAPTER
ELEVEN

"Commander!" Lieutenant Pincote burst into Hing's temporary command post. Less than ten kilometers from the 257th Feldpolizei GSB, the side tunnel was part of an abandoned mine complex where two raiding companies of the Che Loi Brigade were in hiding.

Hing looked up from the computer. He'd been feeding variables to the situation map, testing the plans his staff had developed for a raid on the Feldpolizei headquarters while the Marines were taking the bulk of the force out on patrols. He signed for her to speak.

Pincote grinned and light glinted off the sharp points of her teeth. "The oligarch's lackeys have gone on patrols," she announced breathlessly. "Two companies of them, the same as before." She stood erect and swelled her chest. "They have gone without their Confederation Marines."

A small part of Hing's mind idly considered how impressive Pincote's chest was when she stood that way. But only a small part. Most of his mind was occupied with the implications of what she said. "How good is your information?" If the Feldpolizei were patrolling without the Marines, he could quickly have the brigade in position to do them serious injury.

Pincote looked like she wanted to laugh, but she didn't. "I didn't believe the information, so I went to see for myself. It's true. Arschmann's lackeys are patrolling in platoon strength. I saw no Marines with them." By the time she finished saying this, she was no longer standing with the impressive chest, she had leaned forward with her fists planted on Hing's desk. A manic light shone in her eyes. "If we move soon enough, we can ambush one platoon before it settles in for the night, then strike at another one when it leaves its bivouac in the morning." She threw her head back and stared into that never-never where people look when imagining great possibilities. "We can easily kill two platoons and take their weapons. Then every fighter with us can have a blaster, and there will be more to take back to our base." She lowered her head and focused on Hing's eyes. "The lackeys are moving in the formations the offworlders have been teaching them. Think what it will do to their morale, and to their confidence in the Marines, when two of their platoons are wiped out while doing what they have been taught!"

The sequence of ambushes, the capturing of weapons, and the effect on the Feldpolizei were exactly what Hing had been thinking. Still . . .

"How certain are you the Marines aren't with them?"

"I watched for a long time. I followed one platoon for two kilometers. I saw no sign of the Marines. Then I went to the headquarters to see for myself that they have no aircraft, none of the hoppers the Marines use, or the so-called Raptors. The only aircraft there were the base commander's hopper and a small, civilian cargo carrier."

Hing thought for no more than three seconds, then jumped to his feet, shouting orders as he went.

Lance Corporal Hammer Schultz didn't feel naked the second time he went out on a patrol with the FPs, yet he was even less comfortable and confident than the first time. He didn't have to feel naked this time, because he was wearing his chameleons, the proper Marine uniform for combat. He should have felt more confident, because this time the FPs weren't bumping into each other or wandering off or tripping over things a blind man could see in the middle of the night—they actually looked as if they had a fair idea of how to patrol quietly and alertly. And he should have felt more confident because this time he wasn't the only Marine on the patrol. They weren't patrolling by shifts either, they were in platoons. Corporals Leach and Doyle were with him. Hell, three Marines should be able to deal with anything that came up. Especially if the guerrillas had thirty FPs they could see to shoot at instead of spending their fire trying to hit Marines they couldn't see. Even if the use of chameleons was not restricted to Confederation Marines, the Marines didn't have enough to issue them to the Feldpolizei. This patrol was set up as a double trap for the guerrillas. Not only were the Marines in their chameleons, they weren't directly running the patrol. When a Marine had to give an order, he gave it to the shift leader—platoon commander, in Leach's case—who then gave it to the men. The real object of the patrol was to see if the junior officers and noncommissioned officers of the 257th were learning anything.

Schultz didn't care about that. As far as he was concerned, the FPs were still too incompetent to live. But it bothered him that he couldn't quit wondering what kind of animal would prey on that cow he saw the last time out. When he dwelled on the question too long, his bowels began to feel loose, so he tried not to think about it. But he couldn't help himself.

It was an unusual way for Schultz to feel. He'd been on many operations during his nine years in the Corps, and in more firefights than he could remember. His life had been in serious jeopardy many times—he'd seen so many friends killed, he no longer made friends. There had been several incidents when he believed he was quite literally about to die. Yet he'd never been terrified, and hardly ever more frightened than could be described as mildly apprehensive. Now he was afraid. Actively afraid with the kind of fear that slows a man's reflexes, blunts his senses, prevents him from thinking clearly and acting decisively. That bothered him.

Lance Corporal Schultz needed a good firefight, one that would snap him back to reality, that would let him put his focus back on the human enemies he expected to face, distract him from the predator he'd probably never encounter. At least he hoped he'd never encounter it.

Normally Schultz liked to use his own eyes and ears to observe his surroundings, but the last time out he was so distracted that he didn't see that huge animal until after it moved, even though it had been standing among trees that weren't dense enough to hide it. This time he wasn't taking any chances on not seeing something so big and obvious just because its colors blended into the background. This time he wore his infras in place—if there was anything warm-blooded out there, he'd see it right away. So what if the infras didn't allow him to enjoy the beauty of the landscape he moved through? He never wasted attention on beauty anyway. Anytime a man in a hostile situation paused to smell the roses, he risked getting himself killed. Schultz wasn't about to die over aesthetic considerations.

Despite his infras, Schultz was still distracted enough looking for *large* red spots in his field of vision that he wasn't the first to see the man-size spots.

"Look alert." Leach's voice came over the platoon command circuit. "We've got company up ahead on the right."

Schultz got his attention under control. Sure enough, a stippled line of red began seventy-five meters ahead. He knew that the stippled red line was men lying in ambush in a defilade position. He didn't do it now, but he knew that later he would severely castigate himself for not spotting the ambush first—his shift was in the lead of the platoon; Leach was behind him and still saw something ahead of them before he did.

"Platoon, stop," Leach said.

"Hold them up," Schultz softly told Acting Assistant Shift Sergeant Kharim, who was walking a few meters away. The FP leaders didn't have any of the command frequencies on their radios; the Marines reserved those for communications among themselves.

"Shift, halt," Kharim ordered in a low voice.

The troopers stopped where they were and lowered themselves into firing positions.

"Hammer, stay with them," Leach ordered. "Doyle, come with me."

Schultz's jaw locked. *Doyle, come with me!* Leach was going to scout the guerrilla positions. That was a job Schultz could have done by himself, and done very well—he was the best man in the company at that sort of work. And Leach knew it! Leach should have sent him to scout the ambush. Instead he did it himself. And took Doyle, the damn company clerk, with him! Schultz was mortified.

Mortified, but professional enough not to let it distract him from what he needed to do now, which was check the platoon to make sure everyone knew what was going on and what he had to do. Probably none of the guerrillas had infras, so Schultz figured he could walk upright without being seen. But maybe one or more of them did. Even if none of them did, if they decided to open fire on the platoon, even though it had halted outside the ambush's killing zone, a stray round could hit an invisible man as easily as a visible one. So Schultz crawled to Kharim to tell him what was happening, then began crawling to the second shift leader to tell him. Leach should have told the FP officer, but might not have, Schultz thought, so he told him as well.

Leach got back just as Schultz finished briefing the platoon's leaders and called for them to join him and Doyle.

"There's a guerrilla company up ahead waiting for us," Leach told them. "They've got us outnumbered two to one. I got close enough to hear some of them wondering why we stopped. We don't have much time. Here's what we're going to do . . ."

Lieutenant Sokum Pincote's company lay in concealed positions in a shallow depression that marked an ancient waterway. She knew they were well-hidden because she'd gone out herself to see how close she had to get to them before she could see the ambush. It was a matter of meters. The first time, she was almost within knife range before she saw the closest fighter. Then she did it again from a different direction, and deliberately stepped on the fighter she approached to show him how close she had to be to see him. Three more times she walked toward her company's position from different directions. No matter that she knew where the company was, each time she had to get very close before she could spot any of her fighters. Satisfied, she took her own position in the line.

Their intelligence was good: they didn't have to wait long before a Feldpolizei platoon came toward them. Pincote wanted to laugh out loud at the ludicrous sight. The Feldpolizei were wearing camouflage uniforms in a forest pattern; mottled bands of green, ochre, and black. They tried to make themselves look like miniature sections of forest! But it didn't work, it couldn't make them look like the woods. Certainly not the stiff way they moved. True, they were keeping good intervals and were less awkward than on their first patrols. It was also true that they kept watching the woods around them instead of keeping their eyes to the front as they had formerly done. But they did it all so gracelessly. It was obvious they were unaccustomed to that manner of movement, and uncomfortable with it. Wiping them out was going to be easy.

Suddenly, with the lead shift only seventy-five meters away, the lackeys stopped, with no apparent reason for doing so. No one she saw had given any danger signal to indicate they'd spotted her ambush. The lackeys lowered themselves into defensive positions very casually, as though they were taking a rest. Why did they have to pick that particular place and time to rest? Or were they resting? None that she could see laid down his head to nap, none broke out field rations. As casual as they were about it, all of them seemed to be alert.

What was that? She thought she saw a flicker of movement out of the corner of her eye, but when she looked, she saw nothing but what she expected to see—trees, scattered underbrush, and alert, resting men.

She shook her head to clear it. Maybe she was too tense, too excited about the rich prize that had stopped just short of her ambush's killing zone. She took a deep breath, held it for a few seconds, and let it out slowly. Did it again. After the third breath she felt calm, almost the way she felt when she was lapping the blood her pointed teeth drew from the shoulder of one of her infrequent lovers. She showed those pointed teeth in a tight grin as she thought of how so few men were unafraid to be her lover.

She shook her head to clear it. It wasn't the time to think about men's cowardice when faced with a strong woman; there were Feldpolizei to kill, blasters to take.

There was another flicker of movement at the periphery of

her vision, but she saw nothing when she looked that way. What was happening to her? She'd never experienced this before, not even on any of the occasions when she'd been more excited or tense than she thought she was now. She shook her head. What could be wrong? Then she stopped thinking about the wrongness she felt within her and paid attention to something concrete she saw that seemed wrong.

Three of the lackeys rose to their feet and moved back, almost out of her view. They hadn't moved to any signal she saw or heard. They assembled and knelt in a semicircle, looked the way her own officers did when they knelt in front of her to receive new instructions on a patrol or operation and watched her draw a map in the dirt. But no one was at the center of the semicircle. Something very strange was going on, but she couldn't image what it was.

Then the three Feldpolizei returned to their positions and spoke to the waiting lackeys. Then they all rose into crouches and began returning the way they had come. Why were they going away? They were supposed to continue the way they had been going, they were supposed to walk into her ambush!

"Chan, Godenov, up," Corporal Ratliff said into his radio. Even though none of the FPs had the command frequency on his radio, Ratliff wanted to talk to his Marines face-to-face and not take the chance that anyone unknown might be listening in somewhere.

Chan and Godenov used their infras to find the fire-team leader and joined him.

"Chief's platoon almost walked into a company-size ambush about two klicks south of here," Ratliff said in a low voice as soon as they reached him. "Wang wants to catch the guerrillas. He thinks we don't have time to get our pretty boys in place to do the job. We're going to force-march them to half a klick from the guerrillas and put them in position as a blocking force, then we'll meet Wang and the rest of the squad." He paused to think of how to pass the word to the FPs. He knew they wouldn't like it if they knew what the Marines were thinking. "Tell your shift sergeants first platoon's chasing some bad guys and we're a blocking force to catch them. When we put them in place, tell them we're going ahead to scout the situation. They don't need to know what we're going to do. Understand?"

"Understood," Chan said.

Godenov didn't reply immediately; he didn't quite get it. Why would they put the platoon in a blocking position and tell them they were a blocking force if they weren't a blocking force?

"If the guerrillas run their way," Ratliff explained, "the platoon can do some damage to them. But if we do this right, the guerrillas won't get away. If we take the platoon with us, well, they just aren't good enough to get in close and catch the guerrillas by surprise. We don't want to hurt their feelings by telling them that. Now do you understand?"

Godenov flinched when Ratliff said the FPs weren't "good enough." He'd heard the play on his name directed at himself too many times. But he understood. He wondered if the FPs weren't "good enough" because Godenov wasn't "good enough" to train them right.

"Let's go. We've got to move fast or the guerrillas will leave before we get there." All three sped back to their counterparts in the platoon to tell them as much as they needed to know about what they were going to do. Some four kilometers to the south of them, Corporal Dornhofer was giving similar orders to Van Impe and MacIlargie.

Haste was essential to catch the guerrillas, and the Marines wanted to run. But if one group of guerrillas was in ambush in the area, there might well be another group. They went as fast as they could while using infras to help spot danger. The fire team leaders also used their heads-up displays, which showed where they were and where Leach and his fire team waited. It took more than fifteen minutes for the entire squad to assemble.

"Here's the situation," Sergeant Wang Hyakowa said as soon as they were all present. He transmitted the situation map display he had constructed from Leach's report, and the little bit the string-of-pearls surveillance satellites were able to tell him, to his fire team leaders. "Chief put three FPs in place to keep an eye on the guerrillas. They haven't reported movement, so I think we can assume the ambush is still there."

Schultz snorted softly at the mention of the FPs being trusted to keep an eye on the ambush. MacIlargie rolled his eyes and grinned. No one else showed any reaction.

"My best guess," Hyakowa continued, ignoring Schultz and MacIlargie, "is they don't have infras, so they don't have any idea we're here. Where did you place your platoons?"

Ratliff and Dornhofer gave him the coordinates, which he plugged into his situation map. The four NCOs studied the updated map for a moment, then Hyakowa began talking again.

"First platoon's in the best position for a blocking force," he said, "and we'd be most effective if we rolled up their flank, which would chase the survivors their way. But we'd have to go all the way around the ambush to do that. We may not have the time to go all the way around." He knew that if he was in command of that ambush, he'd probably have moved it already. "I think our best bet is to get on line and hit them from their rear. Comments?"

None of the fire team leaders had a better suggestion.

"Let's do it."

The ten Marines silently sped to get on a line fifty meters behind the guerrilla ambush site.

The more Lieutenant Pincote thought about the way the oligarch's lackeys stopped just outside her ambush and then pulled back, the more it bothered her. She wondered if their scouts had spotted the ambush. But that didn't seem possible; the clumsy Feldpolizei just couldn't move well enough that none of her fighters could see them. She didn't believe that even the Confederation Marines could move that well in the forest; there simply wasn't enough foliage to conceal a walking man that well—and no one could crawl well enough or long enough to be a scout for a patrol. A vagrant thought tickled the back of her mind; somewhere she'd heard that the

Confederation Marines could turn themselves invisible. No, she hadn't believed it when she first heard it, she wasn't going to believe it now.

She looked all around and saw no people but her own fighters, the very few she could spot from her position. No one was standing or walking. Maybe she should send out scouts of her own to see where the lackeys went to? The lackeys couldn't possibly be alert enough to spot her scouts before they were seen themselves. No, no scouts. Something felt very wrong; she wouldn't risk scouts following the Feldpolizei.

What was that? She was facing to her rear, searching for movement, when again something seemed to move at the periphery of her vision. Again, nothing was there. She shook her head sharply. That was the third time she'd thought she'd seen something that wasn't there. Something was very, very wrong. Perturbed, she carefully studied the area again.

Chan froze when one of the guerrillas looked directly at him. If he moved, the shift of patterns created by his uniform would probably give him away. Even someone who didn't know what to look for could spot a fully chameleoned man by accident, if they were looking in the right place when the concealed man moved. And this guerrilla was looking very intently in his direction. Had he seen him? Chan didn't think so, but the guerrilla had seen something that made him look closer.

Nervous sweat beaded on Chan's brow and trickled down his ribs as he stood motionless, watching as the guerrilla peered toward him, eyes probing all around his position. He didn't want to take his eyes off the man, he wanted to know immediately when the guerrilla looked away, or instantly if he aimed his blaster toward him. But he had to have an awareness of the whole situation so he wouldn't be caught by surprise by one of the others. He forced himself to flick his eyes toward the other guerrillas he could see. A few meters to the side of the one watching him, a bearded guerrilla was staring intently in the direction the FP's first platoon had gone. Beyond him another guerrilla, not bearded but unshaven, was also looking in that direction. Chan was shifting his vision to the other side when an anomaly struck him and he looked back at the one who seemed to be seeking him. That guerrilla was totally beardless.

It was odd for a guerrilla to shave in the field. He looked to the next one to the right and saw a heavy mustache—and a five o'clock shadow. Every guerrilla he could see was bearded or unshaven—except for the one who was looking toward him. He lowered his gaze to the chest of that guerrilla. It had a distinct bulge, but it wasn't in the right place for powerful chest muscles. His gaze went lower. The curve of the hips was wrong, and the crotch of the pants was too tight for an active man.

Buddha's blue balls! It was a woman!

In four operations, Chan had never faced a woman in combat. He'd heard of women fighting to protect their children or homes, and he'd even heard of women fighting as members of guerrilla bands. But he'd never encountered it. Women were to be protected and cared for, this he knew and felt deeply. Now he was in a situation where he would have to fight a woman, and to kill her—or risk being killed by her?

His knees weakened. This was wrong. He swallowed to loosen his suddenly constricted throat.

Lieutenant Pincote shook her head, about to give up her search. She'd almost decided she needed to see a doctor about her eyes when she distinctly saw something. Startled, she almost gaped at it, but caught herself quickly enough to keep her gaze roaming.

Centuries ago some philosopher, she couldn't remember who, said that if you eliminate everything impossible, whatever was left, no matter how improbable, had to be the truth. As improbable as it seemed, if she had spotted an invisible man, then an invisible man was there, and she didn't want to stare at him and let him know he'd been spotted. While her head moved and her eyes shifted, she kept examining what she saw out of the corner of her eye. Yes, what she saw remained there. There was a tree forty meters away. Part of its trunk was missing—an irregular line along one side of it was mottled with the browns and greens of the ground and undergrowth as though it was occluded by a man partly blocking it—a man concealed with the pattern of the surrounding ground and underbrush. It was impossible to her that the Feldpolizei could turn themselves invisible. Improbable as it was, the only thing possible—given that an invisible man stood before her—was that Confederation Marines did have a way to make themselves invisible. And the Marines were approaching her ambush from the rear!

Chan watched the woman with growing horror. He was certain she knew he was there. He didn't want to kill a woman; if he had to fight a woman, he'd rather take her prisoner. *Boys don't hit girls* was something he'd been taught since earliest childhood. If he shot the woman, he'd be hitting her the hardest possible way. But she was directly in his path, she was armed with a blaster herself, and he thought she knew exactly where he was. If he didn't shoot her, she'd shoot him. He'd been more frightened at times in the couple of dozen firefights he'd been in on his four previous campaigns, but never more horrified at the prospect of a fight than he was now—he was almost paralyzed by it.

So nearly paralyzed that he almost didn't react when the woman twisted to the side and into a prone position with her blaster pointed straight at him. He almost didn't hear her cry out a warning to the other guerrillas. Almost, but almost wasn't enough to kill him. He flung himself to the side in time to avoid anything more than a singeing. His blaster was at his shoulder when he landed on his belly, and he rapidly depressed the firing lever twice. His combat reflexes took over—she was no longer a woman, she was the enemy. Chan's first bolt hit the ground two meters in front of her. He couldn't tell whether the second was a grazing hit or part of the fireball created when the bolt that struck the ground next to her was deflected onto her. The woman was out of the fight, but Chan didn't have time to breathe a sigh of relief. He turned his attention to another guerrilla and incinerated the man.

While Chan was frozen, trying to avoid giving himself away to Lieutenant Pincote, the rest of the squad continued to creep forward.

When they were twenty-five meters from the ambush line, Hyakowa said one soft word into the command circuit of his comm unit: "Positions." His infra shield was down so he could see his men. He quickly glanced to his sides to assure himself his Marines were lowering themselves to the ground. All but one, who was nearly ten meters behind the line. From the position of the red pillar, he guessed it was Chan. He could think of only one reason a man as experienced as Chan would have frozen instead of moving forward with the rest of the squad. He looked toward the ambush and, yes! One of the guerrillas was looking to the rear. If Chan had been spotted, there was no time to waste.

"Pick your targets," Hyakowa murmured into his mike. He paused for a beat to give his men time to take aim, then said, "Fire!" just as the guerrilla looking toward Chan twisted around and shot at him while screaming out a surprisingly high-pitched warning.

The peaceful stillness of the afternoon was shattered by the ozone cracks of the Marines' blasters and the screams of the injured and dying. The Marines were spread out more than the ambushers, and covered two-thirds of the length of the ambush. Not only were their targets more concentrated than the guerrillas', the guerrillas couldn't see who they were shooting at—or who was shooting at them. In five seconds more than half of the ambushers were out of action, dead or too severely wounded to fight. In the time it took the survivors of the first round of fire to realize they were doomed if they didn't run, nearly all of them in front of the line of Marines had holes blasted through their bodies by plasma bolts. The lucky ones had the bolts pass all the way through and keep going. Others were more severely mutilated when the bolts struck the ground after passing through and reflected back, to set their uniforms ablaze and superheat their bodies so they cooked in their own body fluids.

Nearly twenty guerrillas tried to run, some carrying or dragging wounded comrades. Half a dozen of them were shot down before they got ten meters away.

"Cease fire, cease fire!" Hyakowa shouted. "Fire team leaders report," he ordered as he rose to his feet. He raised his infras so he could watch the flight of the few survivors.

The entire firefight, from the time he gave the order to open up to when he called cease fire, was barely ten seconds.

"First team, all right," Leach replied a second or so later.

"Second fire team, we're okay," Ratliff reported.

"Third team, fine," Dornhofer said.

Hyakowa ignored Schultz's outraged demands that they pursue the survivors, that they could easily wipe them all out, until after the fire team leaders finished their reports. Then he said over his comm unit so everybody could hear his response, "Yes, we could easily get all of them. But we'll let them go. Think of how it's going to affect the morale of the rest of the guerrillas when these few get back and tell how we surprised them, how we killed most of them so fast. They're going to think real hard about it before they go into an area Marines are in again."

He looked around at the carnage in the abortive ambush site. "Let's police up those bodies and see if there's anyone alive who we can maybe keep that way."

As hard as he looked, Chan couldn't find a female body among the dead.

CHAPTER
TWELVE

"Chief Long says before you start your duties in his intelligence unit he wants you to do some patrolling with the Stadtpolizei, get a feel for routine police work and how the Stadtpolizei function," Lieutenant Constantine told Dean and Claypoole one morning. "He wants you to ride all three shifts, and you'll start today with the evening, or Charlie, shift. Roll call is at 1400. You're each being assigned to different stations in the city for the next few days. Let's see. Claypoole, you're going to the Hidalgo Hills Station in District Four. Dean, you go to, um, Kwangtun Heights Station, in District Three. Use your own vehicle to get there. One of you'll have to pick the other up after you're finished. Report to the station commander when you arrive and he'll introduce you to the shift leader. Think you can handle it?"

"Yessir!" they responded.

"Oh, yeah, go light on the 'sir' business, okay? Call me LT or Pete. I blow things up, remember?"

"What's the uniform, LT?" Claypoole asked.

"Utilities. Carry shoulder and side arms. Charlie shift runs from 1500 to 0100. You'll eat somewhere in town. The cops all know the good places. The shift leader will assign you to an officer. Remember this: you have no police powers in this town. You are strictly observers. You'll do whatever the officers you ride with tell you to do. If they need your assistance, they'll ask for it. Otherwise, keep your eyes and ears open and ask questions. It'll make the time pass quicker."

The roll call room at the Hidalgo Hills Station was a mess from the Middle Ages, chairs turned every which way and computer workstations covered with dust, graffiti, and coffee stains. Notices, including advertisements for apartments and houses for rent, were pasted and stuck haphazardly to the partitions. Claypoole was very much aware that he had entered a strange world. One garish, hand-lettered sign boldly announced an Adam shift party that weekend. A graffito Claypoole couldn't help noticing was a pencil drawing on a panel by a workstation of a woman with a huge, gap-toothed leer on her face and hugely exaggerated hips and breasts underneath which someone had scrawled "Shift Leader Gomez's wife" and a telephone number.

Shift Leader Ernesto Lyles was doing his best to make the Marine feel at home. A big, broad-shouldered man with a prominent stomach and flaring mustaches, Lyles spoke with a wad of tobacco stuffed into one corner of his mouth. Occasionally he went *spitooie*, and a thin stream of tobacco juice flew with unerring accuracy into a tiny cup sitting on the floor to one side of his desk. The Marines were soon to discover that the men of the Brosigville Stadtpolizei were much addicted to tobacco products, which pleased Claypoole, an ardent cigar smoker.

"We have fifty officers assigned to this station," Lyles was saying. "We run three shifts, Adam, Baker, and Charlie. You'll note that we use a phonetic alphabet somewhat different from the one standardized throughout the Confederation's military forces. Officers are assigned to their shifts on a permanent basis, so there is no rotation. There are twelve officers on each shift. The remaining fourteen officers are shift leaders, detectives, and the station commander and his lieutenant." Claypoole listened attentively. "There are six stations here in Brosigville, each one with a complement of fifty officers. With another fifty at headquarters, the Brosigville force consists of approximately four hundred sworn officers to serve a population of 100,000 citizens. That's about one patrol officer for each 250 people in the city, not a bad ratio. Our patrol area is approximately four hundred square kilometers, which includes the center city as well as the suburbs of Brosigville and the port area. The citizens of

Brosigville are generally pretty well-behaved. Most of the crimes we investigate are against property, and the crimes against persons are usually assaults, and most of them are domestic in nature. We have few murders or rapes, compared to the"—*spitooie*—"figures I've seen on comparable cities on other worlds in the Confederation."

"What about the other towns and cities in Arschland?"

"Commissioner Landser is—was—also responsible for the Stadtpolizei operations elsewhere throughout the country, but he has a special staff of about a hundred here at headquarters through which he does that. He has subcommissioners in those other municipalities who report directly to him. Of course, we exchange information with those other forces and assist them whenever we can. And since we all train at the same academy and are commanded by the same individual, theoretically a police officer anywhere in Arschland could be transferred between jurisdictions. In practice, if you're assigned to Brosigville or some other town, that's where you stay for your whole career.

"You know how the Feldpolizei is organized? We exchange information and cooperate with them, but their organization is totally separate from ours."

"Do you ever operate at cross-purposes with them?"

"Hah!" Lyles snorted. "Hah! Uniforms of orange and blue? Buzzard guts hanging over their shoulders? Marching around like windup toy soldiers? Lance Corporal Claypoole, the Feldpolizei takes good cops and turns 'em into idiots. Their whole organization is at 'cross-purposes' with ours." He shook his head. "You Marines have your work cut out for you with them."

Lyles appeared to be in his early forties. He was dressed in the standard work uniform of the Brosigville Stadtpolizei, gray shirt with black trousers and a blue stripe along the outside seam. Since he was a supervisor, he was not wearing the standard police equipment belt, but carried a large side arm tucked above his right hip in a black leather holster. His badges of rank, three blue chevrons, open side up, were prominently displayed on each neatly creased sleeve of his tunic. A sterling silver badge glittered above his left breast pocket. His hair was short, like a Marine's.

"How are you armed?" Claypoole asked.

"Ah, figured you'd get around to that." Lyles rubbed his hands together and began an animated and enthusiastic firearms lecture. "We have shoulder-fired projectile weapons in our armory, but they're issued only on an as-required basis, and since I've been on the force, more than ten years, we've never had occasion to issue them. The standard police side arm is a select-fire pistol that fires caseless ammunition. We issue Remchester 4.7mm, 52.5-grain frangible bullets to reduce overpenetration while producing maximum damage inside the target. Other ammunition is available, of course, but on routine patrol our patrolmen use only the frangible type. The issue pistol, the Sig-Smock M-229, is manufactured here on Wanderjahr under license from the parent company. The M-229 uses an 'iron' sight system, as you may be aware, and a thirty-round barrel-mounted magazine. Each patrolman is issued three thirty-round magazines for his piece."

"Never heard of 'iron sights,' Shift Leader," Claypoole said. In fact he didn't know much about caseless ammo and projectile weapons, since the Confederation military forces had abandoned that technology long before he had been born.

"Well," Lyles continued, warming to his subject, "those are just old-fashioned three-dot, low-light-illuminated sights. You line 'em up, and poof! the target goes down. These are fixed sights mounted on the weapon and they can't be jostled or knocked out of alignment, and unlike the laser range-finder devices, the target never knows it's being aimed at. The thing about caseless-ammo weapons is they provide a very stable shooting platform since there are few moving parts. A long time ago, when they used cartridge cases in projectile weapons, you had to eject the spent casings. Since the primer and powder for each round in a caseless gun are consumed in firing, the only ejection required is a small slot for rounds that malfunction. I might add that the propellant Remchester uses leaves hardly any residue.

"I'd like to take my own weapon out and show you all these

features, but only a fool diddles with firearms indoors. Anyway, the Remchester ammo has a muzzle velocity of about a kilometer a second. On full auto the Sig 229 can fire thirty-seven rounds per second, but to conserve ammo, each piece is fitted with a rate limiter that permits only three-round bursts. So your first three rounds are almost always guaranteed to be on target, if you know how to sight properly. I mean, these babies are so smooth there's virtually no felt recoil and barrel climb has been totally eliminated. Vehicles are equipped with ten extra thirty-round magazines, but officers generally don't carry them on their persons unless they expect very serious trouble."

Lyles stopped briefly to expectorate and wipe a droplet of tobacco juice from his mustache. "Are you familiar with the Brady .70 caliber automatic shot rifle?"

"No, sir," Claypoole answered, trying to keep a tone of resignation out of his voice. He appreciated firearms, but this civilian stuff was just not very important to him. He believed that in a pinch he could outshoot the entire Stadtpolizei organization on Wanderjahr—and he was right—but common courtesy and duty forced him to remain alert and to pretend interest. Besides, he had to know this stuff if he was going to work with these people.

"Each patrol vehicle is equipped with the Brady .70 caliber automatic shot rifle. It's potent," Lyles continued. As the shift leader droned on, Claypoole reflected that as a Marine with one combat deployment behind him, he'd seen more action and been shot at more times than probably anybody on the Brosigville police force. "It has five magazine tubes, each with six rounds," Lyles was saying. "Each round is composed of a casing and an explosive primer that when struck ignites the powder charge. Very old technology but very effective and reliable. We decided to use these weapons instead of rifles firing caseless ammo 'cause caseless ammo is seldom used here and the extra weight of the casing is not a problem, and besides, an officer can always defend himself with the Brady using it as a club. Each tube is loaded with a different kind of projectile, one for shot, one for smoke, another for explosive shells, and so on. The tubes rotate around the barrel. You have to be careful which tube the gun is set for. On the range and sometimes on the streets, rookies will select the wrong magazine tube and fire smoke when they want to fire shot. It's a complicated weapon, somewhat similar to the antique shotgun they used to have a long time ago, but it's the most versatile and powerful one available to patrol officers without special issues from our armory. Would you like to fire our weapons someday?"

"You bet!" Claypoole answered. "Do you use body armor?"

"Yes." Lyles tapped his own tunic, under which he wore a lightweight ballistic vest. "These are rated to stop even slugs from a Brady shot rifle. They're no protection from one of those," he indicated Claypoole's blaster, "but we don't encounter anybody armed with plasma weapons on the streets of Brosigville." Claypoole did not have to wonder what would happen if they ever did.

"Do I get one of those vests tonight?"

"You won't need it, Lance Corporal. See, you gotta understand this. We are not a military organization here. A policeman is trained in the use of restraint, not firepower. You military men encounter the enemy and you put fire on his ass until he goes away. A cop, on the other hand, is trained to reduce threats without the use of deadly force. When he draws his weapon, it's an act of last resort and only to protect his life or the life of someone else. That's why we don't use plasma weapons, although under Confederation law, as a legitimate police agency, we could probably get them. But firepower is not what we do best. Another thing, you're more experienced in how to survive a firefight than any of our officers. Hell, most of them have never even fired their weapons in anger; you've not only been shot at, you've killed men with your blaster. But on the other hand, every police officer is on constant patrol when he's on duty, walking point his entire shift, but he sometimes has to exercise unbelievable self-control when confronted with trouble. You can understand the stress this places on the average cop."

Claypoole thought about that for a moment. He thought about "walking point" for ten hours a day, day after day. Yes, he could understand how that could stress a man out. "What kind of crime do you encounter in your district?"

"All kinds," Lyles answered, "everything from murder to drunk in public. But most of the stuff we handle is misdemeanor stuff, where an offender might get up to a year in the city detention facility. There is organized crime in this city, but we have a unit at headquarters that handles that stuff. You'll no doubt get into some of that when you go back up there to help out with the intelligence work."

"What about the guerrillas? You know, the bombs downtown and whoever it was who tried to pot my partner and me out by the port?"

Lyles hesitated before he answered that question. "Chief Long is handling that investigation." He seemed reluctant to continue, so Claypoole did not press him. He made a mental note to discuss the investigation with Chief Long. All the rage he'd felt over Maggie's murder suddenly rushed back. He had not forgotten—would not forget—Chief Long's promise to let him be in on the capture of the shooter.

"You okay?" Lyles asked, noticing the expression that had come over Claypoole.

"Yes," he answered, getting control of himself with an effort.

"Any other questions?"

"No, sir, not right now."

"You'll be riding with Officer Fernandez this evening, Lance Corporal Claypoole. He has patrol area 490C, which is also his call sign. Come over to the map." They walked over to a large wall map of Brosigville. It had been divided up into sectors with dark black lines, each representing a station district, six of them, in different colors. Hidalgo Hills was District Four, so all the patrol designators began with the number 4. The patrol areas within each station area were marked by green lines. The patrol area designations, 490, 520, 621, and so on, were labeled in bright blue. "When I say you're riding in patrol area 490C, that means you're with Charlie shift in this sector here." Lyles ran his hand across a part of the map bordered on the west by the Teufelfluss River.

"Is that a good area to patrol?"

Lyles smiled. "It's one of our quieter areas. This is a weekday, early evening to around midnight, nothing much will be happening. If you stay with us long enough we'll get you into some of the rougher neighborhoods. Tonight you may go on some domestic complaints, maybe a traffic accident, possibly investigate some silent alarms."

Lyles hesitated before continuing, thinking over what he was about to say. "Corporal Claypoole, I know something about your background. More important, I know what you've done since you've been on Wanderjahr. You're a brave man and you got the papers to prove it. I don't exaggerate when I say I'd like to have a man like you on my shift."

Claypoole was flattered and just a bit ashamed that only minutes earlier he'd been making invidious comparisons between his experience and that of these cops.

Soon the officers of Charlie shift began to drift into the roll call area from the locker rooms. They all carried heavy briefcases and laptop computers. They plopped into the chairs and commenced to banter among themselves:

"Sanchez, you look like you just came out of a whorehouse!"

"Hector," the policeman named Sanchez hollered back, "you smell like you live in one!"

"Hell, Hector was born in one!" another officer said, laughing.

They all spoke standard Confederation English very well, but with slight accents that sounded Hispanic to Claypoole. Physically, the officers were all shorter and much darker than he.

"All right, quiet down, quiet down! This is a police department, not a comedy show."

" 'Police department'? Is that what it's called?" one officer hollered.

When the room had quieted down, Shift Leader Lyles introduced Claypoole.

"The Marines have landed!" someone called out, and all the

officers applauded. "Lance Corporal Claypoole," Lyles accentuated *Corporal*, "will ride with Patrolman Fernandez."

Someone yelled out, "You lucky bastard, Lance Corporal!"

Claypoole smiled. He was already beginning to feel at home; the Stadtpolizei reminded him of the barracks back on Thorsfinni's World.

"Lance Corporal Claypoole was a target at the shooting at Juanita's some days ago," Lyles announced, "and three nights ago he and another Marine took on more than forty bandits down in Morgenluft." There was a low murmur among the assembled policemen, who had all heard the story on the media and from police reports. Claypoole breathed a sigh of relief. Juanita's was not in the Hidalgo Hills jurisdiction, so the officer he'd clobbered wouldn't be with these men.

"He also busted Chico's nose!" the man they called Hector shouted gleefully, and two others sitting nearby got up to pat Claypoole on the back.

"Chico, as you may be able to surmise," Shift Leader Lyles told Claypoole, "is a well-known asshole in this department."

Claypoole was definitely at home.

Shift Leader Lyles covered some announcements—lookouts for criminals and stolen landcars—then dismissed Charlie shift to its patrol areas.

Patrolman Fernandez was about Claypoole's age, slim, and in good physical condition. They shook hands warmly.

"I'm at your disposal, Officer," Claypoole told the young policeman.

"Call me Hwang, please! And you are . . . ?"

"Rachman."

The men of Charlie shift filed out of the roll call room into the vehicle compound behind the station, where they entered their assigned landcars. The Brosigville police cruisers were light and dark blue with white reflective lettering. The roofs bristled with antennas and signal lights.

"You seldom get the same car each shift," Fernandez said, "so sometimes you get to clean out all the trash the shift before you left behind. We're supposed to clean up after ourselves, but most of us don't do a very good job of it. You'll see why if

we have a busy shift today. By 0100 you'll just want to get
cleared out of the station and back home." Fernandez began
going through a checklist, inspecting the exterior of his vehicle
and then the interior, the computerized communications
system, and the Brady shot rifle. He carefully unloaded the
rifle, checked all five magazines to be sure they were fully
loaded, each mag with the proper ammunition, then gently
replaced it in its rack. "Press this button here, and the gun pops
out. Charge it with this lever here, then release the safety here,
point and fire."

"Okay with you, Hwang, I'll just rely on my hand blaster."
Claypoole patted his own side arm. "Can I just stow my
shoulder weapon in the storage compartment for tonight?
Don't think we'll need it, do you?"

"Probably not; go ahead, throw it in back there. Hey." He
motioned for Claypoole to watch something. He bent quickly
and snatched a small black object from inside his left leg, down
by his ankle. "Know what this is?"

Claypoole shook his head. It was a pistol of some kind.

"This," Hwang announced proudly, "is a POS .25 caliber
handgun. POS means 'piece of shit,' 'cause these guns are
worthless firearms except at extremely close range. But we all
carry them. To have a POS is a mark of distinction, means
you're one of the team. They're manufactured here on Wanderjahr and are exact replicas of a pistol that was once quite
famous back on Old Earth. It's fed by a magazine that holds six
rounds. We carry 'em with one round in the chamber, so that
gives us seven shots. It's for use in only the most desperate circumstances, like when your service pistol is out of ammo and
you're out of hope." He pulled up his trouser leg. "I carry mine
in this ankle holster. It only weighs about 430 grams; hardly
even know it's down there after a while. Never had to use it
and hope I never will."

Claypoole shook his head in wonder.

Inside the cab, the floor was sticky from coffee or some
other kind of fluid someone had spilled there, and the storage
compartments were stuffed with napkins, plastic spoons, and
soiled blank forms that apparently were used only to sop up

spills. Compartments in the door panels contained extra magazines for the Brady rifle and Fernandez's Sig pistol.

Fernandez plugged in his laptop. "We do as much report writing from inside these vehicles as we can. When you get it all done from here, you can go home when your shift is over. But there are times we have to finish up back at the station, and that's what the terminals in the roll call room are for. The shift leader reviews all his officers' reports from his console and then authorizes them for the central-records database. The station commander reviews all the reports on a daily basis. Lyles is pretty sharp, so hardly any mistakes ever get by him. Otherwise we'd be getting ass-chewings all the time. You'd be surprised how difficult it can be to write a lucid report with all the stuff that goes on out here in the streets on any given night. And when you don't have time to write up each incident, you just have to take notes with a pencil and paper and do all your reports after your shift. Some nights I've had to stay on duty until dawn just catching up with the reports."

Claypoole doubted Fernandez had much trouble writing lucid reports. He'd known the officer only a few minutes and already he respected the man's intelligent professionalism.

"Question?"

"Sure," Fernandez replied.

"Well ... it's just that I've met Commissioner Landser several times, one or two times too often, if you get my drift. And I just wonder ... well, given the kind of officer he is, how do you guys get away with, uh, I mean, manage to be so ... so ... ." Claypoole made a helpless gesture.

"So fucked up?" Fernandez finished the sentence for him, laughing.

"No! I mean, so 'casual' about everything, especially the state of cleanliness back inside the station. You'd think with a guy like Landser in charge, you'd have white-glove inspections every shift."

Fernandez was silent before replying. "You gotta understand something about Landser, Old Allie, as we call him. He's a dandy, that's for sure, struts around like he's a character out of an old-fashioned opera or something. But he understands leadership. He lets his district commanders run their own shows. He knows we have enough to do keeping the streets safe without inspections and formations and all that crap. So long as we're presentable to the public and conduct ourselves professionally, Old Allie concentrates on polishing his shoes and leaves the street cops alone to do their jobs. And you know, when Chairman Arschmann put Chief Long in charge with the authority to fire Landser—we all know that—well, it cut him bad, real bad. Frankly, I don't think he deserved to be treated that way." Fernandez paused. "Not that I think Chief Long and his boys are bad for this department, and there's no doubt we really need you Marines here too. I've met the chief. He came to all the stations and talked to us. He's a good man. But you just don't take an officer like Old Allie and kick him like Arschmann did. And then right after Old Allie's kid brother got himself killed in that bombing."

"I didn't know about that," Claypoole said softly.

At last finished with the checklist, Fernandez turned to Claypoole and said, "Strap yourself in, Rachman, and let's go out and kick some ass!"

Dean was riding with a burly patrolman named Valdez. Valdez did not welcome the Marine's presence in his car, and it was obvious the shift leader had made the assignment as a way to prove a point with the big man. And Valdez resented it. So did Dean, but he decided to keep quiet about things for the present.

"Your patrol area is 310C, down by the river, right?" Dean asked.

Valdez maneuvered his landcruiser into the late-afternoon traffic on the street outside the station. "Yeah," he answered finally.

"What kind of an area is it to work in?"

"Wet, if you go into the river," Valdez responded.

Dean bit his tongue. He'd go along for a while longer. Maybe the ice would melt.

Each landcruiser was connected to a central dispatch facility via its onboard computer system. The policemen logged on to the system each evening and logged out at the end of their shift. Meanwhile, orders and messages flowed across the computer screen all evening long. When something for a specific patrol was transmitted, the console would beep loudly. When an emergency message was transmitted, the dispatcher used the voice channel and requested confirmation, to be sure the instructions were received and understood.

Before they'd left the station, Valdez had given Dean a small wrist communicator set to the same frequency as the cruiser's, so when they left the vehicle for any reason, they'd still be in contact with the dispatcher. "That's so if you get into trouble when you're outside the car, all you do is press this button or shout for help and the dispatcher'll know where to send it. We always tell the dispatcher our exact location when we stop, and we let them know what we're doing. Even when we stop to eat or take a piss."

Inside the cruiser Valdez pointed out some things on the console. "That button there releases the shot rifle. That yellow button there, never touch it unless we need assistance. That transmits what we call a Signal Thirteen, officer down. Mash that fucker by mistake and I'll be the laughingstock of the entire force."

And that was the extent of their conversation for the next five hours. Valdez made several traffic stops, but he never explained to Dean why. He was ordered to stay in the cruiser while the policeman talked to the drivers he'd pulled over. Dean didn't know if the drivers had committed traffic violations or were just friends of the policeman. Valdez also seemed immune to hunger, since he made no mention of supper, and Dean had grown so exasperated at his treatment he wouldn't break down and ask. At shortly past 19 hours, Dean was ready to go back to the station and ask the shift leader to assign him to another officer for the rest of the evening.

Meanwhile, Claypoole and Fernandez were getting along like old buddies. Fernandez carefully explained everything he was doing, and when he made traffic stops, he let Claypoole come along. "Just stand clear of my weapon side, Rachman, in case the situation goes bad. Traffic stops are the most dangerous activity for police officers in Brosigville. If the driver you stop doesn't attack you, you might still get hit by the oncoming traffic."

The neighborhoods in area 490 consisted of rows of small shops along the major thoroughfares and neat residential enclaves on the side streets. Claypoole was impressed at the friendliness of the people they encountered, most of whom addressed Fernandez as Hwang. "I've worked this area for three years," he said. It was hard for Claypoole to imagine the man ever drawing his weapon to shoot someone.

At supper in a local restaurant—"Cops get half price here," Fernandez explained—the two exchanged personal details about themselves. Fernandez was married, with two children, a boy and a girl. He'd been a policeman for six years, all as a patrol officer in the Hidalgo Hills District.

At precisely 19 hours the dispatcher raised them on the voice channel. "Four ninety Charlie, proceed to the Anwar Shipping Company warehouse at 4990D Teufelfluss Promenade. Back up Unit 910C on an Eighty-nine Adam. Priority One event, but do not use lights or sound. All other units stand by."

"Ten-four, dispatcher. Will proceed to 4990D Teufelfluss as backup for 910C. Priority One, no lights or sound." Several other patrol units who'd been monitoring the transmission chimed in, volunteering to go in place of 490C, but the dispatcher put them all on hold.

"An Eighty-nine Adam is a burglary in progress," Fernandez said. "We're the closest unit to the scene right now. Looks like the culprits are still inside the warehouse. That's why the call's a Priority One and they want us to proceed as quietly as possible."

"What if the bad guys are listening on their own radios?"

Fernandez shrugged. "Then there'll be a hot reception, Rachman."

"Who's unit 910C?"

"Ricardo Lanning. When we get there, you stick around the car, monitor the communications system." Fernandez had shown Claypoole how to use the voice system. "I doubt we'll need any Marine fire support, but keep your eyes open."

They pulled up silently behind Lanning's car. Lanning was a heavyset man with very closely cropped hair and tattoos peeking out from under his short-sleeve shirt. He came over to Fernandez. "Hwang, good to see you." They shook hands. Fernandez introduced Claypoole. "Marine?" Lanning asked. "You armed? Good. Stand by. We might need some more firepower. I've called for more backup. The building's too big for only two of us to check."

"What's inside?" Claypoole asked.

"Thule," Lanning answered. He grinned. "I think we've caught ourselves some big-time bad boys here tonight."

Two more cars drove silently up. Since the call was in Lanning's area and no supervisor was yet on the scene, he gave the orders. "Hwang, you and Claypoole cover the front of the place. The rest of us will go in through the back, if we can. Everyone stay in radio contact with Hwang."

Claypoole was about to leave the patrol car when a sharp *ka-pow!* came from the warehouse and Lanning's car erupted in a ball of flame. The four officers who'd been standing in a huddle were all knocked to the ground by the explosion. Fernandez mashed the Signal Thirteen button, released the Brady rifle, grabbed some Sig mags, and rolled into the street, where Claypoole was already crouched behind the car. There were several more shots. This time Claypoole could see bright flashes come from the darkened warehouse, and all four vehicles burst into flames. One of the officers rolled in the street to put out his burning clothes, and all five men hugged the pavement, temporarily out of sight from the warehouse behind the flames of their burning vehicles.

"They're using shot rifles!" someone yelled.

"That's a class-four felony," one of the officers muttered as he tried to squeeze himself between the cracks in the sidewalk.

Then the most frightening noise of all, the flat *hiss-crack* as several plasma bolts lanced out from the warehouse simultaneously and slagged the street in front of the burning police vehicles.

"Dispatcher!" Claypoole yelled into his wrist communicator. "Plasma weapons! They've got plasma weapons. Get Dean over here right now! He's riding in Kwangtun Heights."

"Jesu, it's hot!" someone screamed. The burning vehicles were generating terrible heat. They could not stay where they were any longer.

Dean unholstered his hand blaster, set it on full power, stood up, and began firing rapidly at the warehouse facade, splattering it with bolts. The four policemen did not have to be told what to do—they jumped up and darted out of the street into a nearby building. Claypoole ran after them.

The five men crouched panting inside a storefront whose front windows had been blown out in the explosions. The burned officer's clothing was still smoldering, but he gritted his teeth and kept saying he was all right, despite the burns he'd sustained along the left side of his body.

"They have us outgunned," Lanning rasped. He cursed and spoke rapidly into his communicator. "It'll take a few minutes to get a reaction force down here. Did anyone manage to grab a Brady rifle?" Claypoole said nothing. He'd left the rifle and the extra magazine in the street when he'd dashed for cover.

"I have four bolts left in this thing," Claypoole said, checking the gauge on his energy pack. He did not have a replacement for it. An infantryman, he relied on his shoulder weapon, which was now bubbling goo in the back of Hwang's patrol car.

"Then you're the man," Lanning said.

A plasma bolt hissed through the window and exploded in the back of the shop, spreading fire everywhere.

"We gotta get out of here now!" Lanning shouted.

Claypoole fired three bolts back at the warehouse. They ran through the rising flames into the rear of the store, which consisted of offices and a storeroom. Another bolt exploded in front of the building. Billowing smoke and roaring flames rapidly filled the front of the store. Breathing was becoming difficult with all the smoke in that confined space. Someone slammed the outer door to the storeroom shut, to give them some temporary protection from the conflagration. They stood panting and coughing in the smoky darkness, only partially illuminated by their glowballs as they sought a way out. Seconds later the five desperate men were confronted by a locked and bolted door at the rear of the storeroom. "This goddamned door is against the fire codes," someone muttered. The frangible bullets in their Sigs would be no use against the door's case-hardened steel panels.

"Oh, Jesus Lord, we're going to fry," someone whispered, his voice quavering on the edge of panic.

"Not if I can help it," Claypoole rasped.

"Unit 310 Charlie, you have a Marine on board?" the dispatcher asked.

Startled, Valdez answered in the affirmative and glanced at Dean. "Be advised, 310 Charlie, units in patrol area Four are under fire from plasma weapons and need immediate assistance at—4990D Teufelfluss Promenade. Proceed there at once and render whatever assistance is needed. Do you copy?"

"Three ten Charlie. Copy! On the way!" Valdez came to life immediately and grinned ferociously at Dean. "We got action, Marine! Get your gun!"

Dean, who had been carrying his blaster with him in the cab, checked the safety, glanced at the energy pack indicator light—it was at full charge—and put the weapon on full power. He was forced back into his seat as Valdez shifted the vehicle into drive and mashed the accelerator lever all the way down. The landcruiser leaped forward and within seconds was careening down a broad avenue at nearly 150 kilometers an hour, lights flashing and Klaxons screeching. "Whoooeeee!" Valdez hollered. "This is real police work!" Dean held on for his life.

Two blocks away from the warehouse, they saw the glow in the sky. Valdez slowed down until they were within sight of the place. Three separate fires raged: the warehouse facade was in flames along with a building directly across the street, and a third fire raged in the middle of the street, directly in their way. As Valdez pulled to a stop, a plasma bolt flashed from the warehouse into the burning building opposite.

"What the hell was that?" he asked.

"Hellfire," Dean answered. "You better take the Brady rifle, I don't think your pop guns can handle this." Valdez turned the landcruiser sidewise, blocking the street. They got out and took cover behind it.

"Four ninety Charlie, where are you?" Valdez screamed into his wrist communicator. A multichannel device like the ones the Marines carried, the police communicators were also programmed to respond to voice commands, and 490C should have been receiving Valdez clearly at this distance, but there was no response.

"I think they're in the building that's burning over there, Officer," Dean said. Valdez glanced at him, a sickish expression on his face that turned instantly to rage. He slapped the explosive-shell magazine into place on his Brady. "Let's go, Marine!"

As they stood to walk around the cruiser, two huge trucks came roaring at them out of the flames in the street. Without hesitating, Dean fired at the lead truck. His bolt struck the front of it and bored a hole into the engine compartment. A second later the engine block let out a loud crack as it shattered from overheating. His second bolt hit it squarely on the side of the cab as it slewed off the road and crashed. Valdez fired three explosive rounds at the second vehicle, which impacted in the cab and in the engine block. The truck lurched to a stop. Several men jumped out of the back and began firing at them with plasma weapons. Their bolts went wild, but Dean, target-range calm in the offhand firing position, coolly squeezed the firing lever six times. Each bolt struck its man. Shoulder-to-shoulder, Valdez and Dean marched forward into the maelstrom.

Claypoole fired his last bolt at the door. The blast was so close it singed his eyebrows and the hair on his head, but it was far less intense than the conflagration raging right behind the five men. Without waiting for the molten metal to cool, Lanning pried the door open with his collapsible nightstick and held it open for the others as they rushed through into the cool night air outside. They stumbled in the darkness, breathing in the fresh air gratefully.

"Thank God for the Marines," one officer said, embracing Claypoole.

"You guys can make love later," Lanning rasped. "This alley runs about half a block behind these buildings to a side street. We can follow that back to the main road and see what's happening at the warehouse." He lumbered off in the direction of the side street, the others clomping along behind him. From the main street came the unmistakable firing of several plasma weapons and several explosions.

"It's Dean! It's Dean!" Claypoole shouted. "That wonderful motherfucker's come through again!"

They were at the side street. Lanning turned to his left, and when they rounded the end of a building, they were standing at the opposite end of Teufelfluss Promenade, facing back toward the warehouse. The street was as bright as day from the fires. Two more vehicles, trucks by their size, burned fiercely in the street, and beyond the flames, barely visible through rolling clouds of dense, greasy black smoke, they could just see the outline of an apparently intact Stadtpolizei cruiser blocking the road.

Eight men broke suddenly from the cover of the burning warehouse and ran toward the small group of police officers. They fired as they came. Projectile weapons. Standing two-handed in a boxer stance, weapons on semi-auto, the policemen took aim as the men came on. Bullets whizzed and smacked everywhere around them. The four Sigs went "crack-crack-crack" again and again, but only two of the attackers dropped. It had come down to this: the policemen could not let these men pass, but they could not take cover either.

The attackers stopped advancing about twenty-five meters from the thin line of policemen blocking their way, and paused to take better aim at their targets. Claypoole was unarmed now. Fernandez tossed him his backup pistol.

Survival instinct, honed by training, took over as Claypoole flopped into the prone position. The policemen flopped down beside him. Aiming carefully, using their sights, they began squeezing their rounds off. It took less than thirty seconds for the bandits to crumple under the fusillade.

The five men lay in the street for a full ten seconds before any of them realized the fight was over. After the noise of the firefight, it was almost quiet now, despite the crackling of the flames ahead of them.

Two figures walked slowly out of the roiling smoke between the burning vehicles. The muzzles of all five guns zeroed in on them as one. "Halt!" Lanning croaked.

"Ricardo!" one of them called out. "It's Valdez! Look at all this mess you've made here!" Valdez spoke into his communicator, and instantly it seemed the street was crowded with emergency crews and more police officers; firemen began dousing the flames and medics rushed in with their life-support systems. Chief Long came up with Commissioner Landser close behind. The dapper little commander was highly animated, shaking hands with his officers and loudly congratulating everyone. Lanning and his little group holstered their weapons.

"Well," Dean said, sauntering up to Claypoole, his blaster at sling arms over one shoulder, "you sure manage to draw fire just about everywhere you go."

"Me?" Claypoole exclaimed.

"Where's your blaster?" Dean asked.

Claypoole returned Fernandez's backup gun. "When on Wanderjahr . . ." Claypoole began and shrugged. "We did it the hard way," he said.

"One of these guys is still alive!" a medic shouted. Everyone crowded around a prone figure.

Claypoole, looking over a medic's shoulder, stiffened. "I know this bastard!" he shouted. "Dean, it's Garth! It's that bastard Garth!"

Garth had been hit by two bullets. One had destroyed his left shoulder, and fragments had penetrated his carotid artery on that side of his neck. He'd lost a lot of blood, but it was the wound to his head that was fatal. A large chunk of his skull had been blown away along with pieces of his brain. He was still conscious, however, and he looked up at the faces standing above him and recognized the two Marines.

"My name is not Garth," he said weakly.

"You are Garth, you bastard!" Dean shouted. "I remember you. You work for Multan!"

Garth licked his lips. "My name is . . . my name is Sublieutenant Tang. Peoples Liberation Army . . ." His voice trailed off.

Claypoole knelt at the man's side and shook him violently. "What? What did you say?"

The dying man opened his eyes with effort. They were beginning to glaze over.

"You set off those bombs!" Claypoole shouted. "You shot at us!"

"Easy, easy," a medic cautioned, laying a restraining hand on his shoulder. Claypoole shook the hand off.

The dying man who called himself Tang tried to speak again. "I . . . did . . . not. Spying on Multan . . ." He closed his eyes and lay still. The medic shook his head.

"Don't die, you fuck! You owe us some answers!" Claypoole shouted, oblivious of the crowd that stood silently watching. "If you didn't, who did?" he demanded.

Tang opened his eyes and looked straight at Claypoole. He smiled. "You fools," he said in a normal tone of voice. "You don't understand anything. I never hurt you or anybody."

"Then who did?" Claypoole raged.

Tang stared up at his interrogator, his lips moving but no sound coming out of his mouth. "Titties," he said at last, and lay back on the bloody pavement.

"Okay, that's it," a medic said, and several policemen pulled Claypoole away.

"What did he say, what did he say?" Claypoole asked of the men in the crowd. Dean just shook his head.

" 'Titties' is what I heard," Chief Long said. He took both Dean and Claypoole by the arms and led them out of the crowd. "Are either of you injured?" he asked. When they shook their heads, he said, "You've had enough police work for tonight, lads. Come back to headquarters with me and we'll talk about 'Titties.' "

CHAPTER THIRTEEN

"Back in your bed, Lieutenant," Commander Hing snapped as he stepped into Pincote's small chamber off the main mine shaft. The medics had turned the chamber into a makeshift hospital room. "Your burns aren't bad enough to kill you, but if they get infected, the infection will."

Pincote looked up from pulling her uniform pants on to look up at him. In the dim light of the dying glowball, Hing saw that she was glaring. He also saw that she'd somehow managed to pull on her brassiere without dislodging the synthskin that swathed her left arm, shoulder, and side, and was attempting to put her left leg into her trousers without troubling the synthskin that ran along the outside of her left leg. That was as far as her dressing had gone. Nearby, the IV tubes she'd pulled from her arms dangled uselessly.

"I can move, I can give orders, and I can kill," she snarled. "If I am careful, nothing will go wrong." She grimaced as the waistband of her trousers caught against a patch of synthskin above her ankle, jerking the connections it was growing into the underlying tissue. Just one leg on the ground, she teetered.

In an instant, carefully avoiding her left shoulder, Hing was on her, his left hand firmly gripping her right arm, his right between her shoulder blades. More gently than he wanted to in his anger at her foolishness, he pushed her back and down while keeping her from falling backward. She tried to resist, but in her weakened condition he was much stronger, and she bent with his push until she was back on her narrow bed. Hing released the hold he had on Pincote and squatted in front of her with one hand clamped on her right thigh to prevent her standing again. Almost immediately he regretted his position; his eyes were level with her chest, which was much more impressive covered only by the bra than it had seemed before her disastrous ambush patrol. Only a foot below her chest he could make out the dark triangle of her uncovered pubis. It was too long since the last time he'd been with a woman. But this was the wrong place and the wrong time. And even if she wasn't injured, Sokum Pincote was definitely the wrong woman. He yanked his eyes toward hers.

"We are not sending out another combat patrol. Not yet. Not until we understand what happened to your ambush."

"The Confederation Marines can make themselves invisible, and we weren't prepared for that, that's what happened. Now that we know this, we can take steps." She flexed her leg muscles, but her left leg hurt too much for her to resist the downward pressure he maintained on her good leg. A small muscle twitched in his jaw, and she remembered the way his eyes had flicked over her nearly naked body.

Hing rose to his feet and stood over her, his hand on her good shoulder holding her down. From that vantage, looking down into her eyes, her body was less visible. Not much, but enough that it was less of a distraction.

"Yes, now that we know the Marines can make themselves invisible, we can take steps. But we don't have the equipment for it here. We have to get it. And *you* aren't taking steps of any kind until that synthskin has properly grafted itself to you."

He looked over his shoulder to the chamber entrance and called out, "Cildair!"

A moment later one of the medics rushed in.

"Sedating her for pain isn't enough," Hing said. "She's not good enough at obeying orders to stay in bed and heal. Put her completely out."

Pincote glared up at Hing while Cildair prepared the sedative and pressed the inductor against her good thigh. Then her eyes slowly closed, and she didn't feel the gentleness with which the two men removed her bra and pulled her trousers away from her ankle, then laid her back and covered her with a sheet after Cildair reattached the fluid drips.

* * *

Acting Shift Sergeant Schultz was feeling good. His self-confidence was back. Fear was as much a stranger to him as it had ever been. He no longer gave a damn what kind of animal could kill and eat a Wanderjahrian cow. The one-sided fight against the guerrilla ambush had fully restored his equilibrium. Thinking of the FPs, he had to admit that during the several days since the firefight they had begun to look more like soldiers. Nowhere near like Marines, of course, but maybe as good as Confederation Army recruits halfway through basic training.

Yes, Schultz was feeling good—good enough that he wanted to take his shift back out and find some guerrillas, see how his troops would perform. He was feeing so good he didn't even notice that he was beginning to think of it as *his* shift, as though he actually was the commander, a proper NCO. Nossir. Acting Shift Sergeant Schultz wasn't some kind of NCO, he was a Confederation Marine Corps lance corporal, just what he wanted to be. Not a man in charge, not the responsible one. And his men were finally listening to him, doing what he wanted them to. *His* men were turning into, by-damn! soldiers.

Acting Shift Sergeant Chan had his doubts, but then Chan always had doubts. Was he doing everything he could to turn his shift of FPs into proper soldiers? Were they progressing fast enough? They were improving every day, that was evident. When he looked around at the other platoons and shifts in the 257th Feldpolizei, he saw that his shift was improving as much as any. During occasional moments of objective honesty, he even saw that his shift was improving faster than many of the others. Already he trusted his men to follow his orders in the field. Soon, he thought, they would be able to go on short patrols without Marine supervision and acquit themselves well—maybe they could do that already. He needed to talk to Sergeant Hyakowa, see if something could be arranged.

* * *

Acting Shift Sergeant MacIlargie was experiencing the frustration and pride of mixed emotions. It was almost half an hour since he'd sent his shift—under the leadership of their normal commander, Acting Assistant Shift Sergeant Nafciel—into the woods south of the 257th's headquarters. The instructions he'd given them were simple: patrol the area, don't be seen. He gave them ten minutes, and then, invisible in his chameleons, went into the woods after them. This should be easy, he'd thought. It shouldn't take more than five minutes for him to find them. He'd chuckled quietly in anticipation of how startled they'd be when he began moving along their column, whispering in their ears, tapping them on their shoulders.

Now, after almost twenty minutes of fruitless searching, he was feeling pride in how effective his training in field movement had been. After almost twenty minutes of searching, he hadn't found them. That fruitless searching was likewise the source of the frustration he was feeling. He was a highly trained and skilled Confederation Marine. Something had to be wrong if he couldn't find fifteen half-trained, not very skilled local yokels in a patch of nearly open woodland that was hardly more than two kilometers along its greatest axis.

Then it dawned on him what they must be doing and he got angry. He'd taught them too well about how to avoid their sergeants and officers; they'd probably snuck out of the woods and gone someplace else to goof off, as he would have in that kind of training situation. Well, they weren't going to get away with it. He was going to find them, and when he did, he'd have a piece of every one of their hides. And a bigger piece of Nafciel's hide! Nobody was going to get away with pulling this kind of drek on PFC MacIlargie. Nossir! He knew how to do something they didn't know he could do. He hadn't hunted bunniwolfs when he was growing up back home on Saint Brendan's for nothing. He knew how to track, and he was going to track them down. And then there was going to be hell to pay!

MacIlargie raced back to where the shift had entered the woods and examined the ground. There were the signs, plain as day. A curved line in the semisoft ground showed where someone had planted a foot. A U marked the heel print of someone else. A few meters into the woods he saw a broken-stemmed treelet someone had carelessly stepped on. A little farther, a snapped twig. There, a fragment of another U-shaped heel print. Every five or ten meters one of those clumsy FPs left some kind of sign. He was probably following them faster than they were moving when they left these signs, he thought. It wasn't possible that such clumsy men could evade his view. He'd catch up with them in no time at all.

It didn't occur to him that if fifteen men left one sign every five or ten meters, that meant they were leaving an average of one sign per man every one-hundred-plus meters. If it had, he would have realized the men of his shift were moving very, very well indeed.

After fifteen minutes of tracking, MacIlargie found himself deep in the middle of the woods. He stopped examining the ground, stood erect, and stared unseeing into the trees while he thought about it. His shift had to have been right here *after* he entered the woods looking for them. So if they were in the middle of the woods after he began looking for them, they probably hadn't left them to find a place to goof off. That meant that instead of patrolling, they'd set up an ambush—either that or they found a place to hide and relax while he wasted his time and energy trying to spot moving men.

Well, they weren't going to get away with that either! They were supposed to be patrolling, not sitting in an ambush—and certainly not relaxing in some hidey-hole. He was definitely going to have some hides!

Moments later, MacIlargie found several signs clustered in one small area. He hadn't seen most of them before: shallow cups depressed in the ground—knee prints; a few flattened areas where men had gone prone. The shift had stopped here. Why?

It wasn't long before a suspicion began to grow in his mind. Fifty meters from where the shift had stopped, their signs led to the place where he'd stopped looking for them and backtracked to where they'd entered the woods. From there the signs followed the route he'd taken. Why, why . . .

those . . . They didn't! They couldn't possibly! He was in his chameleons. They couldn't see him. It wasn't possible that they were following him! As impossible as it seemed, the signs continued to follow his route.

Again MacIlargie stopped and thought. Abruptly, he spun around and examined the woods to his rear. Nobody. He shook his head. This is weird, he thought. He resumed tracking. The tracks continued to follow his route almost to where he'd begun tracking them. Fifty meters from the edge of the woods he again found signs of the shift stopping. From there the signs cut across and began following the route he'd taken tracking them.

Again he stopped. "This is absurd," he said aloud. He turned around and carefully examined the woods behind him. He couldn't see any sign of anything animate. What was going on here? He lifted his hand to his helmet and lowered his infras.

Instantly, he saw red splotches. Man-size red splotches.

He focused on one of the red splotches and lifted the infra visor. His focus was on the base of a grospalm about sixty meters away. He dropped the infras back into place and focused on another red splotch. When he lifted the visor, he was looking at a meter-high fernlike bush. He did it a third time with the same result. Shaking his head, he began walking toward the red splotches his infras told him must be his shift. He was less than twenty meters away from the nearest red splotch before he could make out the man with his naked eyes.

No. His men weren't goofing off, they were patrolling. But someone was pulling a joke on him. The FP was wearing a Marine-issue helmet with the infra visor down. Under the lower lip of the visor, MacIlargie could see the man's grinning mouth.

MacIlargie continued into the middle of the shift. He stood tall and looked all around. Even here he couldn't see all of them without his infras. Every one he could see was wearing a Marine-issue helmet with its infra visor down.

"Very good, people," he said loudly. "This exercise is concluded. Fall in on me." Pride returned. His shift had done well. They had learned well. He'd taught well. He wasn't over his anger, he was still going to have someone's hide. But it wasn't going to be his men's. It was going to be the hide of whoever had given them the Marine-issue helmets without telling him. He only hoped it wasn't Staff Sergeant Bass. Or Sergeant Hyakowa. Or Corporal Dornhofer, or . . . He started getting frustrated again. Damn! Unless it was Godenov who gave his men the helmets, he wasn't going to have anybody's hide.

Acting Shift Sergeant Godenov was doing a lot of grumbling since first squad killed the guerrilla ambush. Whenever the Marines weren't actively training their FPs, they engaged in discussion, sometimes heated, about whether or not the FPs were good enough. Godenov flinched every time he heard a Marine say the FPs weren't "good enough" yet—or worse, that they might never be good enough. He particularly hated it whenever someone said *his* shift wasn't good enough yet. Even though intellectually he knew nobody was saying *he* wasn't good enough, emotionally he reacted as though they were. He couldn't help it, he'd been hearing "good enough" and "not good enough" directed at him all his life. Why hadn't his ancestors changed the family name when they began speaking English? The name could be a terrible burden to bear.

Truthfully, the FPs weren't good enough yet. Not by Marine standards they weren't. Of course, by Marine standards nobody who didn't wear the Eagle, Globe, and Starstream was good enough.

Well, PFC Isidore Godenov was tired of hearing "good enough" and "not good enough." His shift was going to be good enough. More than that. He was going to do his best to make his shift the best in the entire 257th Feldpolizei Battalion. He'd show them all he was "good enough"—and then some.

To that end, he had his shift out in the first range of hills west of the GSB headquarters practicing immediate action drills. The Wanderjahrian guerrillas, the self-styled "Peoples Liberation Army," favored the same tactic used by most guerrilla forces for thousands of years—the hit-and-run ambush.

There are three things an infantry unit can do when it walks into an ambush. One is for everyone to run away—in which event many of them will get shot in the back. This isn't considered a viable option, though it's the option of choice of untrained or demoralized troops. The second is for everyone to remain in place, get organized, and fight back. But as the ambush in the Bavaran Hills had demonstrated, that can also lead to disaster. The third choice is an "immediate action drill"; that is, everybody immediately reacts aggressively to the ambush—nobody runs away, nobody waits for orders.

Ambushers always start with the upper hand. They know where you are and have fire superiority before you even know they're there. You're exposed to their sight and fire while they're hidden from yours. Immediate action drills teach troops to get out of an ambusher's lines of sight and fire, quickly build up return fire to match or better that of the ambushers, and to locate them. Not necessarily in that order.

Of course, the best way to react to an ambush is to discover it before you walk into it—as when Corporal Leach spotted the ambush a few days earlier. But that's usually not possible. So good commanders in counterguerrilla conflicts spend a lot of time and energy training their men in immediate reaction drills.

The FPs were in their camouflage field uniforms; Godenov wore his chameleons. He wasn't leading the patrol; he'd placed the men back under the command of their regular shift sergeant, Lahrmann. Instead he walked along watching them. Sometimes he was on one side, sometimes the other. He also followed, or went ahead to observe from the front. All in all, he was pretty satisfied with their movement. They weren't silent, but they were far from noisy. They weren't taking advantage of all the concealment they could, but neither were they walking upright and out in the open. It was a tremendous improvement in a relatively short time.

After giving basic instruction in how to react to an ambush, Godenov began looking for good ambush sites. Whenever he found one before his men passed it, he'd take a position in it and shout "BANG-BANG!" when his men were in the killing zone, and watch how they reacted. After each drill he debriefed the men.

The first time Godenov shouted "BANG-BANG!" his men

must have been suffering from opening-night jitters. They jumped, startled, at the sound of his voice, and most of them stood around for several seconds before they did anything. The second time, they dropped in place and started firing in all directions. The only ones who took advantage of any cover were those who happened to have some kind of cover right where they dropped. And they weren't shooting live, of course, they shouted "BANG-BANG!" and felt silly doing it. They did have live batteries for their blasters, as they had to because of the possibility that guerrillas were in the area, but Godenov made sure their weapons were unloaded—he didn't want to risk getting accidentally fried by one of his own men.

The third time he indicated an ambush by shouting "BANG-BANG!" most of them dove for the nearest cover and BANG-BANGed in his direction. No question, they were improving with practice. Some of them even put some enthusiasm into their BANG-BANGs the third time.

He also showed them how to assault through an ambush if one was spotted in time.

After another three mock ambushes, and a couple where his ambush was spotted before it was tripped, Godenov decided his men were good enough that they needed a force-on-force drill to improve further. Force-on-force was provided; unwittingly, but it came when it was needed.

The woodland Godenov was patrolling his shift through was little different from the woods that bordered the precinct parade ground. It had the near-ubiquitous family groupings of grospalms, but the rolling land wasn't level enough to support as high a concentration of hochbaums, so there were fewer of them. Instead spikers, which seemed to prefer climbing ground, were fairly common. The scattered undergrowth was woodier than the fuzzy and formless fernlike growth on the flatland. This was a grazing area for the huge herbivores the Wanderjahrians called cows and sheep, so the ground was fairly bare.

Godenov was a hundred meters ahead of his shift and a little to the right of their line of march, wondering whether there was any point in putting them through another drill today, when he thought he heard someone say something somewhere in front of him. So far as he knew, he and his shift were the only Marines or FPs in this area. He froze in place and slowly raised a hand to lower his infras. He peered toward the grospalms where he thought the voice had come from, but didn't see any telltale red. Slowly, silently, fully alert, Godenov drifted toward his right front. He listened carefully as he moved, but didn't hear the voice. After he'd gone more than twenty meters, he stopped and listened again. Still nothing. Slowly, he went straight ahead, listening and looking. And then he saw a well-concealed man sitting in a shallow depression from which he could easily watch the animal trail the FPs were paralleling. Quickly, Godenov looked deeper into the grospalm clump. He saw three more men. He wanted to continue checking to see if there were more than four, but they suddenly changed their attitudes and focused sharply in the direction from which he'd come. Godenov looked back. His men were coming into view from behind a row of man-high bushes.

This was an ambush for real.

Still careful not to make any noise, Godenov moved as fast as he could back to his men, easily dodging the few bushes in his way. He was pleased that none of the FPs flinched when his invisible-man's voice said, "Look alive! Lock and load. This is no drill. There's real guerrillas just ahead of us to the right."

The FPs were shifting from left to right as they walked, watching both sides of their path. Godenov was pleased that they all tried to conceal the motions of loading their weapons from the people watching from their right front.

"I know where they're at," he told his men. "I'll give the signal right before we enter their killing zone. When I do, attack to your right front."

By the time he finished giving his instructions, the front of the patrol had already passed the first guerrilla position.

"NOW!" Godenov shouted. Before the word was completely out of his mouth, he pointed his blaster at where he knew the first guerrilla was and pressed the firing lever. The acrid stink of charred, bubbling flesh almost immediately assailed his nose—he got his kill.

His men were doing exactly what he'd taught them. They were rushing in the direction he told them to, yelling fiercely and burning everything in their paths. Two of the guerrillas were able to get off one wild shot each before they were killed. The third was like the one Godenov shot—fried before he had a chance to fire. There were no others. It hadn't been an ambush, it was an observation post.

"Cease fire! Cease fire!" Godenov shouted as soon as he realized they weren't getting any return fire.

"Secure the perimeter," Acting Assistant Shift Sergeant Lahrmann immediately called out. He bustled about, making sure the men were in defensive positions around the observation post, then joined Godenov, who, stomach churning at the grisly task, was inspecting the corpses.

"Not enough of them left to tell us anything," Lahrmann said, shaking his head. Despite his words, he couldn't help grinning. This was the first shift-size action he'd ever been on that was such a clear-cut victory for his side. His eyes shined as he looked at Godenov. "Your tactics really work, Acting Shift Sergeant. You teach us good. We will kill many guerrillas with what you teach us."

Churning stomach or no, Godenov beamed.

"Commander . . ." Fighter Juarez burst into the chamber Hing was using as his field HQ. "A runner just brought an eyes-only message."

Hing made sure the confidential papers he was packing for the move back to the Che Loi Brigade's base were covered before he turned to face Juarez and held out a hand to accept the message. But Juarez had nothing to give him.

"Where is it?"

Juarez looked apologetic and almost stammered as he said, "Commander, the runner refuses to hand it to anybody but you."

That was strange. What could be going on? Hing's voice didn't betray his thoughts when he said, "Bring the runner to me."

"Yessir. Immediately, Commander." Juarez spun about and ran off.

Juarez was back in less than a minute. The runner he brought with him wasn't someone Hing knew. As if in confirmation that the man wasn't a member of the Che Loi Brigade, he wore the green and blue tab on his collar that identified him as being from PLA Staat Command. Hing raised an eyebrow. For a runner from PLA Staat Command to hand-deliver a message to a brigade commander personally was most unusual. And the runner looked surprisingly fresh for having come all the way from wherever Staat HQ was currently located.

The headquarters runner looked at Hing, then glanced at a 2-D image he held in his hand. Satisfied that he was indeed facing the man to whom he was to deliver the message, he snapped to attention and announced, "Commander Hing, I have a message from PLA Staat Command. It is for your eyes only." From somewhere in his uniform he produced a sealed envelope and ceremoniously held it out.

Hing's expression showed nothing of what he was feeling as he accepted the envelope and casually examined it. It was closed, with a self-destruct seal that would open only to the thumbprint of the addressee. Hing remained facing the man as he pressed his thumb against the seal and the envelope popped open. He extracted the single sheet of paper it contained. The paper was printed on one side only, and he continued to face Juarez and the HQ runner as he read it, leaving only the blank side for them to see. Juarez understood the protocol of confidentiality and looked at the floor. The runner boldly kept his eyes on the commander though he didn't look at the paper.

It took only a few seconds for Hing to read the two sentences. It explained why the runner looked so fresh. Hing looked up at the man and asked, "What more can you tell me?"

"Nothing, Commander. I was told simply to deliver the message to your hands only and await your instructions." His words were plain, but his manner of speech told Hing he probably knew more. But Hing had no time to try to get more information out of him, not if he was to obey the instructions he'd just received. He looked at Juarez.

"Assemble the staff. Instantly."

"Yes, Commander. Instantly." Juarez ran off and began calling out names.

They were assembled in moments. All looked curiously at the runner, but no one commented or questioned.

"I have been summoned to Staat headquarters," Hing said without preamble as soon as everyone was present. He held up the message the runner had brought and read it. " 'You will accompany the bearer of this message to Staat headquarters without delay. He has transportation.' " Looking back at his staff, he said, "Lieutenant Harbottle is in command of the movement back to brigade headquarters. Subcommander Sukarnohon will be in command until I return." He looked at Cildair, the senior medic. "Lieutenant Pincote is to remain sufficiently sedated that she can't pull another stunt like she did today until the synthskin grafts. Is everything understood?" Startled by the news, some members of the staff simply stared at Hing, others nodding understanding. "Then carry on," Hing said. He picked up his backpack, which was already packed. "Take me to our transportation," he told the headquarters runner.

Not long after, as impatience about late-returning observation posts began to grow, a runner raced in with a report of a four-man OP that couldn't be found. But there were clear signs of fighting at the OP site.

CHAPTER
FOURTEEN

A dozen heavily armed men dressed in black burst suddenly through the doors of the small chapel. The crash of their entry stopped Reverend Walther Handschu right in the middle of his sermon, which was from Chapter 5 of Paul's Epistle to the Romans: "Therefore, being justified by faith, we have peace with God through our Lord Jesus Christ."

"Who are you?" Gretel Siebensberg asked, standing and facing the intruders. The bright morning sunlight shining through the broken doors outlined the men as huge black hulks crowding into the aisle. Motes of dust swirled about their heads in the golden sunlight streaming from behind them, but their faces were in total darkness.

One man detached himself from the group and strode heavily down the aisle, weapons swinging and clattering, to stand directly over the diminutive woman. As he passed by the other worshipers, they gasped when they saw the leering grin on his face—his teeth had been filed to sharp points. Reverend Handschu stood transfixed in his pulpit, his mouth gaping open, the worn copy of the New Testament from which he was taking the morning's sermon held open in one hand, the other raised as if in benediction. Mother Siebensberg, as she was known among her people, the oligarch of Friedland, the leader and protector of her six million citizens, and the chief religious figure for the Christian congregations in her domains, faced the apparition indignant but without fear.

"Bitch," the man growled, "I am your judgment."

* * *

Gretel Siebensberg was a devout Christian who practiced the simple religious rites of her forebears. She did not demand that her people accept that faith, but all were encouraged to, and church attendance among the people of Friedland was the highest of the Staats on Wanderjahr.

In her household, everyone attended chapel twice a day, at dawn and at dusk. Services were conducted by Reverend Walther Handschu, Siebensberg's personal chaplain, and she attended them whenever she was in her capital city of Kreuz-stadt. For Sunday services she attended the United Brotherhood church in the city or the smaller church in the nearby village of Siebensdorf, where the people who maintained her local estates and farms lived.

The religious tradition of the United Brotherhood was one of utter simplicity. A pacifist sect from its earliest days, the Brotherhood rejected the violence and implicit Jewish nation-alism of the Old Testament for the peace and salvation of the New. Each copy of the New Testament used in Friedland was printed in Old High German and English. Old High German was taught in the schools, and services were often conducted in that language. The United Brotherhood rejected a church cal-endar, and traditional holy days such as Christmas and Easter were not observed by the congregations in Friedland. The only music permitted in their churches were the hymns the congre-gations sang from a common hymnal. And each congregation was independent of any church hierarchy because there wasn't one in Friedland. Pastors were "called" from the congregations themselves. A body of scriptural exegesis was available, com-piled over the centuries by various scholars, and learning those texts was the only education any minister of the United Brother-hood was ever required to have.

Life was good for the people of Friedland. Austere in her personal habits and incorruptible in her public life, Mother Siebensberg nevertheless believed in hard work and enjoying the fruits of honest labor. With the recent rise in income from the production of thule on her farms, she had invested heavily in benefits for her people. There was no need for Feldpolizei garrisons in Friedland, and the Stadtpolizei organization in

Kreuzstadt was a law enforcement agency in name only. There was little banditry or crime in Friedland. Now, on this beautiful early-spring morning, all this was about to change.

"Leave at once!" Mother Siebensberg ordered the grinning hulk standing before her. Imperiously, she pointed toward the chapel door. The other men had taken up positions along the walls and now stood with their weapons leveled at the two dozen worshipers.

The man hit her, so hard that blood spurted from the side of her head. Mother Siebensberg fell heavily between the pews and lay there insensate. A collective gasp of horror went up from the other worshipers, who were kept in their seats only by the muzzles of the guns being pointed at them. The man who had hit Mother, apparently the leader, drew a machete from a scabbard at his side. With one long step he crossed the space between the front row of pews and the pulpit and, swinging the machete, severed Reverend Handschu's head cleanly from his neck. Eyes wide, mouth open, the head flew a bloody trajectory to the wall, then bounced to the floor, rolling under the pew where twelve-year-old Michelle Nguyen sat with her mother, Gretel Siebensberg's chief housekeeper. Michelle, staring in wide-eyed horror at the minister's head, instinctively raised her feet to keep the blood off her shoes. The reverend's body stood erect for a moment, blood pumping out of the carotids in bright red streams, before it crumpled with a thud to the floor. In the total silence that followed the sound of the body hitting the boards, his Bible fluttered noisily down after him.

The man casually wiped the blood off his machete on the shirt of Praxiteles Romero, Mother's chief steward, who collapsed with a heart attack and died right in the front pew.

"Where is your Jesus now?" the man roared, holding his machete high above his head. Michelle Nguyen began to scream, a high-pitched wail that penetrated every corner of the small chapel. As if it was the signal for pandemonium, everyone began to scream and sob and beg for mercy.

"Outside!" the leader bellowed, and his men began to push

and shove the panicked worshipers out through the broken doors. The brilliant morning sunlight and breezes redolent with the perfume of spring flowers contrasted incongruously with the terror of the congregation. The men herded them into a small group in the courtyard outside the chapel. Mothers comforted children, and fathers comforted mothers and children, and all stared fearfully at the armed men. The leader emerged from the chapel, dragging Mother by her hair. He swung her frail body by one powerful arm and flung her hard upon the stones, where she landed with a thud and the sickening crunch of breaking bone. She moaned and lay still.

"My name is Lieutenant Xuyen Phong, and this area is now under the protection of the Peoples Liberation Army," he bellowed. "Those of you who have committed no crimes against the workers of Friedland will be spared. The rest will suffer the punishments prescribed by the party." He snapped his fingers and one of his men stepped forward with a list of names. The man who called himself Lieutenant Phong glanced briefly at the list. "Gretel Siebensberg," he announced, and paused. "Death by burning." The crowd gasped. Two of Phong's men stepped forward and lifted Mother from the stones. Quickly they bound her with wire and then hoisted her semiconscious form into the air and left her hanging from the branch of a nearby tree. Her clothes were quickly saturated with a flammable liquid. Phong stood nearby with a lighted taper.

The drenching had partially revived Mother. She understood she was about to die, but had not heard Phong's pronouncement and so couldn't guess the reason why. "Good-bye, my friends," she whispered to her quaking servants. "God will forgive these men. I am going to see Jesus."

"Witness the death of this traitor to the people!" Phong shouted. He stepped close to Mother and looked into her eyes. "I ask again, where is your Jesus now, bitch?" he demanded, and set her on fire. He stepped back quickly as Mother's clothing burst into flames. In seconds she was a twisting ball of agony. The horrified onlookers watched as her clothes were consumed and then her hair. Her prayers quickly turned to screams, the screams to inarticulate wailing that died away gradually as the flames singed her lungs and her flesh swelled and burst and then began to turn black.

Turning away from Mother's smoking corpse swinging obscenely from the tree limb, which by now was also on fire, Phong announced, "When I call your name, step over here." He pointed to a spot in a corner of the yard by the chapel wall and a thick row of cedars. When he finished reading the list, only the youngest children were left from the original group. They continued staring blank-eyed at Mother's blackened corpse.

"Death by machete!" Phong shouted, drawing his own. To the cowering children, he announced, "Witness the death of these traitors to the people!" With that he and seven of his men set upon the adults, and in moments had hacked all of them to death.

Michelle Nguyen tore her eyes away from Mother in time to witness her own mother fall under the razor-sharp blades. Blood flew everywhere, and soon the killers were drenched in it. The victims screamed piteously and begged for mercy but were shown none at all. The machetes rose and fell again and again. When they struck the cobblestones, sparks flew. Too overcome with terror to cry out anymore, little Michelle watched dumbly as the men went methodically about killing the adults. She remembered afterward the vivid red footprints the men left upon the stones as they walked away from the dismembered remains of her family and their friends.

"They had to die, little ones," Phong said gently to the shivering children pathetically clutching one another in a small group. "That is what happens to traitors. Tell that to those who will come to investigate. As a token of its sincerity, the party wishes each of you to have one of these. Rejoice, little ones. This is the dawning of a new age for the people of Friedland." With that he handed each of the seven survivors a little book brightly bound in red leather. The children accepted the books wordlessly and clutched them tightly in their tiny hands. That is how they were found hours later by a rescue party sent out from the city.

*   *   *

"Ted," Chief Long began without preamble when he'd raised Brigadier Sturgeon on his vid hookup, "I have terrible news." Briefly the chief told him what he knew of the massacre in Friedland. "The subcommissioner of Friedland's Stadtpolizei force has asked me to investigate."

"Guerrillas?"

"Looks like it. Ted, I need fast transportation and firepower. Can you spare a couple of Dragons and some men for me? Whoever did this may still be around."

"I'll send twenty-five men from the landing party security detail. Transportation will be ready for you at the port in, oh, twenty minutes. You'll be in Friedland in less than two hours. Keep me informed." The brigadier's image disappeared from the screen.

"Pete, Alois! To me!" Chief Long shouted.

Commissioner Landser's face turned ashen white when he heard the news. "I knew Gretel Siebensberg," he muttered. "Who in God's name would want to hurt her?"

"That is what we will try to find out, my dear Alois. Get me six of your best detectives. Pete, grab your lads and some personal things. You are all going with me to Friedland. Alois, you come too. Turn over the operation here to your deputy. We'll be gone several days."

The bodies of the victims had not yet begun to stiffen by the time Chief Long and his party arrived on the scene. The subcommissioner of the Kreuzstadt Stadtpolizei, a nervous little man way out of his depth, had done three things correctly: cordoned off the crime scene to prevent contamination of the evidence; isolated the witnesses immediately; and called Chief Long for assistance. Still badly shaken by what had happened, his voice was unsteady as he tried to answer questions.

"It—It w-was the smoke from the f-fires of Siebensdorf burning that f-first attracted our attention," he told Chief Long. "The f-fire department was f-first on the scene. When I got here . . ." His voice trailed off and he gestured helplessly at the mutilated bodies lying about the small courtyard just outside the chapel. Someone had cut Mother's charred corpse down, and it now lay, contorted, under a blanket. The remains of the butchered worshipers lay where they had fallen, crawling with swarms of buzzers attracted by the blood.

Finished at the chapel, the raiders had then marched into the village of Siebensdorf and slaughtered everyone there, over three hundred men, women, and children. After torching the place, they had disappeared toward the mountains in the northeast, little Michelle reported.

Brigadier Sturgeon's twenty-five-man security detail immediately established a defensive perimeter around the chapel. Now the small group of policemen and the two Marines, Dean and Claypoole, stood in the courtyard, surveying the horror. Claypoole, face white, stared at Dean and shook his head. Chief Long pulled the blanket away from Mother's contorted corpse and someone gasped. Its arms and legs flexed into the fetal position, it was impossible to tell who the corpse had been, even whether it was that of a man or a woman. Chief Long hastily threw the blanket back over the cadaver. He turned to the men standing around him. He said nothing for a few moments, just stared off in the direction of the mountains. Then he began issuing rapid-fire orders.

"Lieutenant," he said, addressing the officer in command of the security detail. "I want you to contact the *Denver* at once. We need drone surveillance here, every inch of the continent. If the men who did this are still here and still operating in a group, we must find them.

"Dean, Claypoole. Contact the intelligence officer on the *Denver*. I want you to review every centimeter of tape the satellite surveillance system has taken of aircraft and seagoing vessels arriving and departing from the port of Kreuzstadt back ten days from today. I also want you to review all electronic and voice intercepts the *Denver* has made from this region during that same period. I'll have one of Commissioner Landser's detectives assist you." Anxious to be excused, the Marines hurried off to set up the necessary communications and data-processing networks.

Chief Long then ordered the assembled detectives to collect

and sort evidence, including getting detailed statements from the survivors.

"Pete," he turned to Lieutenant Constantine, "take all of these little red books back to the forensic lab at Brosigville with you immediately. Have everyone here who's touched them fingerprinted. You know the drill. Do what you can to lift and ID latent prints that don't match the kids' or the cops'. I want every detail of these books compared with a genuine article, one of the books we know was taken from the guerrillas." He pointed to the bloody bootprints on the courtyard cobblestones. "Alois, we need to compare those prints with every known type of shoe and boot manufactured on this planet. Start with those that may have been captured from the guerrillas. You men," he addressed the detectives who'd come with him from Brosigville, "scour this entire area. You know how to do it. The murderers must have left more behind them than these little red books."

But they had not.

The survey of arriving and departing vessels and a review of intercepted communications proved fruitless, as Chief Long half expected it would, but it was something that had to be done. Given the disposition of the people of Friedland, he'd been pretty sure all along that the raiders had not come from among them, but had been infiltrated into the country in very small groups as visitors or legitimate businessmen. With virtually no police force available in the country, it proved impossible to conduct a canvass of the population, to identify suspicious persons or strangers who might have been seen anywhere around the capital city before the massacre. The news media throughout the country was cooperative, but after five days no promising leads had been obtained.

Feldpolizei files were scoured for any mention of a man named Xuyen Phong among the guerrillas, but none was found, as Chief Long had also expected.

The security element tracked the murderers into the foothills of the nearby mountains, where they disappeared completely. To the Marines, this meant they had been airlifted out of the

area, but satellite surveillance had shown no aircraft in the
vicinity. They had left nothing behind but the little red books
and some footprints.

Leaving his detectives to follow up on the investigation,
Long and his party returned to Brosigville.

Feeling awkward in civilian garb, Alois Landser sat uncomfortably in a small café off an obscure side street in downtown
Brosigville. He had only just returned from Friedland, and the
horror of what had happened there still hung about him like a
pall. He was not only depressed but angry, so angry in fact that
he had called for this unusual face-to-face meeting with a valuable and very confidential source.

Landser regarded his wineglass darkly. It contained Wein-
bauer Katzenwasser '36, a rare Wanderjahrian vintage that
often graced the table at Oligarch Arschmann's villa, and one
Landser, a connoisseur, normally relished. But that afternoon
the glass sat untouched. Nervously he brushed at some lint on
his trousers and then looked again into the street outside.

Since his appointment as commissioner of the Arschland
Stadtpolizei, Alois Landser had been collecting information on
people. His files were extensive and very confidential. Much of
the information, along with the identities of his informants, he
was sharing with Chief Long and the Marines, as he had been
ordered to do. But he had kept some of it deliberately to himself, files he'd compiled on Wanderjahr's most prominent
people, including the oligarchs themselves.

That afternoon, one of his most highly placed and trusted
informants was to meet with him. Normally Landser did not
meet with informants personally, not even the most trust-
worthy ones. Communication usually took place through drops
and blind signals Landser had worked out with them over time.
Initial contact always had to do with official police business of
some sort, but afterward, information was passed on through
Landser's secret communications system, which he controlled
personally when dealing with the most highly placed contacts.
The man who would be coming through the door anytime now
had agreed to inform because, some years before, his brother

had been charged with a very serious crime and Landser had gotten the charges dismissed. He was now paying the commissioner back for that favor.

Landser never used real names when dealing with his informants. This man's code name was Schlange, and the man he was reporting on, one of the oligarchs, was Verrater, "Snake" and "Traitor" respectively. To Landser the name Schlange fit the man too well; he was also supplying information to the bandits. Verrater? If the suspicions Landser was forming about him proved correct, he would derive the utmost pleasure from making the arrest.

Schlange came through the door. Squinting his eyes in the semidarkness after the bright sunshine outside, he bowed slightly at Landser before sliding into the chair opposite his.

"Good afternoon, most gracious commissioner," he said, smiling unctuously. Landser grimaced as he signed for the waiter to bring another glass. "Thank you," the man said as he was served. Schlange regarded the dark red wine for a moment and gulped half his glass down. "Ahhh," he sighed. Landser was offended. He sipped gently at his own wine, but he was so upset at being in the boor's presence that he could not even savor the bouquet.

"Herr Schlange," Landser began, "if you help me now you are off the hook. I will not trouble you anymore."

The man he called Snake nodded. "This is most generous of you, Herr Commissioner."

"I am not a generous man, Herr Schlange, you know that," Landser replied coldly. "I want revenge, and if you help me get that, you are a free man."

"At your service, Herr Commissioner."

Landser leaned across the table. "Answer some questions." Schlange nodded. "Did Verrater set off the bomb that killed my brother?"

"No."

"You're sure of this?" Landser was disappointed at the answer.

"Absolutely."

"Do you know who pulled off the Morgenluft raid?"

"Verrater." Landser's heart jumped. The raiders nearly killed Commander Peters, an officer of the Confederation Marines. He had the bastard! Maybe Verrater didn't kill his brother, as Schlange believed, but he had him anyway. Landser was a policeman, and he could not suppress a surge of joy at the prospect of breaking a case and bringing a criminal to justice, even if it did not bring the personal satisfaction he wanted.

"He wanted to get rid of his closest rival." Schlange shrugged. "He also wants the Marines to act more quickly against the bandits. Two for one." He passed a microcassette across the table. "I recorded the conversation between Verrater and his agent in Morgenluft. There is other interesting information on there as well." He smiled. Landser pocketed the cassette.

"Oligarch Siebensberg? Do you know who murdered her?"

Schlange shrugged again. "Not the bandits either, that's for sure. But not Verrater either. That narrows the list, doesn't it? I have my suspicions, though."

"Don't play games with me." Landser's voice had turned icy. "Who?"

"Zitze." This was the code name for another oligarch.

Landser sat back in his chair as if slapped in the face. "Impossible!"

Schlange sipped at his wine. "Only a suspicion."

"I cannot believe this," he said after a moment. "I need confirmation of this . . . this speculation."

Schlange nodded. "There is someone, an employee of Zitze's." He gulped the rest of the wine noisily and regarded the empty glass with satisfaction. "Nice, but not sweet enough, don't you think?" Fury silently mounting, Landser glared at the man. "You know, everyone involved wants to eliminate his rivals—"

"The man's name, Herr Schlange!"

"—on the Ruling Council," Schlange continued unperturbed, "and have the Marines step in and eliminate the bandits. The Marines and the bandits are the only ones whose motives are honest in any of this business. That is why I support the bandits, Herr Commissioner. I know you don't care about any of this because you are not political, but I have principles." Schlange grinned and flicked a forefinger against his wineglass, which produced a melodious ping.

The sun glinting off the windshield of a landcar passing very slowly by in the street suddenly drew Landser's attention. "Down!" he shouted, and dived for the floor.

Schlange was not so fast. The first bullets from an automatic weapon shattered the windows, and the next slammed into the informant. The first entered his jaw on the left side at the gum line and exited the right side of his mouth in a spray of blood and tooth fragments. Another struck him just behind his left eye and angled up to exit through the right side of his head, taking much of the right frontal lobe of his brain with it. A third projectile struck his left external carotid artery before plunging down to bury itself in the first cervical vertebra.

Landser drew his own pistol and, as the shooter attempted to reload, fired through the shattered windows at the passenger side of the landcar. The figure sitting there jerked several times before the car sped down the street. Running out into the bright sunshine, Landser took a shooting position in the middle of the street and fired the rest of his magazine at the swiftly departing vehicle. He could clearly see his bullets striking, but they failed to stop the car. Landser stood still for a moment, catching his breath, his still-smoking pistol dangling from one hand. Then he dashed back into the café.

The owner and the waiter stood helplessly over Schlange, who was still alive. A diminishing stream of blood pumped from the side of his neck into a widening pool on the floor. Fragments of gray matter protruded from the exit wound on top of his skull, mixing with the blood beneath him. His one good eye stared up at Landser while his lungs worked spasmodically to expel the blood flowing into them from his destroyed mouth. He gurgled and wheezed as frothy bubbles burst between his bloody lips.

As he calmly reloaded his pistol and slammed it back into his holster, Landser stood over Schlange. Miraculously, the table where they had been sitting remained upright, and Landser's hardly touched glass sat there invitingly. Landser shrugged, picked it up, and took a slow mouthful of the wine. He rolled it around on his tongue before swallowing it. "Ah! An excellent vintage!" he told the owner, who stared at him in horror. "Schlange! Schlange," he said, bending over the dying informant, "the employee's name? His name, please?"

A huge blood bubble burst forth from between Schlange's lips with a sound that could have been someone's name: "Rajinderpal." Landser remained bent over the dying man for a few more moments, but satisfied he would say no more, he straightened up. "Schlange," he said, "you are a mess. Try to clean yourself up before the funeral.

"Gentlemen," Landser bowed toward the owner and his waiter, "you run a most excellent establishment. I shall recommend it to my friends." Landser carefully replaced his glass on the table and strode jauntily out of the café. Neither man thought to ask him who would pay the tab.

"I wish I was back with the platoon, where at least we could shoot back at a real enemy," Claypoole said one night after their return from Friedland. The massacre of Mother Siebensberg and her followers had been the single worst event of its kind in the history of Wanderjahr. Not nearly as many people had lost their lives in the witchcraft frenzy two centuries earlier. That had been due to hysteria; the massacre in Friedland was cold-blooded and calculated murder.

"The goddamned guerrillas," Dean responded angrily, "we should hunt them down and kill the lot!"

They were sitting at their workstations at police headquarters, reviewing the satellite reconnaissance tapes from the *Denver*'s databases for the second time. The search had now been extended to include any information picked up prior to the attack at Morgenluft, with the same results: nothing.

Chief Long came in and asked the pair what they were doing. "Nothing, sir," Claypoole said.

"Come with me, then, lads, we do have something." He led them to the police communications center, where a young lieutenant in the Brosigville police intelligence unit by the name of Bashwa was also reviewing *Denver* intercepts.

"You see," Bashwa explained, "the chief here thought it might be a good idea for a Stadtpolizei officer to review those intercepts since we are familiar with the political and social conditions on Wanderjahr. I went back to just before the raid on Oligarch Keutgens's villa at Morgenluft and discovered this." He played back a recording of two men talking about visitors. "What alerted me was the name 'Ludendorf.' He was a famous German general a long time ago. I concluded that possibly Ludendorf is a code name for Brigadier Sturgeon. I also assumed that whoever made the call was in the party waiting for the brigadier's arrival. I then took that man's voice print and compared it with others on file, and . . ." He punched a key on his console. The picture of a balding, middle-aged man appeared on the screen, with two voice prints beneath it. "The upper one is the recording from the *Denver*'s computer. The lower one is from a speech he made at an international conference on trade last fall. He is Lorelei Keutgens's deputy minister for commerce."

"Wow!" Claypoole exclaimed. "Question the bastard!"

"We are." Chief Long smiled.

"Who owns the other voice?" Dean asked.

"That we do not yet know," Bashwa said. "He was using a voice masker on his end. But we do know the transmission came from right here in Brosigville."

"Damned fine work, Lieutenant," Chief Long said, patting Bashwa on the shoulder. The lieutenant's dark face broke into a wide smile. "And now, my lads, we're having another small conference."

Commissioner Landser and Lieutenant Constantine were waiting for them in Chief Long's office. Landser had gotten used to the presence of the two enlisted Marines at the conferences, but he still had not accepted their presence at high-level meetings that should have been for officers only, and he did not understand why Chief Long persisted in dragging them about everywhere. But the chief had made it very clear to the commissioner and every officer on his staff that the two Marines were Brigadier Sturgeon's intelligence staff and hence deserved all the respect and assistance any police or Marine commissioned officer would expect.

"Gentlemen," Long began, "Lieutenant Constantine has done a technical intelligence sweep of this office, to ensure this conversation remains private. Let's start with what we know about the murders in Friedland. Pete?"

"The little red books were printed here on Wanderjahr," Constantine said. "We've traced the paper to a company right here in Brosigville. We're checking now with everyone who purchased that kind of paper in any quantity. We're getting no cooperation from some of the oligarchs in other Staats, but that should come as no surprise. The books contain the usual Peoples Liberation Army propaganda, mostly junk based on the ravings of an obscure twentieth-century Chinese rabble-rouser.

"The bootprints match the patterns of several popular brands of footwear manufactured on Wanderjahr that are worn by farmhands."

"What troubles me most about these attacks," Landser interjected, "is the level of their violence. The PLA has always preached that the people are their best friends and encouraged their forces not to harm them. What acts of terrorism they have committed up to now have been against prominent individuals, plantation overseers, local officials in the areas where they are strongest. But since they came here," he nodded at the two Marines, "things have turned nasty all of a sudden."

Claypoole resented the implication that somehow the presence of the Marines on Wanderjahr was contributing to these terrible crimes, but he held his tongue.

"There may be some connection," Chief Long said. Both Claypoole and Dean stared at the chief in shock. He merely winked at the two Marines.

"All of this is just too pat," Constantine said. "First the bombing here, then someone tries to kill Dean and Claypoole, then the attack against Keutgens, and now this. Particularly this last act, as if we haven't gotten the point yet that the guerrillas are supposed to be behind all these events. Where does the PLA find the men, material, and time to mount all these terrorist attacks when the Feldpolizei, being led by Marines now, is putting salt on their tails out in the boonies?"

"Yes, and do not forget," Landser chimed in, "that the most severe of these attacks have occurred in Staats where the PLA is weakest. For them to have mounted them there would require a logistical and political organization of more sophistication than they seem to possess, at least outside Arschland and the other two or three Staats where they are strongest."

"Lads?" Chief Long said to the Marines. Dean looked at Claypoole, who shrugged.

"Sir," Claypoole responded, "we're going through the satellite tapes and intercepts for the second time. The detectives here and at Friedland have helped us identify every registered flight and ship entering the territory for the ten days preceding the attack. Nothing. The same with departures up to five days after the attack. We have identified no transport either coming into the place or leaving it that wasn't there on legitimate business. It is our guess—and the detectives back us up on this— that the raiders came into Friedland in small groups, smuggling their weapons and equipment in their luggage. They may have dispersed by air, but so far we can't prove it."

Dean marveled at how smooth the speech was. Was Rachman really becoming a regular staff weenie?

"Sir," Claypoole continued, "the LT and the commissioner have good points too. I thought it was Garth who set off the bomb and shot at us, until he denied everything, and he had no reason to lie about it before he died. By the way, sir, has anybody figured out what Garth meant when he said 'Titties' set off the bomb?"

Chief Long looked at Commissioner Landser. When Landser did not offer anything, he told Claypoole, "Not yet," but he was pretty sure Landser knew.

"And then you confirmed he was spying on Multan for the guerrillas all along," Dean said. "In fact, it was he who turned in the raiders at the warehouse that night," he added.

"It's as if someone was deliberately trying to put the blame on the PLA so we'd go after them," Claypoole said, thinking out loud. Immediately he smiled to himself. So that's what the chief meant!

Chief Long smiled. "That's about what it comes down to."

"Yeah, but who?" Constantine asked.

"Who indeed?" Landser asked.

"Ah, yes, Alois, any new information on who assassinated Kalat Uxmal? Oligarch Arschmann is very anxious that you pursue that case. Why, you were with Uxmal at the time." It was a statement that begged an explanation.

"We go back a long way together." Landser smiled tightly, thinking of Schlange, the Snake, whom he had known for so many years. He exchanged glances with Chief Long. Long knew he was hiding something, but he chose not to pursue it just then. "We found the assassins' vehicle a few hours ago. The passenger's seat was covered in blood, and there were a total of a dozen bullet holes in the rear."

"Good shooting, Commissioner," Lieutenant Constantine said. Landser smiled again.

"Any motive for the shooting?" Chief Long asked.

"Uxmal was spying for the guerrillas, Chief. They may think I turned him."

Chief Long had to be careful how he responded to that nonanswer. Landser was, after all, the commissioner of the Brosigville Stadtpolizei, a good officer too. Calling him out now, in front of the others, would serve no useful purpose.

"Let's recap what we have, then," Long went on, deciding to change the subject. "One: Multan's men were behind the raid at the warehouse. I've got Multan on violation of Confederation law against the unauthorized possession of plasma weapons. As the Confederation's chief law enforcement officer on Wanderjahr, I am going to arrest him, with some help from Brigadier Sturgeon and you, Alois. I do not need the approval for this from your local magistrates either. This is Confederation business and I have the muscle to do what I have to. We'll let the diplomats sort the legalities out—after I have Multan safely in prison offworld. He is history."

"There will be a fight," Landser cautioned.

"So there will be," Chief Long responded. The men sitting around his desk sat up straighter in their chairs.

Landser grinned. "I could never do anything about him because as a member of the Ruling Council he is immune to prosecution while here on Council business, and he is not stupid enough to come here as a tourist. I closed some of his enterprises down and arrested some of his men, but that never stopped him. Chairman Arschmann never seemed to be very upset about it because, frankly, I think he was in on it, although I can't prove it, and as Chairman of the Ruling Council he is always immune to arrest. Until you came here." He nodded at Chief Long. "Now . . ." He smacked a fist into his palm.

Long continued: "Two: the raid on Keutgens was ordered by someone in Brosigville using her deputy minister of commerce as a spotter. The minister is already in custody, and in time we'll know who his contact is here in Brosigville. That person is mine. He is responsible for the attempted murder of a Confederation military officer, and for that he will be extradited and tried by the Confederation.

"Three: we don't know who slaughtered Siebensberg and her people, but the guerrillas are not our first choice for that deed.

"Four: we're not sure who bombed Marine headquarters or shot at my lads here. Of all the incidents, those two are most likely the work of the guerrillas. But maybe not.

"Finally, gentlemen, we have a very complicated situation before us. My guts tell me we're right in the middle of a colossal power struggle on Wanderjahr, of which the war with the guerrillas is only a very small part. Gentlemen, I'll let you know when we're ready to move against Multan. Meanwhile, word of this must stay among us." He looked at each man. "I will need your best men for this operation, Alois, but they shall know nothing of our destination until we are en route. Thank you for your time this afternoon. Alois, please stay behind when the others leave, won't you?"

Alone, Chief Long regarded the commissioner carefully before he spoke. "You are not telling me everything, are you, Alois?"

"No, I am not."

"May I ask why? Your orders were to do so."

"Yes. I disobeyed." Landser swallowed and shifted his weight in his seat. "It is no secret, Chief, that I resent the way Chairman Arschmann forced you on me. I hate him for that, and I only hope my personal feelings have not clouded my judgment in this case."

Chief Long nodded but said nothing.

"But I have come to respect you." Landser's face reddened. Compliments did not come easily to this man. "I will show you that I am a good officer," he said with feeling. "I am just not sure yet about my evidence, but when I am, I will ask for your help."

"I could have you dismissed for this, Alois," Chief Long reminded him.

"Yes, I know." Landser smiled. "But you won't."

"No, I won't." Chief Long sighed. "From now on, Alois, trust me. I am the only one you can trust, you know that. The oligarchs are all at each other's throats. Watch your back, my friend."

"If anything happens to me, Chief, my files will survive." He held out a microdiskette. "Everything is on here. Will you trust me for another few days?"

Chief Long took the diskette. "Yes, Alois, I will do that," he replied.

"Oh, and one more request." Long nodded. "I must leave town for a few days."

"May I inquire where you'll be going, Alois?"

"I'd rather not say, Chief."

"I can always find out, Alois."

"Yes."

Chief Long pretended to consider the request for a moment. "Be careful. Oh, and that was very, very good shooting." Landser was smiling like a schoolboy as he walked out of the office.

After Landser had departed, Chief Long took out one of the cigars Claypoole had given him and lighted it. He puffed contentedly for a time, feet propped on his workstation. Who is doing what to whom? he asked himself. Alois Landser certainly held the key, but Chief Long had already figured most of it out for himself.

Over the next few days, certain individuals in Arschland and Morgenluft mysteriously disappeared from their normal haunts, and wound up incommunicado in a safe house known only to Commissioner Landser and a few of his most highly trusted subordinates. Only then did Landser take Chief Long fully into his confidence. Together, they decided it was time to approach Ambassador Spears and Brigadier Sturgeon. Swift and very decisive action was required, and soon.

CHAPTER FIFTEEN

The headquarters runner, whose name Hing never did learn, led the way to an Arschmann Plantation utility ground car parked a couple of kilometers away, where they got into the cargo compartment. The driver, who wore an Arschmann Plantation foreman's uniform, scowled at them and merely grunted when the runner said, "Take us away." By the time the two guerrillas had changed into the civilian clothes that were waiting for them, the utility car was on a paved road, speeding toward a settlement fifty kilometers north of the 257th GSB headquarters.

Hing didn't bother asking about the driver's identity; he didn't need to know, and understood that he wouldn't be told. Which was all right. He had his own group of informants who were Arschmann employees. For the guerrillas, that was one of the benefits of working in Arschland. The oligarch was so uniformly hated that many people willingly helped the guerrillas, and most of them refused to provide any information or assistance to the Feldpolizei. Arschland was one place where a guerrilla could move as a fish in a school of fish.

The driver stopped the car at a monorail station. Hing wasn't certain, because the settlement was outside his normal operations area, but he thought it was Ulbrichtsburg. For all the cleanliness of its streets, the town certainly was as drab as its name suggested. The few people he saw walked fast with their eyes cast down, as though in a hurry to get off the street and not wanting to be seen. Their clothing seemed gray or brown, as drab as the town itself. The few ground cars he saw were Arschmann Plantation vehicles.

The runner paid their fare at the station's gate and they mounted to the northbound platform to wait. Only one other person waited with them, a stout grandmother type in a rumpled brown dress, with a gray sweater and a head scarf that had once been a bright blue. A large bag sat at her feet.

The wait was blessedly short; the ride wasn't.

Hing had plenty of time to wonder about the meaning of the peremptory summons to Staat HQ. He'd never even heard of a brigade commander getting a peremptory summons. On the rare occasions that a summons was issued, it was done more politely. Some lead time was always allowed, and generally some explanation was given.

Not this time, though. Hing racked his brain, trying to think of whom he might have offended, what he might have done wrong. He could think of no one and nothing. With the possible exception of Lieutenant Pincote's disastrous ambush a few days earlier. And word of that could not have reached headquarters so quickly.

After a half hour of futile mental exercise, he gave up thinking and tried to enjoy the passing scenery. But it was hard to appreciate its beauty when the scenery passed at 150 kilometers an hour. Even the occasional village the monorail stopped in was drab. There were no quaint villages in Arschland. Oligarch Arschmann thought quaintness was a waste of valuable resources—resources that could be put to better use increasing his wealth and power.

They got off the train in Mannerheim, a sparkling clean, middle-size city in the style of an earlier era. In the downtown area, where the monorail station was, most of the buildings were at least five stories high, none more than ten. The architectural team that designed it favored plate glass and bronzed aluminum for facings. The architects eschewed ornamentation. The overall effect was what one visiting critic described as "the boxes other buildings came in." Needless to say, that critic's visitor's visa was not renewed and he was soon ushered away from Wanderjahr.

Hing and his guide left the station through a side exit to a street so narrow it could have been an alley. The runner led the way along ill-traveled side streets for three blocks until a disreputable-looking utility car with faded Arschmann Plantation markings slowed almost to a stop just ahead of them. The runner quickly opened the cargo door and almost bodily set Hing inside the cabin. A dim light cast by a small dome light revealed a bench along each side of the cabin. Hing sat on one, and the runner took his place across from him. A crate against the front wall seemed to be the only cargo. The vehicle sped up.

"Now I have to blindfold you, Commander," the runner said without a hint of apology.

Hing lowered his head to make the runner's job easier.

Several turns and many stops and speed-ups followed. Eventually the vehicle stopped.

"This is where I leave you, Commander," the runner said.

The cargo door opened and there were sounds of one man exiting and another boarding. The doors closed. The car started.

"I'll take you the rest of the way, Commander," a new voice said.

"Yes," Hing replied. There were more turns, slows, stops, and speed-ups before the utility car reached what must have been a highway leading away from the city. Hing doubted there were any roadways in the city where a utility car could go that fast without having to slow or stop.

Blindfolded as he was, and with no conversation with the guide—whom he now thought of as a guard—to pass the time, Hing had no way of knowing how much time passed before the utility car slowed to a complete stop and the driver cut the power to let it whoosh down on its skirts. It was at least a half an hour, possibly much longer.

"You must remain blindfolded until after we get inside, Commander," the guide/guard said.

The cargo door opened and hands helped Hing to get out. Wherever they were, Hing felt bright sunlight on his face. The strong hands of the guides/guards gripped his upper arms to lead him briskly across a slightly spongy surface. Grass, he thought. This was a place with a lawn of imported Earth grass.

Part of his mind wondered what would happen if the grass was allowed to go to seed. Was it strong enough to germinate on its own? What would be the impact on the planetary ecology if it spread? The more active part of his mind wondered if the summons was a trap, if the oligarchs had somehow managed to infiltrate the Peoples Liberation Army at the highest levels and the summons was a ruse to arrest him. There were few places on Wanderjahr where grass grew—and all of them were fully under the control of the oligarchs.

"Step up," a voice on his right said. "There are five steps here." Simultaneously, both hands on his upper arms lifted up, almost pulling him off his feet. He managed to fully recover his balance by the third step.

Hing was marched across a broad veranda and through what must have been a wide doorway, since it didn't feel like either of his guides had to make room to fit through it. Then the echoes of their footsteps told him they were in a large room with a polished wooden floor. A few paces into the room the guides turned him to the right and guided him a few more paces before they stopped.

"When we let go of you, Commander," the voice on his right said, "go forward two paces. When you hear the door close behind you, remove the blindfold."

The hands let go and he heard his guides step backward. Had they then drawn hand weapons to burn him down if he made a wrong move? Hing stepped forward two paces as they'd told him to. The door closed behind him with a solid *chunk*. He listened for a second but didn't hear a lock being thrown, then reached up and removed the blindfold.

After so long without light, his eyes watered. He blinked several times at the sudden brightness of the room. Almost immediately he squinted to see.

He was in a spacious formal dining room with a south-facing wall that was almost completely windowed to allow light to flood in. Draperies could be closed for privacy on dim days or at night. As large as the room was, it was dominated by a table that could easily seat more than twenty people and leave them elbow room. Most of the chairs around it were already occupied by men in civilian clothing. Hing recognized several of the seated men, most of them brigade commanders like he was. One, rising from his place at the head of the table, was a somewhat shorter than average, slender man. Generalissimo Zot, overall commander of the PLA in Arschland. Hing snapped to attention facing him. The Generalissimo extended his hand as he briskly approached Hing.

"Commander Hing," Zot said as he took Hing's hand. "So good of you to come on such short notice. I'm sure you will forgive me the cloak-and-dagger method of your travel, but you understand the necessity of keeping the location of this meeting place absolutely secret." With the hand that wasn't gripping Hing's, he guided him toward an empty chair at the table. "Please, be seated. We should get started very soon. There are only a few more coming, and they will all be here momentarily."

Thoroughly confused, Hing mumbled his greetings and thanks as he took the offered seat. No one other than the Generalissimo spoke. Unless many of his peers and his superior had changed sides and this was the most elaborate charade he could imagine, he wasn't under arrest by the oligarchs. From the position of his seat, slightly more than halfway down one side of the table, neither did it appear that it was a court-martial with him in the docket.

Hing exchanged curt nods with the men he knew, none of whom even opened their lips to say hello, then examined the table. There were twenty-two chairs at it, four of which were unoccupied. Each place was set with a coffee cup and saucer, a dessert plate, a fork, a spoon, and a napkin. Unless he was mistaken, they were fine china, real silver, and imported linen. Each place at the table also had a small computer console, stylus, and keyboard. Coffeepots and plates of cakes were lined down the middle of the table within easy reach of each place. The table itself was dark, deeply polished, and real wood—probably imported from Earth. Hing marveled at the expense of the table and its settings.

"Please, Commander," Zot said, "help yourself to coffee and cake. The coffee is special, it's imported from America

Sud." The Generalissimo grinned. "America Sud *on Earth*. The province of Colombia, I believe."

Hing nodded at Zot. "Thank you, sir. That would be a very special treat." Real Colombian coffee? He'd heard of it, but the only coffee he'd ever had was from locally grown beans, which he was told was vastly inferior to Earth coffee. He glanced about. Everyone seemed to have filled his coffee cup. None of them looked happy or even comfortable, but they all seemed to like the coffee.

Before he could reach for a pot, the door opened behind him. He glanced out of the corner of his eye to see what the others on his side of the table were doing. When they turned, he did the same.

A blindfolded man in tattered and filthy civilian clothing was stepping through the door. The door closed and the man removed his blindfold. Generalissimo Zot was already on his way to greet the newcomer, whom he addressed as Commander Tslotse. Zot guided the man to an empty seat. Tslotse looked as confused as Hing felt.

No sooner had Hing poured himself a cup of coffee than the door opened again and another confused and blindfolded field commander entered the room. Within three minutes all the chairs were occupied by the Staat commander and his twenty-one brigade commanders. There were no guards, no orderlies, and no staff officers. Hing thought this was very peculiar, but it seemed to bode well—at least there were no trappings of court-martial. Everyone sipped at the coffee. It was the best Hing had ever had. Too bad his state of mind didn't allow him to enjoy it, he thought.

Generalissimo Zot looked benignly at each of his brigade commanders, then said, "In case you haven't yet surmised, gentlemen, this is one of Oligarch Arschmann's estates." He looked contentedly around the room and continued slowly and softly, "When this meeting is over, I think I will take a VR recording of myself sitting here and walking around the room." He looked back at his officers. "And have that VR sent to Arschmann. He'll have a stroke when he sees me sitting in his place in his own dining room." He laughed. Then he abruptly turned serious, and angry.

"Four days ago someone raided the household of Oligarch Gretel Siebensberg in Friedland. The commander of the raiding party identified himself as Lieutenant Xuyen Phong of the PLA. My headquarters has no record of a Lieutenant Xuyen Phong—or a person of any other rank going by that name." Zot pounded a fist on the table. "I want to know who he is!" He took a deep breath to calm himself, then said, "Do any of you have anyone in your commands who goes by that name or has ever used it? Have you ever even heard that name?" He looked intently from man to man.

The Che Loi Brigade, like most such units of the PLA, had fewer than three hundred officers, staff, and fighters. Hing knew them all. He looked at Zot, mouthed "Xuyen Phong," and shook his head; it was a strange name to him. The other commanders he could see were doing the same.

"Look at your consoles, gentlemen," Zot said in a calm but firm voice. "See for yourselves what this 'Lieutenant Xuyen Phong' did." He tapped a key on his keyboard.

Hing looked at the console. A moving flatvid image appeared. The vid was recorded by a walking man who angled his camera downward. Occasionally the angle shot upward for a few seconds, but mostly it was down. The image was of bloodied bodies hacked to pieces. The upward shots showed the scene was in a courtyard. A burned corpse dangled from a scorched tree. The cameraman went through a doorway and panned the room beyond, a chapel. Blood stained the front pews. A headless corpse lay in a pool of blood before the altar. Another body with blood on his shirt, but no evident wounds, was sprawled across a front pew. The image blinked out.

"That is what this Lieutenant Xuyen Phong and his men did," Generalissimo Zot said. "The husk in the tree? That was identified by witnesses to the atrocity as Gretel Siebensberg. You don't need to know how we got that vid. Nor do you need to know how I came into possession of this." He flipped a small, red-covered book to the brigade commander on his right. The brigade commander picked the small book up and quickly flipped through its pages. He gave Generalissimo Zot a puzzled look, and passed the book on when Zot indicated he should.

It took a couple of minutes for the book to reach Hing. He blinked at the crudely printed title: *The Beliefs of the People's Liberation Army; as taught by Marks, Linin, Mao, and Guevera.* He opened the book at random to three pages and quickly read brief quotes from it. He passed it on.

"According to Xuyen Phong," Zot said when the book was returned to him, "this book is our bible." He raised his eyebrows at the book. "How curious they didn't bother to spell the names in the title properly. And where would anyone get the idea we're reincarnated Communists?" He looked back to the assembled brigade commanders. "I need to know what any of you know about the book or the atrocity committed on Friedland." He tapped another key on his keyboard and watched his console as the brigade commanders all protested innocence and ignorance. After a moment he cut them off and stood.

"Gentlemen," he said solemnly, "you have my apologies for the way you have been treated today. The coffee was treated with . . . Never mind precisely what it was treated with. An inhibitor that made it difficult for you to lie. There are sensors throughout the room. The sensors agree that you are telling the truth." He sighed and sat back down.

"This thing that happened," he waved his hand weakly at the console, "is a severe blow to us. Many people throughout Wanderjahr believe we are responsible for that. They don't stop to think that we have no reason to murder Gretel Siebensberg. Or that we have no activity in Friedland.

"As you probably know, this is the second incident of an attack on an oligarch's household since the Confederation Marines arrived. Two weeks ago Morgenluft, Oligarch Keutgens's home, was attacked. That time some Marines were on the scene and defeated the attackers. Our sources in Stadtpolizei HQ in Brosigville tell us the investigators are not convinced we were behind it. Interestingly, Morgenluft is also a Staat where we have no activity. Neither of these raids was authorized by PLA high command. So every Staat generalissimo was ordered to assemble his brigade commanders to find out if any of them has been operating beyond his jurisdiction." He smiled wanly. "Before we were charged with investigating our brigade commanders, PLA command subjected us to exactly the same interrogation you have just been through."

Zot rose again. "Gentlemen, enjoy your coffee and cake." He held up a hand to forestall any protest. "I will have fresh coffee brought in that hasn't been treated." He smiled. "Later, in the same order you arrived, you will be blindfolded and escorted away. While you know this is one of Arschmann's estates, you do not need to know which one." He bowed slightly, then left the room.

CHAPTER
SIXTEEN

The planning for the raid on Multan's fortress home proceeded under the cloak of absolute secrecy. The only Wanderjahrian officer included in the deliberations was Commissioner Landser himself. Besides Chief Long, the only other civilian participant was Ambassador Spears. Landser would issue the necessary orders to the Stadtpolizei officers selected to participate, and only after the contingent was on board the *Denver* in orbit would they be informed where they were going; the twenty-five policemen required for the assault would not even be notified they had been picked for the mission until an hour before departure. Aside from the brigadier's immediate planning staff, only the commander of the security party was privy to the attack plan. Of course, as Chief Long's military assistants, Dean and Claypoole were included.

For security, training for the assault would take place on the *Denver*. Although he hadn't been able to track them down, Commissioner Landser was certain that Multan had agents on his force. Spies and informants at every level of government in Arschland were essential to a man like Multan, who depended on intelligence of all sorts to carry out his vast criminal enterprises.

Multan's headquarters was located in the small Staat of Porcina in Wanderjahr's temperate zone, about ten thousand kilometers east of Arschland, on the opposite shores of the Adler Ocean. The installation from which he ruled his domains—the Eagle's Nest—was situated in rugged mountains fifty kilometers from Thigpen, his capital city, population 75,000. Multan was known to have a security force of two thousand well-equipped men who kept order among the inhabitants in Porcina.

Due to the remoteness of their country from the other Staats, and Multan's iron-handed but very effective rule, there had never been any disorder among his people. His security force did not hesitate to exercise brutal authority over the citizens of Porcina. In one infamous incident, they cleared traffic on a narrow bridge simply by pitching the stalled vehicle into the river below. They would have shot the driver and pitched him over too, except he was connected to one of Multan's enterprises. The man's sister, niece, and brother-in-law rode the stalled vehicle into the river. No protest of any kind was ever registered.

Multan's personal bodyguard consisted of over a hundred handpicked mercenaries, and the Marines knew they were armed with at least a few plasma weapons. Since the raid on his smuggling operation in Brosigville, he had refused to leave Porcina even for Council meetings, temporarily putting himself out of reach of any authority. Or so he thought.

"Gentlemen," Brigadier Sturgeon began the initial planning meeting, "bringing Multan in is our number one priority just now. We know he has plasma weapons in contravention of Confederation laws, and for that reason alone he must be dealt with. But we have intelligence," he nodded at Chief Long, "that he is selling arms and equipment to the guerrillas. We don't know just yet if any of these sales have included the latest weapons available on the black market, but I cannot wait to find out. I cannot allow the lives of my men to be jeopardized by Multan. He must be taken out. Quickly. We are going to mount a surprise attack on his headquarters and capture him or kill him. I don't particularly care which."

Brigadier Sturgeon paused. "Finally, I have no choice. I have been ordered directly by the Confederation Council to arrest Multan. As the senior Confederation official in this sector, I must enforce its laws. The order was endorsed by Fleet and confirmed to Ambassador Spears by a communiqué through diplomatic channels."

"How are we going to be sure Multan's there when we bust in on him?" Colonel Ramadan, the FIST's executive officer, asked.

"Very simple," Ambassador Spears said. "Brigadier Sturgeon and I will be there in a meeting with the man himself." A low murmur of surprise circulated among the men in the briefing room.

"That will be very unwise, Mr. Ambassador," Commissioner Landser said.

"Sir," Colonel Ramadan protested to Brigadier Sturgeon, "he's right. You can't afford to put yourself and the ambassador in such a dangerous position. The bastard'll take you hostage if he doesn't kill you outright."

"Relax, Colonel," the brigadier replied, straightening up and leaning forward on the table. "I'll have my two favorite lance corporals with me for security." He grinned at Dean and Claypoole, sitting quietly along the wall of the conference room. Dean's stomach plunged crazily down to his toes at the announcement, and Claypoole's face went white, but neither said anything. "I'm taking you two with me," he addressed the pair, "because Multan will expect it. This must look entirely like a nonthreatening visit to an oligarch's domains. As a result of your accompanying me to Morgenluft, Friedland, and other places, the Wanderjahrians see you as my bodyguard. And since you're both seen constantly traveling between here and police headquarters, people here think you two are a lot more than mere lance corporals on the staff.

"Oh, by the way, report to the FIST surgeon right after this meeting. I want to be sure you two are in tip-top shape for this visit." The brigadier smiled cryptically.

Colonel Ramadan, who had not recovered from the announcement that the brigadier was offering himself as a decoy, spluttered, searching for words. Chief Long drummed his fingers nervously on the tabletop while the other officers in the room glanced apprehensively at each other. There was an uncomfortable silence that seemed to last a long time.

"Well, we've got to be sure he's there," Ambassador Spears said, gesturing with open hands. Nobody responded.

"I decided," the brigadier said, laughing, "to lure him with the most reliable and at the same time the most expendable members of my command." There was a slight pause before the other officers responded with nervous chuckles. "There is no other way," he continued. "If we don't bag the bastard first time out, we won't get him at all. He'll retreat into the mountains over there and then we'll have to give up. We don't have the time or the resources to track him in his own land. I have my hands full with training the Feldpolizei, and if we fail in this and the Confederation still orders me to divert men and resources to capturing this guy, the guerrillas will kick our asses. This is definitely a one-time shot, gentlemen."

"We can't get him to Brosigville," Ambassador Spears added. "He thinks he can sit us out in Porcina, and he's probably right. But he feels safe there right now, so secure he's agreed to meet with the brigadier and me. I have led him to believe we can work out a deal on the weapons charge. That deal will be, 'Come along quietly or we'll fry you.'" Ambassador Spears grinned. It was evident he considered the upcoming raid an exciting diversion. Colonel Ramadan just shook his head.

"Gentlemen, we meet with Multan day after tomorrow," the brigadier concluded. "Let's get with it. We'll meet here again tomorrow and approve the final details. Dean, Claypoole, report to the FIST surgeon after we break up here."

After the staff bustled out, leaving the two enlisted men sitting forlornly against one wall, Claypoole turned to Dean. "Whew!" he exclaimed. "We're in the shit now, Dean-o!" Dean gave a lopsided grin.

"Why the hell does the brigadier want us to report to the surgeon?" Claypoole asked.

"Testosterone shots?"

"Yeah, like you really need a dose," Claypoole replied. He was pensive for a moment, staring at the wall. "Dean-o," he said at last, "this Multan guy, if he does get us, you know what's gonna happen, don't you?" Claypoole could not forget what the Siad had done to McNeal on their last deployment. Neither could Dean.

"Yeah, the ugly bastard's gonna have a real fight on his hands."

The attack plan was very simple. Fifty men would compose the assault team, twenty-five Marines—Team One—from the security force provided by the *Denver*'s captain, and an equal number of policemen—Team Two—from the Brosigville Stadtpolizei. The police officers would back up the Marines by securing a perimeter around Multan's fortress while Team One fought and blasted its way inside. While the odds would be two-to-one at best, more like four-to-one in reality, the assault party would have the advantage of surprise and firepower. They would also have the laser batteries of the *Denver* if needed, and four Dragons on the ground. Everyone would have preferred a battalion-size landing force, but an under-strength Marine provisional platoon was all that was available. The assault teams would be launched from orbit upon receipt of a signal from Brigadier Sturgeon.

Since Multan's living quarters were underground, one minute before the assault force was scheduled to land, the *Denver*'s batteries would sweep the surface clear around the entrance shafts, eliminate any resistance, and even the odds for the landing force. Once on the ground, while the Marines breached the shafts and entered Multan's quarters ten meters below the surface, the police would secure the area. The quarters were reached by stairwells and elevators. One element of Team One, specially trained in the use of explosives and rappeling techniques, would enter through the elevator shafts. The rest of the assault force would use the stairwells, fighting its way down if necessary. These men would use special stun weapons, to reduce the threat of reflected heat radiation, although all carried plasma weapons, to use if needed.

As an added precaution, the brigadier, Ambassador Spears, Dean, and Claypoole would each have a microtransmitter surgically implanted just under the skin of each man's right buttock, so the assault force could locate them once they were inside Multan's fortress—which the latter two discovered when they reported to the surgeon.

It took some convincing, but ultimately Commissioner Landser was permitted to accompany his men on the assault. Landser understood that he and his men would be subordinate to the orders of the Marine officer in charge of the operation, a captain named d'C Merrit Thomas, III. As he sat in field uniform with his officers during the briefings and rehearsals on board the *Denver*, the once resplendent commissioner of Brosigville's police force looked like nothing more than a diminutive policeman wearing a uniform a bit too big for him. But his eyes glittered with excitement. He even deigned to chat with his subordinates.

Since the policemen had never been on an orbital assault in an Essay, this procedure was covered thoroughly, but the coxswain in charge of the craft they would occupy was prepared for quite a mess. "It'll be the longest twenty minutes in your lives," he warned the policemen. He smiled. Marines were no fun on landings since they were used to assaults from orbit, but the coxswain was counting on quite a few laughs from this group.

Satellite and RPV reconnaissance plus agent reports—Commissioner Landser, not to be outdone by a mere criminal, had had a man in Multan's security for some time—gave Captain Thomas a very complete picture of their target. When the signal from Brigadier Sturgeon was received, the assault party would be launched. The party would be combat loaded, in Dragons, already aboard the Essays one hour before the brigadier landed at Thigpen.

"I was in a situation like this once before," Brigadier Sturgeon was saying. "Forty years ago. I was an ensign with the 4th Fleet Marine Landing Force during one of the Silvasian wars, I forget just which one now." They were lounging in the passenger compartment of a hopper as it prepared for suborbital descent to Thigpen. The tension was very high among the four men, and the brigadier was trying to relax them by telling stories. This one ended with the young ensign commanding a platoon surrounded by a vastly superior enemy force, out of touch with his company, and completely on his own. "They demanded our surrender," he said at last.

"What did you do?" Ambassador Spears asked.

The brigadier shrugged. "We surrendered."

There was a moment of silence. That did not sound like anything a Marine, even an ensign, would do. "And then what, sir?" Dean asked.

"They killed us."

Claypoole laughed so hard he choked. Dean started laughing too, and Ambassador Spears cracked a smile. The brigadier leaned back and stretched his legs.

"Well," Ambassador Spears said, getting back to the matter at hand, "this is a lot like attacking under a white flag. It is not what diplomatic protocol would require." He shrugged. "Fuck protocol."

"Sir," Dean asked the ambassador, "were you ever a Marine?"

"No, Lance Corporal Dean, I never had that honor. But I learned how to shine my shoes in the army, many, many years ago. I was a clerk in the 347th Engineer Battalion during that same campaign where the brigadier was killed. We were attached to the 3rd Infantry Division in the assault on Mansara during the Third Silvasian War. The 3rd went up the Mansara-Cremonea Road, and the Marines went up the Mansara-Ilyong Road. The Marines beat us into Mansara by a full fifteen minutes. We never got over it."

"We kicked some ass," the brigadier said.

"Yes, we did, Ted, we certainly did."

Listening to the old veterans reminisce, Claypoole began to feel much better. Their nonchalance about what was going to happen was infectious. He knew the brigadier would bring this thing off. Brigadier Sturgeon winked surreptitiously at Ambassador Spears, who, despite his outward air of confidence, was nauseous.

"Strap yourselves in, gentlemen," the pilot announced over the intercom, "we are about to land."

"You men leave all the talking to the ambassador and me,"

the brigadier said. "I want you two to remain alert. Let me remind you again, the signal for the landing is X-ray, and whoever transmits it will launch the assault party. Any of you can do it. If anything happens, shoot first." Dean and Claypoole wore side arms, but no one else in the party was armed. The brigadier did not add that if they had to shoot, it would be all over for them in a few seconds. The success of the operation depended on overwhelming surprise, not two enlisted men with side arms.

A grim and heavily armed escort met the party at the port. The officer in charge, a burly, unshaven man festooned with weapons, grunted, "I am Captain Ramses," as he showed them to a waiting landcar.

The ride into the hills, surrounded by Multan's men, all of whom smelled heavily of thule and old sweat, took twenty minutes. Multan's fortress home could only be approached by one narrow, winding road blasted out of the sheer face of a mountainside soaring three hundred meters above the plain that stretched from Thigpen to the foothills. Guard posts were situated at intervals all along the road. The men at these posts were alert and well-armed.

Multan's home had been sunk into the living rock on the plateau above the plain. The buildings on the surface housed his security forces in bunkers with very thick, reinforced walls. Surveillance devices and roving foot patrols covered every square meter within a kilometer of the entrance shaft to Multan's quarters. Multan had not clawed his way to a seat on the Ruling Council by taking chances, but now that he was a wanted man, his obsession with personal security had intensified. That he had permitted the visit indicated, however, that he felt secure in his fortress.

The four visitors stood silently as the elevator slowly sank into the ground. Captain Ramses stood with his back to them so he would be the first to go through the doors when they opened. Dean marveled at the back of the man's closely shaved head, which was crisscrossed by a network of tiny scars and indentations that looked like old fragment wounds. His right ear was missing its lobe; the lobe in the other sported a huge diamond that sparkled as he moved his head.

The elevator stopped and the doors hissed open. Ramses wheeled about with lightning speed and buried a fist in Claypoole's solar plexus. As Claypoole doubled over, Ramses slammed his elbow into the side of Dean's head. A dozen armed men rushed in and seized the party. It happened so quickly, all four men were taken completely by surprise. Dean and Claypoole were immediately disarmed and the four were deprived of their wrist communicators. Under heavy guard, they were marched down a corridor and shoved into a large paneled room. The doors were slammed shut behind them and locked.

"Violation of diplomatic protocol for sure," Ambassador Spears gasped, trying to get his breath back. Brigadier Sturgeon put a finger to his lips. "Goddamnit, I shall protest this treatment most strongly," Ambassador Spears said in a louder voice.

"You do that," the brigadier said. "You okay?" he asked Claypoole, who was still trying to catch his breath.

Dean wiped at a thin stream of blood dripping down the side of his head. His vision had cleared by now. "Was I out there for a while, sir?"

The brigadier nodded. "Multan's boys had to drag you down the hallway." He looked around the room, obviously used for conferences or receptions.

A door opened at one end of the room and Multan stepped through followed by Captain Ramses. "Gentlemen," Multan said, "you thought you could fool me."

"Sir, I must protest this—this most unlawful treatment," Ambassador Spears said.

Multan made a dismissive gesture with one hand. "You thought you could trap me, didn't you?" It was a statement more than a question.

"Yes," Brigadier Sturgeon answered. "My two Marines and I came here to take you prisoner and escort you to the *Denver* to hold you there for trial. So let me inform you now, sir, that in accordance with the authority vested in me by the Confederation of Worlds, you are under arrest and my prisoner."

Multan's mouth dropped open in surprise and then he laughed derisively. "Well, do it, then!" He laughed again and held out his wrists for the handcuffs.

Captain Ramses stepped forward, drawing a long-bladed knife.

"X-ray!" Dean shouted, hoping the microtransmitter embedded beneath his skin would pick up the command.

"Kill them!" Multan shouted.

Claypoole snatched a small black object from a holster strapped to the inside of his left leg and pointed it at Ramses, who stopped in midstride and grinned before leaping forward. There was a sharp *crack*. A small hole appeared in the middle of Ramses's forehead. With a look of surprise, he crumpled to the floor. A tiny wisp of smoke rose above the barrel of Claypoole's small .32 caliber automatic. A tiny brass cartridge spun brightly on the floor. "Teach you to sucker-punch me, motherfucker."

"Hands over your head and on your knees!" Dean shouted at Multan. A .32 was almost hidden in his hand. Multan sank to his knees. "You are insane, Brigadier, to think this . . . this kidnapping will work."

Dean stepped behind Multan and pointed his gun at the back of the oligarch's head. "Now lay flat and spread your legs. Come on, come on!" Multan complied reluctantly. "Spread your arms out, palms up! Turn your head to the left! Stay perfectly still or I'll kill you!" He frisked Multan, removing two pistols from him. He tossed them to the brigadier and Ambassador Spears. The door behind him opened and a man stepped through. Claypoole shot him twice in the head and he fell back into the corridor outside.

"What the hell?" Brigadier Sturgeon exclaimed, staring at Claypoole.

The room shook violently as the *Denver*'s bombardment commenced. It lasted thirty seconds. Men shouted and ran through the corridors outside the room.

"How do you work this thing?" Ambassador Spears

asked, fumbling with the unfamiliar mechanism of the pistol
Dean had taken from Multan. It discharged suddenly with a
bright flash and a deafening concussion. The slug plowed a
deep furrow in the large conference table at the opposite end
of the room.

"That's how," the brigadier answered dryly. "Where did
you get those weapons, Claypoole?"

"Officer Lanning of the Brosigville Stadtpolizei gave 'em to
us, sir," he said without taking his eyes off the doorway behind
Dean. "They're reproductions of antique projectile weapons.
The Brosigville cops call them a POS and they all carry them.
Chief Long had the cops teach us how to take down suspects
and all that stuff, sir. Good idea, huh?"

"What's POS stand for?" Ambassador Spears asked.

Claypoole hesitated briefly before replying. " 'Positive,' sir.
They're .32 caliber Positives."

A door behind burst open and several men charged through.
The room erupted in gunfire.

Thirty seconds into the assault, as his stomach matched
the terrific rate of the Essay's descent, the policeman next to
Commissioner Landser vomited profusely. The undulating
mess hung weightlessly in the air in front of his face. Commissioner Landser hardly noticed what had happened, as his
own stomach emptied itself. Men screamed in terror as the
Essay plunged into Wanderjahr's upper atmosphere. They
had been warned what to expect, but the actual experience
was overpowering.

"Gentlemen," the coxswain announced calmly, "thirty seconds to landing."

"Listen up," the commander of the Dragon they were
strapped into said over the net, "we'll hit with a bang. I'll drive
us outside. When the ramp goes down, you perform a combat
dismount just as you did in the mock-up. You know what to do.
We'll give you cover. Good luck."

As the Essay descended deeper into Wanderjahr's field of
gravity, the vomit that had been suspended in the air showered

down on men fastened into assault modules. Those who had not thrown up in the initial seconds of the descent did now.

Landser gasped for breath. "Listen to me!" he croaked into his mouthpiece. "Check your equipment!" That was all he could manage to say. It was all he had to say.

The Essay slammed to earth. The Dragon roared out onto the plateau, then screeched to a halt. Its ramp slammed down and a thick cloud of dust enveloped the policemen as they rushed out in four six-man groups. They had been divided into four parties—Adam, Baker, Charlie, Donald—linked to each other by radio and hooked into the *Denver*'s communications system so the commander of the assault team could maintain contact with Landser. Each party was to establish and hold a segment of the perimeter around Multan's fortress until the operation was clear.

Fires burned everywhere and smoke and ash filled the air outside the Dragon. The remains of the outbuildings and vehicles were smoldering heaps of slag and ash. The entire area above Multan's underground headquarters looked as if it had just been scoured by a huge blowtorch.

Landser was the first out of the Dragon. "Two Actual. Deploying." Landser spoke into the mouthpiece of his helmet as he ran into the swirling cloud of smoke.

"Roger, Team Two is deploying," the communications officer on the *Denver* said, acknowledging the transmission. Team One, the assault element, had already blasted its way into the elevator shaft and the stairwells.

Landser felt panic as he looked around. He couldn't see anything! He couldn't tell which direction was which from where he was standing. So he sent his four team leaders in what he guessed were the four corners of a compass as they dismounted, hoping once they were clear of the fires, they could see to establish their sectors of the perimeter. He moved forward as best he could, talking all the while to his shift leaders. That calmed him down. Abruptly, the visibility cleared. His teams had emerged from the smoke intact and were setting up defensive positions.

The commanders of the two Dragons that had landed with

the assault party checked into Landser's net. Now he had four of the monsters if he needed fire support.

"Team Two Actual, all secure," Landser reported. He was actually beginning to like this military stuff, he admitted to himself.

The radio inside his helmet crackled. "Heads up!" one of the Dragon commanders shouted. "We have bandits, I say again, we have bandits!"

From his vantage point ten feet above the ground, now that a rising wind had blown the smoke away, Landser could see a large cloud of dust approaching from the northwest.

"Team Two, they are too close for us to engage," the communications officer on the *Denver* announced. "Team One, how are you doing?"

"Team One Actual," Captain Thomas replied, his breath coming in labored gasps. "Meeting heavy resistance. Inside not secure! I say again, not secure. Hold them off."

"Team Two, did you copy that transmission?"

"Yes," Landser replied, forgetting proper communications procedure. "We will engage them and hold them."

The Dragon commander who had spotted the approaching relief party focused his opticals more clearly. Several dozen vehicles were roaring toward him at high speed. Each was crowded with armed men. "Gunner, engage at one thousand meters," he said into his mouthpiece.

"Roger that. How about the ones coming up from the southeast?"

Ambassador Spears spun about at the noise behind him and pointed the unfamiliar weapon at the men coming through the door. The first man took the bullet in his chest and staggered back into the second man. Spears, reverting to his long-ago firearms training as an army recruit, took a boxer stance, leaned slightly forward, and, holding the unfamiliar pistol with both hands, extended at arm's length before him, commenced firing into the men in the doorway. Wood, masonry, and pieces of human flesh sprayed about the entrance as the ambassador fired again and again. When no more men tried to push their way through the doorway, he stopped shooting. Footsteps could be heard pounding off down the corridor outside as survivors fled.

The brigadier looked at Ambassador Spears with new respect. "I never had to fire a shot!" he exclaimed.

Spears stood rooted to the spot, his pistol still pointing at the doorway, now blocked by three bodies. Slowly, he lowered it. "Now I need someone to show me how you reload this goddamned thing," he said.

Shooting and screaming could be heard from every direction as the assault teams fought their way into the complex.

"Well?" the brigadier said to Multan, who was still spread-eagled on the floor, Dean's pistol leveled at the back of his head. "Do you believe me now? Normally I'd give you time to pack a bag, but we're in a hurry to get you to a safe place. All this shooting going on down here, somebody could get hurt."

"Brigadier! Captain Thomas here. Don't shoot. We're coming in." The commander of the assault force and several Marines stepped cautiously through the door behind Dean. He lowered his pistol. The captain glanced at Multan and gestured for the Marines to secure their prisoner. "We took some casualties getting in here, sir, and there's a rescue attempt being mounted topside from at least two directions by Multan's men. Let's secure this bastard, get topside, and get extracted."

"You're in charge, Captain," the brigadier said. They followed him into the corridor.

At a thousand meters the Dragons engaged the approaching rescue forces with their main guns. Landser ordered his men to take cover and open fire only when they were sure of good targets. They carried only their side arms and Brady shot rifles. The rifles had an effective range of about three hundred meters, so the approaching men were way out of range. But the Dragons' main guns hissed and cracked and sent streams of plasma bolts plunging into the approaching vehicles. Many slagged and instantly went out of control, but others took sharp evasive action and came on.

"Adam Two," the leader of the party in the southeast quadrant reported, "they are splitting up into multiple targets. We are engaging."

"Donald Two, same here. I estimate forty vehicles now within range."

"This is Landser," he told his officers, "hold your positions! You must hold on. Baker, Charlie, support Adam and Donald. Dragons, can you give us fire?"

"Roger that," all four Dragon commanders replied.

"Team One," Landser shouted. "We are under heavy attack up here. Are you secure down there yet?"

"Team One Actual. All secure. On the way up."

Landser breathed a sigh of relief that was cut short by a gasp as the first incoming rounds from the attackers began to impact within the perimeter. All around him the Dragons' main guns hissed and cracked while the weapons of his own men banged away. The attackers had gone to ground in natural depressions about two hundred meters out and were now taking the perimeter under heavy small-arms fire, despite accurate marksmanship from the Dragons. Fortunately, Multan's men did not have armor-piercing weapons, and Landser's men were using explosive shot shells to good effect, lobbing them accurately into the attackers' positions.

"Essays," Landser said into his mouthpiece, "prepare for extraction." Without realizing it, Landser had taken charge of operations on the surface.

Hunched over and running quickly, Team One came running out of the shafts, carrying its casualties. They began to load into the waiting Dragons.

Captain Thomas ran to where Landser crouched beside the slag heap from where he controlled the perimeter. "We got the bastard!" he shouted into Landser's ear. "Do you need help here?"

"No," Landser shouted back. "We are holding them. When you are secure, we will begin extraction." Thomas nodded and ran to the nearest Dragon, which raised its ramp and roared into a waiting Essay. On board the *Denver* they had practiced extraction under fire. All Landser could remember of the procedure now was that he was to go aboard last. One of the Essays took off with an earsplitting roar.

"Team Two, we are ready to commence loading," the coxswain of Landser's Essay announced over the net. Landser's Dragon began laying down heavy continuous fire on the enemy positions, despite the welcome fact that the incoming had slackened considerably.

Landser ran for the Dragon and stood on its ramp. "Adam, Donald, withdraw to the Essays. Baker, Charlie, cover them." The first two parties clambered aboard as Landser counted them. "Baker, Charlie, go!" He counted another twelve men, some of them wounded. "Shift leaders, are all your men accounted for?" Several seconds elapsed before they responded in the affirmative. Only then did Landser strap himself in and tell the Dragon commander all was clear for take-off. The Dragon lurched into the Essay's loading bay. On an adrenaline high, he never noticed the g forces tugging at him as the Essay roared into orbit.

As the Essays shut down in the *Denver*'s docking bays and discharged the assault teams, crewmen swarmed everywhere, helping the wounded to the sick bay and welcoming the men back. Five men had been killed and eight wounded in Team One; seven of Landser's policemen had been wounded. Best of all, Multan was in the *Denver*'s brig.

Landser found himself standing together with Brigadier Sturgeon, Ambassador Spears, the *Denver*'s captain, and Dean and Claypoole. Landser's uniform was ripped in several places and his face and hands were covered with dirt and scratches. Through the dirt, little streams of perspiration coursed down the policeman's cheeks. "Commissioner, you look like a combat Marine just now," the brigadier said.

Landser came to attention, clicked his heels, and bowed. "Brigadier, I accept that compliment with gratitude," he said.

The brigadier laughed and clapped Landser on the shoulder. "Damn fine combat leadership—for a cop," he said.

Landser turned to Dean. "Lance Corporal, when your headquarters was bombed, you went into the street to help people.

Do you recall assisting one of my officers with a gravely wounded victim?"

"Yes, sir," Dean answered. This was the first time Landser had ever spoken a word directly to him.

"Well, that man was my brother, and I have never thanked you for trying to help him." Dean was so surprised he could not answer. Landser turned to Claypoole. "Lance Corporal, you are indeed a brave man." Landser bowed in Claypoole's direction. "Should either of you men ever quit the Marines, I will gladly offer you commissions on my force."

The small group was silent for a moment, surprised and pleased by this outburst of honest compliments from a man like Landser.

"Well," the brigadier said, finally breaking the silence, "we fried a big fish today, a very big fish."

"Yes, Brigadier," Landser responded. "But now we return to Arschland, and when we get there, I trust that you will all assist Chief Long and me in frying some more of these 'big' fishes, some very, very big fishes."

Years later, visitors to Landser's office were curious to see a certificate framed and hanging conspicuously on a wall. It was the warrant Brigadier Sturgeon had given him after the attack on Multan, appointing him an honorary lance corporal in the Confederation Marine Corps.

CHAPTER
SEVENTEEN

Life had been hectic in the FIST F-2 section from the very day Dean and Claypoole arrived as Commander Peters's assistants, but things got even busier once Chief Long agreed to take over the intelligence functions for Brigadier Sturgeon.

First there were the constant staff meetings at FIST HQ. Usually, Chief Long or Lieutenant Constantine conducted the intelligence briefings, but both Dean and Claypoole were required to be present, sometimes after staying up all night to prepare the computer graphics needed for the next day.

Then Claypoole was assigned to establish a computer link between the *Denver*, the Brosigville city police, the Feldpolizei headquarters, and the FIST F-3 section, so information could be readily exchanged. This required many face-to-face meetings with his counterparts in all three places.

Dean, meanwhile, was kept fully occupied screening agent reports, after-action reports, and spot reports from Marines in the field for information on enemy battle tactics and other activities. He also checked newspaper and magazine articles and television reports, gleaning what information could be had about guerrilla activities in the Staats where they were active. All of this information went into the Enemy Order of Battle database that tracked the movements, strengths, weapons capabilities, and, hopefully, intentions of the guerrilla units. This was made especially difficult because the PLA high command occasionally changed unit designations and the individual brigades were constantly on the move from one operational area to another.

Dean also spent much effort compiling detailed dossiers on

the known PLA leaders and sympathizers, which included not only biographical details but information on their personal habits, friends, associates, anything that would be useful to understanding how the minds of the PLA command worked. The most secret work involved organizing an agent database. Both the field and city police were reluctant to share that kind of information outside their own organizations, and Chief Long suspected what they did share did not reflect all the people on their informant payrolls. But what Long was able to glean, had it become known to the PLA, would have spelled death for dozens of Wanderjahrian informants and seriously damaged his intelligence-gathering capability.

"From now on," Chief Long warned both Marines, "be very careful where you go when off duty, because if you ever fall into PLA hands, they'll pry this information out of you, and you'd better count on it that they know what you're doing up here." Dean resolved that on the rare occasions when he was able to visit Hway, he'd be very careful.

Daily and weekly intelligence summaries had to be prepared for circulation to the field and among the three headquarters groups, and Chief Long delegated the job to his two Marines. In addition, Brigadier Sturgeon and Chief Long regularly briefed the oligarchs when they were in session. Dean and Claypoole accompanied them to Chairman Arschmann's villa on those trips, although they were never invited inside to participate in the actual briefings.

And in addition to all these tasks, Chief Long was responsible for monitoring and improving police intelligence operations within the Staat of Arschland, ferreting out criminal activities of all sorts.

There were trips to the field also, to visit with the Marine training cadre and Feldpolizei commanders, to exchange information, but neither Dean nor Claypoole had yet been fortunate enough to go on any of them.

Claypoole had taken the sign that once hung over Commander Peters's workstation with him to police headquarters. It summarized in one brief statement what military intelligence was all about:

Who Knows What Evil Lurks in the Hearts of Men?
The Two Do.

The intelligence briefing, given that morning by Lieutenant Constantine, had gone very well. The most titillating bit of news was a supposed high-level meeting of PLA brigade commanders that had been held recently in Arschland, but as yet nobody had been able to figure out where or what the subject of the meeting was.

By the time the F-4, logistics, briefing was over, Dean had almost gone to sleep, leaning back in his chair in a far corner of the conference room. Claypoole nudged him in the ribs when he noticed the FIST adjutant glaring at him from across the conference table.

"Gentlemen," Brigadier Sturgeon announced at last, "thank you very much. Now, I know you are all anxious to get back to your duties, but I want everyone to remain seated for a few minutes." He nodded to the Marine from the *Denver*'s shore party who was guarding the door, and the Marine opened it with a flourish.

In walked Captain Conorado followed by Staff Sergeant Bass.

"Gentlemen, I promoted Lance Corporals Claypoole and Dean on the spot that night in Morgenluft, when Commander Peters was almost killed. They earned the stripes. Their service on my staff has confirmed the high opinion I've had all along of the men in Company L. Adjutant?" The brigadier turned to the slim ensign who only moments before had been giving Dean the gimlet eye.

"Attention to orders," the adjutant announced, and then read the promotion orders. Sergeant Major Shiro and Staff Sergeant Bass stepped forward after the reading and pinned the chevrons on, sealing the rite with a stiff punch to each man's shoulder. "Go easy on them," the brigadier said dryly, "I might need them again someday."

"You've done well up here," the sergeant major remarked. "Keep it up."

"Don't turn into worthless staff pogues." Bass shook his finger at the two. "Sir," he turned to Brigadier Sturgeon, "you aren't going to keep these two on your staff permanently, are you?"

"Staff Sergeant Bass, why, I'd rather face the most notorious bandit on Wanderjahr all by myself than cross you," the brigadier said, and laughed.

Sergeant Major Shiro curled his mustaches and grumbled quietly, "Charlie, we need an ops chief in the Three shop. These birds of yours commandeer any of my vehicles again, I'll pull you outta the field to help with map overlays." Bass, who knew better than to ask for details, recoiled in mock horror while the sergeant major stuffed another wad of chewing tobacco into his cheek. He offered Bass a chew, but Bass declined.

"How's it going with third platoon?" Claypoole asked.

"Not easy, but we're making progress. Ever try to teach guys with two left feet how to march? How about up here? I hear you've been into some very bad shit."

"Fine, Staff Sergeant Bass, we're, uh, making progress too, I guess."

"I just bet you are, Marine," Bass answered. He was thinking about the incident at Juanita's, which for a while had been the gossip of the company. He also knew all about the attack at Morgenluft and the fight at the warehouse in Brosigville. "You guys lucked out with this duty," he continued, meaning so far they'd gotten more than their share of the action. He looked at the two. "Listen up. We're proud of what you've done up here. I wish you were back with us again. Sorry about Commander Peters."

Captain Conorado, who had been talking to the FIST executive officer, came over.

"Sir," Claypoole whispered, "I really don't feel I've earned this promotion. Can't you get us back with the company, Skipper?"

Dean nodded in agreement and said, "It isn't that we don't like it here, but we're Marines, sir, not headquarters men." As he was uttering the words, he regretted them. Returning to the company would eliminate any chance he'd ever have of seeing Hway again. But he had to stick with Claypoole.

"Marine, when a FIST brigadier says you earned a promotion, then you earned it, so no more of that from either of you two." The conference room had now emptied out, leaving the four Marines there by themselves. "Look," Conorado motioned for Bass to come close, "a Marine follows orders. I sent you two here because I knew you'd do a good job. You haven't disappointed me. We all know what happened when you were with the city police that night, down by the river. I'd have promoted you both for what you did then. But your job for the duration of this deployment is right here. And if the brigadier decides he's got other plans for you once we're done here, you'll follow your orders. Remember, you don't 'belong' to me, you belong to the Corps." He clapped a hand on each man's shoulder. "Well," he said, "time to go." He and Bass shook hands with them one last time and then they were gone.

Alone in the briefing room, the two lance corporals stared wordlessly at each other for a long moment. They'd been wearing their new rank insignia for some weeks by this time, but it somehow hadn't been real. Now that their company commander and platoon sergeant had witnessed the formal promotion, it was real. Only a year in the Corps and they were both lance corporals, a rank it normally took an infantryman three years to attain.

Claypoole was the first to break the silence. "We gotta find a way to get back to the platoon, where we belong."

"Got that right," Dean agreed.

"So you dislike us that much, huh?"

The two spun toward the voice at the doorway. It was the FIST sergeant major. Claypoole swallowed but couldn't speak. Dean tried not to look guilty and failed miserably.

"I think you're growing soft here," Shiro said. "Maybe you should spend some time with real Marines." He glanced at his watch. "As of eight hours tomorrow morning, you're on temporary additional duty. A forty-eight-hour assignment to the 257th Feldpolizei. Now, get out of my headquarters."

Their eyes popped. "The 257th," Dean said. "That's . . . that's . . ."

"Where our platoon is," Claypoole finished.

"Thank you, Sergeant Major," they both said.

Shiro glowered at them. "What are you doing still taking up space in my headquarters? Has the soft life working with the police made you forget how to obey orders? Get out of here!"

They ran from the briefing room.

The regularly scheduled supply hopper brought something more than the requested food, replacement blaster batteries, and mail. Two Marines in clean garrison utilities got off the hopper, slung blasters over their shoulders, and looked around. An FP pointed out the administration building when they asked directions, and they headed toward it. They were halfway across the parade ground when Staff Sergeant Charlie Bass came out of the administration building. Bass spotted them almost immediately and headed in to intercept the two. He broke out his communicator and spoke into it briefly as he walked.

Lance Corporal Claypoole began with a grin. "Hi, Staff Sergeant Bass."

Lance Corporal Dean was also grinning, but Bass spoke before he could say anything, and the grin fell off his face and his jaw dropped.

"Claypoole, I always knew you were a troublemaker," Bass snarled. "But what's your excuse, Dean? Are you spending too much time in the rear with the beer, you think you're too good?"

"What?" Dean squawked. "I didn't, I'm not, I—"

"What'd I do?" Claypoole demanded.

Bass folded his arms across his chest and glared at them. "First you leave the platoon shorthanded by running off to FIST F-2—"

Dean and Claypoole gaped at each other. They had been ordered to join the intelligence section over their protests.

"—and then you have to go and screw up the entire platoon table of organization by playing hero so you could get yourselves promoted. How am I supposed to reorganize the platoon when you screw up and get sent back? I've got enough lance corporals to go around. You just made me short two PFCs. Do you think I can stick lance corporals in PFC billets?" In fact Bass knew very well he could do exactly that, it was common for meritoriously promoted men to serve in positions below their rank until a position opened to promote them into.

"What?" Claypoole couldn't say anything more; he was too shocked by Bass's reaction. Bass hadn't said anything like that the day before at FIST headquarters. Dean couldn't say anything at all.

Bass let the stunned moment stretch as six other Marines converged double-time on the three. Then he dropped his stern posture and a grin split his face. He grabbed first Claypoole's hand and then Dean's. "Congratulations again, Marines. Everybody's heard all about what you did on Morgenluft and Porcina. Outstanding. Everyone in the platoon's proud of you."

"Nobody more than me," Sergeant Hyakowa said behind them, panting from his run.

"I'm prouder," Eagle's Cry said as he brushed past Hyakowa to face Claypoole. He wrapped an arm around Claypoole's shoulders and squeezed, then extended his free hand to Dean to shake.

Corporals Leach and Keto, their fire team leaders, were the next to arrive and add their congratulations.

Lance Corporal Linsman, the other man in Claypoole's fire team, said threateningly, "Just don't think you're going to replace me, or move above me. I knew you when you were New Guy." Claypoole grimaced, then grinned anew when Linsman pumped his hand.

Schultz was the last to join the group. He hadn't had the farthest to go, he simply ran slower than the others. Schultz knew what the call from Bass was about, and he wanted to have the last word. He planted himself squarely in front of Dean and said slowly, "It's nice to see you've been paying attention to me. Keep it up. Maybe one of these days you'll turn into a Marine." He'd said enough, and he made it clear he was talking to both by turning his head to look at Claypoole as he finished speaking. Then, without warning, his right fist flashed out twice and hit each of them on the shoulder.

"Ow!" Dean yelped. He jumped back, rubbing his suddenly sore shoulder. Claypoole yelped and jumped back as well, but he'd seen the blow coming and didn't get hit as hard.

Leach's eyes glowed. "Pin on the stripes!" he shouted, and pulled his fist back to hit Dean's shoulder.

Bass stepped between them and held up his hands. "Belay that," he ordered. "They got promoted too long ago. It's too late now."

Nobody knew for certain how long after a promotion "pinning on the stripes" with a punch to the shoulder was allowed, but normally the window was the day of the promotion and the day after; rarely did it extend beyond that. The ritual allowed every enlisted man of equal or greater rank to hit a man on the shoulder once for each stripe of his new insignia to "pin them on." Bass and Shiro had been out of line the day before when they "pinned them on."

Schultz knew he was out of line hitting the two so long after the promotion, but he wasn't about to let them get away without someone from the platoon observing the ancient ritual.

"So, what brings you two out here?" Hyakowa asked before anything else could happen.

"We got tired of being with headquarters types all the time," Dean said.

"We needed to spend some time with real Marines again," Claypoole added.

"Well, what are we doing standing around here for?" Eagle's Cry said. His arm still around Claypoole's shoulders, he started walking toward the area where second squad was conducting the training of its company. "You gotta see what we're doing. Hey, did you hear about the way we ambushed a company-size ambush?"

Hyakowa took his leave of Bass and herded Dean toward first squad. "Did you hear what Godenov did the other day?" he asked. "Maybe he's good enough after all."

* * *

The two visitors from Stadtpolizei weren't as impressed by how well the FPs were responding to their training as the other members of the platoon thought they should be, but then, Claypoole and Dean hadn't seen them before third platoon began the training.

"The way this battalion had been trained and ran its operations," Hyakowa told them in an attempt to make them understand, "any one of these shifts today could have taken on the whole battalion and beaten it."

"They used to stand in straight lines, in their dress uniforms, and make targets of themselves," Eagle's Cry added.

Dean looked wide-eyed at the squad leaders, gnawed on his lip, and did his best not to let his disbelief show.

Claypoole was less diplomatic. He didn't say anything— that would be calling the squad leaders liars, and no lance corporal in his right mind would call a Marine sergeant a liar to his face. But his expression and posture said it for him.

Their reactions were understandable. The experience they'd had with the Stadtpolizei had taught them how professional the city police were in their patrol duties. They didn't see how it was possible that the Feldpolizei could be so opposite, no matter what the policemen they worked with in the city said about the field police.

"There's this police investigator from offworld, Chief Long," Dean said after evening chow, when the other men of the platoon were pumping the two of them for details about easy headquarters duty in the big city. "Chief Long was put in charge of all the city police in Arschland Staat."

Claypoole barked out a laugh. "You should have seen Commissioner Landser. He was the police commissioner until Long showed up. Man, he was pissed about an offworlder being put over him. It was like a slap in the face to him."

"But they're working real good together now," Dean concluded.

"And with Marines too," Claypoole said.

"Have they caught the guerrillas who set off those bombs the day we landed yet?" Hyakowa asked. That would be the acid test of how good the city police really were. Dean and Claypoole looked at each other gleefully.

"No. But there's been a lot of other things going on," Dean said.

"Like the guerrilla raid on Morgenluft that almost killed Commander Peters," Claypoole said.

"Only it wasn't the guerrillas who did it."

"And you'll never guess who we busted for that."

Claypoole and Dean were trying to tell the story of the raid on Multan's Eagle's Nest simultaneously, and the telling was getting garbled.

"How about one at a time!" Eagle's Cry said, breaking in.

Embarrassed, Dean and Claypoole looked at each other, and tried to determine without speaking which of them would go first. They nodded as though they'd come to agreement, and both began talking at the same time again.

"As you were!" Schultz barked. He stood directly in front of the two and glared at them until they looked like they wanted to get down on all fours and slink away. "You!" Schultz pointed a finger at Dean. "Talk."

Dean looked at Schultz and swallowed. No matter how experienced he was becoming, the older man always made him feel uncertain. Then he began to tell of the raid on Eagle's Nest. After a moment, Claypoole couldn't restrain himself anymore and began interrupting. He kept interrupting until a growl from Schultz shut him up.

"So maybe it wasn't the guerrillas who bombed out headquarters that first day?" Bass asked when the telling was told.

Dean shrugged. "There's a lot of things the brass think the guerrillas might not have done. That's one thing they think maybe they did do."

"And they think it's possible the guerrillas didn't do it," Claypoole amended as soon as he was sure Dean was finished.

Bass leaned back, lost in thought. The other members of the platoon looked at each other, considering the implications of one oligarch committing terrorist acts in such a way that the guerrillas were blamed for them.

The next day, Claypoole and Dean caught the supply hopper back to Brosigville.

CHAPTER
EIGHTEEN

Over several weeks, Surface Radar Analyst Third Class Hummfree had taken a lot of ribbing from the other junior petty officers in the CNS *Denver*'s Surface Intelligence Analysis section for working on his free time instead of playing computer games or studying for the second class test, the way they were. SRA 3d Hummfree ignored them; as far as he was concerned, what he was doing on his own time at his analysis console was a more demanding and exciting game than the ones they were playing on their personal consoles— and was far better study for promotion than just cracking the books.

Now, after three and a half weeks of puzzling over the surface-movement traces picked up by the *Denver*'s string-of-pearls, and trying to make good intelligence sense of them, he leaned back in his chair and studied the screen he'd just brought up. After a few seconds, he gave a low whistle and leaned forward to tap another series of commands into the computer. His hands hovered over the command nodules while he waited for the computer to bring up his request. He didn't take as much time studying the second screen as he had the first, and he didn't whistle. Instead he immediately tapped in another series of commands. When the third screen appeared, he nodded to himself and hit save-to-transportable, then popped the crystal for his three most recent screens. He could have saved the data to the ship's computer, but it wasn't official work and he would have had to go through the rigmarole of getting authorization from the duty officer. Saving to the crystal was faster.

Hummfree got up from his console and went looking for Chief Petty Officer Peeair, his section chief. As his section was off duty, that meant he had to brave the unknown hazards of chief petty officers' country, a daunting prospect for a third class even when official duty required it—and this didn't come under the heading of official duty. During his nearly four years as a member of the *Denver*'s crew, Hummfree had never been in CPO country. He swallowed, steeled himself, and took the pastel passageway into the unknown. The data was too important to wait for his shift to start.

"What do you want, sonny?" a voice boomed as Hummfree stepped through the hatch into CPO country. "You lost or somethin'?"

Hummfree's head jerked toward the voice. A huge man, someone he didn't recognize, was glowering at him around the stub of a cigar. Water dripped off the end of the cigar and dribbled down his torso to soak into the towel wrapped around his middle. Water dribbling down his legs puddled on the deck around his feet. Wet footprints led behind him to the shower. The many-starred anchor of a master chief petty officer was tattooed on the big man's left deltoid.

Hummfree snapped to attention; master chief petty officers scared him. They scared everyone; a double ration of bile seemed to come with the rate. "Nossir, Master Chief," he managed to say without stammering. "I'm looking for Chief Peeair."

"Well, I happen to know Chief Peeair's off duty. What say you wait until he goes back on duty?" The master chief jutted his jaw aggressively.

"I have some important data the chief needs to see immediately, Master Chief, sir."

"Yer never gonna make second class bothering chiefs when they're off duty, boy. I suggest you get back to your own area and wait until Chief Peeair's on duty." His "suggestion" sounded like an order, but Hummfree stood fast, albeit trembling, instead of scampering away. He cocked his head. "Unless you're carrying orders. You got some orders for Chief

Peeair, boy? I'll give them to him." He held out a hand to take the orders if there were any.

"No-Nossir, I don't have orders," Hummfree croaked. "I'm in Chief Peeair's section, and I just finished analyzing some data that he's gonna want to see. It's important, sir."

The master chief shook his head slowly. "*He*'s off duty, that means *yer* off duty. What do you mean you just finished analyzing it?"

"Sir, this is something I've been working on on my own time. The chief knows about it, sir. He said if I came up with something, he wanted to see it immediately. I came up with something, sir."

The master chief stared at Hummfree hard and rolled the cigar stub to the other side of his mouth. Abruptly he barked, "A-ten-HUT!"

Hummfree, already at attention, stood even more rigid.

"A-bout-FACE!"

Hummfree spun about, facing the entry hatch to CPO country.

"Now stand there," the master chief growled, "just like that until either me or Chief Peeair says you can move." Hummfree heard the squelching of the master chief's feet beginning to walk off. "And don't look around!"

Hummfree stood sweating, hoping some other chief petty officer wouldn't come along and give him an order that contravened the master chief's.

It felt like hours, but probably wasn't more than fifteen minutes, before a gruff voice behind him said, "At ease, Hummfree. What's so important you've got to bother me off duty?"

Hummfree released his tension with a whoosh and turned around. "Chief, you know that project I've been working on on my time?" he said eagerly. "Well, I think I got something."

Chief Peeair, his face otherwise neutral, cocked an eyebrow. "Oh? What do you think you have?"

Hummfree pulled the data crystal out of his pocket. "You gotta see this, Chief."

The chief took the chip and bounced it in his hand. "That good, huh?"

"Better than that, Chief. This might be the piece of the puzzle they need to wrap things up planetside."

Peeair lofted both eyebrows. "Let's take a look." He turned to head back into the depths of CPO country. After three steps he called back, "You gonna come and tell me what I'm looking at, or am I supposed to figure it all out by myself?"

"I'm coming, Chief," Hummfree said, and scampered to catch up.

"Well, gentlemen," Brigadier Sturgeon said to his staff and the commanders of his operational units, who were sitting around a conference table in the briefing room in the Marine headquarters at the spaceport, "it looks like the navy came through for a change." He held up a data chip for everyone to see. "One of their analysts, a petty officer third, came up with this. On his own initiative and time, no less. If it's right, maybe the Corps should hire him away from the navy; he's too good for them." Sturgeon popped the crystal into the console on the lectern while the other officers chuckled at his joke. He glanced at them. "I'm serious."

A map display lit up on the wall behind Sturgeon. "Lieutenant Constantine," he said to Chief Long's assistant, "if you will explain the meaning of this, please." The FIST commander sat down as Constantine limped to the lectern to take over the briefing.

Constantine cleared his throat, then used a laser pointer to indicate the map. "This is a map of the area of the 483rd Feldpolizei GSB. These black lines," he pointed out several curved and jagged lines that seemed to begin and end in random spots and didn't have any immediately apparent meaning, "are movement traces of small groups of people. The *Denver* picked them up on its fourth day in orbit. Some of them have been positively identified. These, for example," he touched a key on the lectern, "are work parties from the farms." Several lines changed from black to yellow. "This one is a group of people heading back to their village after attending church." Another line turned blue. "These are combined Marine-Feldpolizei patrols." Three lines turned green.

"These," the remaining lines, about a third of the total, turned red, "have not been positively identified." He looked from the map to the assembled officers. "We suspect some of them are guerrilla bands. This one we know was." Lightning bolts flashed around one of the red lines. "That was an ambush that killed three Feldpolizei.

"Unfortunately, most of the population of Wanderjahr is rural. Small groups of people are wandering all over the surface of the planet. What makes figuring out who they are even more difficult is the guerrillas also move in small groups and don't assemble until they are ready to act. That makes accurate tracking almost impossible. Especially since the string-of-pearls isn't able to cover the entire planetary surface constantly. And if it did, the volume of data would make it almost impossible to digest and analyze in anything approaching a timely manner.

"There's another problem the *Denver* ran into." Constantine glanced at Sturgeon to make sure it was all right for him to continue with background. The brigadier nodded. "It's doing all its tracking by GSB—rural police precinct," he added for the benefit of anyone who might have forgotten what the initials stood for. "What that means in practice is, once a tracked group of people moves from one GSB to another, it's lost unless the string-of-pearls also happens to have the adjacent GSB under observation.

Commander Van Winkle raised a hand.

"Yes, sir?" he said.

"It's not necessarily germane to this briefing," Van Winkle said, "but why is the *Denver* observing by GSB?"

"I asked them exactly that, sir. It appears that when the GSBs were established, they were overlaid on existing geopolitical divisions. The Ruling Council insisted that people seldom move beyond the bounds of the kreiss, or counties, they live and work in. Those counties correspond to the Grafshaftsbezirk boundaries." He shrugged. "Actual observation tells us the Ruling Council was wrong."

While Constantine talked, the map display behind him continued to change. Each change showed a different precinct on a specific date. While any given map was displayed, black lines of movement turned yellow, blue, green, or red. A few of the red lines had lightning bolts around them.

"A few weeks ago," Constantine said when it was evident that nobody else had any immediate questions, "a junior petty officer in the Surface Intelligence Analysis section got the idea that if he sequentially overlaid maps of given GSBs, the maps might show patterns of movement that didn't match anything the civilians or combat forces would use— even more if he showed two adjacent GSBs. This was the first composite he assembled." He pushed another button and stepped aside so he wouldn't obstruct anyone's view of the map.

The display showed a map of the adjoining 114th and 129th GSBs. Like the others, it had black lines that changed color. As soon as all the lines changed color, all but the red ones blinked out. The map flickered and displayed a different set of red lines, representing movement the next time the *Denver* surveilled those precincts. After a second, it flickered again, and again after another second. In all, there were seventeen different sequential sets of red lines. Constantine looked at the officers. A few looked bemused.

"That almost looks like it should mean something," murmured Commander Iankee, the FIST's composite air squadron commander.

"Look at it this way, sir," Constantine said as he leaned toward the lectern to push another button. Once more the red lines flickered on the display, but at much shorter intervals— this time the display took three seconds.

Van Winkle drummed his fingertips on the conference table.

"That does look like it means something," Captain Halsted, the Dragon company commander, said. "But what?"

"Then the petty officer extrapolated," Constantine said softly, and pushed another button. "He assumed that some lines were continuations of earlier lines—and where some lines might have gone had they continued on their known trajectories."

The red lines appeared afresh on the map. But they didn't

jerk about this time, instead they flowed. Some flowed briefly and vanished before the seventeen displays completed, others started after the beginning, a few ran from beginning to end. Some of them crossed the line that divided the two GSBs.

"Did you see that?" Constantine asked when the display went blank. "Watch it again." The lines flowed. "And then like this."

This time the lines that ended early stayed on the display. When the seventeenth display was reached, all of the terminal lines remained on the screen. Some terminated at places marked as towns or other kinds of settlements. But there were others that seemed to vanish into an irregularly shaped no-man's-land of about eighteen square kilometers.

"What's significant about this, gentlemen," Constantine said as he used the laser pointer to draw a circle around the group of lines that led to nowhere, "is that there is no city, no town, settlement, farm barracks, or other reason for a large number of people to congregate in this area. But detailed analysis indicates that more than two hundred people went into there, and fewer than twenty came out." He paused dramatically, then said, "Somewhere in there, we believe, is the headquarters of the Montezuma Brigade of the PLA.

"Providing, of course, that the petty officer's extrapolations are anywhere near accurate. If they're wrong, this means nothing. At any rate, we have similar displays for the possible headquarters of as many as ten other brigades."

Brigadier Sturgeon stood up. "Thank you, Lieutenant Constantine." Then to the rest, "We have a job to do on Wanderjahr. We're about to do it. The XO will give you copies of my Commander's Intent. F-2 will provide those of you for whom we have intelligence with the data you need to make your operational plans. The F-3 has basics of the FIST operation plan, which will tell you what kind of support you can expect in your plans. See F-4 for your logistical requirements. If you have any personnel problems—and not having enough people isn't a problem—we're Marines, we never have enough people—see the F-1. Gentlemen, I give you to the XO and my staff. Let's get cracking and do this thing."

The officers rose to their feet and stood at attention as their commander left the briefing room. Then a babble broke out as the operational unit commanders asked questions of each other and the FIST staff.

Once Commander Van Winkle had everything he needed from the FIST staff—or everything he could get, which wasn't necessarily the same thing—he returned to his headquarters and called the company and platoon commanders in from the field for a briefing. He deliberately left the Feldpolizei battalion commanders out of the loop.

The infantry battalion commander didn't indulge in any of the theatrics Lieutenant Constantine had, he simply gave the facts—or speculation, as he also labeled SRA 3d Hummfree's maps. He had stripped the battalion headquarters company of men enough to field two platoons, each of which was assigned to GSBs, as were each of the three infantry platoons of each of the three line companies in the battalion. That gave the infantry battalion eleven GSBs to cover. Eight of the eleven had suspected PLA headquarters within their boundaries or in adjacent ones. All eight had to be hit simultaneously to avoid warnings being given to any that weren't hit. What's more, all eight had to be found. All Van Winkle had was an area for each one—the smallest area was a dozen square kilometers, the largest nearly twice that size.

The other three suspected HQs were also covered. Brigadier Sturgeon had stripped enough Marines from his headquarters company to field platoons in two more GSBs. The Dragon company had detached enough men for three platoons, and the Raptor section of the air squadron another two, so the entire FIST covered sixteen GSBs.

The biggest problem the Marines faced was transportation. They needed a lot of it. The FIST had only enough organic transportation to move nine platoons. But two of the Dragon platoons had suspected HQs to deal with, so they couldn't be used. Which meant the entire FIST only had enough transport available to move five platoons of Marines, unless the Dragon GSB that didn't have suspected PLA headquarters pulled out, in which case they could move seven platoons. But even if the Marines had all of their organic transportation available, there still wouldn't be enough to simultaneously move the Marines to all of the suspected headquarters.

And that didn't even begin to count the transportation needed to move the Feldpolizei.

Nor did it account for PLA spies' finding out about the sudden movement of Marine and Feldpolizei forces and giving warning to the guerrillas, which was one reason he had left the Feldpolizei commanders out of the loop. The other was a conviction that it was probable the PLA had spies within the field police organization.

So Commander Van Winkle had to figure out how to move eight Marine platoons and as many FP battalions into position to search eight areas of suspected concentration and destroy or capture whatever units they found there—the eleventh suspected PLA headquarters was covered by one of the platoons from FIST HQ. And he had to move them secretly. There was no way it could be done without organic transportation, which simply wasn't available.

After briefly telling the company and platoon commanders about how the HQ locations were discovered, and distributing map chips, he told them of the need for simultaneity and secrecy.

"What do your battalions have in the way of working transportation?" he finally asked, then held up a hand to forestall quick answers. "I know how much transportation the battalions have, I need to know how much you've got that works. Do you have enough that you could move your entire battalions tomorrow if you had to?"

None of them had enough vehicles to transport their entire battalions. Seven of the eleven, including six of the eight platoons that were going guerrilla hunting, had too many red-lined vehicles.

"When this briefing is over, tell logistics what you need to get the vehicles you do have up and running by the day after tomorrow."

Six ensigns and their platoon sergeants exchanged pained glances.

"Now," Van Winkle looked at his watch, "it's almost 1100 hours. You have your map chips. We will reassemble here at 1500 hours to review your operational plans."

The officers and NCOs rose to attention as Van Winkle left the briefing room. There was no babble when the battalion commander left. The company and platoon commanders stared at each other, appalled by the amount of work they had to do in only four hours.

They reassembled at 1500 hours. The company commanders and three platoon commanders who didn't have plans to draw up had helped the eight who did. None of the plans was complete. Everybody with an operation to run was going to have to walk part of their commands into their assigned areas. For some, it was going to be a four-day walk.

"It's just as well that nobody will see an entire Feldpolizei battalion mount up and head for the field at once," was how Van Winkle brushed aside the objections about not having enough transportation.

The battalion commander quickly reviewed the plans, then told his commanders, "The people who have the farthest to walk move out the day after tomorrow. Lean on your FP commanders to get the rest of their vehicles running ASAP. But don't tell them why. Don't tell any of your Wanderjahrians about this operation ahead of time." He paused and looked off into nowhere for a moment, then said, "Tell them you're under orders to step up patrolling and that's why you're sending more people out now. I'll call the FP commanders in for a briefing the day before your main forces head out. The fewer people who know what's going on, the better.

"I'll coordinate your activities," he said in wrapping up, "not only among you, but with the rest of the FIST. I'll also work on getting additional air support from the *Denver*.

"By the way," he said sternly. "The three of you who didn't have operations of your own to plan—instead of helping the others with theirs, you should have been making plans for functioning as reaction forces or reinforcements.

"But," he glanced at the console monitor on which he'd reviewed the operation plans, "I have to say that under the circumstances, you did an outstanding job in the time you had. Now get back to your commands and get ready to kick some serious ass. To as great an extent as possible, include your Marines in the planning process. They're the ones who'll be leading the FPs in what could be the biggest fight they've ever been in."

The day's briefing was over.

CHAPTER
NINETEEN

The 257th Feldpolizei Battalion had only enough surface and air vehicles to transport half its men, so Company A and part of Company C had to walk to the craggy and crevassed area intelligence had tentatively identified as home to the headquarters of the Che Loi Brigade of the Peoples Liberation Army. When the FPs moved out, all they knew was that they were going on an extended patrol by platoons.

Vanden Hoyt and Bass had been clear in giving the Marines the final briefing before their departure: the day before you reach the area of operations, you will tell your people we just got information about a concentration of guerrillas in the area. They are not to know ahead of time.

What nobody said but everybody understood was that the guerrillas had spies somewhere in the Feldpolizei, even if not in the 257th. Charlie Bass accompanied the Company A command group; Lieutenant vanden Hoyt would follow later with the rest of the battalion. The platoon routes of march and initial objective were tangential to the objective, so no one would know that was where they were headed.

Someone got cute when it came time to assign call radio signs. Commander Van Winkle's battalion headquarters unit was "Farmer." The 257th Feldpolizei Battalion HQ unit was "Henhouse." The 257th's three company HQ units were "Hens," Hen A, Hen B, and Hen C. The platoons were "Chicks," and the sections were "Peeps."

The members of the 257th FP had a confidence in themselves that would have been unimaginable two short months earlier, and, despite some good-natured grumbling, most were looking forward to the operation. Many of them even hoped to encounter bandits. Some of them resented the way they had been used as ersatz blocking forces when Company A's first platoon found the ambush and the Marines wiped it out without any assistance from them, and they wanted to prove to the Marines that they were competent. And ever since Company A's second platoon's second shift had taken out that four-man observation post without suffering any injuries itself, the entire battalion had become almost eager for combat.

The Marines knew where they were going and what their objective was when they got there. Their reaction to walking was mixed.

Chan was glad they were going on ahead of the others because that gave him three more days to train his shift under actual field conditions.

MacIlargie grumbled. He'd been taken in by the recruiting slogan, "Join the Marines and see the universe." He complained about false advertising—the slogan hadn't said anything about seeing the universe one step at a time.

Godenov didn't particularly like having to walk either. But, despite the success he'd had with his shift in wiping out that observation post, he wasn't fully confident that his men would always do what he said, and, like Chan, liked the fact that he had the extra time to train his men in obeying orders in the field.

Being glad or complaining never occurred to Schultz. He was a Marine. To Schultz, there were only three proper ways for a Marine to move into combat—over the beach in a Dragon, on a combat assault in a hopper, or on foot. There was no beachhead to take, no immediate assault to launch. So they walked. It was the natural order of things.

Corporal Doyle didn't voice any complaints. That didn't mean he didn't have any, merely that he didn't say them out loud. After all, he was the senior company clerk. What was he doing out there, walking for three days toward an area thought to be crawling with guerrillas? And then snooping and pooping through that area trying to find those guerrillas? He should be back in a nice, snug headquarters somewhere, he thought, noodling with a computer, instead of being out where there was a high probability someone would shoot at him.

Two days out from the 257th's headquarters the land gradually changed from gently rolling flatlands to low hills, though the flora and fauna mostly seemed to be the same. Hochbaums still climbed toward the clouds, and the grospalms still grew in family groups, but more common among them now were the spikers, trees taller than the grospalms but with narrower boles, from which grew nearly horizontal spiral branches. The undergrowth was a bit thicker by then, patches of low-lying succulents.

The large grazers called sheep chomped contentedly on the tops of the grospalms, and the bigger ones, the cows, stretched up to the juiciest leaves of the giants, but both species avoided the spikers. Smaller quadrupeds the Marines hadn't seen before—beasts a little smaller than Earth elephants—with beaked mouths and knobbly red, green, and gray mottled hides, ripped and nibbled at the spiky foliage and gobbled up the low-lying succulents. The Wanderjahrians said these were called goats. They also told the Marines to keep a respectful distance from them because, like their namesakes, the beaked animals were short-tempered.

Schultz didn't concern himself with the goats any more than he did with the cows or sheep. He'd come to accept that the huge animals were just dumb food animals. So he didn't pay much attention when he saw two bipeds slowly mincing through the underbrush in the direction of an isolated cow. The animals had huge heads with disproportionately large mouths and long, pointed teeth, and he saw that their forelimbs were so small as to be virtually useless. Their hides were coarsely striped grayish green and tan, a good match for the pattern of tree trunks against a green background.

Maybe it was just a psychological defensive reaction on Schultz's part—animals such as he saw on Wanderjahr were too big to understand, so he ignored them. He kept walking and looking all around for danger until he noticed that he was the only member of first platoon's first shift who was on his feet.

Schultz spotted Acting Assistant Shift Sergeant Kharim nearby and dropped to one knee next to him. "Why did everybody stop?" he whispered, peering beyond the animals for any sign of people.

Wordlessly, Kharim pointed at the two bipeds.

"So? They're a couple of pigs, or whatever you call them. What's the problem?"

Kharim twisted around to look up at Schultz's face, which seemed to hover in midair above him. His eyes were wide and his mouth a tight rictus smile. His face was covered with a sheen of nervous sweat. "Shift Sergeant Schultz," he gasped, "those are not pigs. They are tigers."

"Tigers?" Schultz looked back toward the bipeds. They were much closer to the cow now. Both had hunkered down, holding their heads so low their jaws almost brushed the tops of the low bushes. Their massive legs made abrupt, jerky movements, like a bull pawing the ground getting ready to charge. Claws as long as fighting knives on the tigers' feet raked deep gouges in the hard dirt. For the first time, Schultz noticed that the bipeds' eyes faced front rather than to the sides, like the other animals he'd seen—and those front-facing eyes were fixed intently on the huge cow. On every world Schultz had been on, he suddenly remembered, only arboreal animals and predators had front-facing eyes. With massive heads and shriveled forelimbs, he knew the animals were not tree-dwellers.

Schultz lowered himself to his belly and hoped the tigers had no sense of smell.

Suddenly, the tiger nearer the cow screamed and charged toward its front end.

The prey animal snapped its head around at the noise. Then, with an agility and speed astonishing in so bulky an animal, it spun about so it faced away from the charging hunter and swung its tail at it like a whip. The tiger veered off before it got in range of the swing of the heavy tail, and the blow, which looked powerful enough to crush the tiger, missed.

The second predator raced in as soon as the cow began to turn away from the first hunter. The only sound it made was the thunderous pounding of its feet as it charged. The cow's long neck was twisted around so it could watch the first tiger over its shoulder. It saw the second one coming fast, and even faster, spun to swing its tail at it. But that maneuver exposed its flank to the first one, which darted in and tore a hunk of flesh from its side.

The cow honked out in pain, arched its back, bringing its front and rear feet closer together, and stomped those massive feet on the ground, turning rapidly in a tight circle, with its tail slashing from side to side with bone-crushing force.

The two predators weaved around their prey in opposite directions, confusing the huge beast and keeping out of reach of its tail. The cow's head swung about in counterpoint to its tail, its neck jinking up and down as well as side to side in an attempt to keep out of reach of the slashing, snapping jaws of its tormentors.

Trees shook violently from the pounding of the feet of the three huge animals in their dance of death.

Every time one of the tigers saw an opening, it leaped in to gouge out another piece of flesh. The cow's stomping, twirling, and lashing became more frantic as its honks of pain and fear became louder and higher. Blood flowed and flew from the wounds in its sides and belly, and ran from the corners of the predators' mouths as they gobbled the hunks of meat they ripped from its sides.

When the first tiger screamed to begin the attack, all the other grazers had turned to look. The cows and sheep saw they weren't under immediate attack and loped away. The half-dozen goats in the area gathered together and stood in a circle facing outward. They flexed their shoulders and rippled their backs, and long, thick spikes that had lain flat and unnoticed against their shoulders swung forward to protrude past their lowered heads.

The spinning of the cow under attack slowed, and its head swung more slowly side to side—it couldn't keep up the manic movement. The tigers also slowed their weaving and darting and began more methodically looking for openings in the bigger animal's defensive maneuverings. Suddenly, just as one of the tigers moved in front of it, the cow reared up onto its tripod and crashed down, lunging at the tiger with its forelegs.

The tiger jumped back, but not fast enough, and a glancing blow from the cow's foot sent it tumbling and screaming in surprise and pain. The cow bolted past its downed tormentor. But before it could get more than a few steps, the second tiger dashed under the base of its tail and locked its jaws onto the back of its thigh. The cow honked louder than before at the new agony. It again reared up into its tripod and tried to sit on the tiger latched onto its hindquarters, but that tiger jerked its head to the side, pulled back on its powerful hind legs, and staggered backward with a huge hunk of meat in its mouth, which it chomped on once and swallowed.

Off balance, the cow sat heavily and tumbled onto its side.

As soon as the cow began its roll to the side, the first tiger darted in and tore a man-size strip of flesh from the cow's belly. A loop of intestine bubbled out of the wound, and the sight sent the tigers into a frenzy. One of them jumped onto the cow and raked deep gouges in its side with its claws. The cow struggled to roll over onto its legs so it could stand, but the weight of the tiger on top of it prevented that. The first tiger bolted toward the cow's front end with its mouth wide open and bit down powerfully on its neck. As far away as he was, Schultz could hear the shattering of bones.

The cow spasmed, throwing both attackers off. Free of the tigers, it struggled to regain its footing but couldn't. Its head and half its neck lay limp on the ground. Its honks were low and feeble.

The tigers stood watching from a short distance away, their chests heaving from the effort of bringing down the huge prey animal. Then they slowly moved toward its back. When the cow's struggles began to slow, the tigers closed in on it to eat the still-living beast.

Kharim nudged Schultz. "Let's go before the wolves come," he whispered harshly.

"Wolves?" Schultz croaked. He got to his feet. "Lead the way," he said.

* * *

Staff Sergeant Bass brought the Marines together for a final briefing when they reached the turnoff for the possible guerrilla headquarters area. He had very little to say that they didn't already know. They were to tell their shifts about the suspected headquarters. The rest of the 257th Feldpolizei had been transported to the other side of the target area and was about to enter it from there, so the two forces might be able to catch the guerrillas in a pincer movement. They were to break into shifts to search the area. Unusual sunspot activity was building on the local star, so they were told to be prepared for scrambled communications and to be ready to receive on the string-of-pearls frequency if they couldn't hear messages any other way. Unfortunately, if they had to rely on the string-of-pearls, communications would be one-way—their helmet radios weren't powerful enough to transmit to the string-of-pearls.

Deep ravines cut through the area, and jagged crags of igneous rock thrust up through the thin topsoil. The flatland giants didn't grow there; there wasn't enough level ground to support them. Lacking enough space to propagate, the grospalms lived in smaller families. The spikers were more common. Two new types of trees dominated. One was an odd-looking growth with a trunk almost as thick as it was high. Between two and four meters above the ground the trunks split into several massive limbs which quickly split again into less massive branches that twisted and wound about in a Medusa's coif. Gnarly roots splayed widely in the surface dirt to anchor them. The other kind of tree had a slender trunk that seldom rose ten meters. The trees' shaggy branches sprouted along their entire lengths, and they resembled unkempt conifers. The fernlike plants that spotted the ground between the trees grew only a half meter in height; smaller ones grew from cracks in the jutting rocks where trees couldn't gain purchase.

"How are we supposed to find anybody in here?" Godenov complained when Company A's first platoon assembled at the end of the first day's search. The lead elements of the battalion's two forces had met in the middle of the search area, and there had been no contact with or sign of the guerrillas.

Schultz gave him a hard look. "We look for them," he said. Godenov swallowed and stopped complaining.

Vanden Hoyt and Bass joined their command units and set up a battalion command post in a defensible high spot near the middle of the search area. From there they would be able to communicate with all of the platoons and shifts wherever they were in this gouged and tangled wilderness.

"I wonder why the guerrillas aren't using this as an observation post," vanden Hoyt remarked when he first saw the hollowed crown of the basalt mound that was the highest spot in the area. He saw no debris left over from human occupation.

Bass didn't see any sign of occupation either, but drew a different conclusion. "I think they aren't using it now because the observers ran when we got too close."

Vanden Hoyt gave him a speculative look.

Bass nodded toward a narrow crevasse in the side of the hollow. A crack led from the top of the rim down to the bottom of the bowl. Near its bottom the crack enlarged into a hole nearly half a meter wide and more than a meter high.

"A small man could slip through there very easily," Bass said.

"You think the guerrillas are hiding in caves and that's the entrance to one?"

Bass looked away from the crack, out over the rim of the hollow at the surrounding, tortured landscape. Instead of replying, he made a gesture. The gesture said, "Everybody out of here."

Vanden Hoyt looked at the experienced NCO for a moment and glanced at the mysterious satchel Bass had brought along. He decided that Charlie Bass must have a very good reason for wanting everybody to leave quietly. He also gestured the few members of the battalion staff who were in the hollow to leave. He followed his own instruction and left as well.

When Bass was alone, he squatted next to the cleft, his blaster ready in case he needed it. Directing his voice into the crack, he said very clearly, in a conversational volume, "If anybody's in there, I suggest you move back, far back. For your sake, I hope you've got another way out." Then he took the satchel he'd been carrying and exposed its control panel. He made an adjustment on the panel, recovered it, and tossed the satchel into the crack. He remained squatting and listened carefully. He heard a faint sound, perhaps someone moving deep inside the cave. Satisfied that there wasn't someone nearby who would throw the satchel back out, he rose to his feet and left the hollow. Just outside, standing far enough down the side of the peak so only his head showed above the rim, he looked back at the crevasse. Nothing had changed or moved. He pulled a remote control out of a pocket while keeping his eyes on the crack. "Fire in the hole," he said softly, then ducked down and pressed a button.

A loud explosion, magnified by the walls of the cleft and the sides of the hollow, blasted out over the land. The force of the concussion almost knocked Bass from his perch, even though he had a several-foot-thick slab of basalt between himself and the explosion. He regained his balance and listened. All he heard was the sound of falling rocks and gravel. He gave the worst of the dust kicked up by the explosion a moment to begin to settle, then stood and looked back into the bowl. Its uneven floor was covered with rock fragments. Across the hollow, the explosion had opened a second fissure in the rock, and a wedge of basalt had dropped down to fill it in.

"So that's why you wanted us to bring chemical explosives," vanden Hoyt said as he rejoined Bass.

"Satchel charge," Bass replied. "A long time ago Marines called them 'bunker busters.' I knew this area was riddled with caves and that we'd need a way to close them. Sometimes old methods are still very useful."

"You do think they're in caves, don't you?"

Bass nodded. "The string-of-pearls saw a lot more people enter this area than left it. Our people haven't seen any sign of people on the surface. They must be underground." He cocked his head at the lieutenant. "I pulled tunnel rat duty once on Minh. It's a really nasty job. If we go down after them, we have to be prepared to lose a lot of field police. If we were all Marines, we could do it. Even though we outnumber the rebels by more than two to one and our Marines are in chameleons, most of our people are FPs. We could very easily lose this fight."

"Well, we better get our people started finding cave entrances."

Bass nodded. He knew he was going to hate this.

"C-C-Commander," the panting runner reported, "the Confederation Marines and the oligarchs' troops have sealed the entrance to San Juan."

Hing kept his face bland. This was bad news; he'd lost his best observation spot. It also might mean the enemy knew his brigade was in the caves. "How deep did they seal it?"

"To a depth of at least three meters, Commander. They used explosives. A slab of roof fell into the tunnel."

Hing knew explosives were used; he'd felt the tremor. But a slab of rock that big . . . If the Marines or the Feldpolizei occupied San Juan, he wouldn't be able to eavesdrop on them through that thickness of rock.

"Have they occupied any of the other observation posts?"

The runner shook his head. "Commander, all I know about is San Juan is blocked."

Hing ordered the runner to return to his post, then leaned back in his chair to think for a moment. Abruptly, he sat erect and started giving commands.

"We must assume they know we are in caves," he began. "Since they sealed San Juan instead of entering it, either they are going to try to seal all the entrances to this complex and hope we die that way, or they want to seal some so they can enter through the remainder and try to kill us directly. Unseal the escape tunnels. We'll seal them back up on our way out. If they get in, we can be waiting for them when they come back out. And we have our little surprises . . ."

Lieutenant Pincote smiled, revealing her pointed teeth. She was delighted at the prospect of loosing the wolves on the unsuspecting lackeys and their Marines. She still wasn't moving with full freedom, but the synthskin was grafting well.

Medic Cildair had agreed she was ready to return, if not to full field duty.

Hing almost glared at her. "You will not release the wolves until I direct you to," he snapped. "When you do, you will report directly back to me immediately afterward."

Pincote's grin slipped only a little before she nodded acknowledgment of the order.

The next morning, Bass was struggling with the radio to coordinate the movements of all the platoons and sections as they moved into position to blow the cave entrances they weren't going to enter. But a massive solar flare was messing up the ionosphere. The Marine squad-leader company commanders had radios that relayed signals through the string-of-pearls, but the only communication he had with the other Marines was line-of-sight—and the terrain prevented him from having line-of-sight communications with more than a few of them. He had to have the string-of-pearls relay his signals back to the platoon and shift leaders, but those Marines couldn't signal back to him the same way; they had to relay through their company HQ units. Coordination was difficult.

Vanden Hoyt was poring over the small bits of data he'd been able to locate on the subsurface structure of that patch of badlands, leaching out any bit of information he could pass on that would help the Marines and their men when they went underground. A call came in over the high-command net.

"Well, I'll be," Bass muttered as he listened to the gist of the message. Then into the radio he said, "Wait one for the Six Actual." He turned toward vanden Hoyt. "Ensign, you gotta hear this."

The two Marines and their FP counterparts listened to the new orders that came over the scrambled circuit, then looked at each other in stunned silence for a long moment.

Finally, vanden Hoyt took the radio handset. "We're patched through the string-of-pearls?" he asked. Bass nodded, and vanden Hoyt said into the radio, "All Hen, Chick, and Peep Actuals, this is Henhouse Actual. All Hen, Chick, and Peep Actuals up. I say again, all Marines report to the

Henhouse. Leave your Chicks and Peeps in place. They are to take no offensive action in your absence; they may take defensive action only. Chick and Peep Actuals acknowledge to your Hen Actuals. Hen Actuals acknowledge to me once your Chicks and Peeps are on their way." He gave the handset back to the radioman. "Well, what do you know," he said softly.

Bass simply shook his head. Then they settled back to wait. It would take a couple of hours or more for all the Marines to arrive.

CHAPTER
TWENTY

Brigadier Sturgeon's landcar wound its way slowly up the long road to Kurt Arschmann's villa. The drive reminded Claypoole of the first visit he had made there with the Brigadier shortly after their arrival on Wanderjahr. Commander Peters had been with them then. How long ago that seemed now. This time Ambassador Spears sat next to the brigadier. And this time the entire Council would be gathered at Arschmann's villa to hear the ambassador and the brigadier give their final report on the 34th FIST's mission to Wanderjahr.

Claypoole's mind drifted back to Maggie again. He never mentioned her to anyone anymore, not even to Dean, but he was always thinking of her, wondering what would have happened if she hadn't been killed. What was her real name? Goddamn, he couldn't even remember it! His face turned red with suppressed rage and frustration. They'd never found her killer. To young Lance Corporal Rachman Claypoole, that was probably the one piece of unfinished business the Marines would leave on Wanderjahr.

Dean sat in the rearmost seat, gazing back down the road. It was a beautiful day on Wanderjahr. The windows of the taller buildings in the heart of Brosigville glinted in the early-morning sunlight. He'd come to like the place, despite the tragedy that had plagued it in recent months, because it was where Hway lived, and though he'd be leaving very soon and would most likely never see the young woman again, the thought of her warmed him.

Ambassador Jay Benjamin Spears pulled contemplatively at

his beard, not paying much attention to the passing country-side. His beard was full of gray and the once-dark mat of hair on his head was very thin and streaked with gray. The Confederation Council had already approved his request for retirement, and he was thinking ahead to settling down and enjoying his remaining years. He was not thinking of the unpleasant business that would present itself in only a few minutes. He knew what had to be done, and he would do it. He patted the document folded in a breast pocket and then turned his thoughts back to a future of hunting rare books and maps in exotic cities.

Commissioner Alois Landser sat beside Chief Long. He was dressed in his most splendid uniform that morning, as befit a momentous occasion. He knew now who had been responsible for his brother's death, and he was going to see that justice was done to that person. A tiny rivulet of perspiration trickled down the left side of his face.

Chief Hugh Long lounged in his seat. He'd met some truly fine people on Wanderjahr and taken care of some very nasty ones. That was his job. The morning would be a superb finish to a very difficult mission. Some eggs would still be broken, but—he shrugged mentally—they were bad eggs anyway.

Brigadier Ted Sturgeon sat stiffly in his seat, staring ahead at the road as it unwound. By then Arschmann's villa was clearly visible. The rays of the morning sun illuminated its walls brilliantly. He thought back to the morning he'd met Lorelei Keutgens here, and of the sunlit garden behind Arschmann's conference room that wafted such a beautiful aroma through the open windows. They had come a long way since then, he reflected bitterly. But now it was over, and he would do his duty this morning as he had done it every morning all his adult life.

The parking lot was full of landcars when the brigadier's party drove up. They dismounted and entered the villa. "Keep your weapons ready," the brigadier whispered to Dean and Claypoole. Commissioner Landser smiled.

* * *

The composition of the Wanderjahrian Ruling Council had changed significantly since Kurt Arschmann had convinced it to ask for assistance from the Confederation of Worlds. Turbat Nguyen-Multan was now light-years from Wanderjahr, facing the rest of his life in prison. Gretel Siebensberg was represented by her chief minister, until her estate could be settled and passed on to some successor. Death, by natural causes, had come to Oligarch Mannlicher, so Carmago Kampot Khong, as heir apparent, had succeeded to his position on the Council.

The oligarchs sat expectantly about the Council table, waiting for Ambassador Spears to make the special statement that had brought them together that fine morning. With the great successes the Feldpolizei had been enjoying recently over the bandits, there was no doubt in any of their minds that he was going to formally announce that the Marines' mission had been a total success. Already the Marines were beginning to turn the Feldpolizei GSBs back to their commanders, and the Marines responsible for training them were about to return to Brosigville's port, preparatory to their departure.

The table had been arranged so that Chairman Arschmann sat with his back to the window that looked out over his formal gardens. The window was open. The other oligarchs sat on either side of their chairman. Brigadier Sturgeon and his party were escorted into the chamber by the secretary who had recently replaced the dead Kalat Uxmal.

The party bowed respectfully toward the oligarchs, and while Brigadier Sturgeon and Ambassador Spears remained standing, the others took seats opposite the conference table.

"Chairman Arschmann, Mrs. Keutgens, gentlemen," Ambassador Spears began. "On behalf of the Confederation of Worlds, I wish to announce that our mission to secure the safety and peace of the people of Wanderjahr is formally ended." He was interrupted by applause from the oligarchs. "We have a few details to work out before we can withdraw our forces, but essentially the Feldpolizei is now a fully trained, fully equipped combat force capable of ensuring that the rebellion that has plagued your world does not break out again." More applause. "Next week representatives of the Peoples Liberation Army will appear before you to negotiate a settlement."

This statement was followed by amazed silence. They had not been informed about that in the periodic situation briefings Brigadier Sturgeon had given them over the past months. Chairman Arschmann broke the silence. "But you said the rebellion has been crushed. Why do we need to negotiate with anybody?"

"Because you will," Ambassador Spears answered. "The guerrilla commanders have agreed to lay down their arms providing you grant them certain concessions." He pulled the folded piece of paper out of his pocket and handed it to Chairman Arschmann, who read it quickly and, a look of profound disgust on his face, passed it to Lorelei Keutgens as if it were a poisonous reptile. "This is a most irregular demand, Mr. Ambassador," he almost shouted, turning red in the face. "Most irregular—and illegal!"

Ambassador Spears smiled and nodded. "Yes, it is irregular, Mr. Chairman. And considering the finer points of interplanetary law, it may also be, as you say, 'illegal.' But I don't give a good goddamn. Your granting these demands will save many lives and restore peace to this world. That's why you're going to grant them. But did you seriously think you could use the Confederation Marines to shore up this medieval fiefdom you've created for yourselves here on Wanderjahr?" He fixed an icy stare upon the Council members, his face suddenly flushed with righteous anger. "You are a collection of greedy throwbacks to the days of the Hanseatic League. Your ancestors exploited the homeless and poor of Old Earth's most unfortunate populations to settle this world, and ever since, you have held these people in virtual thrall to your own economic interests. That is now over."

Carmago Khong stood up. "And it is about time!" he said loudly. "These bandits are our own children, some of them. I've said all along, Kurt, Lori, all of you, that we should have negotiated with them instead of calling in the Confederation! Well, now we will, and I say it's a good thing for Wanderjahr. Thank you, Mr. Ambassador." He sat down.

"You cannot enforce this outrageous demand!" Arschmann shouted.

"We can and we will," Brigadier Sturgeon announced.

A shadow cast itself across the conference table as a man appeared in the window just behind Arschmann. With the bright sunlight streaming in from behind the figure, it was a solid black to the seated oligarchs, but there was no doubt the man was a combat-loaded Marine, blaster at port arms. He leaped lightly to the floor and stood just behind and slightly to the left of Chairman Arschmann.

Captain Thomas, commander of the landing party, was followed by forty of his men. Silently they took up positions behind the seated oligarchs. Just before first light they had landed by hopper a few kilometers from Arschmann's villa and marched unseen into the woods on the other side of the garden, where they'd remained silently in hiding until a signal from the *Denver* had alerted them that the brigadier was approaching the main entrance to the palace.

"With the redeployment of my men from the field, I now have the combat strength to ensure that these negotiations proceed successfully," the brigadier said. "I warn all of you that any resistance to the peace process will be met with force. And one more thing. By next week those of you who do not now have Feldpolizei garrisons in your Staats will have them, and you will cooperate with the garrison commanders to ensure the peace is kept." This was directed principally at Klaus von Hauptmann and Turbat Nguyen-Multan's factor, a hulking, totally bald man named Bu Lon, who was representing Multan's interests until a successor could be found to replace him.

There was a roar from outside the conference room as two hoppers landed on the lawns in front of the main entrance to the building. Voices sounded, shouting in alarm, and people could be heard running through the corridors of the building. The proceedings in the Council chamber halted for a few seconds and then the doors burst open and in marched Lieutenant Constantine with Shift Leader Lyles and a group of Brosigville city police, escorting three tightly manacled men. Chief Long and Commissioner Landser stood up. They moved forward to the center of the room while Brigadier Sturgeon and Ambassador Spears took the chairs they'd just vacated. The four had choreographed the move carefully to achieve a no-fooling, parade ground effect.

Claypoole turned to Dean and sighed. They both relaxed. With the appearance of the police and Marines, there would now be no need for the side arms they were carrying. Claypoole decided to get himself transferred back to the company ASAP; he was getting mighty tired of being Brigadier Sturgeon's point man.

"I absolutely refuse to be surprised by anything anymore today," Oligarch Hans Rauscher said, and sighed wearily.

"Kurt Arschmann," Chief Long said formally, "as the chief police officer representing the attorney general of the Confederation of Worlds in this sector of Human Space, I hereby place you under arrest." A gasp rose from the oligarchs at this announcement. "You are being charged with the attempted murder of Commander Ralph Peters, a citizen of the Confederation and an officer of the Confederation Marine Corps who was on official duty in the Staat of Morgenluft on Samstag, the fourth day of the month of . . ."

Two Marines grabbed Arschmann and hauled him to his feet. They dragged him around the conference table and shoved him into the arms of the waiting police officers. He screamed and cursed and struggled all the way. Calmly, Chief Long finished his statement of charges.

"Kurt, you bastard! I knew it was you all along!" Lorelei Keutgens screamed.

"I simply refuse to be further surprised anymore today," Hans Rauscher muttered.

"Madame." Chief Long bowed toward the matriarch. "His chief accomplice was one of your very own ministers. He is here now," he nodded toward the three men the police officers had brought in with them, "and we have his full confession."

"Madame." Commissioner Landser made a sweeping bow before Lorelei Keutgens, nearly touching the floor with his right arm. "As the chief law enforcement officer of Arschland, I wish to announce, most respectfully, that I hereby arrest *you* for the bombing of the Marine headquarters that was responsible for the deaths of thirty-seven of our citizens." The remaining oligarchs gasped, and the blood drained from Lorelei Keutgens's face. "And also I arrest you for the murder of Gretel Siebensberg and her people." The blood now rushed back into Lorelei's face and her eyes blazed in fierce anger. Watching her from where he sat, Brigadier Sturgeon thought he'd never seen a woman so alive and beautiful.

"You have no proof and you have no jurisdiction over me," Lorelei answered, keeping her voice under control with difficulty.

"Madame, do you recognize that man, the short one in the gray tunic? You should. He is in your employ. He set the bomb and we have his full confession. You were visiting Arschland the day the bomb was planted. In fact, you met with Brigadier Sturgeon and Ambassador Spears in this very room that day. *That* man was your driver on the occasion. Through him we identified the men in the party that murdered Mother Siebensberg, and they are also in custody. We brought the man along this morning so he could tell your colleagues about his part in the plot."

Landser smiled. "We were able to identify the man because Lance Corporal Dean," he nodded toward the Marine, "smelled explosives residue on him the morning Ambassador Spears and Brigadier Sturgeon met with you and Chairman Arschmann in this very room."

"Brigadier!" Lorelei shouted. "Ted, this—this popinjay is out of his mind! You won't let him arrest me, will you?"

Brigadier Sturgeon did not answer. Instead he nodded to Captain Thomas, who gently placed a hand on her shoulder.

"You have no jurisdiction!" she shouted.

"I don't need any, ma'am," the captain replied quietly. He put one hand under her arm and gently levered the woman to her feet. A Marine took her other arm and together they escorted her into the arms of the waiting police officers.

Hans Rauscher, who was delighted at the morning's surprising developments because they meant now he could relax and enjoy life so long as he cooperated with the new regime, turned to Manfred Kaiserstuhl, sitting beside him, and whispered, "Manny, wake me when the current rash of surprises is over, will you?"

"Gentlemen." Klaus von Hauptmann spoke for the first time. "We require a full explanation of these charges. You can't just barge in here, make allegations, and haul off the members of this Council like—like common criminals." Privately, von Hauptmann was very thankful he hadn't been charged with anything, since he'd cooperated with Turban Nguyen-Multan on several smuggling enterprises. Oligarch Max Ficker, sitting just to von Hauptmann's right, smiled to himself. He'd always left business to his factor, and the other oligarchs, he knew, despised him as a mere playboy. Well, let them fume and fuss over all this mess, he thought. First thing next week he would depart on a long vacation, far away from Wanderjahr, some world where there were plenty of sun-warmed beaches, casinos, and unattached women.

"Sir," Chief Long answered, "our entire investigation will be made available to you, and every stage of the legal proceedings will be open to full public scrutiny. And, sir, I've arrested 'common criminals' all my life, and these two make most of them look like decent, God-fearing citizens."

Commissioner Landser stepped over to where the policemen were putting the cuffs on Lorelei Keutgens. "Madame," he said to her quietly, "I have all the 'jurisdiction' I need to arrest you for crimes committed here in Arschland, and when we are finished with you, I will turn you over to the authorities in Friedland. I understand why you bombed the Marine headquarters, but may I ask, why did you feel it necessary to murder poor old Gretel Siebensberg?"

"I murdered no one!" Lorelei shouted defiantly, wincing as the arresting officer double-locked the cuffs on her wrists. "But I'll tell you what, you ridiculous little fop. That Bible-thumping bitch was a colossal bore all her life. And you," she whirled on Kurt Arschmann, "I only regret I was unable to pay you back for trying to kill me and my family, you bastard! What happened to Gretel was child's play compared to what I had in store for you."

Arschmann made a lopsided smile. "Lori, we should've gotten married after that worthless husband of yours died. We'd have made a perfect team. As it is," he sighed in mock sorrow, "maybe we can convince Commissioner Landser to give us adjoining cells. We could scratch each other to death through the bars."

"No chance. You go offworld," Chief Long rumbled. "She stays here." He nodded to the policemen to escort the prisoners back to Brosigville.

"Wait! One moment, please," Lorelei said. She twisted around and fixed her gaze on Brigadier Sturgeon. "Ted, may I say something to you in private? Just a moment, please?" The brigadier hesitated, and then walked over to Lorelei and lowered his head to hear her. "Ted," she whispered in his ear, "I never meant you or your men any harm. What I did I did for the good of Morgenluft, not for myself. Will you see that Hway and the children are looked after?"

He straightened up and stared at her for a moment, contemplating briefly the possibilities the woman had presented to him. He shook his head. She belonged in jail. "The Council will take care of your family," he replied coldly before making a tired gesture toward the police officers, who led her away. Wearily, he took his seat. "Finish it off, will you, Jay?" he said to Ambassador Spears.

"Gentlemen," Spears announced, "there is one more piece of unfinished business. With Chairman Arschmann, uh, out of circulation, the Council needs a new chairman. We will spare you the difficulty of picking someone. Your new chairman is the Honorable Carmago Kampot Khong. He has our full backing and you will cooperate with him in every way. The guerrilla delegation is due here tomorrow. I suggest you consider seriously how best to meet their terms.

"These proceedings are now ended."

* * *

"So?" Chairman Khong asked. He was sharing a nightcap with Brigadier Sturgeon and Chief Long in his hotel suite. "Did you pull a fast one on us?"

The brigadier smiled. "Tell him." He nodded at Chief Long.

"No, sir, we did not," the chief responded. "It just took us a while to figure it all out. I must say, it was Alois who broke the case for us. He has his spies and informants everywhere, and it was through them we put the finger on the men who acted on behalf of the oligarchs."

Chairman Khong raised an eyebrow. "Well, I surely hope he doesn't employ any of those people in my service."

"He probably does," Chief Long answered, and they all laughed. "You know, Alois and Lorelei Keutgens both had me fooled. At first I thought Alois couldn't do anything but strut. And with Lori, well, I really thought we could trust that woman. She was so . . . so . . ."

"Charming," Brigadier Sturgeon said. "Yes, 'charming'; she charmed me all to hell." He grimaced. "And Ambassador Spears." They were all reminded of the story about the ambassador's marriage proposal and laughed again.

"And me too, gentlemen," Khong added, "and I've known her a lot longer than any of you." He shook his head.

"She and Arschmann were in deadly competition for power on this planet," Chief Long said. "Arschmann conceived the idea of getting us to intervene, to clear up the problem with the guerrillas while he eliminated his competitors among you oligarchs. He was the first one to realize it was Lori who tried to wipe out the Marines' headquarters. She too wanted us to take a swipe at the guerrillas, get them out of the way while she worked on her real competition. And then Arschmann tried to get rid of her."

"And Lori had Gretel murdered? It's hard to believe her capable of such a crime," Khong mused, sipping from his wineglass.

"Well, she knew all along it was Arschmann who'd attacked her, but Gretel was a vulnerable target. Lori set the massacre up so we'd pin it on the guerrillas. She knew we'd see through the ruse eventually, but she thought we'd blame the massacre on Arschmann since it didn't take us long to conclude he'd attacked Morgenluft. It did look at first as if he was methodically eliminating the other members of the Council. But the evidence hanging that deed on the guerrillas was so transparent once we began to look into it that I think she planned all along that we'd pin it on Arschmann. Who'd ever suspect her? Clever woman. We never suspected her until Kalat Uxmal spilled the beans to Alois, just before he was murdered. Kurt knew he was spying for the guerrillas all along, but when he discovered the man was also Landser's informant, he had him silenced. We don't know who the triggermen were, but we know Arschmann ordered the assassination. Proving that will be difficult, but we already have all we need to put him away on other charges."

Chairman Khong shook his head and looked into his wineglass.

"And do you know something?" Chief Long said. "Lori's code name was Zitze, an Old German word meaning 'teat.' Before he was killed, Uxmal told Alois it was 'Zitze' who'd pulled off the bombing. And that guerrilla spy who was killed in the warehouse fight, Garth, he knew too and tipped us when he said it was 'Titties' who'd done the bombing. We just didn't catch on for a while. Incredible, isn't it?"

"They never liked each other, Lori and Gretel, you know?" Khong said. "Then who was it who shot at the two Marines in the bar that morning?"

"That was a guerrilla sniper-assassination team," Sturgeon answered. "We haven't told either of the two Marines involved. I think it's better they just put the experience behind them, especially now that they're going to have to respect the guerrilla peace commissioners. The PLA just wanted to poison relations between the local people and my men. It's an old terrorist strategy."

"I have a cousin with them," Khong admitted. "As you know, I rose from dirt to be Mannlicher's factor and then a member of the Council. Multan and I were the only non-German Wanderjahrians ever to have been admitted that high in the government here. Multan made it by ruthlessly carving out an empire in Porcina, an out-of-the-way Staat nobody gave a damn about until thule came along. I made it because old Mannlicher, he was not like the other German families on Wanderjahr. He believed men should be given a chance to prove themselves by running their own lives. That's what the PLA say they want. Tomorrow we'll find out how sincere they are about it."

Then Carmago Khong snapped his fingers, remembering something. "That Council meeting, when we voted to ask the Confederation to send you here to help us—do you know what Lori said then? She said that inviting you to come here would change everything for us, and she didn't know if that was a good thing or a bad thing. Evidently she thought it would be good for her. But damn, she was right!

"Gentlemen, let us make a toast, shall we?" He raised his glass. "To change!" he shouted. The word seemed to echo in the room for a long time after the toast was drunk.

Later that night, before saying his good-byes, Brigadier Sturgeon turned to Chairman Khong. "I have one question for you, Mr. Chairman. Who's going to take over Lori's government? Just curious."

"Ah, under our laws the firstborn of the same parents automatically inherits their estates when both predecease. But since Lori's only son is dead, it all devolves on *his* firstborn offspring. That would be young Hway. The actual reins of government will remain in the hands of a regent until she attains her majority at age twenty-five. Until then she'll be carefully coached in the art of statecraft and the business of managing the Staat of Morgenluft. Then she will sit with us on the Council. She is a beautiful and accomplished young woman, Brigadier."

"Yes, Mr. Chairman, so I've heard, so I've heard." God-damn, he thought, Lance Corporal Dean has seduced an oligarch!

CHAPTER
TWENTY-ONE

It took two and a half hours for all the Marines to assemble in the hollow peak. They took off their helmets as they sat so they could be more easily seen. Bass and vanden Hoyt refused even to hint to the early arrivals why they'd been called away from preparations to find the guerrillas. So some of them had to sit and stew until Bladon, Goudanis, and Lonsdorf showed up. They hadn't had the farthest to travel, but three deep ravines had slowed them down considerably. They were drenched with sweat when they finally clambered over the lip of the hollow.

Corporal Bladon saw immediately that they were the last ones in. "What's up, boss?" he asked brightly despite his weariness.

Bass and vanden Hoyt looked at each other. They hadn't discussed who should give the news to the men. Bass made a gesture deferring to the officer. Vanden Hoyt nodded and looked briefly at each of the Marines of the third platoon before he spoke.

"I want you all to know," he began slowly, "that I think, Staff Sergeant Bass and I think, that you've done an outstanding job with the 257th Feldpolizei."

There were a few murmurs and the Marines glanced at each other. This didn't sound like a briefing for the operation they were about to launch. Most of them thought there was something ominous about what vanden Hoyt was saying. It was as though he was disagreeing with someone else's opinion of their performance. They steeled themselves for the bad news coming.

"Two months ago," vanden Hoyt continued, "you began working with a paramilitary unit that suffered from low morale, defective tactics, and," he glanced apologetically at the Wanderjahrian officers present, "poor leadership. During these two months you gave the 257th strong leadership, taught them winning tactics, and raised their morale. You have turned them into an effective fighting force. I salute you, Marines." He put his words to action—he came to attention and saluted the men of third platoon. He studied them for a moment, those thirty Confederation Marines. He and Charlie Bass were the only ones above the rank of three-stripe sergeant. Most of the men were PFCs and lance corporals, junior enlisted men. But they had served in positions far above their pay grades, and they had performed magnificently. He felt honored that his first command as a Marine officer was of a unit so good. It didn't cross his mind that during the same two months, he and his platoon sergeant had functioned as a battalion commander and executive officer, several positions above their own ranks.

"Our operation is concluded. Hostilities were declared ended at 0930 hours this morning."

Pandemonium broke out as the Marines jumped to their feet. Some shouted questions, others hooted in glee, more shook each other's hands and pounded each other's backs. Most of them were glad the operation was over before they went into the caves; they knew how deadly that would have been. A few were disappointed; they'd wanted to see how well their FPs would function in this harrowing type of operation.

Bass bellowed and silence thumped down on the hollow. "Some of you asked questions in that melee," Bass said. "Well, if you'll shut up and listen, I've got some answers." He glowered at them, but the glower was a facade, disguising how proud he was of his men's performance. "Third platoon, Company L, 34th FIST, is one of the best outfits I've served with in my twenty-plus years as a Marine. But," he shook his head, "it wasn't us who won this campaign." He paused for a moment to allow the men to express their disbelief. "You're not going to want to believe this," he held up a hand to get their attention again, "but it was a bunch of headquarters pukes who won it."

There were shouts and howls from the men, but Bass raised his voice and talked over them. "FIST HQ, in cooperation with the civilian police experts who came with us, conducted a comprehensive investigation. They also managed to make contact and open discussions with the highest levels of the PLA leadership. The guerrillas weren't responsible for *all* the troubles that were going on. At 0930 hours this morning, Brigadier Sturgeon and Chief Long arrested Ruling Council Chairman Arschmann and Oligarch Keutgens for various crimes, including treason and the attempted murder of Confederation citizens. The brigadier and the chief laid down new rules, which the remaining oligarchs agreed to. Peace talks between the Ruling Council and the PLA are scheduled to begin. We're through."

Bass stood arms akimbo, looking at his men. Aside from a few grimaces, the men didn't express any of the disgust or chagrin he was afraid they might about the "headquarters pukes" winning the campaign.

"You did an outstanding job, Marines. And you gave the proper authorities the opportunity they needed to do what they had to to win this thing.

"Now, I want you to go back to your units and pull them back from the assault positions. Bring them to the designated rally point north of these badlands. Oh, and you may as well turn command back to the regular shift sergeants and platoon and company officers. We no longer have commissions in the Wanderjahr Feldpolizei. They were canceled when peace was declared. Squad leaders, stay behind for a moment."

"Commander," the Che Loi Brigade's intelligence officer said. "All of our observation and listening posts have reported in. I know where nearly all of the Feldpolizei are, though where the Confederation Marines are isn't fully clear." He pressed a button on the console to bring up the situation map. The entrances to the underground were marked on the map. Not all of the entrances went into the part of the cave complex the guerrillas used. The intelligence officer pushed another button and a red X appeared on more than half of the entrances.

"We believe they are about to block those entrances with explosives." He pushed another button. Red circles appeared outside other entrances. "Those are Feldpolizei sections. All indications are that they will enter the complex at those locations."

Hing studied the map briefly and nodded. About half of the marked cave mouths led into short tunnels or single chambers rather than into the complex itself. Fully half of the entrances to the complex proper weren't marked at all. "They are going to have a very difficult time," he said. "Especially when they meet the weapon they don't know we have." He looked at Lieutenant Pincote. "Release the wolves," he said. "And report back to me immediately."

Pincote bared her pointed teeth in a tight grin. "Yes, Commander." And she was gone.

Hing turned his attention to the communications officer. "Do we have contact with anybody yet?"

"No, Commander. The ionosphere is still too disrupted for signals to bounce, and we haven't been able to break the ciphers that would allow us to utilize the Confederation's string-of-pearls."

Hing grimaced. He would have liked to be able to communicate with the outside world, but it wasn't that important. Outside communications wouldn't make any difference in the coming fight. His nearly three hundred freedom fighters would be enough to defeat the three hundred Feldpolizei and their Confederation Marines. His three hundred fighters and the wolf pack.

First squad, minus Sergeant Hyakowa, headed southwest toward where they had left their FPs. Four kilometers from the hollowed peak the guerrillas called San Juan, they reached Van Impe's section and dropped him off in its thicket of unsightly conifers. The position overlooked a cave entrance into a long ridge. The cave mouth couldn't be seen from the position because of the trees, but patches of the ridge wall were visible through breaks in the forest. The three fire team leaders split off there as well to continue on to their platoon HQ groups.

A few hundred meters farther Schultz said, "Let's look for

more cave mouths," and angled closer to the ridge they were paralleling.

"Why?" MacIlargie objected. "Why do we need to look for more, we found all of them. Besides, the operation's off."

Schultz continued looking at the ridge face.

"Because this is a big area," Chan said patiently. "There's not many of us and we didn't have much time. We're bound to have missed some." He didn't want to look for more cave mouths any more than MacIlargie did, but if the guerrillas hadn't gotten the word about cessation of hostilities, some of them might come out looking for the Marines or the FPs. As long as the Marines were in the area, they had to know all the directions danger might come from. And all those coniferlike things along the face of the ridge could hide a lot of openings. Godenov and Doyle followed Schultz, but MacIlargie looked as if he might angle away until Chan jabbed a thumb toward his own collar. Then he stuck his arm out to point the way. Chan was simply reminding the junior man that he had rank and MacIlargie had to obey his orders. MacIlargie grumbled but he followed. Chan brought up the rear.

An almost clear strip from four to ten meters wide ran along the base of the ridge where running water and rocks falling from above had kept trees from taking root.

"Here's one," Schultz said when the others caught up with him. "Whose section is this in?" The cave mouth had been obscured by a small line of grospalm saplings and a rock overhang, but it was big enough for three men to enter abreast without ducking. Schultz pulled a paper map from a shirt pocket and made a mark on it. He gave MacIlargie an I-told-you-so look. MacIlargie looked blandly innocent.

Schultz moved out and the others trailed along.

Seventy-five meters farther, in a place where the clear strip was eight meters wide, Schultz found another cave mouth nobody had seen. This one was smaller, only one man could walk through it at a time, but no trees blocked it at all. He spat to the side in disgust. "I wonder how many more we didn't find."

Chan was horrified; it looked as if they hadn't found very many at all.

"What was that?" Doyle asked.

Chan didn't ask what, he simply listened and looked around. He saw the faces of a couple of the others hovering in midair above their chameleons; they were looking and listening. But the mass of coniferlike trees in front of him was so dense that he couldn't see more than a few meters into them.

The sound came again. A clipped growl or a short bark. Maybe a low-register chirp. Another basso profundo chirp answered it.

"What is that?" Doyle rasped.

Schultz hissed at him to be quiet.

A twig snapped, but not where the chirps were coming from.

"At least three," Chan said softly.

"Four," Schultz replied. Strain showed in his voice. He lifted his left hand to his helmet and lowered the chameleon screen. Of all the shields the Marines had in their helmets, the chameleon was the one they used the least. All of the others gave them information or aided their vision, but left their faces exposed to view. The chameleon screen hid the face the same as the body, but it also obscured vision. Schultz used his less often than most. None of the other Marines immediately thought of their chameleon screens.

There was a rustling of ground cover that sounded closer than the chirps. Chan peered intently into the trees in the direction of the sound. After a moment he thought he saw a shadow that didn't look like it belonged to a tree, but he wasn't sure.

Doyle started to edge back toward the cave mouth. Godenov noticed the movement and began backing up as well.

More rustling came from very close by and an egg-shaped head poked from between two conifers, about two-thirds of a meter long and hanging two meters above the ground. Its open mouth exposed rows of sharp teeth. Its eyes were on the front of its face, like those of a tree-dweller—or a predator.

The animal stood motionless for a moment, apparently looking for something to its front. Then it turned its head to the side and peered for another moment before turning to the other side to look again. It moved its head in sharp jerks. It stepped forward once, pushing its way between the trees. It was similar to the tigers but stood more erect, and its forelegs were much bigger. Each foreleg ended in a three-fingered hand tipped with sharply pointed, in-curved talons. Its powerful hind legs had four-toed feet with even bigger talons. A tapering tail more than two meters long jutted straight behind it. It began to walk forward, bobbing as it moved.

"Oh, shit," MacIlargie said softly.

The wolf froze and turned its head toward the sound. It seemed to see MacIlargie's face suspended in midair two meters away, almost close enough for it to stretch out its neck and snatch from the air. Nictitating membranes slid over its eyes and back, as though it was trying to clear its vision. It stretched its head forward on a neck thicker than a man's thigh. MacIlargie blinked at the hot breath that swept over his face. This was a mysterious thing the wolf saw, a chunk of meat hanging in the air without moving like a flier. Its throat rippled and a deep chirp came out of its mouth.

Chan watched the animal and realized it probably didn't have a sense of smell. It relied totally on sight and sound. He remembered then the helmet-mounted chameleon screens and carefully raised a hand to lower his. "Drop your chameleon screens," he said as soon as his was on the way down.

The wolf flicked its head toward the new sound. It cocked its head at an angle, puzzled about not seeing anything where the sound had come from. Then movement made it flick its head back toward the piece of meat hanging in the air. Another piece of meat approached the first piece and made a downward movement. The first piece of meat vanished. Then the second piece of meat dropped, disappearing long before it reached the ground. The wolf stood erect, a full three meters high. It blinked its nictitating membranes again.

"Slowly," Chan said quietly, "back toward the cave."

The wolf flicked its head toward the sound of his voice and lowered its body back to its search posture. It opened its mouth wide and let out a bass *caw*.

The caw was answered by a chorus of chirps and the

thrashing of many bodies rushing through the coniferous brush. A half-dozen more wolves thrust their heads and shoulders out of the trees.

The first wolf's head bobbed and weaved, and its throat rippled and rolled rapidly as it emitted a series of chirps and caws. Then it lunged its head forward and snapped at the air where it had seen MacIlargie's face disappear.

But MacIlargie had moved by then.

Doyle and Godenov were already inside the cave when Chan reached the cave mouth. Chan dropped his infra shield into place under the chameleon screen so he could see the other Marines. One red blotch was within reach; it was MacIlargie. Chan grabbed his arm and shoved him through the cave mouth. Off balance from being manhandled, MacIlargie stumbled, his blaster clattered against the rock face of the ridge, and he grunted.

The wolves snapped their heads toward the sound. They all opened their mouths and cawed—they heard the sound of food.

"Inside," Schultz said to Chan. "I'll cover." The wolves scared him more than the tigers had. He had to defeat his fear of Wanderjahr's predators.

Hearing Schultz's voice, one wolf, perhaps hungrier than the others, darted toward it.

Schultz pressed the firing lever of his blaster and a bolt of plasma shot at the charging beast.

The wolf screamed several octaves higher than its chirps and caws as the plasma bolt blasted into its shoulder. It tried to skitter to a stop, but the momentum of its three hundred kilos was too great and it slammed into the ridge. Schultz barely managed to dive out of the way of the charge. The wolf staggered from the impact, then stood erect and shook itself. Smoke rose from its charred chest and its right foreleg was missing. The hide of its neck and the uncharred part of its chest bubbled with growing blisters, but it didn't bleed from its missing shoulder; the plasma had cauterized the wound. It cawed loudly, but the caw sounded uncertain. Then it took a wobbly step and lunged toward where Schultz had hit the ground when he dove out of its way. Schultz rolled.

Chan had stopped just inside the cave mouth to cover Schultz. He hadn't been able to fire when the wolf charged because Schultz was in his line of fire. He hadn't shot the animal when Schultz dove out of the way because he thought Schultz's hit would kill it. Then he was frozen with disbelief when the animal stood up and shook off its massive injuries. When the wolf made its second attack, Chan's first shot hit it in the belly and burned away the side of its abdominal wall. A loop of bowel dropped to the ground and tripped the wolf. It raised its head as it began to fall forward. Chan's second shot took it in the head, and momentarily the great beast was haloed in fire. It lifted its head to let out a cry of agony, but no sound came out of its seared lungs. Chan clearly heard bones in its skull pop from the heat of the flames that enveloped its head. The wolf crashed to the ground.

Schultz screamed. He'd rolled out of the way, but not far enough or fast enough. The wolf's chin smashed down onto his legs and one stiletto tooth pierced his thigh. He struggled to free himself, but the animal's head was too heavy for him to lift.

"Hang on, Hammer!" Chan shouted. "I'm coming." With two bounds he was alongside Schultz. He slung his blaster on his shoulder to free both hands to lift the massive head. "Ow!" He jerked his hands off the blistering hot skull. "Hold on, buddy." Chan unslung his blaster and slipped it under the wolf's chin. Grabbing the blaster on either side of the head, he yanked upward.

Schultz grunted in pain as the tooth pulled free and he scrambled out from underneath.

At first the other wolves had watched with passive interest while chirping at each other. But when the first wolf fell, they began dancing toward it. Then Chan's voice got their attention and they advanced faster, cawing at each other, their heads bobbing, flicking from side to side as they looked for the source of the interesting sounds. Two of them tore great gouts of flesh from the body of their fallen companion and swal-

lowed them whole. Another snapped at the creature's feebly
rising head, just missing Chan's hand.

Inside the cave, Doyle peered over MacIlargie and
Godenov's shoulders as the other wolves closed on Chan and
Schultz. Then one of the wolves moved between the two
Marines and the cave.

"We've got to help them," Doyle squeaked. He examined
the situation. Two of the wolves were eating the dead one. Two
others were bobbing and flicking their heads beyond it. One
was edging around its far side.

"We kill this one," MacIlargie said. "Then they can't get
past it and come in here."

Doyle shook his head even though the other two couldn't
see the gesture. "No good. The others'll come to eat it, and
then there'll be more of them between Chan and Schultz and
here. We have to make this one move." The wolf edging
around the far end of the dying wolf was standing where
Schultz had lain, but Doyle couldn't see the two Marines.

"That one," Doyle said. He pulled his sleeve down his arm
so the other two could see which wolf he was pointing at. It
was ten meters away. "If we shoot him, maybe that'll draw this
one away."

"Okay."

"Right."

"Don't shoot until I say so. Maybe if we all hit it at the same
time, we'll kill it right away."

The nearest wolf, the one blocking the way for Chan and
Schultz, was sidling toward the cave mouth, trying to locate the
source of the sounds coming from it.

Doyle carefully sighted on the wolf, but the sight picture
shook from his trembling. He wondered if it was possible to
miss a target that big from this short range. He suspected it
was. The near wolf was about to stick its head inside the cave;
there was no more time.

"Now!" Doyle shouted. Three bolts enveloped the wolf in
flame. A huge hole in its abdominal cavity, the wolf stood for
a few seconds, then collapsed straight down.

The snout of the nearest wolf was scorched by a bolt as it

shot past. The creature reared back and screamed as the one closing on Chan and Schultz from the other side jerked its head toward its newly dead companion and took several tentative steps in its direction. The two wolves nearest the second dead one tore into its carcass.

But the wolf closest to the cave stuck its head and shoulders inside to locate the source of the unfamiliar sounds and the heat. MacIlargie wound up and hit the wolf squarely on the snout with the muzzle of his blaster. The wolf screamed and hopped backward, then lowered its shoulders and stretched its neck forward in a fighting posture. It cawed.

"Kill it!" Schultz shouted as he fired at the wolf. The other Marines also fired, and, totally engulfed in flames, it toppled over.

Chan dashed into the cave, half supporting Schultz. The five Marines scurried five meters deeper inside.

"Now what?" Godenov asked, his voice shaking.

"Now we wait," Doyle said. "There are three dead ones. The other four will eat their fill and go away. I hope."

"How's your leg?" Chan asked Schultz. He pulled a glow-ball out of his pack to give him light to examine the injury.

"I'm all right," Schultz said. He made motions to push Chan away, but didn't push very hard.

Chan used his combat knife to cut away a flap of fabric on Schultz's trouser leg so he could examine the bite. He whistled. Blood slowly oozed out of a four-inch slit. Around it the flesh of Schultz's leg had blistered from the heat of the wolf's head. "If we don't get you to a corpsman in a hurry, that's going to infect," Chan said.

"We aren't going anywhere in a hurry," Schultz said.

"What do you mean?"

"Out there." Schultz nodded toward the cave entrance.

Chan looked. Outside, several wolves were dashing about. He realized then that he'd been hearing a lot more chirping than before. "Damn!" He stared at the narrow bit of the outside he could see, then said, "Wait here." He stood and took a couple of steps toward the opening. The area in front of the cave was filled with wolves feeding on the three they had killed. He backed up, careful not to make any noise.

"Schultz is right," he said.

Godenov looked at Doyle. "Now what do we do?"

"What do you mean asking me what we're going to do next?" Doyle squealed.

"You're a corporal," MacIlargie said. "You're the only NCO here. That means you're in charge."

Momentarily panic-stricken, Doyle looked at the others. Schultz was clearly disgusted, Chan seemed pained. MacIlargie and Godenov merely looked back at him waiting for his orders—all they knew was that Doyle was the ranking man. He might be a clerk instead of infantry, but he did have a Bronze Star.

Chan shook his head. If nobody had mentioned that, he, Chan, would have taken command. But now it was out in the open. "You've got the rank," he said. "You're in command, Doyle."

Doyle swallowed. This situation wasn't like being in charge of another clerk. This was combat, or it could be if somebody—he—made a mistake. People's lives depended on the decisions of the man in charge in a combat situation. "Oh, shit . . ." They weren't going to let him off, he could see that. He, Corporal Doyle, had to make the decisions.

CHAPTER
TWENTY-TWO

"The wolves are out, Commander." Pincote grinned around her pointed teeth. Her eyes glowed manically.

Hing glanced at her. Satisfied that she had obeyed his orders to return immediately, he almost dismissed her from his mind. "The rest of the brigade has taken its combat positions and laid out its routes of withdrawal," he said. "You will bring your company with me when I retire to the southwest. I think that's where their major effort will come."

Pincote swelled her chest. It was only right, of course, that Commander Hing use the company of his best officer to take on the enemy's main thrust. She didn't swell her chest from pride; gratitude was unnecessary. No. From the way Hing looked at her from time to time, she knew he enjoyed the sight of her body. So she puffed out her chest to reward him for doing the right thing.

Hing didn't notice Pincote's chest, as he was focusing his attention on the reports he'd been receiving all morning. The Feldpolizei hadn't launched their attack yet, and the sun was already nearing the zenith. Some of his observation posts reported that the oligarchs' men had withdrawn from their positions outside the cave entrances through which he expected them to assault. He wondered why they hadn't yet destroyed the many cave mouths they were known to have mined. He wished he had communications with the outside. He wished he was able to intercept Feldpolizei communications. Well, wish in one hand and . . .

That was an unproductive train of thought. He stood.

"Assemble your company. Move them out. I will meet you there."

"Yessir." Pincote swelled her chest again and raced from the command post to get her fighters.

"There's really a lot of wolves out there?" Doyle asked.

Chan nodded glumly.

Doyle looked at the size of the tunnel they were in and remembered the wolf that had started in after them. "They'll come in after us, won't they?"

Schultz spat to the side.

"Then we're going to have to find another way out of here."

Schultz spat again.

"That means we have to go deeper into this cave." Doyle gave the darkness behind them a worried look.

Schultz had no more saliva to waste.

Chan looked apprehensively deeper into the cave. "I hate caves," he muttered.

"Anybody know anything about spekung—ah, spelunk— uh, going in caves?" Doyle asked.

"We've all been in caves," Schultz said.

"Oh," Doyle said brightly. "Then we're going to be okay. Since everybody is experienced, do you want to draw straws or something to decide who leads the way?"

MacIlargie and Godenov exchanged a look—they were beginning to get the idea that not all corporals are created equal.

Favoring his injured leg, Schultz stood. "The leader's supposed to tell someone to take the point," he growled. He headed into the tunnel, feeling his way as the darkness increased. He wouldn't get out a glowball to light the way until the tunnel made a turn, or until they squeezed through a spot too narrow for the wolves to get through.

The others followed.

Time doesn't move at the same speed at night as it does during the day—just ask anybody who's ever spent a night on a defensive line, knowing there were enemy forces out there somewhere, waiting for the beginning of an attack he wouldn't be able to see coming. Neither does it move at the same speed in a cave. Dark-time is slow-time no matter what way you cut it. So the ten minutes it took the five of them to get from the tunnel just inside the cave mouth, through a man-made baffle that allowed people to pass but kept out man-size animals, past an unoccupied checkpoint to a chamber with a rock-littered floor, seemed a lot longer, especially since they were also on the alert for booby traps. That ten minutes was long enough for Chan to start feeling very claustrophobic. Long enough for Godenov and MacIlargie to begin to fear that they would wander underground forever. Long enough for Doyle to get the idea that maybe they should have stayed where they were and hoped the wolves wouldn't try to come in after them. But then, Doyle had never been in a cave before, so time moved a lot more slowly for him than it did for the others.

They had just entered a small cavern strewn with rocks when Schultz sensed light ahead. He didn't see the light directly—another tunnel curved out of the opposite side of the cavern—he saw light reflected off the wall of that tunnel. He stopped, flicked off his glowball, tucked it into his pack, dropped to one knee behind a boulder, and, readying his blaster in both hands, prepared himself to fight. Close behind him, Doyle stumbled and almost tripped over Schultz when the glowball disappeared. Then he saw the reflected glow ahead of them.

"We made it!" Doyle gasped. "We're saved! All we have to do is follow the lights. They'll lead us out of here. Let's go." When Schultz didn't move immediately, Doyle patted him on the shoulder and stepped around him.

Schultz calmly reached out and yanked him back. "We don't know what's there," he whispered.

"There's light; there's a way out," Doyle replied.

"Quiet!" Schultz snapped. "We don't know who's there."

"The fighting's over," Doyle said somewhat less loudly. "It doesn't matter who's there."

"We don't know they got the word."

"Sure they did. Everybody got the word."

Chan joined them during this exchange. He grabbed Doyle's shoulder and pulled him close. "We don't know that," he said softly into the corporal's ear. "Communications are screwed up, remember? Solar flare, remember? Remember how we can only receive line-of-sight or from the string-of-pearls? They can't use the string-of-pearls. Unless they've got hardwire communications, they probably don't know about the cease-fire."

"You think so?" Doyle's voice betrayed his doubt.

From up ahead they heard sounds, and the glow from the tunnel dimmed. Someone was approaching. A voice said something. Another voice replied indistinctly.

Doyle's head snapped toward the voices. Whoever was in command had to make quick decisions, had to be very decisive. A cease-fire was in effect. If those people didn't know about it, someone had to tell them. Even though he didn't want to be, he was in command. So it was up to him to make the tough decisions. Around him, he felt the other Marines getting ready for a fight. It was wrong to fight when there was a cease-fire. But he thought that if his companions knew what he had in mind, they'd stop him. He waited until he saw a moving shadow on the tunnel wall, put his blaster down, and jumped to his feet.

"You in there," he shouted rapidly as he stumbled across the rocky floor of the cavern. "Hold your fire. This is Corporal Doyle of the Confederation Marines. There's a cease-fire—"

There was a wild shot—the bolt close enough to blister Doyle's left arm and set the sleeve of his shirt on fire. Doyle stopped talking and started screaming.

The other Marines returned a quick volley and one guerrilla was immediately set aflame. He jumped up and twirled like a fiery dervish until someone shot him in the chest. Another guerrilla, who was missing a leg, began to whimper. A third had either been killed outright or was doing his best to hide. The last of the guerrillas who'd made it into the cavern was scrabbling across the rocks, trying to reach the safety of the tunnel.

"Cease fire," Chan shouted when he saw the guerrillas weren't shooting back. With Doyle down, he was taking over.

The Marines stopped shooting.

"Doyle, how bad are you hit?" Chan shouted.

"I'm alive," Doyle called back. "I'm alive!" His voice cracked.

"Hold your fire," Chan shouted at the guerrillas. "A cease-fire is in effect. Let's not shoot each other."

"You lie," a female voice replied.

Chan blinked and swore. He'd been right, the guerrillas did have women in their ranks. "No, I'm not. It's true. Do you have radio communications with anyone?"

The female voice laughed harshly. "If there's a cease-fire, why are you hunting us in the caves?"

"We aren't hunting you. Some animals chased us in. We came in to get away from them."

The woman laughed again.

"Listen . . ." Chan thought desperately; the way that woman sounded, she wanted to keep fighting. "We both have wounded out in the open. Let's make a truce to retrieve them."

"If there's a cease-fire, we don't need a truce. Go ahead, try to retrieve your wounded. Our wounded will willingly suffer for the cause."

"She wants to fight," Schultz growled. He took aim at the tunnel mouth. "I can take the fight out of her."

Chan pushed the barrel of Schultz's blaster down, then shook his hand. The barrel was still hot.

Then a man's voice penetrated the cavern, his words clear. "What's going on here?" The woman answered him excitedly. The man lowered his voice and they talked. Chan had trouble understanding the rest of the exchange, but he caught the words "cease-fire" and "lies" from the woman. Then the man spoke up.

"How can we believe you?" he asked. "What proof do you have?"

"Check with your higher headquarters, they'll tell you."

The man laughed. "You know we can't use our radios now."

Chan swore. He'd hoped the guerrillas had some kind of hardwire communications. Evidently they didn't.

"Let's do this, then," Chan said. "There's some animals outside this cave. We came in to get away from them. Tell us how to get out of here. We're all pulling away. Give us a half hour from the time we leave the cave, then come out. I think I can get my commanding officer to leave a string-of-pearls radio someplace where you can find it. You can use it to call your headquarters."

"How can we trust you? Suppose it looks like you've gone away but you haven't, and when we come out, you ambush us?" There was a pause, then the man continued. "The animals you're hiding from, what do they look like?"

What did that have to do with a cease-fire? Chan wondered. "They're about two meters tall, striped, and a lot of teeth. They run in a pack."

"Wolves. Very dangerous. How many of you did they kill?"

"None. We killed three of them. The rest of them were eating the dead ones. We came deeper into the cave so they couldn't come after us when they were through."

"I apologize. I knew there were wolves out there. I just wanted to make sure you were telling the truth about them. All right, you asked for a truce to move the wounded. Let's do that and then continue talking. I am Commander Hing, commander of the Che Loi Brigade. I'll come out for my side. Who am I talking to?"

"Lance Corporal Chan, Confederation Marine Corps. I'm also an acting shift sergeant in the Wanderjahr Feldpolizei." Chan swore at himself. He'd added the FP shift sergeant because he knew lance corporal didn't sound like much. As soon as he said it, he realized FP shift sergeant sounded like even less.

Hing chuckled softly. "A Marine lance corporal, a Feldpolizei shift sergeant. You don't have a lot of men with you, do you?"

Chan didn't answer.

There was a quick, angry exchange in the tunnel that ended with Hing shouting, "That's an order!" Then he said,

"All right, I'm putting my weapon down and coming out unarmed." There was a scraping sound, then a handgun slid into view in the tunnel mouth. "I'm unarmed. Don't shoot." A shadow moved on the wall and a man sidled into view. He held his hands open and out to his sides. "See, no weapons. I'm going to get one of my wounded. Who's acting for you?"

"I am." Chan put his blaster down and stood up with his hands open and to the sides, the same as Hing's.

"Where are you?" Hing asked. "I'm in the open, but you're still hidden."

"I'm here. Look for my face and hands." Chan held his hands at shoulder level and shook his arms to slide his sleeves down to his elbows.

Hing saw the movement, then focused on Chan's visible forearms. He looked, and above the hands saw Chan's face. *"Mein Gott,"* he said softly. "It's true, you really can make yourselves invisible. How do you do that?"

Chan grinned wickedly. "That's a Marine secret."

Hing chuckled again, with an edge of nervousness this time. "Keep your secrets. But I'd like you to tell me sometime. Let's get our wounded."

"Yes." Chan lowered his sleeves and slipped his infra screen down so he could see Doyle. But before he could take a step the woman in the tunnel shouted, "No, it's a trap!" and ran into the chamber with her blaster leveled to fire.

"Don't shoot!" Hing cried as he snatched the weapon from her hands. He threw the blaster back into the tunnel. There was a surprised gasp and a slap as someone caught it. He grabbed the woman by the arm and shook her. "Lieutenant Pincote, I declared a truce to retrieve the wounded." He pushed her back toward the tunnel and looked around for his nearest wounded fighter.

Lieutenant Pincote staggered when Hing shoved her, but quickly caught her balance. She stood, trembling with anger, and glared briefly at her commander, then quickly scanned the chamber. She saw Doyle's face in the rocks where he lay more than halfway across the cavern from the Marines' position.

With a howl of triumph, she dashed toward him, pulling a combat knife from her belt as she ran. She leaped.

"NO!" Chan and Hing shouted simultaneously. Both of them raced toward the woman and her intended victim.

Schultz got there first. Throwing a body block into Pincote while she was still in midair, he knocked her sprawling, away from Doyle. He grunted at the pain in his injured leg when he landed. Schultz glanced toward Doyle as Chan reached to pull him to safety, then turned back to face the woman's attack. But Hing's doubled-up free hand connected with her jaw. The *crack* reverberated loudly in the chamber and the woman went limp.

Schultz and Hing stared at each other for a moment. Hing's chest heaved. His bent arm held the unconscious Pincote upright.

"Truce," the guerrilla leader finally said, while looking at a face that hovered before him.

Schultz nodded, then said, "Truce."

The two turned and went back about collecting their wounded—a much easier task for the Marines, as they had only one casualty.

Doyle's wound was fairly minor, first- and second-degree burns on his left arm and side where the uniform had burned away. Chan quickly applied a dressing to numb the pain and protect the burned flesh.

"We'll get you to the battalion surgeon," Chan said as he finished the job, "he'll fix you up. In another week you won't even have any scars. All you'll have to show for this is a wound stripe on your dress reds."

"I'm really going to get a wound stripe?" Doyle asked eagerly.

"Injured as a direct result of enemy action? You better believe it."

"Wow," Doyle whispered, awed. "A wound stripe to go along with my Bronze Star." He didn't know any clerk who had a medal for bravery *and* a wound stripe. Maybe he'd get a promotion to sergeant and a transfer to battalion headquarters, where he'd never again have to risk being in battle.

Schultz hawked off to the side. What was his Marine Corps coming to when a clerk could see so much action?

"Lance Corporal Chan," Hing called a few minutes later when he'd retrieved all of his wounded. He was out of sight in the tunnel. "We have an impasse here that requires a resolution. Do you agree?"

"If you really don't have communications, I guess that's true," Chan called back. "Unless I can convince you there's really a cease-fire on."

Hing laughed softly. "I don't know how you can." After a pause he asked, "Why is there a cease-fire? Why is today different from yesterday?"

"This morning Confederation authorities arrested Ruling Council Chairman Arschmann and Oligarch Keutgens. The remaining oligarchs and your high command agreed to talk. That's what's different."

Hing barked out a laugh. "The tyrant and the bitch-queen arrested? Now I understand why Lieutenant Pincote called you a liar."

"It's true."

"Let me think on this."

The Marines waited with nervous patience while Hing thought.

"All right, Marine," the guerrilla commander finally said. "I don't know how many of you there are. I think you are few enough that if I send my fighters in they could kill all of you quickly. But they can't see you, so you might kill too many of them even though they kill all of you. I don't want to lose many of my fighters—especially if the fighting is truly over."

Pincote screamed her disagreement. The Marines heard the sharp report of a slap on human flesh.

"Lieutenant, *I* am the commander!" Hing shouted. "I make the decisions, not you. Everyone will do as I say. Is that understood?" There was a pause during which soft whimpering was audible, then Hing resumed talking to them again.

"On the other hand, Lance Corporal, that's an outrageous story you tell about the arrests. But it doesn't sound like something a lance corporal would make up, which means there is a chance you are telling the truth. So. I will tell you of another way out of here. It leads to the top of the ridge. You won't have to worry about the wolves up there, they never go to the ridge top because they can't climb well." He laughed softly. "You might have to worry about them when you descend the ridge, though."

"If we can get to someplace where there aren't any wolves, we can deal with them if we run into them again."

Hing chuckled. "Such confidence. You Confederation Marines must be very fierce fighters."

"We think so. And so does everybody we've ever fought."

Hing laughed again. "Here's where you go . . ."

Chan and his men didn't encounter the wolves again when they climbed down the ridge side. Before they descended, Chan managed to make contact with the 257th's headquarters unit via line-of-sight communications. Bass told them their shifts had been located and withdrawn and where they should go to rejoin the battalion. It was midafternoon by the time they reported in and gave a more detailed account of the action in the caves.

When the debriefing was over, vanden Hoyt said, "Well done, Marines. Now rejoin your shifts, we're going back to GSB headquarters."

Bass gave them a grin and a thumbs-up.

It was several more days before the solar flare ended its storm in the ionosphere and the guerrillas were able to confirm the cease-fire. But by then Hing had a different problem that was occupying entirely too much of his attention.

Lieutenant Pincote was looking at him with altogether new eyes. At last, she had found a man who didn't grovel when she bared her pointed teeth at him, a man willing to stand up to her. She wondered what his blood would taste like after she punctured his shoulder with the sharp points of her teeth.

CHAPTER
TWENTY-THREE

"I'll be back in a while," Dean told Claypoole some days after the oligarchs' arrest. They were scheduled to return to the company the following morning, and so were at police headquarters to clean up their workstations. Commission Landser had scheduled a formal going-away party for later that afternoon, and both were looking forward to that almost as much as they were to their return to the Corps. But Dean had private business to attend to first.

After Dean departed, Claypoole asked Lieutenant Constantine for the loan of his landcar. The lieutenant gave him permission without question. That's one thing Claypoole had come to like about the police: once they trusted you, nobody ever asked you any questions when you went somewhere. If it'd been the FIST sergeant major, he'd be on foot—with full field gear—for asking for the loan of a vehicle without full justification, and especially for personal business.

With Claypoole's contacts in the police department, he had no trouble learning where Maggie had been buried. He stopped at a florist's on the way to the cemetery and bought a beautiful bouquet of pinekiss flowers. Hoffnungsberg Cemetery lay on a high bluff just across the river. It was the oldest burial site in Brosigville, with graves going back more than three hundred years. Since most Wanderjahrians were Christians, the graves had stone monuments, each of which bore at least the name and dates of the deceased. Many had Bible verses and something about the lives of the individuals that lay beneath them.

The original cemetery had been carefully laid out by the first settlers, but over the centuries it had expanded as Brosigville grew from a village of huts and mud streets to a modern city. Long ago the caretakers had given up assigning graves and let the families of the deceased pick burial spots wherever they wanted. The bluffs held thousands of graves, most arranged with little thought for the original grid, but each burial was accurately recorded in the chief caretaker's office.

The boards in the floor squeaked under his feet as Claypoole walked up to the caretaker's desk. A shriveled old man with wild wisps of gray hair floating about his head like an overgrown halo looked up and smiled as Claypoole approached.

"You are a Confederation Marine!" he exclaimed, and stood to extend his hand. "Thank you for what you have done for us, young man." He bowed slightly.

Somewhat embarrassed, Claypoole stood awkwardly, the flowers grasped tightly in one hand. "Sir, I would like to visit someone," he said at last.

"And who might that be, young man? Oh, yes, I think I know! A young woman. A recent burial. Most unfortunate case. You knew her." It was a statement, not a question. Claypoole nodded. Maggie's full name had just slipped completely out of his mind. The caretaker took down a huge folio volume from a shelf. They had always recorded the graves at Hoffnungsberg by hand, painstakingly making each entry in huge leather-bound ledgers using only black ink in a big, old-fashioned hand.

"Here," the old man said at last, and turned the ledger so Claypoole could see. "That's Section Six, Line Thirty-nine, Grave number 193906." He jotted the figures down on a slip of paper. "It is very nice back there. Quiet. I'll give you directions."

Claypoole drove slowly through the vast cemetery. Hundreds of hectares in extent, it was crisscrossed by roads and pathways interspersed with parks and ponds and flower beds, altogether a very pleasant and restful place. Hochbaums everywhere provided deep shade from the bright sunlight. He marveled at the variety of monuments. A big metal marker with an Arabic numeral 6 on it soon appeared.

He parked and got out of the landcar. He realized that,

judging from the simple stone markers, the people buried here were not very well-to-do. He found Line 39 with no trouble, then walked down it, searching for Maggie's grave. Most of the stones carried only the briefest entries, just the name of the deceased and their dates of birth and death. Here and there, however, more elaborate monuments poked up from the closely cut grass. One bore the carving of a child embracing some kind of small animal. The child, buried fifty years before, had been only eight years old when he died. As he walked farther down Line 39 he passed into the shade of a beautiful hochbaum. The dates of death were closer to the present. Maggie was at the far end of the line, clearly one of the most recent interments in that section.

Claypoole stared down at the simple stone. He was surprised to discover that she had been several years older than he. The grave was still fresh, the earth still slightly mounded. He closed his eyes. In his mind he heard her singing that exciting, lascivious song. He knelt down and put the pinekiss flowers into a metal vase fitted into the front of her stone. The bouquet was so big that when he stood up he couldn't see the stone behind it. Then he removed all but one flower, a gorgeous thing of deep red on a long green stem, and stuck them onto the grave next to Maggie's. "Here you go," he said, carefully placing the single remaining beautiful red flower into her cup. It looked nice. He stood a while longer and then walked to the car and drove back to the caretaker's office.

"How much would it cost to have a new stone made for Miss . . . Miss, uh, excuse me, sir, for Miss, er . . . ." Again his memory had failed him. "For Maggie's grave?"

Dean knocked lightly on the door. A servant girl opened it. "I'm here to see Miss Hway Keutgens."

"Who is it?" Hway's granduncle asked from inside the house. The servant girl opened the door wider and the old man came to stand in the doorway. "Lance Corporal Dean, you are no longer welcome in this house."

"I—I've come to see Hway," Dean replied.

"After what you have done to my sister, young man, you are not wanted here." He began to close the door in Dean's face.

Dean grabbed the door and held it. "I did nothing to your sister, sir! You go ask Gretel Siebensberg's family about what she did to them. Hway is here, sir, and I want to see her. Please?"

"No!" the old man shouted, and leaned harder against the door.

"Goddamn you!" Dean swore. "Get out of my way or I swear, I'll blow this fucking door all to hell on you!" The old man was strong, but Dean was angrier than he'd ever been in his life, and he began to win the shoving contest.

"Uncle! Let him in," Hway shouted from behind the slowly opening door.

"No!" her uncle shouted back.

"Uncle, I am the oligarch of Morgenluft now, and as such I am also the head of this family. Let Joe in."

The door swung open. Dean and Hway's granduncle glared at one another as they panted.

"Come, Joe, let's walk in the field again." She took Dean by the hand and led him outside and around the house. The door slammed behind them.

"I know you had nothing to do with grandmother's arrest," Hway said as they walked hand in hand. "But I just can't believe she did those things, Joe! Gram is not the murderer they are saying!" She began to cry.

"Aw," Joe said, "I don't know, Hway." He held her in his arms. "There'll be a trial and all that. Maybe all this will work out." Of course, he knew it wouldn't.

They walked along the rows of tomato plants. "They will begin the harvest tomorrow or the next day," Hway said.

"Yeah. Hway, I'm going back to the company tomorrow, and the day after we'll go back to Thorsfinni's World. I—I—goddamn, I'll start crying next! I came to say good-bye—" His voice broke on the last syllable. He took her and held her close. She put her arms around him and hugged her tightly. "Honey, can we stay in touch? Can we write? Let's not lose contact." Joe was finding it difficult to get his breath.

Gently, she pushed him away. "Joe, no; it's over between us. If I were an ordinary citizen, I'd take the next ship for Thorsfinni's World and live there outside your camp and wait for you to come to me. But I am not an ordinary citizen. I am no longer a free agent. I'm going to succeed Grandmother. My responsibility now is to the people of Morgenluft. You're going back to your Marines, Joe. That's where you belong." She was crying again. He reached out to touch her, but she shook her head. "Joe, my life is here. Yours is—out there." She gestured toward the sky. She leaned forward slightly and kissed him gently on the lips. "My brave Marine," she whispered, and stroked his hair lightly. "I am going back to the house now, Joe. We shall never see each other again."

Dean stood helplessly watching the only woman he'd ever loved walk away from him. He remained between the plants for a long time after Hway had disappeared into the house. Then he began to pick some tomatoes to take to the guys in the barracks.

Hway Keutgens, soon to be oligarch of Morgenluft and ruler of millions of people, watched stoically as Joe Dean drove away from her granduncle's home. She ran her hand thoughtfully over her still-flat, hard belly. No, she would never forget Lance Corporal Joseph Finucane Dean. She had just missed her period.

Don't miss this exciting new series by Brian Daley!

SMOKE ON THE WATER
GammaLAW Book 1

Though they contemplated a final suicide mission of blood, guts, and glory, the Exts knew their warrior superskills were no match for the LAW— Legal Annexation of Worlds—who were sent into space by the mighty Periapt potentates to colonize new populations against the evil, alien Roke.

Among the Ext draftees bound for Periapt were Allgrave Burning, his technowizard cousin Lod, and beautiful, death-scarred Ghost, all sworn to a greater purpose, destined to fight in a star-torn war like none other. For a mysterious, danger-shrouded planet beckoned them—along with a disgraced starship captain and a powerful high priestess—for the greatest battle of their lives . . .

Published by Del Rey® Books.
Available in bookstores everywhere.

STARFIST

Book I
FIRST TO FIGHT

by David Sherman and Dan Cragg

Stranded in a hellish alien desert, stripped of their strategic systems, quick-reaction force, and supporting arms, and carrying only a day's water ration, Marine Staff Sergeant Charlie Bass and his seven-man team faced a grim future seventy-five light-years from home. The only thing between his Marines and safety were eighty-five miles of uncharted, waterless terrain and two thousand bloodthirsty savages with state-of-the-art weapons in their hands and murder on their minds.

But the enemy didn't reckon on the warrior cunning of Marine's Marine Charlie Bass and the courage of the few good men who would follow him anywhere—even to death . . .

Published by Del Rey® Books.
Available in bookstores everywhere.

STARFIST
Book III
STEEL GAUNTLET

by David Sherman
and Dan Cragg

Published by Del Rey® Books.
Available now in bookstores near you.

A SCREAMING
ACROSS THE SKY
GammaLAW Book Two

by Brian Daley

Arrival on the ominous planet of Aquamarine
was a splashdown into danger and death for
Periapt high priestess Dextra Haven and her
ragtag force of scientists and Ext warriors. Yet
Dextra was undeterred, certain that
Aquamarine held the key to peace between
humans and a fierce alien race.

But the priestess and her mighty warriors
would need to summon all their powers, for
the sea-planet was rife with many deadly
mysteries—and conquerors both seen and
unseen lurked in cyberspace and outer
space waiting to invade, possess,
and destroy . . .

Published by Del Rey® Books.
Available in bookstores everywhere.